Changing of the Guard:
Book Five in the Tori Cooper Novels

By Vicki Stewart

First Sight – Book One in the Tori Cooper Novels
4 out of 5 stars

"Stewart weaves an intriguing story, combining realistic characters performing day to day activities with supernatural abilities. The reader is immediately drawn to Tori and Ben and their relationship of friendship and love. Stewart's writing moves the reader forward from scene to scene with colorful descriptions and fast paced dialogue. I found myself caring for Tori and Ben and thinking about them even when I wasn't reading the book. The book is nicely layered with a plot of crime investigations at the forefront and sub-themes of romance, family bonds, grief and spirituality interspersed, providing substance deeper than the storyline. This book is a tremendous example of a story involving crime, romance, and paranormal without becoming macabre and erotic. Praise to Stewart for finding this balance in her writing. I look forward to the next book in the series, and the next after that."

~ Kathi Nidd, Readers Favorite

The Enlightenment – Book Two in the Tori Cooper Novels
5 out of 5 stars

"Tori Cooper is an amazing character with depth and heart, and this is an incredible story. Vicki Stewart has created a wonderful series based on Tori's unique abilities and her quest to become an FBI agent attached to the Behavioral Analysis Unit. Well written dialogue, fast-paced action, terrific supporting characters and a strong paranormal sub-plot make The Enlightenment, Book Two of the Tori Cooper Novels well worth reading on many levels."

~ Melinda Hills, Readers Favorite

Guardians of the Chosen – Book Three in the Tori Cooper Novels 5 out of 5 stars

"From the very first page of Guardians of the Chosen, I was hooked. I loved that some of the characters were quite complex. Vicki Stewart has delivered a story of epic proportions, incorporating those of so many different realms into one place, with the help of Tori's special gifts. My only regret is that I read the third book in the series first, before reading the others, but I will be quickly rectifying that, having discovered that there are four books in the Tori Cooper Novels so far, each of which looks just as mesmerizing. Seeing the murders, not only from the view point of the FBI but also of the killer and the victim, was a first for me. Most of the characters were likeable, and watching Lucifer receive a good dressing down for being mischievous was definitely a first. I would recommend this book to all those who love a good murder mystery entwined with a gory supernatural element in their read."

~ Rosie Malezer, Readers Favorite

Children from the Light – Book Four in the Tori Cooper Novels 4 out of 5 stars

"I enjoyed Children from the Light: Book Four in the Tori Cooper Novels very much. Vicki Stewart has written a story that depends on the heroine having supernatural powers. The villains are so well-hidden; the mark of a superb paranormal fantasy. Tori herself comes over as an authentic first-time-pregnant married woman and it is easy to empathize with her, even when Luc, thrown out of heaven, appears to gloat over the forthcoming child. "All of the heavens are abuzz with the news of the prodigal Remial son!" Children from the Light is a fascinating story, sure to attract readers to the whole series.

~ Sarah Stuart, Readers Favorite

ISBN: 978-0-9894186-3-8

Books written by Vicki Stewart

The Tori Cooper Novels:
First Sight, 2013
The Enlightenment, 2014
Guardians of the Chosen, 2015
Children from the Light, 2016
Changing of the Guard, 2017

Dedication

This book is dedicated to all of my sisters.

Laurie, Cathleen and Julie, the truest soul-mate is that of a sister. We may look old and wise to the outside world, but to each other, we are still those four little girls from Tuckaway Drive, whispering to each other in the dark long after our bed-time. We've seen each other at our best and our worst, and know we would defend each other to the end.

Garnet, Laura and Kendra, you've become such valued and respected women in my life. I no longer see you as just my best friends, you too are my sisters.

I love you all dearly.

I would also like to dedicate this book to my faithful canine companion, Cooper, who keeps me company while I write, and speaks volumes to me through his eyes. You are my Goliath, my sweet old man, and I will treasure the time we have left together.

~~~~~

"Carry out a random act of kindness, with no expectation of reward, safe in the knowledge that one day someone might do the same for you."

-Princess Diana

Chapter 1

Zander stared at the man looking back at him in the mirror, wondering for the millionth time how his life had gotten so incredibly screwed up. The deepening lines on his forehead and corners of his eyes revealed the tell-tale signs of the stress he'd been under the past three years. Listening for the sound of footsteps behind him every time he was out in public and setting booby-traps on the door to his room to make sure no one entered it when he was gone was now second nature to him.

He was so incredibly tired. Tired of not knowing how long he would be able to stay in one place; tired of not being able to sleep through the night without the slightest sound making him jump up and check every door and window; tired of not having a life of his own; just plain tired. Every time he started to feel settled somewhere, the little voice in his head would tell him the FBI was starting to close in on him, and he would have to pack up his things and run to somewhere new.

"Oh how I wish things could go back to the way they were," he thought wearily. *"Before...,"* his thoughts trailed off, remembering why he was staring at the face of a stranger in a cracked mirror of a run-down, rent-by-the-week motel room.

"Go ahead, say it," the voice in his head taunted.

"...before I shot and killed three innocent men and almost killed an FBI agent," Zander whispered to his reflection.

"See how easy that was to admit?" the voice continued to tease.

"But that's not the man I am!" Zander argued. "I'm a decorated Marine! I served my country, I protect people, not kill them!"

"I beg to differ considering the obvious circumstances you're in," the voice argued back.

"Enough," Zander whispered, closing is eyes wishing the buzzing pain in his head would go away.

"You need to face the truth and stop fooling yourself! You're a murderer, Zander. And no matter how far you run, or how well you try to hide, you will always be a cold-blooded murderer. It's not a matter of who you once were it's who you are now. And right now, you're Agent Hunter's primary objective. And he won't stop looking for you until he finds you," the voice accused.

"I said enough!" Zander shouted angrily at his reflection, banging his palms on the edge of the basin. The reverberation of the impact shook the walls of the tiny room, causing the suspended light bulb above the sink to gently sway back and forth.

As he glared angrily into the glass, his eyes picked up a shadow on his hairline as the bulb swung overhead. He leaned forward to take a closer look at his short cropped hair and recognized the blonde roots of his natural hair color starting to emerge, indicating it was time for him to pick up another box of brown hair dye the next time he was at the store. He sighed in resignation and surveyed his mustache and beard noticing they too needed a touch-up.

He hated the facial hair, always had since he was a kid. His father had a mustache, and Zander remembered it always felt scratchy and rough. He used to think it looked like a brown caterpillar crawling on his father's face.

"What does it feel like?" he had once asked.

"It's a little itchy when it starts to grow in, but after a while, you get used to it," his father had said.

But Zander couldn't get used to it. It felt foreign to him and tickled his nose while he slept. He didn't like living in disguise. What was even more unsettling was catching his reflection in a store window and failing to recognize himself. It had been so long since he had someone he could trust, someone to talk to. It was a very lonely life on the run. He had used so many aliases at this point even he forgot who he was sometimes. A once proud and decorated Marine was now a fugitive, and a wanted man with a price on his head. The only people wanting to talk to him were those who wanted to put him behind bars.

"Or shoot me," he thought sadly. *"I miss Rhea. She always knew what needed to be done to make things right. If only she had stayed with me and let me explain!"*

"Explain what? That you're a killer?" The voice in his head tried to reason. *"Why would she have stayed with you and risk becoming your next victim?"*

"I would never have hurt her!" Zander argued at his reflection. "I loved her! I still love her," he murmured, looking away.

"*Love,*" the voice spat in disgust. "*Love is a cancer of the heart. It deceives you into thinking you have some fatalistic connection to another human being and then it eats away at you slowly until you're too weak to fight back. Eventually, you lose yourself completely until you're just lying there pathetically, incapable of remembering who you once were. Then it finally kills you. Once upon a time there was just you, and then you fell in love, the end.*"

"That's not what love is," Zander argued.

"*Whatever,*" the voice mocked.

"Why won't you just go?" Zander begged. Wincing at the increasing pain in his head as another migraine began to settle in he whispered, "Why won't you just leave me alone and torture someone else for a while?"

"*What and miss all the fun we're having?*" the voice snidely exclaimed. "*Don't I always take care of you? Don't I always make sure you have a roof over your head and food in your belly? Don't I always warn you when they're getting close, so you have time to get away? You'd be lost without me, Zander! We're friends you and me!*"

"No," Zander choked, staring at his face in the mirror. "You and I are most definitely not friends."

"*Oh, that hurt, Zander,*" the voice whined.

"I seriously doubt that," Zander muttered. "It may have taken me a while to figure out who you are, but I know you are most definitely not my friend."

Impressed by Zander's bravery, the voice taunted, *"What makes you think I'm not just your subconscious talking to you from your diseased, twisted little mind? Aren't I just the nasty little voice inside your head?"*

"You're not," Zander insisted defiantly.

"If you're so sure I'm someone else, tell me, who am I?" the sound of the voice oozed.

Terrified of the conversation he was having, Zander met his eyes in the reflection steadily and swallowed hard. "You're the devil," he croaked.

"Well, well, look at you," Lucifer applauded. *"It took you long enough. Most people figure it out much sooner than you did."*

"I've suspected you for a while," Zander growled. "I just wasn't sure I was willing to admit it."

"So, now that you've come to terms with your predicament, what are you going to do about it?" Lucifer threatened quietly.

"I haven't figured that out yet," Zander whispered.

"Perhaps I can help," Lucifer leered, ominously.

Feeling his headache intensify Zander shook his head a few times, trying to push the pain away, but as usual, he was unable to stop it. "Stop," be begged. "Please don't do this anymore."

"Too late," Lucifer chuckled as Zander's mind slipped away into the darkness. *"Time to go..."*

Chapter 2

"We've needed this time alone together," Tori thought to herself as Goliath danced around her feet happily, waiting for her to throw the stick again. She smiled down at the large brown dog, whose mouth was open in a wide grin, his lolling tongue hanging out on one side, dripping saliva.

"Ready my little grizzly bear?" she teased.

"Yes!" she heard him quickly reply, eyeing the stick.

Pulling her arm back behind her head, she gathered her strength and flung the stick forward as hard as she could across the open field. "Go get it, Goliath!"

Immediately, the dog lunged forward, trying to catch the stick before it hit the ground. Tori smiled in satisfaction when she saw the stick drop into an area of overgrown grass and weeds several hundred yards away.

"That ought to keep him busy for a few minutes," she thought to herself, happily.

While she waited for Goliath to return, she pulled her phone from her pocket and glanced down at the screen to make sure Ben hadn't tried to reach her. She sighed in relief when she saw the screen was clear. *"No news is good news in our house,"* she thought, pocketing the device.

Feeling a slight twinge below her left shoulder blade, she rotated her arm gently around in a circle to release the tension. Even after three years, sometimes the scar from the bullet wound still pulled when she moved a certain way.

Glancing across the field, she saw Goliath foraging through the grass looking for the stick. Thankfully the scarring from the shared bullet hadn't seemed to affect his gait, and he moved without any sign of pain or injury. She shuddered as the memory replayed in her mind of the day Goliath jumped up to take the bullet for her. His selfless act of devotion risking his life had slowed the bullet down as it passed through his body into her shoulder, ultimately saving her life. She knew it was only by the grace of God neither of them died that day.

"And to think he was in a shelter, about to be put down before Remy found him," she thought to herself. *"Not to mention how much you argued with Remy the day he gave you Goliath, insisting you didn't need another guardian."*

"You need someone to protect you when I can't be there," Remy had insisted.

"Little did I know then how much my life was about to change," she thought to herself, wryly. *"I now have a Guardian Angel, a dog with telepathic abilities, a son who can control the elements and a daughter who can heal, and do things you only read about in science fiction novels."*

Looking up to the sky above her, she prayed, "*I know you have a plan for my children, God. And I know I need to have faith and remember that it's all out of my hands. We've entered a new era, and my children are the future heirs in the line of the Archangel Remial. Please continue to keep me strong and focused on You so I can be a positive example for them.*" Then the image of her husband Ben's face appeared in her mind, and she closed her eyes and sighed, contentedly. "*Another blessing in my life and thankfully so wonderfully normal,*" she added.

Hearing a quiet 'woof' from Goliath, she opened her eyes and looked across the field as he emerged from the grass and began running toward her. Then she noticed he was no longer smiling. His eyes told her something was wrong.

"What is it Goliath?" she asked running toward him.

"*Someone needs Tori's help,*" she heard him announce frantically, dropping the stick at her feet.

Confused, Tori frowned slightly and asked out loud, "What do you mean? Who needs my help?"

"*Brought it back to show you,*" she heard him reply.

When she looked down at the ground by her feet, she realized it wasn't a stick Goliath had brought back: it was a large bone. Drawing in a surprised breath, she pulled an evidence glove from her pocket and carefully picked up the bone, examining it closely. Then she looked intently into Goliath's eyes and demanded, "Show me where you found this, Goliath."

Immediately the dog spun around and began running back in the direction which he came. Tori followed closely behind him, praying the bone was from a large animal like a deer or an elk.

By the time they reached the spot in the grass, Tori knew the bone was human. As they got closer, she could see the spirit of a young girl, not more than sixteen years old, shimmering semi-transparently beside her corpse, clothed in a white t-shirt and denim jeans, both heavily stained with blood. Mentally preparing herself and not wanting to frighten the girl, Tori slowed her pace and walked the rest of the way toward her.

"Hello?" the girl asked Tori, timidly. "Can you hear me?"

Tori nodded and replied, "Yes. I can see and hear you. My name is Tori, what's yours?"

The girl looked down at the skeletal remains of her body on the ground where they stood and whispered, "My name is Amber, Amber Reynolds." Making eye contact again with Tori, she asked, "Am I dead?"

Tori leaned down to place the right femur bone Goliath had given her back in position on the ground and stood up to face the girl.

"Yes, sweetie, I'm afraid so," Tori admitted.

"Oh," Amber whispered. "I thought so."

"Do you remember what happened?" Tori asked, gently.

Amber shook her head and murmured, "Not really. The images are all fuzzy."

"What's the last thing you remember?" Tori asked.

The girl frowned, trying to think back and replied, "I think I was supposed to meet someone here."

"Do you remember who you were supposed to meet?" Tori asked.

The girl shook her head no in response.

"Was it a boy?" Tori probed gently.

The girl nodded her head guiltily. "Yes, I think so."

"Do you remember his name?" Tori suggested, hoping to jar the girl's memory.

Tears began to flow down the girl's cheeks, and she shook her head again, "I can't remember," she sobbed.

"That's okay," Tori soothed. "You're in shock which is totally normal. You may remember later, okay?"

"Okay," the girl agreed.

"Amber, I need to make a phone call to the police so they can come out here and recover your body. When they show up, you may hear them say things that are very scary and confusing so try not to get too scared by what you see or what you hear, okay? They won't be able to see or hear you, so they won't know your spirit is still here," Tori advised.

"How come you can see and hear me?" the girl frowned.

"I have a special gift," Tori explained slowly. "I can communicate with the spirits of murdered victims. I don't tell many people about my gift because sometimes it's difficult for people to understand. Does that make sense?"

Amber nodded and whispered, "Yes. I understand." She glanced back down at her body and added, "I'm scared Tori. I didn't want to die."

"I know you didn't, sweetie. It's important that you know none of this was your fault," Tori insisted.

"But what if I my coming out here to meet William was something I wasn't supposed to do? What if my parents didn't know? What if I snuck out of the house? They're both going to be so mad at me. Oh, why can't I remember?" Amber wailed, turning away.

Not realizing she had given Tori the first name of the boy she was supposed to meet, Tori stored that nugget of information away and replied, "Amber, it's important for you to know none of this is your fault."

"How could you know that?" Amber argued.

"I had an older sister who snuck out to meet a boy when she was eighteen years old, and it turned out not to be a boy: it was a sick, demented man with delusions of having feelings for her and he caused her death. I understand what may have happened to you. That's why I want you to know whether you snuck out of the house to meet a boy, or just ended up in the wrong place at the wrong time, this," she demanded while pointing down at Amber's body, "was not your fault."

"I'm sorry about your sister," Amber whispered.

"Thank you," Tori replied. "It was a long time ago, and it took a while for my family to come to terms with what happened to her, but we're in a good place now. Your parents will go through the same thing once they learn of your death, but I'll try to help you and them when the time comes."

"What do you mean?" Amber asked. "Help how?"

"I'll explain later. We don't have time for that now. I need to make that phone call now, okay?" Tori advised.

"Okay," Amber whispered.

"I promise I'll come see you once they've taken your body to the morgue and we'll talk more then. Maybe you'll have remembered some details about that night, or I can help fill in some of the pieces once I've had a chance to look into a few things. Would that be okay?" Tori asked.

"Yes," the girl whispered, her eyes glistening with tears. "I would like that."

"Okay. Here we go," Tori replied, removing her phone from her pocket. Quickly unlocking the phone, she dialed the police and waited for the dispatcher to answer on the other end of the line.

"9-1-1, please state the nature of your emergency," the dispatcher answered.

"Hello. My name is Agent Tori Cooper. I'm with the FBI Behavioral Analysis Unit Division Two. I've located human remains of what appears to be a young girl in Hadley Park behind the pavilion in the field to the right of the pond," Tori replied.

"Were you working a case Agent Cooper, where you had prior knowledge of the body's location?" the dispatcher asked.

Understanding the protocol, Tori replied, "No, I was not aware the body was here. I was here recreationally with my dog."

"Is the body in a secure area? Is there anyone else there with you other than your dog?" the dispatcher asked.

"Yes, the area is secure. There's no one else here," Tori replied patiently.

"I'll need you to remain with the body until the police arrive," the dispatcher advised.

"That's not a problem. Would you like me to remain on the line with you until then?" Tori asked.

"Yes, that would be preferred. Hold the line please while I send a unit to your location," the dispatcher advised.

"Ma'am?" Tori interrupted.

"Go ahead Agent Cooper," the dispatcher replied.

"Would you or someone on your team be able to call my supervisor? I'll need him to know that I will be out of communication for the time being, in case he tries to reach me," Tori requested.

"Yes, go ahead with his information," the dispatcher advised.

"Thank you. My supervisor's name is Agent Gabriel Hunter, and his cell number is seven, zero, three, six, three, zero, nine, nine, one, one," Tori replied very slowly.

"Thank you, Agent Cooper. We're contacting Agent Hunter now. Please remain on the line," the dispatcher advised.

"I will," Tori replied. Covering the speaker on her phone, she whispered, "The police are on their way."

"Okay," Amber murmured as a wave of fresh tears streamed down her cheeks.

Chapter 3

"Hello!" Tori called out from the front door as she and Goliath returned home.

"In the kitchen making dinner," Ben called out in reply.

Catching the scent of food in the air, Goliath instantly headed in the direction of Ben's voice. *"Goliath treat!"* Tori heard the dog declare as he trotted away from her side.

"Mama!" chimed two tiny voices from the direction of the twin's bedrooms. The sound of little feet running toward her quickly followed.

Bracing for impact, Tori held her ground while the two mini torpedoes launched at her, each grabbing one of Tori's legs in a strong hug. "Hello, my sweet angels," she greeted, hugging them against her body.

Pulling back to look up into her mother's face, Gemma soothed, "Poor Mama. Is the girl okay now? Did you send Amber to heaven?"

Registering surprise, knowing Ben would not have told the children, Tori glanced over at RJ who was also looking up at her with a concerned expression. "We knew as soon as you found her," he confirmed.

"What do you mean you knew as soon as I found her, sweetie?" Tori asked, in surprise.

"We saw her. Standing in the grass by her body, waiting for you," Gemma replied calmly.

"How on earth could they have seen her?" Tori wondered, glancing back and forth between the faces of her children.

"We don't need the amulet as you do, Mama," Gemma answered Tori's question out loud. "We can see the things you see without it."

"That's right!" RJ smiled at Tori happily. "Remy says me and Gemma are special, and we can use our gifts without it. Isn't that cool, Mama?"

"Mmmm, yes," Tori murmured, making a note to have a conversation with Remy later about what to and what not to talk about with the children.

"All right you little monkey's," Ben chided as he joined them. "How about you let go of Mommy and wash your hands for dinner."

"What are we having?" RJ demanded, excitedly.

"Turkey Parmesan sliders and baked potato tots," Ben replied.

"Yum!" RJ cheered, letting go of Tori's leg. Running toward the powder room, he yelled, "I'm gonna beat you!" teasing his sister.

"Bet you won't!" Gemma insisted, chasing after him.

"And not just water, use soap!" Ben called out loudly. Turning to Tori, his expression softened, and he pulled her into his arms. "How are you doing?"

"I'm okay," Tori sighed, leaning her head against his shoulder.

"Man, you can't even take Goliath to the park without stumbling over a body, can you?" he teased, rubbing her back gently.

"I guess not," Tori admitted.

"You sure you're okay?" he asked, again.

"Yeah, I'm fine. Just sad for yet another innocent girl who trusted the wrong person," she replied.

"It made you think about what happened to your sister didn't it?" he asked.

"The pattern is eerily similar to what happened to Bree," Tori confessed, pulling back to look at him. "It's so strange how close the details of the case are."

"What did you tell the police?" he asked.

"I wasn't able to tell them too much without disclosing more than I should know, based on what the girl told me," she admitted.

"Did you get a chance to talk to her afterward?" he hoped.

Tori nodded and said, "Briefly, but there were a lot of people coming in and out of the morgue area, so I had to be discreet."

"Did she want to stay and find out what happened to her?" he wondered.

"No," Tori admitted. "That girl was so scared, Ben. I told her she could wait, but she was so overwhelmed with what was going on, I can't blame her for not wanting to stay."

"Well she's at peace now, and that's all that matters, right?" Ben offered.

"Peace for Amber, yes. Not so much for her parents. Their nightmare has just begun," Tori noted.

"You did what you could," he consoled.

"I just wish there was more I could do to help them," Tori sighed.

"Do you think it would help to meet the parents and share the story of your sister with them? Maybe give them someone to talk to if they need to, considering you've already been through a similar situation?" Ben suggested.

"I don't know. You know how sometimes getting too close to a victim's family can do more damage than good?" Tori shrugged.

"Well, I know you'll figure out the right thing to do. You always do," Ben praised.

"Thanks, honey," Tori smiled. "Tell me about your afternoon. Did the twins behave themselves?"

"Well," Ben hesitated, exhaling loudly, "Yes, they behaved themselves. But something did happen that you probably need to be aware of."

Groaning, Tori said, "Tell me."

"I took them to the library to get some new books because they've already read through the stack you picked up a couple of days ago," Ben advised.

"They did? That's crazy! I even picked out a few books at a more mature reading level to see if it would slow them down!" Tori exclaimed.

"I know. I guess we need to find some more challenging reading material." Ben shrugged.

"So why the exasperated breath?" she asked curiously. "What happened?"

Glancing toward the kitchen to make sure the twins were out of earshot, Ben quietly replied, "The books they picked out were pretty advanced, Tor. They were historical biblical references about angels and the origins of demonology. I didn't know if should have let them check them out, but they seemed pretty insistent."

"Well, I guess at some point we had to expect they would start doing research of their own but I never guessed it would be at three years old!" Tori admitted.

"That's not all," Ben warned, glancing again toward the kitchen.

"What?" Tori frowned.

"When the clerk behind the counter was scanning the books, she looked at the titles and jokingly said to me, 'My goodness I hope you're not reading these as bedtime stories for your children!'" Ben replied.

Grimacing, Tori groaned again, "Let me guess, Gemma replied?"

"Yep," Ben nodded.

"What did she say?" Tori sighed.

"Without blinking, she said, 'Oh, those aren't for Daddy. They're for me and my brother'."

"She didn't," Tori winced.

"She did," Ben advised.

"Then what happened?" Tori asked, already suspecting the outcome.

"The woman just stared at Gemma, obviously not understanding how a toddler could not only speak so maturely at her age but understand the context of the conversation," Ben replied. "Well, that and the subject matter of the books. She was pretty dumbfounded."

"Then what did you do?" Tori asked.

"What do you think I did? I grabbed the books before either one of them said anything else and high-tailed it out of there!" Ben exclaimed, trying not to raise his voice.

"I'm sorry, sweetie," Tori soothed, not knowing what else to say.

"There's nothing for you to be sorry about. It's not your fault! It's just the way our life is going to be from now on," Ben admitted. "We have two exceptionally gifted children, years in maturity beyond their little bodies and stuff like this is going to happen."

"I know," Tori agreed. "It's just starting to happen more often than I would like. Do you know how hard it is trying to explain to a toddler what it means to keep a low profile? I'll talk to them about it again tonight before bed. Well, after I read them one of those devilish bedtime stories of course."

Ben laughed and put his arms around her comfortingly. "You're funny."

"And you're wonderful," she sighed, holding him tightly.

Hearing the onset of the twins arguing in the kitchen, Ben kissed Tori on the forehead and suggested, "Sounds like the natives are starting to get restless. We better get in there before something get's broken."

Tori snorted a laugh and said, "Agreed. Thank you for making dinner, Ben. The sliders sound great."

"My pleasure," he smiled, taking her by the hand and leading her toward the kitchen. "When I saw we had ground turkey, shredded cheese, pasta sauce and the Hawaiian sweet rolls, I knew the sliders would be a hit. Plus it's a quick, easy meal that I know they'll eat so it worked out well for everyone!"

"It's perfect!" she agreed.

"Oh, and I poured the twins glasses of milk, but you get something a little stronger. I figured you would need a glass of wine after the day you've had."

"And you claim you can't read minds," she teased, following him into the kitchen.

"I know, right?" he teased back.

"What can I help you with?" she offered as she washed her hands and surveyed the food on the countertops.

"If you would be willing to toast the rolls in the toaster oven while I get the slider patties ready that would be great!" he suggested.

"I'm on it," she nodded, making her way to the other side of the counter.

"Can I help?" RJ asked, excitedly. "I'm hungry!"

"May I help," Tori gently corrected her son.

"May I help?" RJ asked properly.

"You bet, buddy! You can put the cheese on top of the patties," Ben offered, picking RJ up and placing him on a stool alongside the counter beside him.

"Okay!" RJ agreed happily, grabbing a handful of the cheese and stuffing it into his mouth. As he chewed, he reached one arm behind his head and fiercely scratched his shoulder blade.

"Is that itch on your back still bothering you, sweetie?" Tori asked, noticing the momentarily distracted look on RJ's face.

"Sometimes, I'm okay," RJ replied, stuffing another fist full of cheese in his mouth.

"Let me take a look," Tori suggested, walking toward him.

"Mom, I'm okay!" RJ argued. "I put the lotion on like you said."

"Okay, okay. Don't get sassy with me," Tori warned gently.

"Sorry, Mama," RJ replied quietly.

"What may I do?" Gemma asked, not wanting to be left out.

"You are in charge of the sauce!" Ben insisted, placing her on a stool on the other side of him. "Are you both ready?"

"Yes!" they chimed in unison.

"Okay, Gemma you're first," Ben advised.

"Why does she get to go first?" RJ pouted, glaring at his sister.

"I was born before you! That makes me first!" Gemma glared back.

"That's not why, Gemma. Come on sweetie we talked about this. RJ, do you want to do the sauce instead?" Ben mediated.

Realizing that meant he would no longer be able to eat the cheese freely, RJ shook his head sullenly and replied, "No, I'll do the cheese."

Nodding in approval, Ben instructed, "Okay, thank you RJ. Gemma, take the spoon from that bowl of pasta sauce and put some sauce on top of each patty. Got it?" Ben instructed.

"Got it," Gemma replied, furrowing her brow in concentration as she spooned the sauce.

"RJ, when your sister finishes with the sauce, you sprinkle a big pinch of the shredded cheese on top of each one, okay?" Ben asked.

"Got it," RJ mumbled through a mouth full of cheese, watching Gemma closely. "You missed one!" he added pointing at one of the burger patties.

"I did not!" Gemma argued, adding a bit more sauce to the one RJ pointed out.

"There! That looks better," RJ admitted.

"Thanks," Gemma muttered, quietly.

"Okay, way to compromise! Good job you two!" Ben praised, glancing back at Tori with a mischievous wink.

"Good job, Daddy!" she mouthed silently winking back.

Chapter 4

"So, what have you found?" Agent Hunter asked Piper as he entered the room.

"Very similar evidence we've found at the last two locations, sir," Piper advised, sealing a small evidence bag containing several pieces of hair from the bathroom floor. "I'll send these samples to the lab to check for DNA markers but do you notice how the hair color is darker than before?"

Slipping his sunglasses into his pocket, Agent Hunter looked at the hair and replied, "Meaning he's dyed his hair a different color than last time."

"Looks like it," Piper agreed.

"What else?" he asked.

Pointing to a stack of cards in the evidence case, Piper replied, "Several good fingerprints, and a dried piece of skin from the sheets on the bed. More than likely it's a scab from a cut. It will be another possible DNA marker for us to use to positively ID him."

"Any dried fluids on the sheets?" Agent Hunter asked, glancing over at the bed.

"None that I could find," Piper admitted. "Zander has been alone here from what I can tell."

"That does seem to be his pattern," Agent Hunter paused, thinking.

"I did find one thing I wasn't able to identify. I'm hoping the lab can ID it," Piper admitted, sorting through her evidence samples to find the right bag. "Here it is," she offered, handing it to him.

Agent Hunter held the bag up to the light and squinted, trying to get a closer look at two tiny yellow beads inside the bag. "Hmm...they're symmetrical in shape, so it's something manufactured," he noted, opening the seal on the bag. Sniffing the contents he asked, "Is that ammonia I smell?"

"That's what I thought too," Piper agreed, taking the bag back from him and returning it to the case. "My aunt is an avid gardener, and she uses a type of organic fertilizer that I remember always smelling like those beads. From what I remember, the most common ingredients in most fertilizers are nitrogen, phosphorous, and potassium. The ammonia could be from nitrogen."

"So we need to figure out why you found those beads in this room and what relationship they would have to Mr. Wells," Agent Hunter challenged.

"He could have just stepped on them somewhere, and they got caught in the treads of his shoes," Piper suggested.

"Or they could be part of an incendiary device," Agent Hunter noted. "Fertilizers are often used in home-made bombs."

"Agreed, there's that possibility too," Piper grimaced. "I seriously hope he's not carrying a bomb around with him."

"Hey," Riley greeted them both as he entered the room. "Find anything good?"

"Possibly," Piper nodded. "We'll have to wait for the lab results, but I found several good prints, some skin and hair samples which should help positively ID our guy, and these little yellow beads Agent Hunter and I were just discussing."

Riley looked at the contents of the bag and asked, "What's so interesting about the beads?"

"Take a whiff," Agent Hunter suggested.

Riley opened the bag and tentatively breathed in, frowning when his sensory glands picked up the aroma. "That's ammonia," he declared, meeting Agent Hunter's eyes. "Are we concerned he's made a bomb?"

"That's what Agent Stirling and I were discussing when you came in," Agent Hunter advised.

"Huh. Well, we'll need to take that into consideration then," Riley agreed, resealing the bag and handing it to Piper. "All of this evidence will be good for trial purposes, but I don't think we need to be concerned about the ID. We're in pretty good shape as far as positively identifying Zander as our guy."

"I guess the motel owner was helpful then?" Agent Hunter surmised.

Riley nodded and said, "Their video surveillance system isn't the best, but the owner did have a few decent recordings of the parking lot, and the occupant of this room. His hair is darker, and he has a full mustache and beard, but our facial recognition software still confirmed it's him."

"When was the last recording dated?" Piper asked as she labeled another evidence bag.

"Two days ago," Riley replied. "He hasn't been back here since."

"I wonder what tipped him off that we were getting close," Piper frowned.

"Or who," Riley suggested.

"You mean Luc?" Piper guessed.

"Who else could it be?" Riley shrugged. "From everything we've been able to determine, Zander is on the run, alone and each time we get close, he suddenly disappears. We've been too careful not to disclose our whereabouts for him to find out where we are."

"So you agree with Agent Cooper's theory that Lucifer still has control over Mr. Wells and is directing his movements?" Agent Hunter asked.

"As crazy as that sounds, yes," Riley nodded. "It's the only theory that makes even the remotest bit of sense."

"Perhaps," Agent Hunter replied, unconvinced. "Did you get any other information from the motel manager?"

"Yes," Riley replied, pulling a piece of paper from his jacket pocket. "According to him as well as what I confirmed on the video surveillance, Zander is driving a silver older model Ford Focus with a license plate B, V, six, H, D, four. Obviously stolen but that's the car he was driving when he left. I've already called the state highway patrol and asked them to put out an APB on the vehicle so hopefully someone will spot it, so we know what direction he went."

"Nice work, Agent Hughes," Agent Hunter praised. Looking around the room, he added, "Is there anything else we need to check while we're here?"

"Nope," Piper replied, snapping the case on her evidence kit closed. "I've checked every register vent, every light socket, the tank on the toilet, the trap in the sink and the bathtub, and the dumpster behind the back of the building. All clean. Well, you know what I mean."

Riley chuckled and winked at her humorously.

"Okay, nice work as well, Agent Stirling," Agent Hunter applauded. "Let's pack up the car and make our way into town and see if we can find out what Mr. Wells was doing to earn a living while he was here."

"Yes, sir," Piper and Riley both replied.

"Here, let me take one of those from you," Riley offered, picking up one of the cases.

"Thank you," Piper smiled, following behind him with the other case.

As she secured the cases in the trunk of the car, Piper gently pushed her rifle case towards the back, wishing there was time for a quick round of target practice. It had been weeks since she had an opportunity to fire her rifle which was a long time for her.

"*Soon*," she thought to herself.

"All set?" Riley asked as she got into the back seat of the car.

"Yep, we're good to go," she nodded, closing the door.

"All right," Agent Hunter replied, starting the engine. "Agent Hughes shotgun makes you the navigator. Where are we going?"

Glancing at the GPS on his phone, Riley replied, "Looks like we should head north out of the parking lot. That should take us to the more commercial part of town where most of the restaurants and business are."

"Roger that," Agent Hunter nodded, engaging the turn signal and merging the car into traffic. "How many miles are there to town from where we are now?"

"Just shy of three, sir," Riley advised.

"Okay. Let's keep our eyes on the surrounding area. Speak up if you see something you think we need to check out," Agent Hunter instructed.

"Yes, sir," Piper and Riley both replied.

Looking out the window as they drove, the glint of the sun reflected off the diamond on Piper's left hand, drawing her eyes down to her engagement ring. The large solitaire stone shone brilliantly in the sunlight and appeared to float on top a circle of small mystic fire topaz stones surrounding it.

"To represent how much I love you and show you how much I appreciate all of the radiant colors you bring to my life," Riley had told her when he proposed. "I see the world in a completely different way since I met you." It was the perfect proposal and the perfect ring for an Auric, who spent her life analyzing the auras of the people around her.

They hadn't set a date yet, but that was mainly because of her. She loved Riley and wanted to marry him, just not yet. There were too many painful memories of her past, watching her parents argue and tear their love for one another away, piece by piece. Their eventual divorce was brutal, and Piper became the pawn they both used to hurt one another. In the end, it was Piper's aunt who took her in and raised her. It took years for Piper to forgive her parents. Their role models on marriage taught her never to let someone too close. At least not close enough to hurt you. It was a lesson that was very hard to unlearn. Riley understood her hesitation and promised her he would wait until she was ready.

"He won't wait around forever, Piper. Don't take too long," Tori had gently warned her.

Piper looked at Riley's face as he and Agent Hunter talked about the case, and smiled, comforted by the happy orange and gold aura around him, gently pulsing in time with his heartbeat.

"I'm nearly there, Riley," she promised him quietly.

Glancing back out the window, she saw a tree and flower nursery coming up on the left side of the road which instantly triggered the return of the ammonia smell in her nostrils. "Make a left at that nursery!" she blurted out suddenly.

Agent Hunter immediately engaged the turn signal and turned into the parking lot. "What made you think to come here, Agent Stirling?" he asked as he parked the car.

"The ammonia smell from the yellow beads," she replied excitedly. "What if the beads did get picked up in Zander's shoe because he worked here?"

"Or they got picked up in his shoe because this is where he bought the fertilizer to make a bomb," Riley suggested.

"Both possibilities worth checking out," Agent Hunter agreed. "Let's go find out, shall we?"

"What alias did the motel manager say Zander was using this time?" Piper asked Riley as they walked toward the building.

"Andrew Rhea," Riley replied quietly.

"Well that's out of character for him, don't you think?" she frowned, stopping short in her tracks.

Agent Hunter stopped abruptly and turned to face her. "What do you mean, Agent Stirling?"

"Has anyone else not noticed how close his aliases have always tied back to his real name?" Piper whispered excitedly. "Alex Anders as in Alexander, Andy Wells who is still pretty close to Alexander Wells...," she offered as examples.

"And?" Riley frowned, not seeing her point.

"And now he's using 'Andrew Rhea' which has nothing to do with his name. Where in the heck did 'Rhea' come from?" she demanded.

"Maybe he's run out of other monikers, or he's just not very creative," Riley suggested.

"Or maybe he thinks we wouldn't expect him to use an alias so close to his real name to throw us off his trail, however since that's not working, he's trying something new?" Agent Hunter suggested.

"Maybe, but something still doesn't feel right. There has to be some significance to the name 'Rhea' that we don't know about yet," Piper insisted.

"Why don't you ask Agent Cooper to run a search on the name and see what she finds?" Agent Hunter suggested.

"That's a great idea!" Piper agreed, taking her cell phone from her pocket. "You guys go ahead, I'll catch up."

Chapter 5

"Finally," Logan grumbled when he saw the highway sign indicating Blacksburg was the next exit. Anticipating the ability to stretch his cramped legs after the long drive, he checked his mirrors to make sure there weren't any state highway patrol cars nearby and then applied a bit more pressure to the accelerator to shorten the remaining distance. As he exited the highway, he glanced briefly down at the GPS app on his phone and followed the signs directing him into town. Seeing he only had a few blocks to his destination, he turned into a gas station to fill the gas tank and take advantage of the restroom inside.

Once he was settled back in the car, he noticed the time displayed on the car dashboard and thought, *"I better check in with the boss and let him know where I am."* Dialing Agent Hunter's number, he heard the call connect and immediately go to voicemail. "Agent Hunter, this is Agent Chase calling to give you a brief update. I just arrived in Blacksburg and am on my way to interview the veterinarian here in town. I'll let you know what I find out later this evening."

Back on the road, it was only a few minutes later when he heard the mechanical voice of his GPS application informing him he had arrived at his destination.

Pulling into the parking lot, of the Blacksburg Animal Hospital, he surveyed the small one-story red brick building, noting the freshly painted white trim around the doors and windows and the manicured shrubbery shading bright, colorful flowers along the ground. There was a single entry glass door centered between two windows, flanked on either side by cartoon-like plastic statues of a smiling dog sitting up on his hind legs with his tongue hanging out of his mouth, and a striped tabby cat playing with a ball of yarn.

"How adorable," Logan muttered sarcastically, already envisioning how the interior of the building would look.

As he got out of the car and approached the building, the entry door of the clinic flew open, and a large black Labrador puppy bolted from the opening, followed by a young boy frantically trying to keep his grip on a long leash. As soon as the dog saw Logan, he immediately changed course and galloped toward him.

"Buddy stop!" the boy cried out, planting his feet firmly on the sidewalk trying to regain control.

"Whoa there," Logan chuckled, noticing the boy was losing the fight. "Do you want some help?"

"No thanks," the boy grunted, pulling the puppy away as he began jumping up on Logan's legs. "Mom says I need to learn how to control him myself."

"Well then let me show you a little trick," Logan offered the boy. "Buddy, down!" he demanded loudly, gently kneeing the dog in the chest forcing him to back up. As soon as the dog was on all four legs, in a very stern voice, he said, "Sit!"

Although his tail and back end were still wriggling on the ground, Buddy immediately sat down.

"Good boy," Logan praised, petting Buddy on the top of the head.

"Gee, Mister, how did you get him to do that?" the boy exclaimed.

"It's all a matter of attitude and control," Logan explained. "You need to let Buddy know he's not in charge, you are. And make sure your voice is strong and confident when you correct him. If you sound unsure, he won't want to listen. Do you want to try it?"

"Okay," the boy agreed, nodding his head.

"Okay, get ready," Logan warned, backing up a few feet. Turning his attention back to Buddy, Logan said, "Come here, boy!"

Instantly Buddy's hindquarters were off the ground, and he was lunging in Logan's direction.

"Buddy, down!" the boy demanded sternly, pulling firmly back on the leash. As soon as Buddy's paws were all on the ground, the boy commanded, "Buddy sit!"

And Buddy sat.

"Hey! Look at you!" Logan smiled, happily. "Great job!"

"Thanks, Mister!" the boy replied.

"No problem!" Logan grinned.

"Well, I gotta get going," the boy advised, pulling Buddy down the sidewalk. "My mom's waiting for me in the car. Thanks again!"

"You're welcome," Logan waved as he entered the clinic.

Once inside, Logan gave his eyes a few minutes to adjust to the fluorescent lighting as well as the unexpected interior décor. The small lobby was currently void of any patients; however, the room nearly overflowed with animals. Large aquariums with various colorful fish and living coral lined the walls, and in each corner of the room stood a tall cylindrical floor to ceiling cage, containing a beautifully colorful, and exotic looking parrot. Then Logan noticed the clear plastic tubing of a hamster habitat suspended above his head, extending across the room, disappearing through a hole in the wall above the reception desk.

"It's like a pet store without any price tags," he marveled, watching the hamsters running through the tubes.

"Hello," one of the birds welcomed.

"We'll be with you in a moment," another bird advised.

"Please have a seat," the third parrot instructed.

"Ding!" the fourth one squawked.

Noticing a domed silver bell on the counter top, Loan smiled and decided to take the last parrots suggestion.

"Ding!" the parrot repeated as Logan pressed the button on the bell.

"Be right with you!" a woman's voice called out down the hallway.

A few moments later, a young woman with long dark brown hair braided down the center of her back appeared. She had a slightly freckled complexion across the bridge of her nose and a natural rosy glow on her cheeks that matched the bubblegum pink shade of lip gloss on her lips. Glancing around the room, she noticed Logan didn't have an animal with him. "May I help you?"

Then Logan noticed her white coat with the name 'Dr. Laura Andrews' stitched on the left pocket. Showing her his badge, Logan smiled and replied, "Dr. Andrews, my name is Agent Logan Chase from the FBI. We spoke on the phone yesterday."

"Oh, of course!" she exclaimed. "It's very nice to meet you, Agent Chase."

"Likewise, thank you for agreeing to see me," he replied, pocketing his badge.

"Have a nice day!" one of the parrots behind him squawked.

Dr. Andrews laughed and said, "Perhaps we should talk in my office. We'll be less distracted."

Logan smiled and admitted, "Your lobby is pretty cool. Did you do all this by yourself?"

Dr. Andrews laughed and looked around the room smiling. "No, my veterinary assistants and receptionist are the masterminds behind what you see. The parrots are mine, so I contributed partly, the rest of it is all them."

"All four of the parrots are yours?" Logan asked, somewhat surprised.

"Yes, I've had them since I was a child. Well, they first belonged to my parents. Then after they passed away, I inherited them," Dr. Andrews replied. "Parrots are a huge investment in time. More than most people realize."

"What do you mean?" Logan frowned, looking at the birds more closely.

"For example, the one in front of you, that's Moe. He's a blue-and-yellow Macaw. Macaws can live up to fifty years," Dr. Andrews advised.

"Fifty years!" Logan exclaimed in shock. "Wow! I had no idea! So how old are your birds?"

"Moe is thirty-six," Dr. Andrews replied, pointing at each cage. "Larry is thirty; Curley is thirty-four, and Shemp is twenty years old."

"I like your parent's sense of humor," Logan chuckled.

"Yeah, we were big Stooges fans. Shemp was my high school graduation gift from my dad. He and I used to watch the Three Stooges movies all the time," she grinned.

"That's a great memory to have," Logan replied.

"Ding!" Shemp agreed loudly.

Dr. Andrews laughed, embarrassed and suggested, "Like I said, we should probably go talk in my office. Would you like some coffee or a soft drink?"

"No, thank you, I'm fine," he replied, following her down the hallway. Glancing in the empty exam rooms as they walked, he asked, "Where's your staff?"

Sitting down at her desk, Dr. Andrews replied, "It's just me and Gwen, my receptionist, today. She's at lunch right now. We didn't have many appointments booked."

"Ah, got it," Logan replied, sitting down in one of the chairs across from her desk.

"So, what can I do for you today, Agent Chase?" she asked politely. "You mentioned on the phone yesterday that you were looking for a dog you believe may be one of my patients? I'm curious why the FBI would be looking for a dog. Is he an escaped criminal?" she winked, teasingly. "They are quite gifted when it comes to escaping confinement you know."

Logan laughed and replied, "No, nothing like that. It's not so much the dog it's the connection the dog has to a person of interest we're looking for."

"How can I help?" she asked.

"The dog I'm looking for is an eight-year-old Dalmatian by the name of Butler," Logan replied. "The family who adopted Butler moved to this area about two years ago so I'm contacting all the veterinarians nearby to see if perhaps the family is a client. Do you currently have a Dalmatian patient by the name 'Butler'?"

"As a matter of fact, I do," she replied calmly, eyebrows raised. "Butler belongs to the Murphy family and they have been my clients for about two years. They seem like really nice people, and Butler loves their little girl. Have they done something wrong? I would hate for that little girl to have to give up her dog."

"No, they've done nothing wrong! I have no intention of taking him away from them," Logan assured her. "Butler was dropped off at an animal shelter in Kentucky by the former owner who we believe is the wife of one of our suspects. We think the woman was afraid of her husband and obviously having a dog so distinctly recognizable would draw attention, so she gave up her dog and has been in hiding ever since."

"How sad for her," Dr. Andrews sighed. "That must have taken a great deal of courage and sacrifice to give away her pet like that. I don't think I could make that kind of sacrifice with any of my birds."

"I agree, that would be very difficult," Logan nodded. "How often do you see Butler?"

"Once a month," Dr. Andrews advised.

"That sounds pretty frequent. Is there something wrong with the dog?" Logan frowned.

"Butler is a Dalmatian as you know," Dr. Andrews explained. "And that breed of dog tends to have a condition known as hyperuricemia. Butler is one of those dogs afflicted with the condition."

"What is hyperuricemia?" Logan asked, making a note in his notebook to research the term later.

"It's a health condition associated with the buildup of uric acid in the blood. Uric acid normally gets excreted in high concentrations in the urine leading to the formation of stones anywhere in the urinary tract, especially the bladder or kidneys. Uric acid levels in Dalmatians are usually higher than in any other breed," Dr. Andrews replied.

"So this isn't something that will shorten his life, just something they need to monitor to make sure he has a healthy quality of life," Logan surmised.

"Exactly," she nodded. "Special food designed for dogs with the condition as well as an adequate amount of water each day are usually all an owner needs to do to have a happy, healthy pet."

"Got it," Logan smiled. "Thanks for explaining that in layman's terms."

"You're welcome," she grinned. "So if you're not planning on removing possession of Butler from the Murphy's, what are you hoping to find now that you've located him?"

Not wanting to give too much information away, Logan replied, "The woman in question has a veterinary degree and used to own a practice back in Kentucky. If she and Butler had a close bond, there's a possibility that she would try to remain in contact with him, even at a distance."

"I see," Dr. Andrews replied, deep in thought. "What is the woman's name?"

"Veronica Wells," Logan replied.

"Hmm, the name doesn't ring a bell," she admitted. "Does she go by Veronica or Roni?"

"Both. Mrs. Wells may also be living under an assumed name," Logan advised. "How long has your staff worked for you? Have you hired anyone new in the past two years?"

"Just Rebecca, but she's not from Kentucky. I think she's from somewhere in Illinois," Dr. Andrews shrugged.

"What's Rebecca's last name," Logan asked, making a note of the name in his notepad.

"Rebecca Stone," Dr. Andrews replied. "But I seriously doubt she's the woman you're looking for."

"Does Rebecca show any special attention to Butler when he comes into the office?" Logan pressed.

"My goodness, she shows special attention to every animal that comes in here!" Dr. Andrews laughed. "Becca loves animals period. And they love her. We're a boarding kennel as well as a veterinary clinic so whenever we have a pet staying with us, Becca always asks to be the one to come in after hours and take care of them."

"What about Butler? Does he show an unusual amount of affection towards Miss Stone when they're together?" Logan pressed again.

"Butler is a very high energy, loving dog. He thinks anyone he meets is the best person in the world," Dr. Andrews laughed. "I don't think you need to worry about Rebecca, Agent Chase."

Getting the feeling she couldn't be more wrong, Logan smiled and said, "Well considering your experience with animals, I'm sure you would know best, Dr. Andrews."

"What does this Veronica Wells look like?" she asked, trying to help.

Not wanting to risk having Dr. Andrews tip off Rebecca once he left, Logan falsely replied, "She's a little shorter than you, has blonde hair, blue eyes, and a fair complexion."

"Well, there you go! That can't be Rebecca. She's a few inches taller than I am, she has dark brown hair, hazel eyes, and olive complexion," Dr. Andrews advised.

Having just described Veronica Wells exactly, Logan smiled and admitted, "Well there you go then! She's not the same woman!"

"I'm glad we settled that!" Dr. Andrews smiled. "Is there anything else I can help you with, Agent Chase?"

"No, you've been most helpful, Dr. Andrews, thank you for your time," Logan replied, getting up from his chair.

Rising from her chair as well, Dr. Andrews walked around her desk and shook his hand firmly. "I'm glad I could help and also glad you finally found your missing Dalmatian!"

"About that," Logan hesitated. "There's no need to mention this to the Murphy's. I don't want to alarm them unnecessarily. As I said, they adopted Butler legally. And since this is an on-going investigation, I would appreciate you keeping our conversation here today between the two of us."

"All right," she nodded.

"That includes your staff as well," he stressed.

"Understood," Dr. Andrews replied, leading him back down the hallway toward the reception area. "Mum's the word!"

"Thank you. Here's my card if you come up with any other information you might find helpful," Logan said, handing her a business card.

"I'll let you know if I come up with anything," she nodded, taking his card. "Goodbye, Agent Chase."

"Goodbye, Dr. Andrews," he waved as he left.

"Have a nice day," Shemp squawked as the door closed behind him.

Chapter 6

The next morning, Logan parked the car at the far end of the parking lot of a donut shop across the street from the veterinary clinic. Hearing the growl of his empty stomach, he glanced over at the 'fresh baked donuts' sign glowing from the storefront window and decided to give in to his desire for a bag of donut holes and a cup of fresh coffee. The clinic wouldn't open for another hour, so he decided to take advantage of the convenience of a quick breakfast.

"So much for the joke about law enforcement officials and their obsession with donuts," he chuckled, getting out of his car. Fortunately, he had anticipated spending a lot of time sitting today, so he opted for a polo shirt and a pair of khaki pants instead of the usual dark business suit and tie.

A few minutes later he was settled back behind the steering wheel, sipping a steaming cup of coffee and savoring the fresh baked goodness of cinnamon-sugar dusted donut holes.

As he was popping the last sugary sphere into his mouth, he saw a vehicle pull into the clinic parking lot. Wiping his fingers, he quickly positioned his wide-angled lens camera on the vehicle and snapped several quick shots of the back bumper, providing the make model and license plate.

When the drivers' door opened, the first glimpse he saw of the occupant inside was a very long, tanned and well- toned female leg clad in a pair of Bermuda shorts, wearing a high-top sneaker.

"Nice form," he mumbled quietly, snapping a few more shots. "Come on let's see the rest of you."

As the occupant of the vehicle emerged, Logan felt his heart skip a beat. "Damn," he breathed quietly, taken off guard. Through the lens of his camera, Veronica Wells was just a few feet from him, in the flesh. Even though the pictures they had of her on file had shown she was an attractive woman, seeing her in person revealed that pictures did not do her justice. She was positively stunning. She was wearing her hair much shorter than in the pictures they had of her, but it was very flattering and framed her face, accentuating her features.

When Logan saw her hazel, almond shaped eyes he knew for sure that it was her. He took several more pictures of her as she walked to the building, then he sat lost in his thoughts for several minutes after she went inside.

"Now what," he thought to himself. *"I can't go back inside the clinic, or Dr. Andrews will give me away. I'm going to have to find a way to meet this Rebecca Stone outside of work."*

Realizing that meant a lot of patient surveillance of her movements, he glanced at the time and made a note in his notebook. Then he adjusted the recline position of his seat, leaned back and began to wait.

~~~~~~~~~~

Four hours later, as the clock struck Noon, Rebecca Stone emerged from the clinic carrying a small insulated cooler and began walking down the sidewalk, in the opposite direction of the clinic.

Remembering a park up the street that he passed earlier that morning, Logan assumed that was the direction she was going. Giving her a few minutes head start, he started the ignition and guided the car onto the street. When he saw her walk across the grass into the park toward one of the benches, he pulled over to the side of the road and turned off the ignition.

Using the lens of his camera to zoom in on her, he noticed her watching something and smiling as she ate her lunch. Angling the camera in the direction of her gaze, he realized this part of the park was a dog park, and there were several people inside a fenced enclosure, allowing their dogs to run freely and play with other dogs.

"She still misses Butler," Logan thought to himself. *"So she comes here hoping he shows up. I wonder how often she does this?"* he asked himself when suddenly an idea came to him. *"That's brilliant!"* He declared, making a note on the notepad.

A half hour later, Rebecca packed up her cooler, and began walking back toward the clinic. Following slowly behind her, Logan returned to the donut shop parking lot and waited again.

~~~~~~~~~~~

After watching the clinic door open and close several times throughout the afternoon as patients came and went, Logan saw the door open again at four o'clock and Rebecca emerged with her cooler in her hand.

Sitting back up at attention, Logan waited until she got into her car and then started the ignition. Easing his car slowly to the exit of the parking lot, he waited until he saw her pull into traffic and then he turned onto the street a few cars behind her.

Just shy of ten minutes later, Rebecca turned her car into the parking lot of a small apartment complex. Following a safe distance behind her, Logan saw her turn her car into an empty spot by one of the buildings so he did the same, picking a spot where he could still see her. Then he quickly aimed his camera in her direction and took a few pictures as she walked up the sidewalk to a row of mailboxes. Snapping several pictures as she checked her mail, he continued to watch her approach the building until he saw her enter the door on the far end closest to the parking lot. Taking a few more pictures of the door to remind him which apartment she was in, he made another note of the time in his notebook and resumed his position of watching and waiting.

~~~~~~~~~~

After two weeks of continual surveillance and switching rental cars every few days so as not to arouse suspicion, Logan had Rebecca's routine carefully logged.

Deciding to follow up on an idea he had the first day he saw her visit the dog park, he called Agent Hunter to propose his next steps.

"Hello Agent Chase," Agent Hunter greeted, engaging the call. "How is your case coming along?"

"Hello, sir. It's coming along very well," Logan replied.

"Did you receive an email from Agent Cooper containing the last known photo of Mrs. Wells?" Agent Hunter asked.

"Yes, she sent it last night along with a copy of the marriage license," Logan replied.

"So now that we know Miss Stone is Veronica Wells, the estranged wife of Alexander Wells, you'll have to proceed with caution, Agent Chase.

"We have no idea why she left her husband, but it was important enough for her to give up her pet and assume a new identity. She's still a flight risk, so you need to be very careful," Agent Hunter warned.

"Yes, I understand, sir," Logan agreed.

"So how do you plan to proceed?" Agent Hunter inquired.

"Well, I have an idea I would like to run by you," Logan said. "It's a little on the fringe, but I'm hoping you'll see where I'm going with it."

"All right, go ahead," Agent Hunter agreed. "What is your idea?"

"Well, sir. I have Miss Stone's schedule carefully logged and have become familiar with her routine. She's very structured and follows the same pattern almost every day."

"As most people do," Agent Hunter pointed out.

"Agreed," Logan replied. "What I would like to do is temporarily rent an apartment in the same complex as Miss Stone."

"I see," Agent Hunter hesitated. "And what do you hope to accomplish by doing that?"

Logan cleared his throat, hoping his second idea wouldn't sound too ridiculous to his boss and confessed, "Well, the apartment is only half of my idea. The other half would be asking for permission to requisition a Dalmatian puppy to use as bait."

"Bait?" Agent Hunter replied, not hiding the surprise in his voice. "How exactly will a Dalmatian puppy be bait, Agent Chase?"

"Well, sir, as I said, Miss Stone has a fixed routine. She visits a dog park every day during her lunch hour and watches the owners play with their dogs. I think she misses being with Butler, her Dalmatian. The visits to the park must be her way of remembering spending time with him. I thought if I were to move into her complex and have a Dalmatian puppy to take to the park at the same time she's there, I'll use the puppy to draw her in. That way we could meet, and I can find out what she knows about her estranged husband," Logan replied.

Pausing long enough for Logan's idea to visualize in his head, Agent Hunter said, "That's a very interesting plan, Agent Chase."

"Uh, thank you, sir?" Logan replied with a question in his voice.

"Agent Cooper also found a picture of Butler, so I would assume we should try to find a puppy with as close to the same markings, wouldn't you agree?" Agent Hunter proposed.

"Uh, yes, that would probably be a good idea?" Logan guessed was the correct reply.

A few paused moments later, Agent Hunter said, "I'll submit the paperwork for the requisition of the dog in the morning."

Blinking in surprise, Logan asked, "That's it, just like that?"

Agent Hunter laughed lightly and reassured, "You've obviously put a lot of thought and consideration into this plan of yours, Agent Chase. If you feel you have Miss Stone's routine clearly mapped and this approach would be an organic means of working your way into her life, I applaud you for your creativity. It's worth a shot. Just be careful. You can't let your guard down at any moment once you've made contact with her."

"I understand, sir. Thank you, sir," Logan breathed in relief. "I'll contact the apartment manager in the morning to secure the space, and then arrange for delivery of some rental furniture."

"You're welcome, Agent Chase. I'll let you know when you can arrange for pick up of the dog," Agent Hunter replied.

"Thank you, sir," Logan agreed.

"Is there anything else?" Agent Hunter asked.

"No, sir, that was all I had to report tonight," Logan replied.

"Very good," Agent Hunter replied, "Goodnight, Agent Chase," he added.

"Goodnight, sir," Logan replied, ending the call. Breathing a sigh of relief, Logan leaned back against the driver's seat, pleased the call had gone so well. "Okay Logan," he told himself, "This is your shot to show your stuff. You better not screw it up!"

Chapter 7

"Wow, I agree with Agent Hunter, Logan. That is a pretty clever plan you came up with!" Piper praised.

"Thanks, Piper," Logan's voice crackled through the speaker on the conference room phone.

"So what's it like out in Blacksburg? I don't think I've ever been out in that part of Virginia," Ben asked.

"It's a pretty decent size city, about forty thousand people. It's not too far from a forest with some hiking trails, and there's a river where I can do some white water rafting, so I think I'm going to check that out once I get settled," Logan replied. "If I'm going to look like I fit in here, I'm going to have to take in some of the local sites."

"The hiking trails will be a good exercise for a puppy too!" Tori advised. "I hope you realize what you're getting yourself into with a puppy. It's a lot like having a baby, Logan. You're on call twenty-four hours a day, and you won't be getting much sleep."

"We'll be fine!" Logan replied. "I've had a dog before. I'm looking forward to it!"

"Are you a dog sleeping in a crate or a dog in the bed person?" Riley asked, curiously.

"Crate? Heck no! I'm a dog in the bed person, man!" Logan chuckled. "Seriously, if you're going to have a dog, let it be part of the family! Don't stick it in a crate and let it cry by itself all night!"

"I'll remind you of that when your body is covered in flea bites," Piper giggled.

"Yeah, it's tough to crate train a dog when you're living in an apartment," Reagan chimed in. "Your neighbors would hate you!"

"Exactly!" Logan exclaimed.

"We were able to find a breeder in Roanoke, Virginia who has a puppy with very similar markings as Butler, Agent Chase," Agent Hunter advised. "It's a male Dalmatian, and he's seven weeks old. You'll be able to pick him up at the end of next week."

"That's perfect, sir! Thank you," Logan replied.

"You're going to have to come up with a name for him!" Piper exclaimed.

"I've got a few ideas in mind, but I want to wait until I meet him to decide which one fits him best," Logan confessed.

"What are you going to do about a job?" Reagan winked at the others.

"What do you mean?" Piper scowled. "He already has a job!"

"He can't be an investigating FBI agent while he's investigating a witness, slash possible accessory to a crime can he?" Reagan challenged.

"She's right," Logan interrupted. "I've already thought of that too. Tori, how's it going getting a hold of that computer equipment we talked about?"

"All packed up and ready to go whenever you give me an address," Tori replied.

"Excellent, thanks!" Logan replied.

"Computer equipment?" Reagan asked Tori.

"We're going to set Logan up to appear as if he's a web developer who works out of his home," Tori announced proudly. "I came up with the idea myself which I'm pretty proud of."

"Logan, a web developer?" Piper snorted. "He can't even program a thermostat much less a computer program."

"Hey!" Logan's voiced objected through the speaker. "That was harsh, Pip."

"Not to worry," Tori intervened. "I've written a few simple programs Logan should be able to follow, should an opportunity come up where he needs to play the part. He'll be fine."

"Thanks, Tor! You're the best!" Logan praised.

"You're welcome," Tori smiled.

"Speaking of an address, how are the arrangements coming along with the apartment?" Agent Hunter asked.

"Great. I signed the paperwork this morning and planned to have the furniture delivered on Thursday during the time when I know Miss Stone will be at work," Logan advised.

"Excellent, keep me updated on your progress," Agent Hunter said.

"Will do, sir," Logan agreed. "How did it go in Greenville?"

"I think we came up with some good information. Agent Stirling, would you like to give the update?" Agent Hunter offered.

"Sure!" Piper brightened eagerly, sitting up in her chair. "We found the usual evidence Zander leaves behind, some hair and skin cells. This time, however, I found several small yellow spheres in the carpet that stumped us for a while."

"Yellow spheres?" Reagan scowled.

Reaching into an evidence box beside her, Piper pulled out a small plastic evidence bag and showed it to Reagan. "These yellow spheres," she advised.

Taking the bag from Piper, Reagan squinted closely at the contents and asked, "So what are they?"

"Fertilizer," Riley announced.

"Why does our suspect have access to fertilizer?" Ben grimaced. "I don't like the sound of that."

"We didn't either at first," Piper addressed the group. "But then we stopped at a plant nursery and landscaping center in town and found out from the manager that Zander has been working for him for the past four months as a landscaper. The same yellow fertilizer is available for purchase at that nursery, so we assume the spheres got picked up in the treads of his shoes."

"Four months, wow." Tori murmured. "That's a long time for Zander."

"Agreed," Riley nodded. "That's the longest place of employment he's had since he started running."

"Our boy is starting to slow down," Logan's voice announced through the speaker. "Think he's getting tired of running yet?"

"I would be if it were me," Piper admitted.

"Same," Reagan agreed.

"So what did this landscaping manager say about our guy?" Ben asked. "Was he the role model citizen again as his former bosses have claimed?"

"Pretty much, yep," Piper shrugged. "The manager paid Zander in cash each week, so we have no money trail. Zander gave the same sob story that he was wrongly incarcerated and had trouble finding a job so the soft-hearted manager gave Zander a shot and after a while, he proved to be a decent, hard-working employee. He had nothing but wonderful things to say about him."

"I bet," Reagan grumbled.

"You've got to give the guy some credit for the 'wrongly incarcerated' story," Tori admitted. "It would keep someone from digging into Zanders alias if he admits to having done time in prison."

"But he's never even done any time!" Reagan argued.

"That's exactly my point!" Tori exclaimed.

"What name was he going by this time?" Logan interrupted.

"Andrew Rhea" Riley replied.

"Which is not following the naming convention he's been using for his aliases up to this point," Piper pointed out.

Suddenly the light bulb went off in Tori's head hearing the name. "No it's not the same naming convention he's been using, but it makes perfect sense to you and I, doesn't it, Logan?"

"Yep," Logan agreed quietly.

"Why does that name make sense?" Piper insisted. "I've been racking my brain trying to figure it out!"

"I found a copy of the marriage license between Alexander and Veronica Wells. His middle name is Andrew, and hers is Rhea," Tori announced.

"He still loves her," Reagan stated quietly. "He wouldn't be using her name as his alias if he didn't still love her."

"Sounds like he does," Agent Hunter agreed. "Would you agree, Agent Chase?"

"Yes, sir," Logan agreed, understanding why his boss was asking the question.

"Which is even more concerning considering the position you're about to put yourself in," Agent Hunter warned.

"I understand, sir," Logan replied firmly.

"What do you mean, sir?" Piper asked, not seeing the reason.

"We don't know if Veronica or Rebecca as she's calling herself now, still loves Zander or not, but it seems Zander still loves her," Tori replied.

"Ah, so if he still loves her, he may also be looking for her," Piper deduced.

"Exactly," Agent Hunter confirmed. "I meant what I said the other day, Agent Chase. Under no circumstances can you let your guard down for one moment once you make contact with Miss Stone."

"I understand, sir," Logan promised. "I'll be careful."

"That's all I had for today. Does anyone else have any other business we need to cover?" Agent Hunter asked the group.

Other than the sound of Goliath's breathing in the room as he slept everyone around the table shook their heads. Then the sound of Logan's voice broke the silence. "I don't have anything else, sir."

"All right, that's all for today. Thank you, everyone," Agent Hunter advised, indicating the meeting was over.

"We're hanging up on you now, Logan," Tori announced, reaching for the end call button.

"Okay, chat with you guys later!" Logan replied quickly before the call ended.

Glancing at the time on the clock, Agent Hunter gathered his paperwork from the table, picked up his coffee mug and rose from his chair. "Excuse me," he murmured as he quickly left the room.

"Where's Agent Hunter off to in such a hurry?" Piper asked quietly.

"I would assume another meeting," Tori shrugged.

"Do you guys want to hang out a bit while Riley and I check our evidence into the system? Maybe grab a bite afterward?" Piper suggested.

"Sure, we could hang out for a bit, right, Tor?" Ben proposed.

Glancing at the time, Tori winced and admitted, "Actually, the meeting went a bit longer than I expected, so the nanny will be expecting one of us home pretty soon."

"Oh yeah, you're right. We'll do it another time," Ben agreed.

"Why don't you stay for a bit?" Tori suggested. "I have to make a quick stop at the store for a couple of things but can make it home in time to relieve the nanny."

"Are you sure you'll be okay by yourself?" Ben worried.

"Tori not by herself, Goliath with her!" Goliath growled, irritably as he stretched.

Not needing the translation from Tori, Ben patted Goliath gently on the head and replied, "Sorry, Goliath. I know she's never alone when she's with you. No offense, buddy."

Satisfied with Ben's reply, Goliath's tail began to wag, and his mouth opened into a big grin.

"We'll be fine!" Tori smiled, giving Goliath an affectionate look. "I've got my big grizzly bear of a dog with me, don't I, Goliath?"

"Always!" Goliath vowed.

"All right then, it looks like I can hang out here with you two for a while," Ben agreed.

"As long as you're sure," Piper asked Tori again.

"Of course, I'm sure!" Tori exclaimed, getting up from her chair. "Everything will be fine! We'll see you guys later! Come on, Goliath."

Chapter 8

"Everything is SO not fine," Tori sighed heavily as she took a sip from her glass of wine, watching the Gemma and RJ play their favorite game of 'Monkey in the Middle' with Goliath in the backyard. Fortunately, Goliath enjoyed the game as much as the children, so he was now happily romping back and forth between them, trying to catch his favorite ball.

When finally it looked like the ball would be within his reach, Goliath increased his speed and jumped up in the air to try and catch it, not realizing how close he was to Gemma. Tori's heart quickened slightly, and she drew in a breath, foreseeing the collision that was about to happen when suddenly Gemma disappeared from where she was standing and re-appeared a few feet away, safely out of harm, ball in hand.

Exhaling, Tori shook her head and muttered, "I don't think I'm ever going to get used to that." She took another sip from her glass, closed her eyes and leaned her head back against the chair, relishing this rare moment of quiet inside the house. Her enjoyment, however, was short-lived as the sound of the garage door broke the silence, announcing Ben's return home.

"Hello!" he called out from the front hallway.

"In the living room," Tori replied.

As Ben entered the room, his eyes were immediately drawn to the bottle of wine on the table, the glass in Tori's hand and the look of weariness in her eyes. "Uh, oh," he frowned, glancing out the window at his children. "Which one was it this time and what did they do?"

"Grab a glass and have a seat," Tori motioned to the cushion on the couch beside her.

Nodding grimly, he said, "Hold that thought," and headed toward the kitchen to wash his hands.

While she waited, Tori took another sip of her wine and continued watching the children play.

"Okay, what happened?" Ben asked as he sat down beside her and filled his glass.

"Well," Tori paused trying to decide which part to tell him first. "For starters, Maria quit today."

"Are you serious?" Ben frowned in frustration. "Which one did it this time?"

"Are you seriously asking me that question?" Tori asked, sarcastically.

"What did he do?" Ben sighed.

"Apparently he wanted grilled cheese for his afternoon snack today, and Maria had already made peanut-butter and jelly because that's what he wanted yesterday. She didn't ask him what he wanted today, so he got mad, and made it rain in the kitchen."

"Well, I was just in there. It didn't look like there's any damage this time," Ben began to reason.

"Oh, that's the frustrating part!" Tori exclaimed. "When I told him how disappointed both of us were that he couldn't control his anger and his rain thingy, he argued back that he listened to us and only made it rain over Maria so the rest of the kitchen wouldn't get ruined this time!"

"Well at least he listened to what we said…..," Ben tried to argue.

"Ben!" Tori scolded sternly.

"Okay, okay. Then what happened? Where was Gemma in all of this?" he asked.

"Oh yeah! Gemma sat there giggling while she explained to me how creative RJ was and how apparently this little storm cloud began to form over Maria's head as she was trying to reason with RJ that she would make him a grilled cheese sandwich tomorrow. Then apparently thunder and lightning began to erupt from within the cloud and then it began to rain, right on Maria's head and ONLY on Maria's head!" Tori advised, angrily.

"Man…..," Ben muttered, looking out the window at his son.

"Oh, that's not the worst of it!" Tori declared excitedly, almost spilling her wine.

"What else?" Ben sighed, leaning back against the couch cushion.

Setting her glass down on the table, Tori turned to him angrily and said, "Okay, so I'm at the store, picking up a few things for dinner tonight and my phone rings. I see its Maria so I take the call and she starts screaming in the phone at how I need to come home right now, and how soon could I get there. So I drop everything, leave my cart in the middle of an aisle, which I hate doing, and I immediately come home.

"She must have been watching for my car from the front window because I hadn't even pulled into the driveway yet when suddenly she's out the front door, running down the sidewalk toward me. So I get out of the car, and she immediately starts gesturing with her hands in the air and yelling at me at a hundred miles an hour, half of which I couldn't even understand because I don't speak Spanish! Next thing I know, she's headed to her car, still spouting off in Spanish, slams the car door, peels away from the curb and drives away!"

"I was wondering where the black skid marks in front of our house came from," Ben muttered.

"That was her!" Tori replied, with a wave of her hand.

"Anything else?" Ben cautiously asked.

"Actually yes!" Tori declared. "About a half hour later I got a call from Regina Black who's the head of the placement agency where Maria is employed, and Ms. Black told me Maria would not be coming back. When I asked her if she had a recommendation for another nanny we could use, she said no and to please remove them from our list of agencies to contact from now on. She went even further to say that perhaps a nanny is not who we should be looking for, maybe we should be looking for a priest!"

Ben scowled, understanding the implication and replied, "Well I don't think that was a very nice thing for her to say, our children are not possessed by the devil!"

Tori's shoulders dropped, and she sighed heavily, glancing back out the window at her children. "To the outsider, they look like they are, Ben. They're too young to understand how to control their abilities and we have to stop pretending things can go on the way they have."

"Oh come on!" Ben argued. "Let's not give up so soon! We can find another agency!"

"The nannies aren't the problem, Ben. I need to step up and take responsibility for my role in raising these children, and focus on them from now on." Tori reasoned.

"But you love your job!" Ben continued to argue.

Patting his hand gently, she smiled at him and admitted, "I love my family more. You, Gemma, RJ and Goliath are my priorities. I've already decided to talk to Agent Hunter about it so he can plan to replace me on his team."

Snorting in derision, Ben insisted, "Like he could ever replace you! At least consider staying on the team in a consulting role. We can find a way to make that work, right? That would give you time to be with the kids and still be able to use your abilities to help the FBI!"

"I guess we could give that a try if Agent Hunter would agree," she shrugged.

"Of course he would agree! At least promise me you'll ask," Ben pleaded looking into her eyes intently. "I know how much you love what you do. No one else can do what you do. I don't want you to give it all up. There has to be a way to compromise."

"Fine, I promise I'll ask," Tori conceded.

"Thank you," Ben whispered, leaning forward to kiss her tenderly on the lips. "I love you."

Tori smiled and replied, "I love you too."

"What do you say we go have a talk with our little demons?" Ben asked wriggling his eyebrows.

Tori laughed and replied, "I guess I've put it off long enough. Let's go."

Chapter 9

"Kids, Grandma, Grandpa and Aunt Aubrey are just a few minutes away!" Tori called out from the front hallway. "Do you want to come outside with Daddy and me and wait for them?"

"Coming!" she heard RJ shout from his bedroom followed by the pounding of feet running down the hallway toward her.

"Me too!" Gemma shouted, following closely behind him.

Preparing the runway, Ben opened the front door and stood back as RJ raced past him out the front door, followed by Gemma, immediately followed by Goliath who as usual, left a trail of hair and saliva on the floor in his wake. "Maybe we should have taken all three of them to the park earlier to burn off some of their energy," he chuckled, watching the trio jump around excitedly in the front yard.

"Ugh, or at least taken the hairbrush to Goliath to get rid of some of that loose hair," Tori grimaced in disgust. "I love that dog to pieces, but that hair completely drives me nuts!"

"Well, considering Corkey is about to add to that collection on the floor, I don't think your parents or your sister are going to be grossed out by a little dog hair," Ben smiled, rubbing her back supportively.

"Yeah, but Corkey is about one-eighth the size of Goliath!" Tori exclaimed. "Maybe we should get him shaved for the summer?"

"Oh, please tell me you're kidding. Between people shaving the hair off their dogs and dressing the dogs in clothes, humans have completely taken the dignity out of letting a dog be a dog!" Ben complained.

"I was almost kidding," Tori winced.

"There's their car!" Ben nodded in the direction of the street.

"They're here; they're here!" RJ and Gemma cried out happily in unison.

"Stay back until the car pulls into the driveway, okay?" Tori insisted, walking toward them. "Grandpa isn't used to having to avoid little munchkins running around everywhere."

"He'll get used to it pretty quickly around here," Ben murmured out the side of his mouth.

"Shh!" Tori laughed, playfully hitting him on the shoulder. "And remember, no sudden movements or we'll scare them away!"

Laughing with her, Ben nodded and added, "At least until they have their car unpacked."

"Agreed," Tori snickered.

As soon as Tanner had the car in park, the front passenger door flew open, and Sarah jumped out of the car with her arms wide open. "There are my little darlings!" she cried out as the twins raced toward her.

"Grandma!" they chimed in unison flinging themselves into her arms.

"Oh, how I've missed you both," Sarah declared, hugging the twins tightly against her.

Frantic barking ensued as soon as Tanner opened his door, so he reached behind him to open the rear door to release Corkey from the back seat. "Okay, okay, settle down, Cork," Tanner gently scolded as the dog launched from the car toward Goliath. "There. Go see Goliath!"

While the usual tail wagging and butt sniffing ensued between the dogs as they re-familiarized themselves with one another, Tanner walked around the car and embraced Tori in a tight hug. "Hi sweetheart," he murmured affectionately. "How's my girl doing?"

"Hi Dad," Tori smiled, breathing in the familiar smell of her father's aftershave as she held him close. "Much better now that you're here. I've missed you."

"I've missed you too, baby girl," Tanner murmured, pulling back to kiss his daughter on the forehead. Noticing Ben waiting patiently nearby, Tanner held out his hand and pulled Ben into a warm embrace. "Hi, Ben, it's good to see you too, son."

"Likewise, Tanner," Ben smiled, patting Tanner on the back affectionately.

"All right, Grandpa. It's your turn," Sarah warned letting go of the twins.

"Come here you little monkey's!" Tanner teased as the twins rushed into his arms. "Gosh, I've missed you two! Look at how big you're both getting!"

"They've missed you too! They've been so excited since we told them you were coming to visit!" Tori laughed watching her father try to keep his balance and not fall.

"Hi sweetie," Sarah soothed gently pulling Tori into her arms. "Everything is going to be okay, honey."

"Thank you and Dad so much for offering to stay with us for a while until we figure things out. I don't know what I would do without you guys," Tori confessed quietly into her mother's ear.

"Hey, don't forget about me!" Aubrey demanded loudly behind her.

"Oh like you would ever let that happen," Tori teased, turning toward the sound of her sister's voice. "Hi, Bree."

"Hey, Tor," Aubrey smiled, her spirit shimmering as she floated a few inches above the ground.

"Your sister has a surprise for you," Sarah whispered mischievously. "She's been so looking forward to showing it to you."

"Does she now?" Tori exclaimed, her eyebrows rising, expectantly. "Do tell!"

"Close your eyes!" Aubrey demanded with an excited smile.

"All right, my eyes are closed," Tori complied. "Now what?" she demanded.

"One second," Aubrey murmured, her voice filled with concentration.

Suddenly Tori felt fabric wrapping itself around her like a soft, warm hug, followed by a scent she hadn't smelled since she and her sister were both teenagers.

Her eyes flew open, and she looked down recognizing her sister's favorite shawl wrapped around her. "Oh, Bree," she whispered, her eyes filling with tears as she reached up to pull the shawl more tightly around her shoulders.

"Since I can't physically touch you, this is the closest thing I can get to giving you a hug," Aubrey admitted sweetly.

Burying her face into the fabric, Tori inhaled a deep breath and shook her head in amazement. "Where on earth did you get a bottle of Debbie Gibson's Electric Youth perfume?"

Laughing out loud, Aubrey pointed her finger at Sarah and cried out, "I told you she would know it as soon as she smelled it!"

"Yes you sure did," Sarah admitted, conceding an apparent bet.

"Seriously, where did you find it?" Tori marveled as a flood of memories from her and Aubrey's childhood filled her mind.

"Mom found it on eBay," Aubrey confessed. "I wanted to attach a memory to this so neither one of us would ever forget it."

"Gosh, remember how much we used to love this stuff?" Tori laughed, taking another whiff. "It smells like orange scented cotton candy!"

"I know, right?" Aubrey laughed.

"That was very sweet of you, thank you, Bree," Tori smiled fondly at her sister.

"You're welcome!" Aubrey beamed.

"Did you bring anything for us, Aunt Aubrey?" RJ interrupted loudly.

"RJ!" Tori scolded gently. *"That's rude to ask, sweetie,"* she directed at him telepathically.

"But Aunt Aubrey always brings me and Gemma something," RJ silently argued.

"He's right, Mama," Gemma silently agreed.

"That's true, but you're not supposed to ask," Tori reasoned, giving both RJ and Gemma a look of warning.

Confused, RJ frowned and turned back toward Aubrey sullenly. "Sorry, Aunt Aubrey," he mumbled, staring at the ground. Instantly agitated, RJ reached one hand behind his head and began scratching furiously at one of his shoulder blades.

Frowning at the intensity of his scratching, Tori reached over and pulled the collar of his shirt away from his skin so she could look down the back of his shirt. "Is your back itching again, honey?"

"It's okay," RJ grumbled, reaching over to scratch the other shoulder blade.

"I swear I don't see anything," Tori complained, pulling up the bottom of his shirt to expose his entire back.

"Mom," RJ argued, trying to push her hand away.

"Just let me look, honey," Tori pleaded, feeling along his back with her fingertips. "Mom, do you see anything?"

Sarah leaned forward to take a closer look and also ran her fingers over RJ's shoulder blades. "Hmm, other than the redness on his skin from him scratching, no, I don't see anything," she agreed.

"Hmm, maybe I should make an appointment with Max and have him checked out," Tori thought out loud.

"You're still using Max as the kid's pediatrician?" Sarah asked.

Tori nodded and replied, "For now, yes. At least until we find another doctor who we can trust with our secret. Even though Max retired from his practice, he still wants to treat the twins while they're little."

"That's very kind of him. He really came through during your delivery that's for sure," Sarah agreed.

"Yeah, Max is great. Finding someone to replace him will be hard," Tori sighed. Letting go of RJ's shirt, she advised, "We'll put more lotion on your back when we get inside, okay sweetie?"

"Okay," RJ shrugged, pulling his shirt down. Then he cast a sideways glance over in Aubrey's direction.

"What were we talking about again?" Aubrey teased, pretending she'd forgotten.

Sliding his eyes over at Tori, RJ paused long enough to form an acceptable response and said, "Mom was telling me it was rude to ask if you brought Gemma and me a present."

Narrowing her eyes at her son, Tori scowled disapprovingly, knowing her son had just successfully mastered this round.

"Well, fortunately for you young man, I did!" Aubrey teased again.

Instantly flipping his sullen expression to joy, RJ tensed with excitement and asked, "What is it?"

"I don't know. You might want to help Grandpa and your dad unload the back of the car. There might be two wrapped boxes in there with yours and Gemma's names on them," Aubrey suggested calmly.

Quick as a flash, RJ was grabbing Gemma by the hand, pulling her toward the car. "Come on! Aunt Aubrey brought us something!" he insisted urgently. Eager to follow suit, Gemma ran with him.

"Very smooth, Sis," Tori conceded to her sister. "What did you get them? Do I need to be worried?"

Laughing ominously, Aubrey's spirit floated across the driveway toward the car and replied, "I guess you'll just have to wait and see."

~~~~~~~~~~

"This is fun. I miss girls only cooking therapy," Tori admitted as she stirred a steaming pot filled with grits.

"I second that motion! We need to do more of this while we're here," Sarah agreed, pouring a small amount of olive oil in a large sauté pan adjacent to the pot.

"Especially now that Bree has found a way to be a part of it," Tori smiled, watching her sister transport the lettuce from the cutting board into the salad bowl. "I still can't get over how much you've improved since the last time I saw you! Is there anything you can't do?"

"I still can't physically touch anyone, but I'm still working on that," Aubrey replied, concentrating on the bottle of dressing floating a few inches above the salad bowl. "I've pretty much mastered the ability to manipulate everything else physical. How much dressing should I add to the salad?"

"About half of what's in that bottle and give it a good toss," Tori advised.

"Got it," Aubrey replied concentrating on the bottle as it tipped forward slowly.

"How much time do you need for the scallops, Mom?" Tori asked.

"About three minutes per side. I only need a quick sear on them," Sarah replied, carefully arranging the large scallops in the pan.

"Perfect, that works for me too," Tori nodded.

"Do you want me to go tell everyone dinner's almost ready?" Aubrey offered.

"Yes, please!" Tori replied as she measured shredded Gouda cheese into the pot.

"Thanks, honey," Sarah called out as Aubrey's spirit floated toward the window.

"No problem, Mom!" Aubrey replied, her voice trailing off once her form passed through the panes of glass.

"Does she ever use a door anymore?" Tori wondered.

"Why would she? She doesn't need to," Sarah replied, carefully turning the scallops over.

"I'm just curious how long it will take until Gemma notices," Tori admitted, quietly. "She doesn't need to use doors anymore either. She can transport her physical form through any solid material like its water. I think the main reason she still does is that of RJ. She doesn't want him to feel left out."

Sarah glanced at Tori's worried face and smiled reassuringly. "You're going to have to learn how to roll with the punches more effectively as the kids grow up, sweetheart. They're going to do some things that may totally throw you off balance. You need to be strong for them and encourage them. That may mean one of them can do something the other one can't."

"I know," Tori sighed. "I'm just so worried about how the world will treat them because of how different they are. The experience with the nanny was just the start of it. They don't understand why people react to them the way they sometimes do."

"Which is why your sister, and your dad and I are here," Sarah advised firmly. "It's going to take the entire family to show Gemma and RJ that they can be special and still be part of society at the same time. It may take a few repeated attempts before it sinks in, but they'll learn, sweetheart."

Exhaling a deep breath, Tori nodded in agreement and murmured, "We'll see."

Deciding they needed a distraction to lighten the mood, Sarah broke one of the scallops in half with a fork and presented a half to Tori. "Here taste this and tell me if you think they've cooked long enough."

Taking a bite, Tori chewed for a moment, debating. "Um, that's perfect! And you only used olive oil, salt, and pepper on those?"

"Yep," Sarah replied, popping the other half of the scallop in her mouth. "That's all they need. Scallops are so sweet and buttery. They don't need anything else."

"Yum, I agree that was delicious. Here try the grits. Let me know if you think they're seasoned okay," Tori asked, handing Sarah a spoonful of the grits.

"Oh wow," Sarah marveled as the flavors hit her tongue. "Those are really good! I'm not a big grit fan, but the smoked Gouda cheese gives them such a rich, smoky flavor! Wow, your dad is going to love those!"

"Thanks! Ben and the kids love this dish. That's why I made such a big batch just in case you were wondering," Tori chuckled.

"Well, I can see why!" Sarah grinned, happy that her diversion worked. *"Cooking therapy is the perfect cure for a troubled mind!"* she thought to herself, happily.

"Hey! Rumor has it dinner is just about ready," Ben declared as he entered the kitchen. "I'm all washed up and ready to go. What may I do to help? Do you want me to set the table?"

"I've already set the table so you can get everyone drinks," Tori suggested.

"Okay. What do you two beautiful ladies feel like drinking this evening?" he inquired.

Motioning to two glasses on the counter, Tori replied, "We've already started on a bottle of the Vouvray Chenin Blanc in the fridge if you wouldn't mind topping us off please?"

"Oh, that sounds good. I might join you. We're having seafood tonight, right?" Ben asked, retrieving the bottle of wine.

"Yep," Tori confirmed, scooping the grits from the pot into a decorative serving bowl. "Seared scallops with applewood smoked Gouda grits and a Caesar salad."

"Oh, that sounds amazing!" Ben exclaimed. "I'm starving!"

Shaking her head in disbelief, Tori argued, "What? You guys had the veggie tray and the anti-pasta platter an hour ago! You shouldn't be starving after all that!"

"Well, you know how the kids are when they see cheese, sausage, and crackers. They wolfed that plate down almost between themselves!" Ben admitted, sheepishly.

Giving him a disapproving scowl, Tori replied, "And as their father you have the parental right to portion control them and make them eat some of the vegetables too."

"Yeah, but come on, Tor, what kid wants to eat vegetables when there are cheese and sausage?" Ben tried to argue.

"Anyway, dinner's ready so it doesn't matter at this point," Tori smirked, rolling her eyes at him. "Go see what Dad wants to drink. The kids get milk."

"Yes, Ma'am!" Ben saluted before heading toward the dining room.

"What a goofball," Tori muttered under her breath as she picked up the bowls for the grits and the salad.

"I've got the platter with the scallops, the Parmesan cheese, and croutons for the salad," Sarah chuckled, following Tori.

"Thanks, Mom. All right, everyone take a seat," Tori instructed, setting the bowls on the table. "Who would like to say, Grace, tonight?"

"I would!" RJ immediately raised his hand.

"All right, thank you RJ," Tori smiled, sitting down in the chair beside Ben.

While everyone grabbed hands around the table, Aubrey floated over to the spot directly behind Gemma and RJ's chairs and hovered silently with her head bowed and eyes closed.

"Dear Heavenly Father," RJ began. "Thank you for safe travels for Grandma, Grandpa, Aunt Aubrey, and Corkey. Thank you for Mom, Dad, Gemma and Goliath. Thank you for forgiveness, God. I know what I did to Maria was wrong and I'm sorry I made her leave. She was nice. I promise I'll try to do better, so Mom and Dad won't be mad at me. Amen."

Opening her eyes, Tori looked at RJ's sad expression and replied, "We're not mad at you, sweetie. We know you can't always help how you feel. We'll work on the anger control together, okay? By the way, that was a really beautiful prayer."

"Yes it was, son," Ben agreed.

"Thanks," RJ grinned.

"I agree! Nice job little man!" Aubrey praised loudly, leaning forward closer to RJ's chair.

"Thanks, Aunt Bree," RJ smiled, looking over his shoulder at her. As he turned, his shoulder lightly brushed up against Aubrey's arm. "Hey, I touched you!" he exclaimed excitedly, letting go of Gemma's hand so he could turn around.

"Oh my gosh, you did!" Aubrey's spirit shimmered with excitement. "How did you do that? Do it again!"

Reaching his hand toward her, he frowned when it passed through her. "Aw, it didn't work," he complained.

"Are you sure you felt him?" Tori exclaimed in surprise.

"I swear I did!" Aubrey cried out.

"She did," Gemma announced quietly.

Glancing at Gemma's calm expression, Tori asked, "How do you know that for sure, honey?"

"I felt it too," Gemma replied innocently.

"How could you have felt it, sweetie?" Tori asked. "RJ is the one who brushed up against Aubrey."

"Here, I'll show you!" Gemma shrugged. "RJ, grab my hand again."

Immediately, RJ grabbed Gemma's hand.

"Now touch Aunt Bree," Gemma demanded.

Obediently, RJ reached out his hand and placed it on Aubrey's arm, causing Aubrey to jump in surprise.

"You can feel me," she whispered, staring down at her arm. With tear filled eyes, she grabbed hold of RJ's hand and exclaimed, "You can feel me!"

Gemma reached over to take Aubrey's other hand and together, the children's faces beamed with joy. "We can both feel you," they replied in unison.

Quickly getting up from her chair, Tori rushed around the table and reached her hand out toward Aubrey. Disappointed when her hand passed through her sister, she shook her head in amazement, noticing that the children and her sisters' hands were still intertwined. "I don't understand. Why can't I feel you?"

"It must be something only Bree, and the twins can do," Sarah suggested, wiping a tear from the corner of her eye. "It's truly a gift from God."

"I'll say," Tanner added his voice thick with emotion.

Dropping to her knees, Aubrey pulled the twins into her arms in a warm embrace. "Oh, it's been so long since I've felt another human being!" she exclaimed happily. "You both feel so soft and squishy!" Breathing in deeply, she added, "I can smell the baby shampoo in their hair!"

"Uh, Aunt Bree, I can't breathe," RJ grimaced, squirming in her arms.

"Oh, I'm sorry RJ," Aubrey giggled, releasing her hold slightly. "I'm just so blown away by what just happened! It's incredible, it's amazing, it's, it's...."

"It's a miracle," Tori whispered happily for her sister.

Meeting Tori's eyes, Aubrey smiled sadly and admitted. "I wish it would have worked for you too."

"Maybe one day it will," Tori replied.

"Can we eat now? I'm hungry," Gemma interrupted, squirming out of Aubrey's arms.

"Of course we can, honey," Tori laughed, walking back to her chair and sitting down. "Okay, everyone! You heard Gemma. It's time to eat!"

Chapter 10

"I'm stuffed," Ben groaned, leaning back against the cushion on the lounge chair.

Adding another piece of wood to the fire pit, Tori chuckled and replied, "I would hope so after all you ate!"

"I know, right?" he winked playfully.

"Once again, you ladies prepared a wonderful dinner, thank you," Tanner praised, taking a seat by the fire.

"You're welcome, Dad," Tori smiled, sitting on the chair beside Ben.

"Where are your Mom and the twins?" Ben asked, glancing toward the house.

"The twins just got out of the bath and are brushing their teeth. I told them to come out and join us afterward," Tori advised.

"Man, they're going to sleep well tonight! That yard sprinkler with the water fountains Bree picked out for RJ is perfect for him! Did you see how much fun he was having freezing the fountains into sculptures earlier? He was having a blast!" Ben chuckled.

"Yes, he was," Tanner grinned. "She hit the nail on the head with that present."

"Well I had to get them something cool since we didn't get to see them on their birthday," Aubrey replied, appearing beside Tori.

"Bree said she needed to get them something cool since she missed their birthday this year," Tori recited for the guys, so they knew Aubrey was there.

"What did you get Gemma, Bree? I didn't see what she got," Ben asked loudly.

"Tell him I got her memory flash cards," Aubrey addressed Tori. "I have an idea I want to try with her and RJ once they're done brushing their teeth."

"She said she got Gemma memory flash cards. She wants to try something with the twins using the cards," Tori repeated.

"Ah, those should be fun," Ben nodded.

Suddenly a burst of barking from Goliath and Corkey broke the silence, followed by the sound of clawed feet on pavement running toward them.

"Both of you quiet down," Sarah scolded, holding something in her hands above her head as she walked. As soon as both dogs quieted, she looked between them, and insisted, "Sit!"

Goliath's and Corkey's hind quarters immediately hit the pavement. Smiling at their obedience, Sarah revealed that she had a large beef bone in each of her hands, one slightly larger than the other. Giving the larger bone to Goliath, and the other bone to Corkey, she nodded and said, "Good boys!"

"Where did you get the bones, Mom?" Tori wondered, knowing the exact contents of both the house and garage refrigerators.

"We picked them up from the butcher in town today on the way to your house," Sarah grinned, wiping her hands on a napkin she had stashed in her pocket. "I had them in the cooler and put them in the garage fridge when we got here."

"Man, you are their new best friend, Sarah," Ben chuckled as both dogs lay by the fire pit, hungrily gnawing on their bone. "Look at them go!"

"Well, they've both been good today, so I thought they deserved a treat," Sarah shrugged, sitting in the chair beside Tanner. "Whew, it feels good to sit down!" Looking at the table beside her, she frowned and said, "Shoot, I must have left my wine in the kitchen."

"I'll go get it!" Ben insisted, quickly getting up from his chair. "Tor, Tanner? Want me to bring another round out for you too?"

"Sure, I'll take another glass," Tori admitted.

"Count me in, thanks, Ben!" Tanner replied.

"No problem! I'll check on the twins while I'm at it," Ben advised, heading toward the house.

"I'll come with you," Aubrey replied, following him.

"Bree's coming with you," Tori called out as Ben walked away.

"Got it," he replied. Once inside, Ben noticed the twins were spreading Gemma's flash cards out on the coffee table in the living room. "Don't you guys want to come outside by the fire pit with Grandma and Grandpa?" he asked.

"Naw," RJ mumbled, continuing to spread out the cards.

"We need the light, Daddy," Gemma noted, pointing to the lamp on the table.

"Ah, yes you do! That was silly of me wasn't it?" Ben teased, winking at Gemma.

"That's okay, Daddy. You came to get drinks for everyone outside, didn't you?" Gemma asked, focusing her attention back on the cards.

"How did you…," Ben started to ask when Gemma interrupted him.

"I heard Mama say that she would take another glass. She must be thirsty," Gemma replied innocently, laying out another row of cards on the table.

Turning back toward the door, Ben noticed the screen was closed, and none of the windows were open for the kids to have heard what the grownups were discussing. *"How did she hear Tori say that?"* he thought to himself.

When she realized Ben was still standing there, Gemma looked up, saw the expression on his face and calmly replied, "I can hear what Mama thinks, Daddy. It's okay. You don't have to be worried."

Taken back by her response, Ben blinked in surprise and stammered, "I-I'm not worried, sweetie. T-That makes total sense. Thank you for explaining it to me."

"You're welcome, Daddy!" Gemma smiled sweetly at him.

Doing her best to suppress the giggle in her throat, Aubrey remained silent, her spirit hovering beside the table next to the twins.

Still a little shaken, Ben smiled back at Gemma and then immediately headed for the kitchen. As he rounded the corner out of the children's line of sight, he gripped the countertop tightly with both hands and blew out a deep breath. "Okay, man. Be cool," he whispered to himself. "This is just another one of those moments when you learn something new about your kids. Take a deep breath, act normal and go tell Tori."

Quickly assembling the drinks, he hurried through the living room, making sure the kids were still sitting on the floor beside the coffee table, and made a bee-line for the back door. As calmly as possible, he made his way out to the group outside and set the drink tray on the table.

"Here you go, my dear," he said handing Tori her glass.

"Thank you, sir," Tori said.

"My pleasure," he replied.

"Thanks, Ben," Sarah smiled, taking her glass.

"You're welcome, Sarah," he smiled back.

"Appreciate it, Ben!" Tanner grinned, happily.

"Anytime," Ben gave a quick nod. Picking up his glass, he took a very long drink and felt the tension in his body release. "Ahhhhhh," he sighed, loudly when the glass was empty.

"Ah, are you alright there, sweetie?" Tori eyed him suspiciously.

"That's an excellent question, Tor," Ben replied calmly. "I'm not sure if this is just news to me or not, but I wanted to let you know that Gemma can read your mind," he announced, watching her closely for her reaction.

"Excuse me?" Tori blinked, her hand pausing in mid-air as she was about to take a sip of her wine.

"What?" Tanner exclaimed in surprise.

"Oh my," Sarah murmured quietly.

Eyeing Tori carefully, Ben frowned and replied, "You seriously didn't know?"

Setting her glass down on the table, Tori stared at him wide-eyed and exclaimed, "Well, of course I didn't know!" Pausing as a thought came to her, she added, "Well, now that I think about it, that makes sense considering some of the conversations I've had with her." Then another thought occurred to her, and she cringed. "Oh my, I wonder what she's heard that I don't know about."

"Is it just Gemma, or can RJ read Tori's mind as well?" Sarah asked Ben.

"I don't know," Ben admitted. "It happened so fast, and then I didn't want them to see me freak out, so I quickly grabbed the drinks and hurried back out here to tell you."

"Well, I guess I need to have a talk with Gemma then," Tori sighed, getting up from her chair.

"I'm coming with you," Sarah announced.

"Same here," Tanner agreed, getting up from his chair.

"This should be fun," Ben muttered under his breath, following everyone back into the house.

As they all filed into the living room, Gemma looked up and announced, "Hi, Mama! Daddy told you I said you were thirsty."

Sitting on the floor by the table between Gemma and RJ, Tori nodded and replied, "Yes he did, sweetie."

"You're not angry," Gemma stated in a very matter of fact manner.

Realizing Gemma hadn't stated it as a question, Tori replied. "No, Mommy's not angry." Looking at both Gemma and RJ's innocent faces, she asked, "Can you always hear what Mommy's thinking, sweetie? Thoughts Mommy doesn't say out loud?"

"Pretty much," Gemma nodded.

RJ nodded silently along with his sister.

"Ah," Tori noted. "So you can both hear what Mommy's thinking," she surmised.

Again, both Gemma and RJ nodded their heads in response.

"How long have you been able to hear what Mommy's thinking?" Tori worried.

Gemma looked at RJ and exchanged what appeared to be a silent conversation with her brother. Then RJ gave a quick nod to his sister and looked back at Tori.

"It started the day you found the girl in the woods," Gemma advised.

Tori gulped hard, thinking back in her head how long ago that was.

"Were you and RJ just talking to each other with your minds, honey?" Sarah asked Gemma, quietly.

"Uh huh," Gemma nodded.

"Is that something the two of you often do?" Sarah prodded.

"Uh huh," Gemma nodded again.

Glancing over at Tori, Sarah asked, "You didn't hear them did you?"

"No, I didn't," Tori admitted.

Looking over at Aubrey, Sarah asked, "Did you hear them?"

"Nope," Aubrey replied.

"So what are you saying? The twins can communicate with one another telepathically with and without Tori knowing, as well as hear Tori's thoughts without her knowing?" Ben exclaimed. "What does that mean?"

"It means they share a bond between them they don't share with their mother," Sarah replied calmly. "It's not a bad thing, Ben," she added, inclining her head in the direction of the children, reminding him they were listening. "It's just something new."

"Of course it's not bad!" Ben agreed, smiling at Gemma and RJ, praying that neither of them could hear the panic starting to rise in his voice.

"So you're not angry with us?" Gemma worried, looking back and forth between her parents.

"Of course we're not angry with you, sweetie," Tori soothed, reaching out to gently cradle her children's faces in the palms of her hands. "We don't ever want you to be afraid to tell us something new, okay?"

"No matter what it is?" Gemma pressed.

"No matter what," Tori assured her.

"Okay," the twins replied.

Glancing at the memory cards, which had been laid face down on the table, a thought materialized in Tori's head, and she looked up at Aubrey. "You had a feeling about this, didn't you?"

Shrugging her shoulders, Aubrey nodded and replied, "I can't explain it, but the last time we saw the twins at Christmas, I thought I saw a silent exchange between them. It was so subtle, though I wasn't sure, so I didn't say anything. I thought about it afterward and decided to find out. I thought the flashcards would be a good test to find out for sure."

"Well, let's say we find out?" Sarah suggested, easing down the floor to sit by the table. "Who else wants to play?" she added, giving the rest of the grownups an intense stare.

"Well, I do, of course!" Aubrey replied.

"Me too," Tori nodded.

"I'm in," Ben agreed, taking a seat on the floor beside RJ.

"Well don't leave me out!" Tanner chuckled, always prepared for something unexpected from his family.

Once everyone took a seat on the floor around the table, Ben asked, "So how does this game work?"

"Traditionally, memory cards are played by each player taking turns turning two cards over one at a time to find a match. But for this first round, let's try something a little different," Sarah suggested.

Picking up one of the cards, she peeked at the other side, not letting anyone else see it, and placed it face down in front of her. "Can anyone tell me what my card is?"

Tori shook her head and replied, "I can't."

"Me either," Aubrey admitted.

"Me either," Ben replied.

"Nope," Tanner shrugged.

RJ and Gemma both shook their heads no.

"Okay," Sarah shrugged making eye contact with Tanner. "Grandpa, it's your turn."

"All right," Tanner replied, picking up a card and taking a look at the other side before placing it face down in front of him. "Can anyone tell me what my card is?"

Again, everyone around the table gave the same response.

Tori shook her head and replied, "I can't."

"Me either," Aubrey admitted.

"Me either," Sarah replied.

"Nope," Ben shrugged.

RJ and Gemma both shook their heads no.

"Okay," Sarah replied, calmly. "It's your turn, RJ."

RJ eagerly picked up a card and quickly took a peek at the other side. Before he could even set the card down in front of him, Gemma exclaimed, "It's a bunny!"

Frowning, RJ threw the card down and shouted, "You're supposed to wait until I ask, Gemma!"

Playing mediator, Sarah quickly said, "There will be no shouting. Is that understood?"

"Sorry, Grandma," RJ sulked, glaring at his sister.

"We didn't state the rules before we started playing, so Gemma didn't know. From now on, we wait until the player asks the question before anyone answers, is that clear?" Sarah demanded.

Tori quickly nodded, winking at Sarah encouragingly and replied, "Understood."

"Agreed," Aubrey choked out, trying not to laugh.

"Got it," Ben replied, doing the same.

"Yes Ma'am," Tanner promised.

RJ quickly nodded his head and glared at Gemma who reluctantly agreed.

"All right, good," Sarah announced. "RJ, turn your card over. Is it a bunny?"

RJ obediently turned over his card revealing the image of a bunny.

"Okay, that's one point for Gemma," Tori noted, handing Gemma the card. "Hold on to this, honey. The person with the most cards at the end of the game wins."

Gemma smiled, quickly grabbed the card and placed it in her lap.

"Gemma, it's your turn, sweetie," Tori advised. "Remember we all wait until Gemma asks the question," she reminded everyone, noticing RJ was already poised and ready.

Knowing she had control of the round, Gemma slowly chose her card and paused, glancing at everyone's faces around the table before looking at the other side.

"Look at the card, Gemma!" RJ demanded, scowling at Gemma in frustration.

"RJ," Tori warned quietly.

"But she's doing that on purpose!" RJ complained.

"It's Gemma's turn," Tori reminded him quietly. "Gemma...," she urged calmly.

While they all waited, Tori and Sarah exchanged a look, and rolled their eyes, suppressing their urge to laugh at the silent battle being waged at the table.

Then Gemma took a quick peek at her card and laid it face down on the table in front of her. Instantly RJ's face lit up with excitement, and he held his breath in anticipation.

That is until Gemma decided to sit calmly with a secretive look on her face torturing her brother. After almost an entire minute, Tori became worried RJ would pass out from holding his breath, so she pressed her daughter for the question. "Go ahead Gemma."

Glaring at RJ as if to tell him he was under her control, Gemma slowly asked, "Can anyone tell me what my card is?"

But RJ had a plan of his own. As soon as the last word left Gemma's lips, it was if RJ was a balloon and someone stuck him with a pin. He slowly released the breath he'd been holding and then simply sat there, looking bored, glancing at everyone around the table, not saying a word. His eyes stopped on Gemma who was now seething with anger, furious at him for spoiling her fun.

Barely able to keep from bursting out laughing, Tori looked over at Ben and saw that he was having the same trouble. Not daring to make eye contact with anyone else around the table, she squeaked out, "I can't."

"Me either," Ben croaked.

"Same," Aubrey giggled.

"I'm out," Sarah whispered, obviously having difficulty keeping her composure.

"Nope," Tanner smiled, not looking up at anyone.

"It's a tree," RJ announced, reaching his hand out toward Gemma for the card.

"Gemma, is your picture an image of a tree?" Tori asked, clearing her throat. Reluctantly, Gemma turned the card over revealing a picture of a tree. "Give the card to RJ, sweetie," Tori added.

Not moving fast enough for him, RJ reached over and took the card off the table, knocking a vase filled with flowers over in the process.

"My cards!" Gemma cried out while the water from the vase began to spread.

Immediately, a shadow crossed over the table; the vase returned to its upright position, the flowers reassembled in place, the liquid was back inside the vase and the cards, as well as the table, were completely dry.

"What was that?" Tanner exclaimed, looking around the room.

"Karla?" Ben asked Tori, inclining his head toward the table.

"Nope, that time, it was Elsbet," Tori replied, grinning. "Thank you Elsbet," she called out. The amulet around her neck glowed brightly in response. "See honey? Your cards are fine!" she explained to Gemma.

"Does that happen often?" Tanner exclaimed in surprise. "Elsbet coming to the rescue I mean?"

"Surprisingly yes, with these two going at it the way they sometimes do," Tori replied.

"So all of the times you and Aubrey mentioned seeing shadows moving across a room, it wasn't Lucifer as the shadow, it was Elsbet instead?" Tanner asked, curiously.

"Yes," Tori admitted, cradling the amulet in her hand. "She was watching us, well she was watching me. She wanted to make sure it was safe to contact me before she revealed herself. She and the other sisters practice reaching out to our plane of existence to strengthen their powers. You see them as shadows. The vase and the flowers were another exercise in control for them."

"Well, it was very much appreciated!" Sarah admitted.

"And at least now we know we don't have to worry about it being Lucifer hovering over us all the time causing trouble," Tanner confessed.

"Oh he's still there hovering nearby," Tori advised. "Goliath senses him sometimes, but he's become more cautious in his attacks. He knows Remy is still looking for him. We can't let our guards down no matter what."

"Ugh, just talking about him gives me the chills," Sarah replied, rubbing her hands up and down her arms. "Let's talk about something else."

"It's your turn, Mama," RJ interrupted, quietly.

"Perfect timing, RJ," Tori smiled appreciatively. Pausing to give both Gemma and RJ a stern look, she said, "If we're going to keep playing this game, there are a couple of additional rules I'm going to add. First of all, once you've drawn a card, you have thirty seconds to look at the other side and ask the question. If you take longer than thirty seconds, you lose your turn."

Thinking Tori was taking his side, RJ sneered at Gemma.

"Second, there will be no grabbing of another players card while it's still their turn. If you take a card, you also lose your turn, and you do not get the card even if you guessed correctly," Tori continued.

Surprisingly taking the higher ground, Gemma nodded her head and replied, "Okay, Mama."

Not wanting to look like the bad guy, RJ nodded his head in agreement too and replied, "Yes, Ma'am."

"And third, once the active player asks the question, you must raise your hand if you know the answer you cannot blurt it out loud. If you say what's on the card before the player has indicated, you can answer, you also lose your turn, and you do not get the card even if you guessed correctly," Tori warned. "Does everyone understand and agree to these new rules?"

Everyone around the table, including the twins, nodded their heads in agreement.

"Okay," Tori replied, picking up one of the cards. Trying to see if she could block her thoughts, she looked at the side of the card with the image and then set it to face down on the table in front of her. "Can anyone guess what my card is?"

Immediately both Gemma and RJ's hands went up.

"Gemma," Tori pointed to her daughter.

"Aw...," RJ moaned.

"It's a flower," Gemma replied proudly.

"That is correct," Tori nodded, handing Gemma the card. "Okay, Daddy, your turn," she added, looking at Ben.

Knowing the kids wouldn't be able to read his mind, Ben noticed Goliath sitting next to Tori, watching them play the game. With a mischievous grin, Ben picked up a card, held it out to where only Goliath could see it and then placed the card face down on the table. "Can anyone tell me what my card is?"

Instantly, Tori's, Gemma's and RJ's hands all went up. Then they looked at each other and began giggling.

"Wow," Sarah whispered, immediately understanding what happened.

Grinning in satisfaction, Ben replied, "That was cool."

"Daddy," Gemma interrupted him.

"Yes, Gemma?" Ben asked.

"You need to pick someone before your thirty seconds is up," she reminded him.

"Ah, you're right, thank you, sweetie," Ben chuckled. Looking back and forth between the three of them, he said, "RJ."

"Yes! It's a ball!" RJ exclaimed excitedly.

Turning the card over for everyone to see, Ben replied, "You are correct. Here you go RJ."

Taking the card from Ben, RJ's face beamed knowing he and Gemma were now tied.

"How did you know that would work," Tori laughed, impressed by her husbands' cleverness.

"I didn't," Ben admitted. "I knew they couldn't read my mind so when I saw Goliath sitting there, I knew you could read his mind so I was curious if the telepathy would work as a conduit through you to the twins."

"Oh, we're going to have a lot of fun with this game," Aubrey laughed, thinking of other ways they could test the boundaries of the twins' telepathy.

"Bree's got a look on her face that makes me very worried," Tori laughed watching her sister. "We better watch out. This game could get dangerous!"

"Oh, just you wait. You have no idea," Aubrey smiled ominously.

Chapter 11

Zander stared at the computer screen, slowly clicking through the results of his web search, trying to ignore the young woman at the circulation desk, arguing with the librarian over a fine on her account for an overdue book. The grey-haired matriarch, who had probably sat at that very same desk for the past seventy years, maintained her voice at the perfect library volume, patiently explaining the rules of responsible book reservation to the woman.

Today was the fourth day in a row Zander visited the library, and like a small theatrical stage, each day resulted in a humorous altercation with the seemingly unflappable librarian. Monday it had been a man suffering from dementia who wandered away from home, without his pants, or his library card. A call to the local sheriff helped to discreetly remove the man from the building and return him to his family.

Tuesday it had been two young boys running around the circulation desk shooting imaginary guns at one another while their mother waited in line. One stern, disapproving look from the librarian had been enough for the mother to chastise the boys and send them outside to wait for her.

On Wednesday, the town drunk stumbled in and proceeded to pass out on the floor. Another call to the local authorities took care of that minor disturbance.

It wasn't necessarily the individuals in question being at fault for their circumstances. The summer heat made people do strange things sometimes. It was mid-July in the south which meant rising temperatures and humidity were forcing people off the street and into the nearby air-conditioned buildings to experience a few moments of cool air on their damp skin before returning to the sweltering heat outside.

Most of the people who came inside this building, however, had a reason for being there. The historic monument located in the center of town housed the public library as well as the city clerk and county public records. It was one of the few places Zander could go without having to provide a form of identification or spend any money. So far the town of Ravenswood West Virginia was showing promise of being his next temporary home. It was small but not quaint, people went about their business without asking too many questions, and the local law enforcement consisted of only one sheriff and two deputies who spent most of their day drinking coffee and shooting the breeze with the local folk at the town diner. It was the perfect cover for a man on the run trying to hide from the rest of the world. Now all Zander needed to do was to find a job. He was running low on cash, so he needed to find something soon.

Giving up on the apparent injustice she was being subjected to; the young woman slammed the book she was attempting to check out on the countertop and stormed out the door. As the door closed behind her, a vacuum of hot air pulled in from the street outside, triggering the sensor on the ancient air conditioning system hidden behind the yellowed plaster walls. The machine moaned in protest as the fan reluctantly kicked in, pushing out the barest breath of tepid air through the rusty vents along the floors. Meanwhile, a row of dusty, unbalanced ceiling fans wobbled and creaked slowly overhead.

Hearing the scrape of a chair against the slats on the wooden floor, Zander raised his eyes a few inches above the screen and watched as the librarian slowly pushed herself up from her seat. Grabbing onto the top of the desk for a moment to find her balance, she picked up the book the young woman had left behind and begun shuffling her way toward the shelves. Glancing over at Zander, she noticed him watching her.

"Are you still doing all right over there, Mr. Butler?" she politely asked, peering at him through a pair of spectacles with lenses he estimated had to be at least an inch thick.

"Yes, thank you, Miss Norma," Zander smiled back at her.

"You let me know if there's anything I can do for you," she advised quietly.

"I will, thank you, Ma'am," Zander smiled again, feeling slightly uncomfortable by her intense stare, magnified severely by her glasses. With the intention of bringing their polite exchange to a close, he dropped his eyes back to the monitor and pretended to show interest in whatever was on the screen.

Taking his dismissal as an indication that Zander didn't require her services at the moment, Miss Norma returned the book to its spot on the shelf and shuffled back to her seat.

Jotting down the name and address of the last job advertisement he qualified for on the cities classified ads, Zander glanced over his list and nodded in satisfaction. He had a few strong possibilities to look into further. *"I guess there's nothing else I need right now,"* he told himself, preparing to gather his belongings.

Then another idea came to him. Casually glancing across the room where Miss Norma presently sat perched at the desk waiting for her next customer he clicked back to an open web browser and entered a new search string reading 'Dalmatians, Butler, Kentucky'. Executing his search, over a hundred and sixty thousand results pulled back.

"You've got to be kidding me," he whispered in protest. "There's seriously a town in Kentucky called Butler?" Knowing he wouldn't find anything helpful in those results, he cleared his search and entered another search string. 'Veronica Rhea Wells.' As he pressed the enter key, he held his breath waiting for the results of the search to pull back. "Nine hundred thousand," he sighed shaking his head in frustration. *"I'm never going to find them,"* he thought to himself.

Seeing her name displayed on the screen unlocked a flood of memories. He stared at the screen unmoving as his favorite ones began to replay in his head.

The sound of her laughter at one of his corny jokes...

Her long dark hair that flowed like silk through his fingertips...

The way the sun reflected a kaleidoscope of colors through her hazel colored eyes....

The smell of her perfume...

The feel of her skin as his hands explored her body...

The taste of her mouth when he kissed her...

"Mr. Butler," a woman's voice called out, breaking him from his trance.

Blinking in surprise, Zander recovered quickly to find Miss Norma standing on the other side of the table facing him. *"How in the heck did she get over here so fast?"* he wondered. *"How long was I sitting here daydreaming?"*

"Mr. Butler," she repeated, a bit louder.

"Y-yes, Miss Norma?" he stammered, obediently sitting up in his chair guiltily.

"I said it's time for the library to close for lunch," Miss Norma replied curtly. "As you know, I take my lunch every day at twelve o'clock sharp until exactly twelve thirty. I'm afraid you'll have to leave and come back later."

"Y-yes, Ma'am," Zander replied as he quickly cleared the search history on the computer. "I'm sorry, Ma'am. I didn't hear you the first time," he added, picking up his things and getting up from the chair. Hurrying toward the door, he paused as he grabbed the door handle, glanced back, gave a slight nod of his head and said, "Enjoy your lunch."

Unprepared for the wave of heat that enveloped him as soon as he stepped out onto the sidewalk, he paused, as his lungs filled with the stagnant hot air. *"Come on this is nothing!"* he told himself. *"You served two tours in this kind of heat! You've gone soft Lance Corporal Wells! Suck it up, rip off those panties, put on your big boy pants and get moving! That's an order!"* Inspired by his little pep talk, he quickly determined his present location against the first job opportunity on his list and began heading toward the Ravenswood Parks and Recreation department.

~~~~~~~~~~

"You say you've had prior experience in landscape maintenance and construction," Mr. Rhodes gruffly read from the single page application in his hand.

"Yes sir," Zander replied politely, his eyes briefly glancing down at the engraved name plate on the desk reading 'Walter Rhoads, Human Resource Manager.'

Clicking the pen in his hand several times as he continued to scan the page, Mr. Rhoads paused and glanced up at Zander suspiciously. "You didn't fill out the reference section. Is there a reason why?"

"Yes sir," Zander lied, having already prepared an answer to this question in his head. "My prior experience has primarily been having worked for my father. He owned and managed a hardware and garden center back home in Kentucky, and I worked for him before joining the Marine Corps. My father passed away while I was serving my second tour. The business was in pretty serious financial trouble by the time I got home so I had to sell it to pay off the debt," Zander continued to lie. "Since my father is no longer with us, God rest his soul, I'm afraid I don't have anyone to put down as a work reference."

"Hmmm...," Mr. Rhoads muttered, debating the believability of Zander's story. "You'll have to get a West Virginia driver's license if you get the job," he warned, glancing back up at Zander. "Is that going to be a problem?"

Having already prepared for this question as well, Zander previously obtained a social security number from another individual named Alex Butler so that he could assume that person's identity. "No, sir, I'll make that the first thing I do, once I get the job."

Impressed by Zander's boldness, the man chuckled and set the application down on the desk. Opening the top drawer, he reached inside and pulled out a business card. Handing it to Zander, he said, "Here's the name and address of who you'll need to talk to about the job. His name is Zeke Edwards. It's hard work, especially this time of year so don't waste his time if you're not serious about the position."

Taking the card, Zander nodded appreciatively and smiled. "Thank you, sir, I won't."

"I'll give him a call and let him know you're on your way over," Mr. Rhoads replied, reaching for the phone on his desk, indicating the interview was over.

Thankful for no more questions, Zander stood up from his chair, extended his hand across the desk and replied, "Thank you, sir."

"You're welcome," Mr. Rhodes replied. Returning the quick handshake, he motioned Zander to the door and barked instructions into the phone. "Clarice put me through to Parks and Recreation!"

Chapter 12

"Tori, can you hear me?" a woman's voice pleaded. "Please, we need your help!"

"What? Who?" Tori mumbled, turning over in her sleep. Finding the cool spot against her cheek on the pillow, she sighed and felt her mind clear. Floating downward like a feather on a summer breeze, she lay like that for several minutes, allowing her mind to drift as she transitioned into a deeper level of sleep.

Suddenly, she heard the woman's voice again. "Please help us, Tori. We need you!" she begged. "Open your eyes and talk to me!"

Reluctantly, Tori opened her eyes, surprised to find herself standing alone in the open white space her dreams tended to take her. *"Man, I was just getting to REM level,"* she thought, looking around for one of the other daughters. *"It's been a while since I've had one of these dreams yet here I am again in the creepy white room."*

"Well, I might as well find out why I'm here," she sighed. "Elsbet?" she called out hopefully.

When Elsbet didn't appear, she tried again.

"Karla, are you there? Hellooooooo?"

Then she heard footsteps behind her. Turning toward the sound, she saw the figure of a young woman approaching her through the fog. As the mist cleared away from the woman's face, Tori realized she didn't recognize her. The woman was close to Tori's age with shoulder length hair, a slightly brighter shade of copper than Tori's hair color, and her eyes were the shade of robin egg blue as opposed to Tori's sea-green color.

When the woman reached Tori, she gave her an apologetic smile and said, "I'm very sorry to have invaded your sleep like that. I've been trying to reach you for a while; tonight is the first time you responded," she confessed.

"Who are you?" Tori frowned, trying to place the woman's face with a name.

"My name is Gretchen Mallory," the woman replied.

Still not triggering a memory, Tori shrugged and replied, "I'm sorry, Miss Mallory. Your name doesn't sound familiar to me. Have we met somewhere?"

"Not directly, no," Gretchen admitted. "But we do have a connection to one another. That's why I reached out to you. I need your help, Tori. Well actually, we need your help."

"Who are we?" Tori asked, looking around for someone else.

"Me and the Cutler family," Gretchen replied.

"The Cutler family," Tori frowned. "Do you mean Sam, Ashlyn and Miranda Cutler?"

"Yes," Gretchen nodded encouragingly.

Frowning again in confusion, Tori asked, "I don't understand. What is your connection to the Cutler family?"

"Sam and I worked together for about ten years. We were friends," Gretchen replied.

"Are you alive or dead?" Tori asked.

"I'm dead," Gretchen replied.

"Are yours and Sam's deaths connected?" Tori asked.

"We think so, but we can't prove it. That's why I'm here to ask for your help," Gretchen advised.

"How do you even know about me?" Tori wondered. "How are you able to reach me here? I haven't even met the Cutler family yet."

"I brought her to you," Karla interrupted, appearing beside Tori.

"Karla!" Tori cried out, embracing her friend. "Oh, it's been so long since I've seen you!"

"I know I'm sorry. I've been working on strengthening my powers. We all have," Karla replied.

The amulet around Tori's neck glowed with a bright blue-green light in response.

"So why did you bring Gretchen to me?" Tori asked.

"She can help you solve the Cutler family murders. And in return, I told her you could help her," Karla suggested.

"How so?" Tori asked, looking at Gretchen.

Smiling sheepishly, Gretchen replied, "We know all about you, Tori. We've heard stories from people visiting our cemetery about a woman who possesses an amulet from a heavenly angel giving her the power to send souls trapped on earth to heaven."

"People are telling stories about me?" Tori frowned, worriedly. "What kind of stories?"

"About how you visited Arlington National Cemetery, and you gave the soldiers peace by sending them to heaven," Gretchen marveled. "Well most of the people," she added quietly. "The ones which you and God thought were worthy."

"Is that seriously what people are saying?" Tori exclaimed in frustration. "That's not it at all! I don't pick and choose who gets to go and who has to stay!"

Gretchen gave Tori a puzzled expression and asked, "Then why can't everyone go?"

"My abilities are limited to only murdered victims," Tori explained. "If someone dies and they have killed another human, they don't leave. Maybe they will be during the rapture or purgatory, but that's God's decision, not mine!"

"Oh," Gretchen nodded sadly. "We were hoping you knew."

"Besides, that was an experiment we tried to test how far the range of the amulet would travel. It worked, but it drained the energy from the stone, and my sisters are now just starting to regain their power again," Tori explained. Looking at Karla, she asked, "How is everyone?"

"They're all fine, Tori. The test worked," Karla assured her friend. "We're almost back to full power again."

"That's good," Tori nodded. Turning to Gretchen, Tori asked, "So what do you think I can do to help you and Sam?"

"It would probably be easier to show you than to try and explain," Gretchen replied, taking a step closer to Tori. Reaching out her hand, she asked, "May I?"

Karla stepped in between Tori and Gretchen, taking each of their hands. "I need to complete the connection between you."

"Are you sure you're strong enough?" Tori worried.

"I promise, I am," Karla nodded.

"All right," Tori agreed. Exhaling a deep breath in preparation for whatever was about to happen, she reached out and bravely clasped Gretchen's hand. Almost instantly an onslaught of images began playing out in her head. "Oh!" she gasped in surprise.

The images began with Gretchen, Sam Cutler and another man sitting at a table in a bar with several empty shot glasses laid out on the table. They were laughing and seemed to be having a good time.

Then the image changed, and Gretchen and the man were in a car together late at night. The man was driving while intoxicated and was having trouble keeping the vehicle on the road.

The next image surprised Tori. The car appeared to have gone off the road and hit a tree. The driver had a few minor cuts on his arms and face and was standing over Gretchen's body which was lying on the ground covered in blood. The hole in the windshield suggested she hadn't been wearing her seatbelt and her body thrown from the vehicle upon impact.

A bright flash of light temporarily blinded Tori, and she saw the two men arguing on a sidewalk. Behind them, an apartment building was in flames. Through one of the third-floor windows, Tori could see Gretchen's spirit looking down, watching the men.

Tori flinched as another flash of light blinded her, followed by a deep booming sound of thunder that rolled across the sky, shaking the ground beneath her feet.

She looked up and all of a sudden, the clouds parted, and she saw a human form falling from the sky, plummeting toward the earth. Then she realized it was a young boy with a pair of small wings protruding from his back, his arms flailing. As the boy tried to regain control, he turned his head, and Tori saw his face.

"RJ!" she cried out frantically, sitting up in bed startled awake.

"I'm okay, Mama," RJ replied taking her hand.

Tori looked beside her and saw Goliath, Gemma, and RJ standing next to her side of the bed, watching her. "Oh, my sweet angel," she exclaimed, pulling RJ up into her arms, holding him tightly.

"What?" Ben blubbered loudly, rousing from his sleep. "What's going on?"

"Mama had a bad dream, Daddy. She'll be okay," Gemma advised, patting Tori gently on the arm. "Don't be scared, Mama."

"*Need Remy?*" Tori heard Goliath ask.

"No, not yet, Goliath," Tori wept.

Reaching over to turn on the light, Ben sat up and saw tears streaming down Tori's face while she rocked RJ back in forth in her arms.

"I'm okay, Mama," RJ repeated, quietly.

Looking over at Gemma, noticing her calm expression, Ben asked, "Did you and RJ both see the dream, sweetheart?"

Nodding her head, Gemma whispered, "Yes, Daddy."

"Come here, Peanut," he beckoned, motioning with his hands that she should join them on the bed.

"Come on, Goliath!" Gemma invited, quickly climbing. She scrambled across the bed into Ben's waiting arms as Goliath crawled up over the comforter resting his head on Tori's lap supportively.

Kissing Gemma tenderly on the head, Ben whispered, "I love you, my sweet girl."

"I love you too, Daddy," Gemma whispered back, snuggling in closer.

Giving Tori the time she needed, they sat quietly holding each other as her breathing returned to normal.

Several minutes later, Tori released RJ, sat him on her lap facing her, and wiped her tears away. "Did you know about them, before you saw my dream, sweetie?"

RJ nodded his head guiltily and murmured, "Yes, Ma'am. Remy told me not to tell you."

"He did? Why?" Tori frowned.

"He said when the time was right, you would find out," RJ replied.

"Told RJ about what?" Ben asked, trying to keep up in the conversation.

Suddenly Tori sensed the air in the room change. "It sounds like you have some explaining to do, my friend. Might as well show yourself and join the conversation."

Instantly Remy appeared at the foot of the bed, looking very uncomfortable. "Hey."

"Remy!" both children cried out, scrambling across the bed toward him.

Rubbing his hands over his eyes thinking he was the one having the bad dream, Ben sighed and muttered, "Hey look the gangs all here!"

"Sorry about this, Ben," Remy apologized.

"That's all right, Remy. I appreciate how much space you usually do give us. So what's all this about?" Ben shrugged. "What was RJ not supposed to talk about with Tori or me?"

"RJ's wings, Daddy!" Gemma exclaimed, gleefully.

Blinking in surprise, Ben asked, "His what?"

"His wings, Ben," Tori advised.

"His w-w-wings," Ben stammered in bewilderment. Looking over at RJ, he noticed his son watching him carefully. Then the realization came to him. "The itching on his shoulder blades," he murmured, turning to Tori.

"Yes," Tori nodded.

"Oh, wow," Ben whispered.

"Yeah," Tori breathed. Glancing over at Remy who was doing his best not to make eye contact with her she said, "This wasn't part of what you showed me the day the twins were born."

"No," he murmured, finally looking at her. "It wasn't."

"Why?" she demanded angrily. "Why would you keep something like this from me?"

"You know I can't answer that question," Remy argued back. "At least not the answer you want to hear! Father reveals what He feels we need to know when He feels the time is right. I have no part in that decision!"

"But this is huge!" she exclaimed, pointing at RJ. "I'm his mother! Was it okay to tell him? He's just a baby!"

"I'm not a baby," RJ mumbled quietly.

Heaving a deep sigh, Tori looked at RJ and explained, "I'm sorry, sweetheart. I didn't mean it like that. It's just this is something I feel Mommy and Daddy should have known about."

"What would you have done?" Remy challenged quietly.

"Well, for starters I would have …," Tori's voice trailed off as the realization set in that she had no idea.

"So what do we do now?" Ben asked.

"I guess I need to make an appointment with Dr. Max," Tori sighed.

Chapter 13

"Hello, hello!" Max sang as he entered the examination room. "How are my two favorite little angels doing today?"

"Hi, Grandpa Max!" Gemma cried out, rushing forward for a hug.

"Hello, sweet Gemma," he smiled, hugging her in return.

Glancing down at his arm, she noticed a cut on his forearm. "You have a boo-boo."

He smiled and replied, "Oh, that's nothing. It's just a scratch. I got caught on a rose bush this past weekend while gardening. I'll be fine."

Reaching out her hand, Gemma gently laid it on top of Max's cut. When she pulled her hand away, the wound was gone. "There! All better!"

Never growing tired of experiencing these little miracles from the twins, Max smiled and said, "Thank you, my dear."

"You're welcome," she smiled up at him sweetly.

Turning to RJ, he asked, "What about you? You're not too big to give Grandpa Max a hug are you my boy?"

Wrapping his arms around Max, RJ replied, "Never!"

"Wow, you're getting strong!" Max teased. Tousling the boy's hair affectionately, he looked at Tori and Ben and asked, "So why did you ask me to meet you here at the agency medical office today? Is something wrong with one of the twins?"

Clearing her throat nervously, Tori replied, "No, nothing's wrong per say, just something we need to have checked out with either an ultrasound or an x-ray."

"Hmm....All right, who is my victim today," Max growled, turning toward Gemma and RJ with extended hands prepared to tickle them.

"RJ," Gemma giggled, moving out of Max's range.

"Is that so?" Max exclaimed, focusing his approach on RJ. "So what do we need an X-ray of, RJ? Do you have another nose growing somewhere on your body?"

"No," RJ giggled, slowly backing away.

"Hmm..... Is it a sixth toe sprouting out on one of your feet?" Max continued to tease.

"No," RJ giggled again.

"Hmm.....well those are the only two super cool things I can think of," Max shrugged, giving up.

"What about a pair of wings growing from his shoulder blades?" Tori asked, wincing slightly.

Max blinked in surprise and exclaimed, "What did you say?"

"RJ is going to have wings, Grandpa Max!" Gemma announced excitedly, jumping up and down.

Chuckling quietly, he looked back and forth between Gemma and RJ's faces in awe and said, "Sometimes I forget how gifted you both are. You're both such sweet, normal, looking children." Focusing his attention back on RJ, he asked, "So you have an emerging pair of wings have you?"

"Yes, sir," RJ replied proudly.

"That's most definitely cooler than an extra nose or a sixth toe," Max admitted, winking at the boy.

"I agree," RJ giggled again.

"Are you having any pain?" Max asked.

"No, sir, just some itching like normal," RJ shrugged.

Glancing over at Tori, Max admitted, "Yes well obviously it's not eczema as I originally suspected is it?"

Tori shook her head and said, "Nope."

"Very well, let's see what we've got! Why don't you remove your shirt RJ and let me take a look," Max instructed, adjusting his eyeglasses.

"Here let me help you, buddy," Ben offered, picking RJ up in his arms and setting him down on the examination table. "Raise your arms and I'll pull your shirt up."

"Okay, Daddy," RJ obeyed, raising his arms over his head.

Stepping back from the table, Ben advised, "There you go, Max."

"Thank you, Ben," Max smiled, patting Ben on the arm comfortingly. *"I can't even imagine what's going on in your mind right now, my friend,"* he thought. Using his fingertips, he felt along both of RJ's shoulder blades. "Hmm....," he murmured quietly.

"Do you feel something?" Tori asked, anxiously.

"I feel a slight thickening of the bones but since RJ said he's not having any pain, that's a good sign," Max admitted. "I don't think an ultrasound will give us enough information; I think an x-ray is the best route to take. Lie down on your stomach with your head facing that wall, RJ," he instructed. "Let's take a look at what's going on."

"Okay," RJ agreed, lying down on the table.

Positioning the x-ray machine over the table, Max paused before pressing the button and turned to Tori. "The three of you should probably step out of the room for a moment, just to be on the safe side."

"Oh, right!" Tori exclaimed, realizing they were all at risk of unnecessary exposure. "Come on, Gemma; we need to go out into the hallway for a couple of minutes."

"Why? I want to stay with RJ!" Gemma scowled.

"It's just for a couple of minutes, Peanut," Ben reasoned, scooping her up in his arms and following Tori out into the hallway. She gave Ben an appreciative smile as she closed the door behind them, which he returned with a playful wink. Setting Gemma down gently he said, "Okay little monkey you need to stay here until Max says it's okay to go back in."

"But it's boring out here," Gemma whined.

"You can still hear RJ's thoughts through the wall, right honey?" Tori suggested.

"Yeah," Gemma nodded sullenly.

"Well then you're not missing anything, right?" Tori reasoned.

"I guess," Gemma reluctantly agreed, poking at the floor with the toe of her shoe.

"Hey, how about you and I play a game while we wait?" Ben suggested excitedly.

Piquing her interest, Gemma looked up at Ben curiously and asked, "What kind of game?"

"How about we test how far away you and RJ can still hear each other's thoughts? Have you two done that already?" he tempted.

"No," Gemma admitted.

"Well, then this will be fun! Tell him what we're doing and then you and I will start walking down the hallway," Ben suggested. "Your mom will stay here just in case Max needs her for something. Is that okay with you, Mommy?" Ben asked Tori, giving her another wink.

"I think that sounds like a lot of fun!" Tori agreed. "I can't wait to find out how far that is!"

"Okay!" Gemma grinned, getting into the spirit.

"All right, let's go!" Ben encouraged, starting to walk away.

"Wait let's go this way, Daddy!" Gemma demanded, pointing in the other direction.

Reading her daughter's thoughts, Tori giggled, appreciating her daughter's masterful art of negotiation.

"What? What am I missing?" Ben frowned. "Why do we need to go this way?"

"Because this way has the candy machine we passed on our way in," Gemma advised, walking in the opposite direction from him.

"Did she just fleece me?" Ben whispered as he passed Tori to catch up with Gemma.

"Yep," Tori grinned. "She sure did."

~~~~~~~~~~

Ten minutes later, Tori and RJ were in the examination room reading a book waiting for Max to return. Suddenly the door flew open, and Gemma burst into the room.

"Three hundred and fifty feet," she declared excitedly, jumping up and down. "Daddy said that's almost as long as a football field! Isn't that amazing?"

"That is very amazing, sweetie!" Tori agreed.

"Here's your M&M's RJ," Gemma declared happily, handing a snack sized bag to her brother.

"Here are your M&M's," Tori corrected gently.

"Thanks!" RJ grinned, taking the bag from his sister.

"You're welcome! That was fun, Daddy!" Gemma exclaimed twirling in a circle so the skirt of her dress would billow out like a bell.

Recognizing the signs of a sugar rush, Tori gave Ben a raised eyebrow stare and asked, "How much candy did you let her have?"

"Just one package of the Skittles," Ben chuckled. "They're her favorite candy, Tor; she's fine."

"They're Mama's favorite candy too!" Gemma noted, still twirling. "Right, Mama?"

"That's right, sweetie," Tori agreed.

"Which reminds me," Ben grinned, revealing a small bag of Skittles he had hidden behind his back. "We got you a bag too."

"Thank you, that was very sweet of you both," Tori smiled. Tearing open the bag, she poured a few of the colorful candies into her hand and popped them into her mouth. "Yum, sometimes I forget how good these are!"

"Don't worry, Mama, as long as I'm here, I won't let you forget," Gemma declared, losing her balance as the dizziness took over. "It's like eating a rainbow!"

"Whoa there munchkin," Ben exclaimed, grabbing her before she fell. "Why don't you sit down for a few minutes until your head stops spinning? You don't want to see that rainbow come back up do you?"

"Ben," Tori choked, unable to keep from laughing.

"What? Halloween last year remember? I don't want to see that again," he teased.

"Daddy," Gemma giggled, watching double images of everyone swim around the room.

"Still no word from Max?" Ben asked.

"Not yet," Tori shrugged. "He said it might take a while for the technician to get the films read. He wanted to make sure he had another pair of experienced eyes checking the x-rays with him."

"Sounds like a reasonable plan," Ben agreed, sitting down in the chair beside Gemma. "How are you doing over here?"

"I'm fine," Gemma smiled looking somewhere beside his left ear.

"How many fingers am I holding up?" he asked, showing only his pointer finger.

"Three!" Gemma announced, blinking a few times to clear her vision.

"Hmm...you better sit there a little bit longer," Ben advised.

"Sorry that took so long," Max apologized as he entered the room. "The technician and I decided to consult with an Orthopedist just to be sure what we saw on the films was correct."

"So what's the verdict?" Tori asked, taking a deep breath.

Giving Tori a wide-eyed grin, Max replied, "It's quite fascinating!"

"Meaning what?" Tori exclaimed.

"It will be easier for me to show you while I tell you," Max replied, walking over to the row of light boxes on the wall. As the panels flickered to life, he began sliding films out of one of the envelopes in his hands and clipped them into the brackets at the top of each panel. "Okay, for comparative purposes, this first set of films belong to another three-year-old boy the Orthopedist had on file.

"As you can see, the shoulder blade, also known as the scapula, is a flat, triangular-shaped bone, protected by a complex system of surrounding muscles. It forms the back part of the shoulder connecting the arm to the trunk of the body. It also provides a socket allowing for arm movement, such as up, down and rotation of the arm. Are you both following so far?"

"Yes, nothing too complicated there," Ben noted.

"Agreed," Tori nodded.

Sliding another set of films from the other envelope into the next panel, Max turned to Tori and Ben and advised, "These are RJ's films."

Stepping forward to take a closer look, Tori immediately saw what Max wanted them to see. "RJ's scapula is much thicker and bigger than the other image."

"Yes, it is," Max nodded, excitedly.

"What's that ridge, right there?" Ben asked, pointing to a long ridge above the scapula.

"That's called the acromion. It forms the summit of the shoulder. Along with this area here called the coracoid process, together the bones extend laterally over the shoulder joint. The acromion is a continuation of the scapular spine, and articulates with the clavicle collar bone to form the acromioclavicular joint," Max explained.

"Man. Proportionally, RJ's is huge!" Ben exclaimed.

"Yes, it is," Max agreed.

"Does any of what you see indicate the formation of wings?" Tori asked tentatively.

Pausing to look at RJ and Gemma, who were both listening intently with eyes as big as dinner plates, Max removed one final film from the envelope and clipped it into the remaining bracket.

"This image is the one we wanted. Do you see this area right here?" Max pointed to one area on the film.

"Yes," Tori nodded.

"This area shows the formation of new bone tissue along the humerus which is the longer bone between the shoulder and the elbow. I'm not sure if you can see this as clearly, but if you look close, you can see the formation of another set of the humerus, ulna and radius bones directly in front of the scapula," Max advised.

"I see them!" Tori breathed. "What are these two tiny images here? Are they fingers?"

Pushing his eyeglasses up higher on the bridge of his nose, Max pointed to the spot Tori was referring to and replied, "Well, if we truly are going with the assumption that these new bone formations are in fact wings, these two tiny bones would be the alula and the phalanges, making up the tip of the wing."

"Wait, aren't phalanges another name for a finger?" Ben frowned. "Are you saying underneath their feathers, birds have fingers?"

"In a sense, yes," Max shrugged. "Phalanges are not restricted terminology to the human anatomy. They are known as a homologous structure, which means they are an example of an organ or bone that appears in different animals with underlining anatomical commonalities. In other words, it's when very different animals have bones that appear very similar in form or function and seem to be related."

Stepping back to look at all the films again, Tori exhaled a deep breath and thought, "*Well, if this is what God has planned for RJ, I guess all we can do is have faith and wait and see what happens.*" Turning to look at RJ, she asked, "What do you think about all of this, sweetie?"

Giving her a crooked smile that always reminded her of Ben, RJ shrugged and replied, "I feel the same way you do."

Realizing he had heard her thoughts, Tori chuckled and reached over to pull RJ into a hug. "You're a funny boy, you know that, RJ? And I love you dearly."

"I love you too, Mama," he whispered, holding her tight.

"So what do we do now?" Ben asked Max.

"We have faith and wait and see what happens," Gemma announced calmly.

"Well said, Gemma!" Max agreed.

Chapter 14

"Come on, Scout," Logan urged, gently tugging on the leash. Still not used to wearing a collar or the sound of his new name, the puppy pulled away, flinging his body around like a fish trying to get off a hook. "Come on, buddy; you were doing so well earlier this morning! We've got to get going!"

Not wanting to miss his window of opportunity, Logan scooped the puppy up into his arms and began walking the rest of the way toward the park. Happy to be close to his human companion again, Scout wriggled up against Logan's chest and began enthusiastically licking his master's face. "Okay, okay, that's enough, Scout," Logan chuckled, secretly loving the overwhelming show of affection as well as the smell of the puppy's breath.

Making sure to place them in direct line of sight to the park bench where Rebecca always sat, Logan set Scout down on the ground and looked down at him sternly. "All right, Scout, it's time you learned some basic commands. Scout, sit!"

Of course, Scout had other plans. As soon as the scents from the other dogs at the park began filling his nostrils, he proceeded to ignore Logan and began sniffing the area around him. Then he heard one of the dogs across the park bark, and he looked up curiously for the origin of the sound. When he saw the dog, he began barking excitedly in return.

"Scout, no!" Logan scolded sternly, which Scout ignored.

"Scout, no!" Logan repeated, a bit louder, snapping his fingers, startling the puppy into cowering silence. "Good boy!" Logan praised, giving the puppy a dog biscuit from his pocket.

Greedily swallowing the treat, Scout's interest in Logan returned now that he knew there was food involved.

"Yeah, I'm a lot more interesting now, aren't I?" Logan chuckled patiently. Getting the puppy's attention with another treat, he pushed gently on the dog's hindquarters until he sat and commanded, "Sit! Good boy!"

They worked intently on sit, good boy, treat, for another fifteen minutes until Logan realized what time it was. When he glanced over to the park bench, Rebecca was eating her lunch watching them. *"Shoot! When did she show up? How could I have missed that? How long has she been there? Okay, here we go,"* he thought nervously.

Having practiced this scenario in his head several times in preparation for today, he smiled and gave her a casual wave. Not seeming to care that he noticed her watching them, Rebecca smiled, waved back politely and then looked away. *"Huh, okay, not bad for step one,"* he thought.

But again, Scout had other plans. When he realized the woman on the bench also had food, he lunged forward and began galloping in her direction. Unable to grab the leash in time, Logan called out to the dog to no avail. "Scout no!" Chasing after the dog, Logan was able to stomp on the end of the leash just as Scout was preparing to pounce. "Gotcha!" Logan declared triumphantly, picking up the end of the leash.

Impressed by Logan's fast reflexes, Rebecca's smile broadened, and she nodded at him approvingly. "Nice catch!"

"Thanks," Logan grinned, trying to regain his breath. "Man this guy's fast!"

"Have you had him long?" she asked politely.

"Just a few days," Logan replied. "We're still getting used to one another."

"He's a beautiful dog," she admitted, reaching out her hand so Scout could smell it. "What's his name?"

"Scout," Logan replied.

"That's cute," she smiled. "Scout, come," she beckoned in a soothing voice.

Eagerly advancing toward her, Scout's tail began wagging, and he stood obediently in front of her, waiting for his treat.

"Sit," she demanded, firmly.

And Scout sat.

"Great job, buddy!" Logan praised his dog silently.

"Good boy!" she praised, giving Scout a treat from her pocket.

"You keep dog treats in your pocket?" Logan exclaimed, mocking surprise.

Rebecca laughed and admitted, "Not something most people do, I know. I work for the vet down the street and always keep treats in my pockets when I'm at work so the animals remember me as the nice lady with the treats and not the bad lady with the needle."

"That's clever," Logan replied. "Which vet the one on Elm?"

"No, the one down the street on Main," she pointed in the direction opposite to where they were.

"Ah, I didn't realize there was more than one vet in town," Logan lied.

"If you haven't already picked a vet for Scout, you should come check us out!" Rebecca invited. Pulling a business card out of her other pocket, she handed it to Logan and said, "It's the Blacksburg Animal Hospital."

"Gosh, that's very nice of you thanks, but I have already chosen a vet, well I guess you could say my sister has," Logan continued to lie. "Ironically enough, my sister is also a veterinarian. Her practice is out in Newport. But I'll keep this card, just in case."

"Okay," Rebecca agreed. "So you're already aware of the possible health conditions prone to Dalmatians and are giving him the right kind of food and all that."

"Yep, my sister, has us all taken care of," Logan replied.

"That's great," Rebecca smiled. Looking down at Scout's face, she leaned forward and cupped his chin in her hand. Rubbing Scout gently on the head, her smile saddened slightly, as a memory of doing this same thing to Butler came back to her. "He is such a sweet boy," she added softly.

Not wanting to overstay their welcome or ruin the moment, Logan quickly said, "Well, we've taken up enough of your time. Sorry for barging in on your lunch like that."

"No worries, it was nice meeting you both," Rebecca sat up, recovering quickly.

"I'm Logan by the way," he tactfully offered.

"Oh, right! I'm Rebecca," she blushed, realizing they hadn't formally introduced themselves.

"It's very nice to meet you, Rebecca," he replied, giving her his most charming smile. "Perhaps we'll bump into you again sometime."

"Perhaps you will," she replied.

"Come on, Scout," Logan commanded, strolling away as casually as possible.

As soon as they were out of Rebecca's line of sight, Logan scooped Scout up into his arms and gave him a big kiss on the head. "What a good boy you are! You totally nailed it back there; you know that? We couldn't have rehearsed any better had we tried! You are going to be the best wingman - I mean wing-dog ever!" Happy to be back in his master's arms, Scout wriggled excitedly, covering Logan's face again with kisses.

Once they were back in their apartment, Logan unclipped the leash from Scout's collar and set him gently on the floor. "There you go, buddy, good boy." Then he filled Scout's water bowl with fresh water and sat down at his desk to check for any new messages.

Lapping up some of the fresh cool water, Scout gave his empty food bowl a hopeful sniff. Disappointed to find it empty, he walked over to where Logan sat and stared up at him with the classic puppy dog face.

"Not right now, buddy," Logan advised, forcing himself not to cave in and pick the dog up. "I've got work to do. Go lie down." After a few minutes of unsuccessful staring, Scout gave up and curled up on the floor beside Logan's chair. Not long afterward, he was fast asleep.

Chapter 15

The unexpected sound of the doorbell jolted Goliath out of his sleep, and he quickly scrambled to his feet and barked loudly to get Tori's attention while he ran toward the front door.

"Easy, Goliath," Tori gently scolded as she followed behind him. Glancing out the side window, she smiled and advised, "It's your buddy, Agent Sullivan!"

Hearing Agent Sullivan's name, Goliath's anxiety instantly dissolved, and was replaced with anticipation. He retreated a few steps back and sat down excitedly beside Tori and told her, *"Goliath treat!"*

"You're such a goofball," she chuckled, unlocking and opening the door. "Hello, Agent Sullivan! What a nice surprise," she greeted.

"Hello, Agent Cooper," he answered. "I hope I haven't caught you at a bad time."

"Not at all, please come in! What brings you out to our neck of the woods?" she asked, stepping aside so he could enter the foyer.

"Well I have a meeting with Gabriel in a couple of hours, but since I was in the general area, I wanted to come and discuss something with you that a friend of mine contacted me about," he replied, noticing Goliath waiting patiently by Tori's side. "Hello, Goliath! How is my favorite canine today?" he asked, pulling a large dog biscuit from his jacket pocket.

Goliath's mouth opened in a wide grin in response, eyeing the treat eagerly.

"Here you go," Agent Sullivan smiled handing the treat to Goliath. Gently petting Goliath on the head, he murmured, "You're such a good dog."

"He sure loves it when you come over," Tori smiled watching Goliath devour the treat.

Agent Sullivan chuckled and admitted, "My wife doesn't understand why I always have a box of dog biscuits in the pantry, yet I don't want a dog of my own. I guess she doesn't understand the attachment I have to Goliath."

"Well, you were the one who drove him to the vet the day we were both shot, and you stayed with him the entire time until he came out of surgery. You showed him how much you cared for him that day. I can't imagine the two of you not having formed a common bond after that," Tori replied.

"Yes, well, I started out doing it for you so you would let Ben get you to the hospital, however after seeing how brave Goliath was that day, willing to sacrifice his life to save yours, gave me a new perspective on the bond between you two. It's something I've never seen before," Agent Sullivan admitted. Deciding he didn't want to bring his mind back to that horrible day, he said, "Well, let's get back to the reason why I came. Are you sure this is a good time?"

"Oh, right!" Tori snapped to attention. "Of course, please come inside. We can sit at the table in the kitchen. Would you like a cup of coffee?"

"Oh, no, I'm fine, thank y..," he began to reply as he followed her into the kitchen. Then he noticed a domed covered plate on the counter. "What have you got there?" He asked, looking through the glass.

Knowing his weakness for pastries of any kind, Tori laughed and replied, "Those are my homemade sugared lemon and rosemary scones. Would you like to try one?"

Licking his lips in anticipation, he looked over at her with an eager expression, and admitted, "Well, perhaps just one."

"I know you also have an appreciation for food with a little kick so would you like to try a spoonful of my habanero, bourbon, and pear jam to go along with it?" she tempted, wiggling her eyebrows.

"You made jam too? Oh that sounds lovely, I would!" he quickly agreed, setting his briefcase down on the floor beside his chair. "If you don't mind, may I wash my hands first?"

"Of course, you know where the powder room is," Tori smiled, grabbing a plate from the cupboard and the jar of jam from the refrigerator. "And was that a yes or a no on the coffee?" she added.

Eyeing the coffee pot, he asked, "Do you already have some made?"

'I do!" she confirmed.

"Then yes, please," he agreed quickly making his way to the powder room.

"No problem!" she replied, going back to the cupboard for a coffee mug.

"Where are your parents and the children?" he asked when he returned, suddenly noticing how quiet the house was.

"Ben took them all to the park for some fresh air and to burn off some energy," Tori advised, pouring the coffee. "I had some work I wanted to catch up on, and for obvious reasons, someone needed to stay with me, so Goliath opted to hang back here with me today."

"Speaking of obvious reasons, have you had any recent encounters with Lucifer?" Agent Sullivan asked, whispering the last word.

Tori smirked and said, "You know, if you make him all big, bad and scary, he'll end up being big, bad and scary, Agent Sullivan. We already know Satan exists so you might as well say his name boldly."

"I know, I know," he chided himself gently as he eased himself down into the chair. "It's still difficult for me to admit sometimes how real Lucifer is. Until I met you, all I knew of the devil was from what I read in books and supposition from fellow theologians. I had never really considered him as a person. And how you describe him as having a personality much less a sense of humor, no matter how twisted it may be. Honestly, it's very disturbing to envision him as a flesh and blood human."

"I totally understand," Tori replied, noticing Agent Sullivan wince as he sat down. "Ben still has trouble with it too sometimes. When Luc wants to, he can be utterly charming."

"If you say so," he grinned, wryly.

Setting a plate, spoon and mug down on the table in front of Agent Sullivan, she asked, "I noticed you wince when you sat down. Is your arthritis acting up again?"

"It's just old age," he shrugged. Looking at his plate his eyes lit up like a child at Christmas, and he said, "Oh my, this looks delicious!" Quickly picking up the pastry, he took a large bite. "Oh," he groaned as he chewed. "As usual, you've completely outdone yourself!"

"Thank you," Tori beamed.

"What did you say was in this scone again?" he asked trying to pick out the flavors in his mouth. "I can taste the lemon, yet I'm getting savory too."

"That's the rosemary," Tori advised.

"That's it! Rosemary is the other flavor I taste," he declared, taking another bite. "My goodness, that's good! I would have never thought to put those two flavors together in a pastry."

Pointing to the jar on the table in front of him, Tori suggested, "Now try it with the jam."

"Oh, right," he nodded, quickly picking up his spoon and dropping a dollop of the jam on the scone. Taking another bite, he paused as the explosion of flavors hit his tongue and he looked at her with a look of utter surprise.

"Too spicy?" she winced, not able to tell if his expression was joy or shock.

Savoring the rest of the bite quietly, he shook his head and continued to chew. After he swallowed, he looked down at the remaining bite of scone in his hand and said, "That was most definitely the perfect bite, Agent Cooper! More so than anything

I've tried in a very long time. Both the scone and the jam are delicious on their own, however, when put together and tasted at the same time it's like a kaleidoscope of colors and flavors swirling all around me. You have such a gift with food."

"Thank you," Tori blushed, happily. "That means a lot coming from you knowing what a foodie you are."

"You know," he paused taking a sip of coffee. "Were you not already perfectly suited to your role with us in the FBI, I might suggest you consider opening up a café or pastry shop and sell these! You have an artisanal quality to your food that I know people would enjoy!"

"I'll keep that in mind if I ever decide to change professions," she chuckled.

"Just don't ever tell Gabriel I suggested it," he teased.

"He's still getting used to the idea of me changing roles and remaining on the team part-time as a consultant. Any other changes might be a bit much right now. Your secret is safe with me!" Tori vowed, crossing her heart with her left index finger.

"Speaking of secrets," Agent Sullivan suddenly remembered the reason for his visit. Popping the last bite of scone in his mouth, he brushed the crumbs off his fingers and reached down beside his chair for his briefcase. "As I mentioned, a friend of mine found something very interesting that he shared with me. Something I thought you would find interesting as well."

"Okay. Where is this friend from?" she asked.

"He lives in Matera, Italy," he replied.

"Matera? Where's that? I've never heard of it," Tori wondered.

"Oh, it's a very, very old city east of Naples. Antonio, my friend, moved there many years ago, primarily because of its history and lack of tourism. He's a very private man and lives a very secluded life," he admitted.

"He never married?" Tori asked.

"Antonio? My goodness no, he's married to his work, he always has been. Even when we were in school together, he rarely went out or did anything outside of studying," Agent Sullivan advised.

"So what did he find that you feel I should see?" Tori inquired as Agent Sullivan set several items on the table.

"Come have a seat, and I'll show you," he eagerly motioned to the chair beside him.

"All right," Tori agreed, sitting in the chair.

"So first, let me explain a little bit of Antonio's background," Agent Sullivan began to explain. "As I mentioned he was a student of theology like I was, however, his interests were always in the historical documentation of religion, the life of Jesus while he was here on earth, and information not included in the Bible."

"Not included in the Bible? Like what?" Tori puckered her brow.

"Well for example, when I told him about you and your connection to the Archangel Remiel, he was fascinated with the realization that angels are in fact real and that they walk among us here on earth as many of us have often wondered," he admitted.

"Was it safe for you to tell him about me?" Tori worried.

"Oh, absolutely," he exclaimed emphatically. "Antonio may be an odd duck, but I trust him completely. Don't worry. Your secret is safe with him."

"Well if you trust him, then I guess I can too," she inclined her head in agreement.

"You may trust him, even more, when I show you what he found," Agent Sullivan smiled mysteriously as he unfolded a piece of cloth covering one of the items on the table.

"Oh it's beautiful," Tori breathed, leaning in to take a closer look. "Is that glass?" she asked.

"Yes," Agent Sullivan confirmed. "It's a section of a stained glass window that Antonio indicated came from a very old church. Someone made a point of saving this piece of glass from one of the windows."

"Why this piece?" she asked eagerly, wanting to see it more closely. "May I pick it up?"

"Of course, just be careful. The edges are a bit sharp," Agent Sullivan warned.

As Tori gently picked up the glass, the sunlight from one of the windows reflected off the glass surface and cast an array of colors over the table. Intricate borders of green and golden leaves and mauve colored flowers intertwined along the outer frame, separated by a double red border and scallops of ivory fleur de lis. Her eyes traveled to the center of the glass, featuring a cherub face of a young boy with auburn curls, surrounded by a circle of colorful feathered wings.

"It's positively breathtaking," she whispered, enthralled with the face of the young boy. "Who's the boy? Is he a cherub?"

"I don't think he's a cherub," Agent Sullivan replied quietly. "I think he's someone else. Someone you already know."

"Remy?" Tori frowned.

"No, not Remy," Agent Sullivan replied.

Her frown deepened, and she looked into Agent Sullivan's eyes, questioningly. "You're not trying to tell me the face in this piece of glass is RJ!"

"As a matter of fact, I am," he admitted unwaveringly.

Tori laughed, thinking he was teasing her, but then she noticed he wasn't laughing back.

"Oh come on, seriously?" she argued.

"Seriously," he shrugged.

Looking back at the face in the glass, Tori shook her head slowly and admitted, "Okay you're going to have to sell me on this one because I don't see the connection between this ancient piece of glass and my three-year-old son."

"All right, first let's set that aside," he said, gently taking the glass from her and placing it back on the fabric. Moving the item to an open spot on the table, he unfolded another item which appeared to be a very old piece of parchment paper.

Tori glanced at the document briefly and shrugged. "I can't read Latin."

"That's okay. Fortunately for you, I can," Agent Sullivan smiled patiently, angling the document between them both.

"Oddly enough, it was Antonio who brought this document to my attention, and that was before he told me about the stained glass he found. He sent me an email about a month ago, asking me if I had ever encountered any written translations about a winged human boy."

Slightly startled, Tori swallowed hard and said, "Go on."

"I didn't tell him anything about RJ," Agent Sullivan promised. "However I did tell a little white lie and implied that I might have heard rumors of a story like that many years ago, but had never found any proof to support it, so I assumed it was probably a myth or urban legend. That's when he told me about this document."

"Why the little white lie? I thought you said you trusted Antonio?" Tori asked.

"With your story, I do," Agent Sullivan replied. "Since we don't yet know what the future holds for RJ now that we know about his wings, I would rather not bring others into our circle of confidence."

"Thank you for that," Tori smiled, relieved.

"You're welcome," he replied.

"Okay. So what does the document say?" Tori asked, anxiously.

"As you can see, the text aligns with several drawings, the first one being of what appears to be an angel, mainly because you can see his halo and his wings," Agent Sullivan noted. "Do you see that?"

"Yes. And this image above the angel, is that the sun?" Tori asked.

"It's either the sun or the representation of heaven or God," Agent Sullivan replied. "The text doesn't explain the glowing object above the angel."

"Okay, so the smaller figure next to the angel, he looks like a normal boy," Tori noted, pointing to the picture.

"Correct. In this first part, the boy appears to be normal. The text explains the origin of the winged boy. There are many different interpretations depending on your lineage. Norse mythology refers to a winged human as a Valkyrie, other parts of the world referred to it as a Seraph or an elite angel with multiple wings. There was even an Archeologist many years ago from New Zealand who claims to have found the fossilized remains of an entire nomadic civilization of winged humans," he explained, excitedly.

"I agree, that sounds fascinating, but what does this specific writing say?" she insisted, tapping the document with her index finger.

"Oh, right, sorry," he winced apologetically. "As I said, this first part of the text mentions the origin of the boy, who seems to have a direct relationship with the angel." Moving his finger down to the next section of text, he translated, "This section relates to the second image of the boy, who now appears to have newly emerged wings sprouting from his shoulder blades. Do you see it?" he asked growing excited again.

"Yes," Tori agreed, leaning in closer to look at the drawing. "The expression on the boy's face looks surprised, whereas the face of the angel doesn't. Why do you think that is?"

"I'm not entirely sure; I noticed that as well. From what you told me of Remy's revelation to you right after the twins were born, RJ has a destiny of his own that is far beyond what any of us could have imagined. One might assume that at the time of this writing, the author wouldn't have known how advanced our technology would have been where we would have been able to see the formation of RJ's wings using X-rays?" he suggested. "Thus it would have been a surprise to all of a sudden learn of them as they emerged."

Tori shook her head, bewildered and admitted, "I've got nothing. Consider my mind blown at this point. What about the next section where it looks like the boy is learning how to fly. If this depiction is truly RJ, and that's Remy, then it looks like Remy is teaching him?"

"Yes, that's what the text indicates. The angel is instructing the boy how to use his wings. What I found very interesting was the clouds around the boy. Look closely at his hands. What do you see?" he asked.

Tori's brows furrowed together as she analyzed the image more closely and replied, "It looks like he's pushing the clouds away from him."

"As if he has control of the elements," Agent Sullivan suggested.

"As RJ does," Tori admitted.

"Exactly," he replied.

Heaving a deep sigh, she sat back in her chair and looked at Agent Sullivan with a resigned expression. "Okay, I have to admit, this does seem to have some validity to being about RJ. Now, what? How do we prove one hundred percent that it is?"

Agent Sullivan leaned back in his chair and met her eyes candidly. "I'll continue digging through the resources I have available to me, as well as ask Antonio to do so as well."

Angling the document to face her fully, Tori leaned forward and began studying the page carefully. As she neared the bottom of the document, Agent Sullivan saw her expression change and her eyes quickly began scanning the page again.

"What do you see?" he asked.

"It's what I do not see," Tori advised, fully distracted by the document.

"What do you mean?" he frowned, leaning forward to look at it again.

Pointing to the end of every paragraph, Tori noted, "See how there's a punctuation mark at the end of every paragraph? Even though I can't read the words, I can see the author of this document was very precise in proper punctuation. Every 't' is crossed, every 'i' is dotted, every comma is in the proper place, and every paragraph ends with a period. Except this last one," she pointed, angling the document back towards Agent Sullivan. "This is not the entire document. There's more."

Watching his eyes carefully as he scanned the page, she saw his expression change from concentration, to realization to complete surprise.

"You're right," he whispered, meeting her gaze.

"So if that's true, you need to ask yourself, who has the other piece to this document and what does it say? What if it's your friend Antonio? Would he do something like that? Would he intentionally keep something like that from you?" she challenged.

"I don't know," he admitted. "But I promise you I'm going to find out!"

Chapter 16

"Yes, Gumdrop Pass!" Gemma announced happily, moving her green plastic gingerbread man over to the adjacent purple square across the path.

"Aww," RJ moaned, jealously.

"Your turn," she smiled sweetly.

Suddenly feeling Remy's presence enter the room as he checked on them, the twins paused a moment waiting to see if he would appear. When they felt him leave, they went back to their game.

"He never wants to play with us," RJ frowned.

"He's busy. He doesn't have time to play with us," Gemma replied.

"He's very angry at his brother," RJ noted, picking up a game card from the stack. "Yes! Peanut brittle!" he declared triumphantly, moving his blue game piece ahead of Gemma's.

"Yes, he is," Gemma agreed, selecting her next card. "Double blue," she added, moving her game piece.

"Father doesn't like the anger in Remy's heart. Single yellow," RJ added, moving to the yellow square closest to his game piece.

"No, He doesn't. Single green," Gemma agreed.

"Do you think Remy realizes that's why Father hasn't let him come home yet?" RJ asked. "Double red."

"Father wants Remy to figure it out on his own. That's the only way he can return to heaven. You can't tell him RJ," Gemma warned looking at her brother sternly.

"I know. But I want to help Remy," RJ argued.

"I do too, but we can't. Father specifically told us not to," Gemma argued back.

"What about Mama? Can she tell Remy?" RJ asked.

"No! Father said Remy has to figure it out on his own," Gemma insisted. "Besides, Mama and Remy can't know that Father talks to us, remember? He said we couldn't tell anyone."

"But why can't we tell Mama?" RJ argued.

"It's not our place to question Father's wishes," Gemma whispered, fiercely. "Whatever He tells us to do, we do it."

"I guess," RJ reluctantly agreed.

"I'm serious, RJ, you promised!" Gemma pressed. "Double orange."

"I know! Single blue," RJ exclaimed defiantly, moving his game piece.

"How sweet, listen to the little angels worrying about poor Remy's salvation," Lucifer chuckled quietly to himself as he watched the twins play.

"And even better, the poor dears were sworn to secrecy by the head honcho up in the clouds himself," he continued to muse. *"I think I might be able to use that to my advantage,"* he grinned as his mind began planning all sorts of devious things. *"I wonder if they would be interested in someone other than Remy joining them in their game,"* he thought wickedly. Extending his powers into the children's room, Lucifer picked up RJ's game piece and moved it to the blue square just beyond the frost queen.

Sensing the presence of someone else in the room, yet knowing it wasn't Remy, the twins stopped arguing and stared at one another quietly. Waiting for a sound or some sign of movement, RJ looked down at the game board and drew in a sharp breath when he saw his game piece had moved.

He looked back up at Gemma and whispered, "I swear I didn't...,"

"I know you didn't," she interrupted him, her eyes shifting around the room sensing the change in the air.

Then they heard a scraping sound coming from the game board, and they both looked down to find a new player on the board near the starting point, the red gingerbread man.

"We don't want to play with you," Gemma called out loudly.

"Gemma...," RJ whispered fearfully.

"It's okay RJ," she advised confidently. "We don't have to be afraid of him. Besides, he's not staying. Put your hand out like this," she instructed holding out her hand palm facing her brother.

RJ immediately stuck out his hand toward her and asked, "Like this?"

"Perfect," She nodded. Pressing her palm firmly against RJ's, a small electrical charge surged between them, followed by a crackling sound and a slight smell of smoke.

"ARGH!" Lucifer cried out as the force of the charge threw him backward, repelling his power out of the children's room. "Little brats!" he spat fiercely, retreating quickly away from them.

"How did you know that would work, Gemma?" RJ marveled, looking at his hands.

"Shh….," she whispered, anticipating what would happen next.

Suddenly Remy was there standing in front of them; his wings extended and his fists clenched. "Where is he?" he demanded angrily, looking around the room.

"Where's who?" Gemma innocently asked, giving RJ a warning look before turning to Remy.

"I thought I felt…," Remy began to say but then he stopped short.

"Would you like to play with us?" Gemma offered, discreetly pushing the red game piece off the board.

The hard edge on Remy's face softened, and he gave her a small smile. "Not right now, sweetie. Maybe later, okay? I need to find someone right now."

"Who do you need to find?" she asked, innocently.

Suddenly sensing where he thought Lucifer might have gone, the hard edge returned to Remy's face, and he extended his wings in preparation to leave. "I'll see you both later, okay?"

"Okay," Gemma replied, pretending to be interested in the game again.

"Bye," RJ waved calmly, copying his sister.

A moment later, Remy was gone.

"Why did you lie to him?" RJ whispered worried Remy could still hear them.

"Don't worry; he's gone. He can't hear you," Gemma advised. "Besides, I didn't lie to him. He didn't tell us who he was looking for."

RJ frowned at his sister and argued, "You know darn well who he was looking for, Gemma!"

"Do you want to make things worse between them?" Gemma argued back, angrily. "Lucifer was testing the waters, and we showed him we're able to defend ourselves! Remy was the one who made sure we could handle situations like this. We have to learn how to protect ourselves. Remy and Mama won't always be with us."

"But should we make Lucifer angry with us right away?" RJ worried. "Maybe he was trying to be nice."

"Nice?" Gemma gasped, shocked at her brother's response. "Do you think he was trying to be nice the day he had that man shoot Mama and Goliath?"

"No! Of course not," RJ exclaimed. "But Mama always tells us not to judge someone based off of someone else's opinion. She said we should get to know that person and decide what kind of person they are by ourselves."

"I don't think that included the devil!" Gemma scoffed. "I don't want to talk about this anymore. Do you want to keep playing or not?"

Exhaling a frustrated sigh, RJ nodded and muttered, "Fine, let's finish the game."

Nodding satisfactorily, Gemma insisted, "Fine. Put your game piece back where it should be. It's my turn."

Chapter 17

Zander critiqued his reflection in the mirror, satisfied with the comfort of his new city of Ravenswood uniform. Already accustomed to wearing military BDU's, he fingered the thin cotton fabric as he buttoned the short-sleeved tan oxford shirt, thankful that both the shirt and the cotton green khaki pants were standard issue for the hot summer months.

"Well, don't you look all spiffy in your new uniform," Lucifer taunted quietly in his head.

Zander's hands froze in mid-air, and he drew in a surprised breath. It had been weeks since he had heard the voice. His eyes darted over to a prescription bottle on the shelf in the bathroom and suddenly realized he had forgotten to take his pill last night.

"Did you forget something?" Lucifer taunted again.

Silently admonishing himself, Zander ignored the voice and strode over to the bathroom. Quickly popping the top off the pill container, he tipped the bottle forward and shook the pills down into the palm of his hand. Drawing in another surprised breath, he saw there were only three pills left. Turning the pill container over to read the label, he realized there were no refills remaining.

"Uh oh!" Lucifer continued to torment him.

"Dang it!" Zander thought angrily, tipping two of the three pills back into the bottle. Placing the remaining pill into his mouth, he swallowed hard, ignoring the bitter taste on the back of his tongue, and set the bottle back on the shelf. *"I've been so caught up in getting this job I wasn't paying attention to how many pills I had left. I'm going to need to get another prescription written before I can get another bottle filled."*

"When are you going to have time to do that I wonder?" Lucifer feigned surprise.

Still ignoring the voice, Zander went over to a small dinette table by the window and flipped through the pages on his notepad until he found the notes he made during one of his visits to the library. *"Okay, there are two VA outpatient clinics that aren't too far from here, one in Parkersburg and the other one in South Charleston."*

Mentally calculating the distance between the towns to Ravenswood he thought, *"I should be able to make it to Parkersburg on my day off on Wednesday. I'll be cutting it close because I'll be out of pills by then, but I guess I don't have much choice."*

"Oh, I wouldn't worry about it, Alexander," Lucifer taunted again. *"I'll take care of you if you don't make it in time."*

Making a concerted effort to continue ignoring the voice in his head, Zander glanced over at the clock on the nightstand and saw he should have left for work already. "Crap!" he exclaimed, grabbing a green ball cap with the city emblem stitched on the front. Pulling the cap firmly onto his head, he grabbed his sunglasses, wallet, and the car keys and headed out the door.

~~~~~~~~~~

Later that morning, Zander and another new guy on the team, were assigned to weeding and dead-heading the flower beds surrounding the city hall building in the center of town. It was another hot, humid day so both men were drenched in sweat, desperate for even the barest of breezes to cool the wet fabric stuck to their skin.

"Looks like you've got a couple of new guys out there, Zeke," Roger noticed, rocking back and forth in his chair.

"Yep," Zeke nodded, his rocking chair creaking in the opposite direction.

"Where'd you pick them up from?" Roger pressed.

Shrugging his shoulders, Zeke replied, "Don't know. Rhodes interviewed them and sent them to me. They both seem like decent enough guys. Besides, it's not like I've got a line of applicants begging to work outside in this heat."

The sheriff chuckled quietly puffing on a cigar, from a chair adjacent to the men, listening to the conversation.

Friends since high school, Zeke, Roger, and Jethrow, more commonly known as 'Sheriff,' sat on this porch every day, smoking cigars, drinking iced bottles of cola, and watching the inhabitants of the town live out their lives while the trio of men gossiped like a bunch of old women. Over the years, the salt and pepper in their hair had slowly transitioned to mostly salt, along with a hearing aid for Sheriff, a pair of orthopedic shoes for Zeke, and a walking cane to go along with the blown knee Roger brought home with him from the war many years earlier.

The porch belonged to the town's general store, of which Roger and his wife, Betty, owned and managed. It offered mainly staple groceries and a few hardware items, but what drew people inside the store were Betty's baked goods, candies, and homemade fudge.

"I heard the blonde haired fella is staying at the motel down the highway. What's the story?" Roger pressed further.

"He's a former Marine. From what I've heard, it sounds like he's gone through some rough times. His father passed away while he was serving his second tour, and when he got home, the family business was in debt, so he had to sell off everything to cover it," Zeke replied.

Squinting as some of the smoke from his cigar got into his eyes, Roger asked, "What kind of business?"

"What?" Zeke snapped, getting annoyed with the twenty questions.

"What was his family business?" Roger asked.

"I don't know! He said it was a hardware and garden center back in Kentucky! If you want to know more about him, maybe you should go ask him and quit bugging me!" Zeke scolded angrily. "Don't you have customers inside you should be taking care of?"

"Geez, calm down!" Roger exclaimed defensively. "I was just making conversation. Besides, Betty's got the store covered."

"Bull! I know what you're up to," Zeke growled, pointing his finger accusingly. "You're looking to pair that homely daughter of yours up with someone, and you're sniffing around my men since they're the new meat in town."

"Aw Zeke, that's not a nice thing to say. Mae's not a homely girl; she just ended up looking more like her father than her mother," Sheriff Ford teased, trying to ease the tension between the two men.

"Ha, you got that right!" Zeke guffawed, slapping his hand on his knee, knocking ash from his cigar onto the porch.

"Aw, come on guys," Roger cried out, protectively. "My Mae's a good girl. I just want what's best for her."

"We're just messing with you, Roger," the sheriff continued to tease. "Your girl's got a heart of gold, and she'll be a fine wife for someone someday."

"Thank you, Sheriff," Roger nodded appreciatively. "That's very kind of you to say."

"If she can cook like your Betty, that's all she'll need. Cause' your wife can cook!" Zeke exclaimed appreciatively.

"Oh, Mae's a wonderful cook," Roger grinned. "She's saving up her money to go to culinary school. She says she wants to be a chef in one of those fancy restaurants in the city."

"If that's where the good Lord calls her, then it'll happen," Sheriff Ford noted quietly, puffing on his cigar.

After a few more creaks of the rocking chairs, Roger's curiosity got a hold of him again, breaking the silence. "But you've got to admit it's strange, a young man like that living in a weekly rental motel, not knowing anyone in town. He eats by himself in the diner, and he doesn't talk to anyone. Maybe he's in some sort of trouble, and he's using Ravenswood as a place of refuge!"

"A place of refuge," Zeke groaned, his patience wearing thin. "Roger, you need to stop watching those crime detective shows on TV!"

"Hey, it happens more often than you realize!" Roger argued.

"Miss Norma says he's a polite young man and maybe he just likes to keep to himself," the sheriff advised, again trying to mediate.

Roger looked at his friend, curiously and asked, "Norma said that?"

"Yep," the sheriff nodded.

"Huh. When has Norma had a chance to talk to him? She never leaves her post at the library," Zeke wondered, now curious as well.

The sheriff shrugged nonchalantly and said, "Apparently he likes visiting the library."

Roger scowled at his friend, unconvinced and said, "You're trying to tell me he sits in his room all night reading books?"

"I didn't say that," the sheriff shook his head. "I said he likes visiting the library."

Catching on to what his friend was saying, Zeke said, "Ah, so maybe it's not the books he's interested in, it's the library computers."

The sheriff nodded and admitted, "So it would seem."

"What do you think he's doing on those computers? Did Miss Norma say?" Roger asked, his interest growing.

"Don't know," the sheriff shrugged.

"Well, she can check, can't she?" Roger pressed, leaning forward eagerly.

"Yep," the sheriff inclined his head in admission.

"Well, what did she find when she looked?" Roger demanded, nearly falling out of his chair.

"Nothing," the sheriff replied, making eye contact with Zeke.

"Search history cleared?" Zeke asked, understanding the meaning behind the look.

"Yep," the sheriff replied.

"Want me to let him go?" Zeke worried, having just filled the position.

"Not yet," Sheriff Ford replied. "He hasn't done anything wrong. You said it sounds like he's had a rough time. Like Miss Norma said, maybe he just likes his privacy and keeps to himself."

Nodding his head in agreement, Zeke acknowledged, "But you still want me to keep my eye out for anything suspicious."

"Yep," the sheriff nodded.

"What about my other new guy? Anything I need to be worried about there?" Zeke asked.

"I'm not sure yet. It's probably a good idea to keep an eye on them both," the sheriff advised.

"What about me? What can I do?" Roger insisted, intent on getting in on the action.

"You don't do anything," the sheriff warned his friend. "I mean it, Roger. Like Zeke said, this isn't one of your TV shows. We respect the people living in our town and give them the benefit of the doubt unless or until we have reason to think otherwise. You got it?"

Disappointed, Roger sat back in his chair and frowned. "Yeah, I got it."

"I'm serious!" the sheriff warned again.

"I said I got it!" Roger insisted.

"What are you going to do in the meantime?" Zeke asked his friend.

Tampering his cigar out on one of the boards on the porch, the sheriff stood up to leave and said, "I've got some feelers out with a few law enforcement agencies. I'll let you know what I find."

Chapter 18

"Hello, who just joined the call?" Agent Hunter asked, hearing a beep on the speaker phone.

"It's us, sir," Piper's voice replied crisply throughout the room.

Then a second beep broke the silence. "Agent Chase is that you?" Agent Hunter asked.

"Yes, sir," Logan replied.

"All right, we have everyone," Agent Hunter advised loudly. "Agents Cooper, Vincent, and Nichols are with me in the room. Let's get started. Agent Stirling, why don't you and Agent Hughes go first?"

"Yes, sir," Piper replied. "As we suspected, the image Tori's facial recognition software picked up in Parkersburg, WV is, in fact, Alexander Wells. Agent Hughes and I met with the director of a VA outpatient center there in town. We showed them the picture of Alexander Wells, and although he's using a new disguise, they confirmed it was the same man."

"So what is his new look?" Tori asked so she could tweak the settings on her search program.

"Very short cropped hair, almost back to a military cut, and bleached light blonde. No facial hair anymore but Zander is now wearing dark-framed glasses which probably have clear lenses," Piper advised.

"So he's trying to pull off the Clark Kent look," Logan remarked sarcastically.

"Did they tell you why he was there?" Agent Hunter asked.

"Yes, sir, he was there for a refill on a prescription for a medication called Quetiapine," Piper replied.

"Quetiapine?" Agent Hunter frowned. "What is Quetiapine?"

"It's a drug often used to decrease hallucinations and improve concentration," Piper advised. "It's also known to help patients think more clearly, reduce anxiety, improve sleep, appetite, and energy level. According to the woman we spoke with, it's a fairly common drug given to people who have PTSD."

"Interesting," Ben noted quietly.

"Very, especially the part about the treatment of hallucinations," Reagan agreed.

Tori sighed and added, "That's like Luc's M.O. It sounds like he's still got a hold of our guy."

"We don't know that for sure," Agent Hunter warned.

"Agreed, however, it's starting to sound a lot like suspects we've dealt with in the past. Dare I mention the name Talman Mahmid?" Tori suggested.

"Ugh, I wish you wouldn't," Regan shuddered. "That guy was a psyco."

"A psyco who was controlled by the devil through his thoughts," Tori pointed out.

"If Zander filled the prescription at the VA center, then he has to come back every month for a refill, right? We should be able to catch him on his next trip into town," Logan suggested.

"No such luck," Riley's voice chimed in. "Zander asked for a written prescription. He'll be able to fill that anywhere. Plus he gave a sob story about how he lives in a remote location, and it's difficult for him to get to town on a regular basis, so they gave him a three-month refill script."

"That makes it harder but not impossible. We can still track it!" Tori advised. "All I need to do is write another web search program, designed to search for all new prescriptions for Quetiapine in a three hundred mile radius of that outpatient clinic and we should be able to find him."

"All right," Agent Hunter nodded in agreement. "Let's give that a shot and see how it goes."

"Will do!" Tori replied, making notes on her notepad.

"Do you have anything else, Agent Stirling or Agent Hughes?" Agent Hunter asked, directing his question to the speaker.

"No, sir," Piper replied. "We'll keep our eyes and ears open and report anything new as we find it."

"Very good," Agent Hunter agreed. "Okay, Agent Chase, you're up next. How's your progress going with Veronica Wells? I mean Rebecca Stone?"

"It's going very well, sir," Logan replied. "Scout and I are getting along great, and his training is going well. He's a smart dog. It turns out he's also quite a charmer. My plan was to expose him to Miss Stone gradually and have her slowly come to us, but Scout had other plans. The first day out, he saw her and made a b-line directly for her. So we ended up meeting the first day."

"Like father like son," Reagan snorted. "See a pretty girl, run toward the pretty girl."

"I was thinking the same thing!" Tori giggled.

"You know I can hear you, right?" Logan chastised.

"They know," Ben chuckled, rolling his eyes.

"So what's she like?" Piper chimed in. "The pictures you sent us, by the way, were great! Scout is adorable! I can't wait to meet him. And I agree with Reagan and Tori. Mrs. Wells is quite a looker. Are you going to be able to handle being around a woman that attractive and not make a move on her?"

"Hey, I am a total professional," Logan advised. "I've got this."

"Let's hope so," Agent Hunter replied firmly. "When is your next anticipated encounter?"

"Tomorrow at lunch," Logan replied. "She goes to the same park bench at a dog park down the street from the clinic where she works every day like clockwork."

"Okay, I look forward to your next report," Agent Hunter replied. "Do you have anything else?"

"Nope, that's all I have for now," Logan replied.

"All right, Agent Cooper, do you want to go next?" Agent Hunter asked.

"Sure," Tori agreed. "So after the dream I had about Gretchen Mallory, I did some research and confirmed that she and Sam Cutler did, in fact, know one another. They worked together at the same insurance agency for just over ten years. Even more interesting is the man I saw in my dream with them. It turns out he worked with them as well. His name is Pierce Andrews. He's the same suspect the detective in charge of the Cutler family case suspected of starting the fire in their home."

"Well that's quite the coincidence," Regan noted wryly.

"That's what I thought!" Tori agreed. "So I called the detective who originally worked the case, and spoke with him at length about his take on the suspect and his relationship with Gretchen Mallory and Sam Cutler. He said, Mr. Andrews was an arson investigator for the agency and seemed to have some suspicious connections to other arson investigations in the surrounding area. There wasn't enough evidence to physically tie him to any of them and before they could focus on him, Mr. Andrews quit his job and left town. The detective tried to keep tabs on his location, but after a while, Mr. Andrews just disappeared."

"Yeah and that didn't make him look guilty at all!" Piper scoffed.

"Exactly," Tori nodded. Pausing to phrase her next point carefully, she turned to Agent Hunter and added, "Since the murders of Gretchen Mallory, Sam, Ashlyn and Miranda Cutler equate to multiple homicides by a single individual; technically the murders fall under the classification of a serial killer. And since the possible related arson investigations crossed state lines, it permits the FBI to have jurisdictional entitlement."

"So it would seem," Agent Hunter mused quietly.

"And," Tori added, taking a deep breath, "As I am now officially deemed a part-time contracted agent with the FBI for a special assignment as directed by my immediate supervisor, I would like to ask you, sir, as my immediate supervisor to be assigned to this case."

Agent Hunter pursed his lips, regarding Tori quietly as he considered her request.

Familiar with his stone-faced demeanor, Tori sat quietly, staring back at him steadily.

No one else in the room dared to make a sound, knowing this was a pivotal moment and a case close to Tori's heart she had been hoping to work on for the past several years.

"Put all the information you have together in a report, and I'll review your findings," he finally replied.

"You'll have it by the end of the day," Tori exhaled in relief.

"This isn't a yes, this is an 'I'll take a look at the information.' I want to make sure that's clear," Agent Hunter advised, with eyebrows raised.

"Yes, sir. I understand," Tori nodded.

"Very well," Agent Hunter replied. "Since you brought up your change in status regarding special assignments, I do have one additional agenda item to cover before we adjourn. Agents Stirling, Hughes, and Chase, feel free to drop off here if you have other things you need to do."

"I need to take Scout outside for a potty break, so I'm going to jump off. Have a productive rest of your day guys and gals," Logan advised.

"See you later, buddy! Give me a call tonight if you feel like catching up," Ben quickly answered.

"Will do," Logan agreed.

"Bye, Logan," Tori added.

"Goodbye, Agent Chase," Agent Hunter replied.

A moment later, a quiet beep indicated Logan had left the call.

"We're going to stay on, sir," Piper advised.

"Very well, Agent Stirling," Agent Hunter agreed.

"All right, what is the additional agenda item?" Tori asked curiously.

Sliding three manila folders over to her, Agent Hunter replied, "Agent Sparrow's team in Richmond is working on a case involving three young college women murdered at the University in Norfolk. All three women were sexually assaulted and strangled in their apartments after returning home intoxicated from college parties. He has asked for your help on the case."

"Did he now?" Tori asked, mildly surprised. "Sounds like our friend has finally decided my gifts do not equate to witchcraft and I'm a useful human being after all."

"It has taken him a while to accept your abilities. However I believe he sees the value in them now, especially since he's reached out for your help," Agent Hunter admitted.

"Well then, I'll do my best not to disappoint him," Tori agreed, arranging the files in a line in front of her. Opening the cover of each file, she noticed a small silver dolphin charm in plastic evidence bags, stapled to the interior of each folder. "Is the killer leaving these charms at each crime scene?" she asked.

"Under the victim's tongues," Agent Hunter nodded.

Comparing the photos of each crime scene, Tori noticed each woman's body posed in the same manner, which was common behavior for serial murderers. "So after he rapes them, he strangles them, poses their bodies and the puts the charm under their tongues," she summarized for the rest of the team.

"Basically, yes," Agent Hunter nodded. "None of the women were in sororities, they focused on different majors, so they didn't have the same classes, nor did they work together. Agent Sparrow and his team interviewed the women's friends; their former classmates and teachers, and have come up with no leads as to who the killer might be."

"So we need to find the connection," Tori noted, feeling her fingers begin to tingle in anticipation of touching the evidence. Breaking the seal on the first bag, she prepared to drop the charm into her hand.

"Wait," Ben exclaimed, placing his hand on her arm. "Will the twins be able to see any of this?"

"Ah, good catch," Tori hesitated. "Goliath and I have been working on some exercises to block our thoughts from them so yes, I can keep them from seeing any of it." Turning to look at Goliath, who was, as usual, patiently sitting by her side watching her, she advised, "Goliath, no sharing what we're about to see, okay? RJ and Gemma cannot see this."

"Goliath won't share," he promised.

"Good boy," Tori praised. Turning back to the bag in her hand, she glanced down at the corresponding file and said, "Okay, this is the first victim, Cassy Burns." She tipped the bag forward, and as the charm dropped into her opened palm, she felt the icy cold of the metal quickly warm as her skin made contact. Closing her eyes, she began to watch the visions unfold in her mind.

"Okay, we're looking for a white male; mid-to-late twenties, and looks like he works at a gas station with one of those convenience stores attached. He's wearing a name badge with the name 'Brock' printed on it. There's a small display by the register with a bunch of charm necklaces, mood rings and stuff like that, so he's probably getting the charms from where he works. I see the girl, Cassy. She's buying beer, and he's carding her. She's underage, but he's still selling it to her."

"So he's getting their names and addresses from their driver's licenses," Agent Hunter realized.

"Yes," Tori replied breathlessly as her pulse began to quicken from the disturbing images she was seeing.

"Are you okay, Tor?" Piper worried, unable to see Tori's aura which she typically monitored during evidence readings.

"I'm fine," Tori gasped as the horrific acts of violence Cassy experienced played out in her head.

A few moments later she opened her hand and dropped the charm on the table. Wiping away the tears she was unable to stop from flowing down her cheeks, she exhaled a trembling breath and advised, "The man who raped and murdered Cassy Burns is the same man from the convenience store."

"Did you pick up on any additional details about him we can share with Agent Sparrow?" Agent Hunter asked.

Tori nodded, doing her best to regain her composure and replied, "He's wearing an ankle monitor, so he's already in the system for something. Agent Sparrow should be able to check the GPS locations of all white males in that area for all three victim's locations and find him."

"Excellent work, Agent Cooper," Agent Hunter praised. "I know these evidence readings are tough to experience. I hope you know how much I appreciate the sacrifice you make doing them."

"I do. You're welcome, sir," Tori replied, reaching for the second file.

"Are you sure you're ready to do it again, Tor?" Ben frowned, worried about the strain he saw on her face.

Giving Ben a small smile, Tori nodded and replied, "I have no choice. I have to read the other two charms to make sure they're the same guy." Breaking open the seal on the second bag, she noted, "Okay, this is from the second victim, Grace Lindsey...."

~~~~~~~~~~

"Yes, that is correct, Agent Sparrow, Agent Cooper confirmed all three of your victims were assaulted and killed by the same man," Agent Hunter advised. "I sent you an email with all the details."

"Yep, I got it. I can't thank you both enough for your help," Agent Sparrow's voice crackled through the conference phone speaker. "I've already got my guys working on canvassing the convenience stores in the area looking for a man matching the description you gave us. The addition of the GPS ankle tracking device should narrow that list down pretty quickly. Hopefully, we catch this guy before he kills anyone else."

"Agent Sparrow," Tori interrupted.

"Yes?" he replied.

"Would you mind sending me the locations where the three victims were buried or where their families determined to be their final resting places? I would like to visit each of them at some point and give them closure," Tori asked.

"After what you just did for the agency and those families, that's the least I could do. I'll send it to you as soon as I have it," he promised.

"Thank you," Tori replied.

"Keep us informed on how things go, Agent Sparrow, good luck," Agent Hunter requested.

"I'll do that. I'm hanging up now," Agent Sparrow advised.

"Goodbye, Agent Sparrow," Tori replied quickly, seconds before they heard the beep of him hanging up. Pressing the end call button on their phone, she reached over to re-organize the evidence bags into their respective folders but then noticed Ben was staring intently at the picture of the third victim.

Feeling her eyes on him, he looked up at her and quietly admitted. "This was someone's little girl. A little girl they prayed for, loved, protected, and nurtured her entire life until she was a strong independent young woman capable of living life on her own. I can't even begin to imagine what her parents must be feeling knowing they weren't there to save their little girl while she was dying. Their little girl who was probably crying out for someone to help her but no one did. I don't ever want to be one of those parents, Tor."

"Neither do I," she whispered, blinking back tears.

"I can't tell you the number of times Miranda, and I have had this same conversation over the years as Willow was growing up," Agent Hunter admitted. "As soon as you become a parent, you live the rest of your life with your heart walking around outside of your body."

"That's it exactly!" Tori exclaimed dramatically.

"I wish I could tell you it gets better," Agent Hunter added. "We see the darker side of humanity in our job. All you can do is appreciate the moments when you see the good and teach your children to be good. After that, it's all up to them as to whether they choose the right path."

"Dang, you guys keep talking up the joy of parenting like that and single people like me are going to steer clear of that whole part of life," Reagan warned, sarcastically.

"Just you wait, your time will come," Tori teased, trying to laugh off her tears.

"Speaking of which, I may have actually met someone worth pursuing," Reagan announced, casually.

"What?" Tori cried out, happily. "Who is it?"

"Someone I think might be close to having the same high level of standards and moral fiber I feel Ben and Agent Hunter have," Reagan admitted.

"That's a very flattering thing to say, Agent Nichols, thank you," Agent Hunter replied.

"You're welcome, sir. You guys set the bar pretty high," Reagan smiled.

"Really?" Ben smirked. "Did you hear that? I have a high level of moral fiber."

"You sure fooled her! You're such a dork," Tori laughed, rolling her eyes at him.

"Ouch, that hurt, Tor," Ben clasped his hand over his chest, pretending to be wounded.

"Uh-huh, I can see the blood from here." Turning back to Reagan, Tori asked, "So where did you meet this honorable guy?"

Laughing nervously, Reagan grimaced and replied, "Ah, actually in my kitchen, along with the rest of his fire crew."

Gasping audibly, Tori burst out laughing. "You didn't!"

"I kinda did," Reagan winced.

"What were you cooking and how bad was the damage?" Tori demanded, still laughing.

"Well, it was my first, and the last attempt at making fried chicken and I'm still waiting on the damage report from my insurance company," Reagan admitted. "I basically cannot use my kitchen right now. Let's put it that way."

"Oh sweetie, I'm so sorry!" Tori attempted to reply without laughing. "Grease fires are the worst! I'm just glad you're okay!"

"Yeah, no more Food Network for me," Reagan laughed. "I am officially culinary challenged."

"But you got a hot date out of it, so it wasn't a total loss!" Tori giggled.

"And he's an amazing cook. The first night he cooked for me, he made me fried chicken," Reagan smirked.

"Oh, that was so sweet," Tori crooned.

"And how was it?" Ben asked curiously.

"The chicken was perfect!" Reagan exclaimed, wide-eyed. "It was seriously the most delicious fried chicken I've ever had."

"So when do we get to meet this young man?" Agent Hunter asked, packing up his briefcase.

"Um, I'm not sure. I'll check and to see what our schedules look like and let you know," Reagan replied.

"What's his name?" Tori prodded.

"His name is Brice Corbin," Reagan replied.

"Brice.....that's a sexy name. Is he featured in the fireman's calendar by chance?" Tori teased.

"No!" Reagan laughed. "Well, at least not that I'm aware of!"

"Well, I look forward to meeting him," Agent Hunter advised, getting up from his chair. "You all have a nice evening. Good work again today, Agent Cooper."

"Thank you, sir. I hope you have a nice evening as well," Tori replied.

"Goodnight, sir," Reagan nodded.

"Goodnight, sir!" Ben waved as Agent Hunter left the room.

"So are you going to see Brice tonight?" Tori teased, wiggling her eyebrows.

Reagan shrugged and said, "No, he's on shift the next two nights at the station."

"Oh right, they have weird on and off days don't they?" Tori asked.

"Yeah, so far it hasn't been a big deal. We've only known each other for a few weeks so for now; the time apart is fine. Plus considering how much our job takes us out of town when we're actively pursuing a lead, we'll have to figure all that out," Reagan admitted.

"Well, since your man is busy and you don't have a kitchen, why don't you come over and have dinner with us tonight? I know the kids would love to see you and my mom has been asking about you," Tori offered.

"You sure it will be okay on such short notice?" Reagan asked.

"You're like family to us, Reagan, you're welcome anytime," Ben assured her.

"Okay, thanks! What time should I be there?" Reagan grinned.

"How does six o'clock sound?" Tori suggested.

"It sounds perfect; I'll see you then!" Reagan confirmed.

Chapter 19

"Come on Scout, bring it back!" Logan coaxed, grinning at the sight of the small dog dragging a large stick slowly behind him. "Good boy!" he praised when Scout dropped the stick at his feet. Eager to please his master, Scout's tail wagged furiously, and he barked, indicating he was ready to go again. "You know you could have picked a smaller stick, buddy. This one's a little big for you."

"Bark!" Scout insisted.

"All right," Logan agreed, reaching back and throwing the stick across the field. "Go get it, Scout!"

"Bark!" Scout replied again darting after the stick.

"That's one way of tiring him out!" Rebecca's voice announced from behind him.

Logan spun around and smiled when he saw her standing there. "Hi!"

"Hi, back," Rebecca smiled. "Couldn't find a bigger stick?" she teased.

"Well you know, it's like picking a switch from the tree in the backyard. Scout chose the stick, so I have no choice but to honor his decision," Logan chuckled.

"I see," Rebecca replied. "Remember, you're the alpha in this relationship, not him."

"Yeah, I know," Logan admitted.

Finally noticing Rebecca, Scout dropped the stick, barked happily and raced toward her.

"Hi, sweetie," Rebecca crooned, crouching down to rub Scout's ears and face. "You are such a sweet boy! I just love this cute little face! Ironically enough, I used to have a Dalmatian a few years ago who had very similar markings."

Surprised at her readily giving up that information, Logan tried not to show it and asked, "Really, that is a coincidence considering I've heard how varied Dalmatian markings are, like Zebras. What happened to your dog?"

"He died of old age," she lied.

"Oh, I'm so sorry to hear that. Did you have the dog as a puppy?" Logan asked, disappointed at how easily she had just lied to him.

"Yes. Since the dog was about Scout's age," Rebecca replied, standing up to face him.

"Did you give him a unique Dalmatian name like so many other people do like Spot or Domino?" Logan teased.

Rebecca laughed lightly and nodded her head in admission. "Domino," she lied again.

"Funny!" he replied, his disappointment in her growing.

"Did you bring your lunch today?" she asked, changing the subject.

Logan nodded toward the park bench behind them and replied, "It's in the cooler over there on the bench."

"Let's have lunch first, then work on Scout's training, I'm starving!" she suggested, motioning toward the bench.

"Works for me," Logan agreed, walking beside her. "Come on, Scout," he commanded.

Noticing how quickly the dog responded, Rebecca nodded her head in approval and said, "That's a good sign. He's learning his name and responding to your commands."

"Thanks, we've been working on it pretty steadily the past several days," Logan admitted. "And thanks again for agreeing to help me train him. I've never trained a dog before." Realizing the lie he just told her was equally as bad as her lying to him a few minutes earlier, he admonished himself for being so judgmental of her.

"You're welcome," she smiled, unwrapping her sandwich. "I love training dogs. Maybe someday I'll become a dog trainer."

"That would be a rewarding job I would think," he agreed, keeping the conversation light. "What do you do now in your spare time? Couldn't you start doing some of that now?"

"Well I would have to be licensed with the city to do that, and I don't have the money to start a business right now. I'm trying to save up enough to at least get that far," she admitted. "What about you? What do you do when you're not training Scout?"

"I'm a software developer by day and a bit of a baker at night," Logan winked, taking a bite of his sandwich.

"A baker! Really? Who would have thought?" Rebecca laughed.

"I know, right?" Logan grinned. "It's therapy for me. When I need to clear my head, I bake. What's your favorite cookie? I'll make you some."

"Peanut butter," she grinned. "So you get to work out of your apartment for your day job, that's nice. Speaking of which, I still can't get over the coincidence of us living in the same apartment complex. Imagine the odds of that happening!"

"Well, it's not too far from the park. I picked it mainly because of Scout so he could get some regular exercise. But I agree, it is a bit of a coincidence," he chuckled nervously, realizing for the second time the dishonest role he was playing in this scenario. "And yes, being able to work from home is one of the perks. And I get to set my schedule," he noted.

"Don't you get lonely not having direct contact with other people?" she wondered.

"Not when I meet interesting people like you," he confessed.

Rebecca blushed and quickly replied, "Well perhaps you need to expand your range outside of the park then."

"Well, that's the beauty of being able to manage my work schedule. It gives me an opportunity to work in some recreational fun now and then. While we're on that subject, I was thinking about taking Scout out to the hiking trails by the river this weekend and start working on building the muscles in his legs like you suggested. Would you like to join us?" Logan offered.

"Ah," she hesitated, unsure how to respond.

"I want to make sure I do it right so having you there to show me would be helpful," he almost begged.

Turning to face Logan, Rebecca searched his eyes and asked, "I'll go as long as you understand this won't be a date, okay? We'll be going strictly as friends."

"Would that be such a bad thing?" he asked. "I enjoy spending time with you and you know Scout enjoys spending time with you."

Nodding admittedly she replied, "I do enjoy spending time with you both but again, only as friends. I can't offer you anything more than that Logan."

Not wanting to push her her further, Logan nodded agreeably and said, "Okay, strictly as friends. So is that a yes to Saturday morning at eight?"

"Deal," she smiled.

"And I'll bring lunch that day so don't worry about bringing anything," he insisted. "Consider it payment for your services."

"Okay," she agreed. "Are you done with your sandwich? We could do a little training now."

"Sure," he replied, getting up to throw their garbage in the trash can. "What are we going to work on today?"

"It's a command called 'watch.' We're going to teach Scout that whenever you say that word, that means he should turn to face you and wait for your next command," she instructed.

"Okay, sounds good. Let's get started!" Logan agreed. "What do I do first?"

"Did you bring the bag of dog treats as I suggested?" she asked.

Pulling a small plastic snack bag from his pocket, he held it up showing her he did. "Got it," he revealed.

Remembering Logan putting treats into the bag earlier, Scout's attention focused on Logan, his tail wagging eagerly for a treat. "Not yet, buddy," Logan laughed.

"Good. So for starters, we're going to sit down opposite from one another on the ground and have Scout in between us," Rebecca instructed.

"Okay," Logan agreed, sitting down cross-legged on the ground. "Scout, come," he commanded, firmly. Responding obediently, Scout bounced over and stood in front of Logan. "Good boy, now sit. Good boy!" Logan praised, giving Scout one of the treats when he immediately sat down.

"Nice," Rebecca smiled, sitting down on the other side of Scout facing Logan. "So the next thing we're going to do is wait for Scout to look away from you, and then you're going to position the pointer finger of your dominant hand in front of your face, and you're going to say, 'Scout, watch.' When he returns his attention to you, give him a treat."

"Got it," Logan nodded, shifting his position on the ground to get ready. While he waited for Scout to look away, Logan's eyes drifted past the dog, and he saw Rebecca watching him. *"Dang, she has the most beautiful eyes,"* he thought, distractedly. *"Remember this is a job, dude. You don't get the girl on this one. Besides, she clearly stated she wants to be friends. Keep your mind focused."*

"Logan," Rebecca whispered.

"What?" he whispered, snapping free from the inner dialog going on in his head. Then he realized Scout had looked away from him. "Oh, right." Positioning his pointer finger in front of his face, Logan commanded, "Scout, watch."

Immediately, Scout turned his head and regained his attention back to Logan. "Good boy!" he praised, giving Scout a treat.

"That was great!" Rebecca praised. "Keep doing it, just like that. Eventually, the praise will be all he'll need, and you won't need to food reward him. Remember, rewarding with food shouldn't be your primary objective. Praise for good behavior and obedience is your goal."

"Got it," Logan agreed, rubbing Scout on the head. "Good boy, buddy!" he praised again.

"Try it again," she demanded.

"Okay," Logan agreed, resuming his earlier position. As soon as Scout looked away, he commanded, "Scout, watch."

As before, Scout immediately turned his head and regained his attention back to Logan. "Good boy!" he praised, giving Scout a treat.

"Man, he's a smart dog," Rebecca admitted, shaking her head in disbelief. "I swear I've never seen a dog learn so quickly."

"Yeah, he's pretty smart," Logan lied again, not wanting to admit to her that he and Scout were already working on this command at home. "Or it could be our trainer."

"Ha," Rebecca laughed.

"Again?" Logan suggested.

Glancing down at her watch, Rebecca sighed and admitted, "I'm afraid not for me. Time flies when you're having fun. I have to get back to work."

Bounding to his feet, Logan extended his hand and said, "Understood. Here let me help you up."

"Thanks," she smiled, taking his hand.

Pulling her to her feet, Logan intentionally pulled a little more firmly than he needed to so Rebecca's balance would be slightly off, and she would fall in his direction. Bracing her hand on his chest when she did, she quickly recovered her balance and removed her hand.

Embarrassed, she glanced up at his face and paused as their eyes met. Then just as quickly, she stepped back and blushed again. "I'm sorry, I lost my balance."

"That's okay. I had it under control. I wouldn't have dropped you," Logan grinned, secretly pleased at Rebecca's reaction. "Same time tomorrow?" he asked, allowing her a quick subject change.

Appreciating his gesture, she nodded and replied, "I'll see you then!"

Chapter 20

"No go on Morgantown," Agent Hunter reported as he opened the car door and slid into the driver's seat.

"Well boo," Piper objected from the back seat. "Scratch another one off the list."

"Did the pharmacist give you an acceptable description of the customer to confirm it wasn't our guy?" Riley asked, once again riding shotgun.

Agent Hunter nodded and replied, "Even better, she showed me the video footage of the customer who picked up the prescription. It was a thirty-year-old Jamaican male, definitely not a disguise. He's not our guy."

"Should we consider the possibility that Zander could be sending someone to fill his prescriptions for him? Did the pharmacist visually check a photo ID against the man who picked up the prescription?" Piper asked.

"Hmm, that's an excellent point. Now that you mention it, I don't think I saw the pharmacist do that on the video. I'm going to go back and ask for confirmation whether the pharmacist is one hundred percent certain the man who filled that prescription matched the name on the original doctor's script. I'll be right back," he advised, getting out of the car. Firmly closing the door behind him, he paused a moment for traffic to pass, quickly crossed the street, and then disappeared through the automatic doors of the pharmacy.

"We're going to have to be more aware of things like that," Riley admitted, wishing he had thought of it earlier. Glancing back at her, he praised, "That was good instincts there, Piper."

"Thank you," she smiled reaching forward to touch his arm gently.

Taking advantage of the opportunity, he took her hand in his and turned it over, kissing the top of her hand tenderly. "You know how much I love you, right?" he asked sincerely, staring intently into her eyes.

"I do," she smiled, enjoying how his aura changed to a deep red when he talked to her like this. "You know how much I love you, right?"

"I do," he grinned. "So how much longer are we going to wait until we're saying those exact words to each other in front of our family and our friends? Have you thought more about it?"

"Honestly I have," she admitted, slowly pulling her hand away, and nodding her head at him, indicating Agent Hunter was returning to the car. "Let's talk about it tonight when we're at the hotel."

Glancing over, seeing Agent Hunter's approach, Riley quickly repositioned himself in the seat and nodded. "Okay."

Resuming his position behind the wheel, Agent Hunter closed the door and advised, "The man is a long time resident here in town, one who the pharmacist has known for years. She also confirmed he has a slight mental disability and the Quetiapine was a recent change from a previous drug which wasn't working for him. I feel it's safe to continue and mark this one as not a match to our search."

"Okay, I agree. Where's our next stopping point?" Riley asked, turning to Piper.

"Johnstown, Pennsylvania," Piper advised, reviewing their list.

"How far away is that from where we are?" Riley asked.

"Two hours north from here," Piper replied. "I just sent the address to both of your phones so you can set your GPS."

"Tori's search sure cast out a wide net," Riley noted, checking his phone.

"Well, she said she was going to cover a three hundred mile radius so hopefully one of these leads pan out soon," Agent Hunter admitted, buckling his seatbelt and starting the car.

"We sure could use a break and get some good direction somewhere," Riley admitted.

"I reached out to one of my friends who used to be a nurse who has had extensive experience treating patients with PTSD, and asked her what she knew about the drug Quetiapine," Agent Hunter admitted as he drove.

"Is that the woman who was married to your friend Whit who passed away last year?" Piper asked.

"Yes, Cecilia," Agent Hunter replied, forgetting they already knew about her. "She mentioned that Quetiapine hasn't always been the standard drug administered to people who have PTSD. In the past, the drug of preference was called Nortriptyline."

"What were the advantages of prescribing Nortriptyline over Quetiapine?" Riley asked.

"Well, Nortriptyline is used to treat mental conditions like depression, mood swings and to relieve anxiety and tension. It also increases energy level and a sense of well-being in many patients. It belongs to a class of medications called tricyclic antidepressants, and it works by affecting the balance of certain natural chemicals in the brain," Agent Hunter advised.

"And how is that different from the Quetiapine?" Riley asked.

"Well, as we've learned, Quetiapine is an antipsychotic. However, CeCe said it's also used to treat certain mental conditions such as schizophrenia, bipolar disorder, or episodes of mania or depression associated with bipolar disorder. Like the Nortriptyline, it also helps to restore the balance of certain natural substances in the brain, however, what I found interesting was she said the Quetiapine often helps PTSD patients think more clearly and positively about themselves and take a more active part in everyday life."

"So they're able to function more mainstream in society using the Quetiapine," Piper surmised.

"That's what it sounds like," Agent Hunter agreed.

"Man, forgive me for how this sounds but I'm curious about laying eyes on Alexander Wells," Piper admitted, boldly. "If he's this twisted and tormented on the inside like we think he is, I would bet his aura is pure chaos."

"That brings up a good point," Agent Hunter replied. "Do you typically see people's auras change color or are they pretty constant?"

Surprised by his question, Piper leaned forward between the seats and said, "Actually a person's aura does change, depending on their mood, but they typically don't stray too far from their baseline color. For example, remember Chet Arrant one of the guys in our forensics class at the academy?"

Agent Hunter chuckled and replied, "You mean the guy you all had a special nickname? What was it again? Wasn't it something like 'Arrogant Arrant'?"

"Yes!" Piper exclaimed, impressed he remembered such a trivial detail. "His aura was always an ugly shade of brown which means that person is selfish, greedy and egotistical. He's one of those people whose aura rarely changed. He was pretty much always a selfish, greedy and egotistical person. On the other hand, there've been people we've interviewed whose auras are normal healthy colors. Depending on the situation, I've seen where the color of their aura becomes threaded with either a dark muddy blue which translates as their fear of speaking the truth or a dirty gray which means guardedness and unwillingness to reveal certain pieces of information. It's pretty fascinating to see the choices made by a human mind externally translated into color."

"What about being able to look at someone's aura and know whether they're an honest or dishonest person? Can you take one look at someone and immediately think, they're the bad guy, and we should watch that person?" he asked.

Piper shook her head and replied, "No because honesty is a choice a person makes, not a trait of their personality. That's another one where a healthy aura will change and show tinges of murky dark pink which reveals a dishonest decision they're in the process of making given their current situation."

"It's too bad there aren't more people like you," Riley admitted. "I think it's a huge advantage for someone with your ability to work in the field of law enforcement or criminal justice."

Piper inclined her head in agreement and said, "I agree, that is an upside. However, it does have its downside. I've seen people wrestle with guilt trying to make a decision, sometimes swaying their mind in the wrong direction, only to find out later that their sense of goodness later came into play, and they end up making the right decision. If I were to act too hastily and accuse someone of wrongdoing, before they've made the realization to do the right thing themselves, then I would be affecting their life in a negative way. I would be taking away their power to choose for themselves."

"Huh, I hadn't thought of it that way," Riley admitted.

"I agree. That's another layer of complexity I hadn't thought about either," Agent Hunter admitted. "Here's a random question. Have you and Agent Cooper ever done any experimentation on combining your abilities together when profiling suspects or trying to solve a case? I'm curious how effective that would be."

"We've dabbled a bit here and there but not to any extent where we've conclusively found we're more effective as a team or as individuals. Tori's gifts are so powerful and specific, most of the time I feel like I'm hovering around her on the fringe but not breaking through. If that makes any sense," Piper shrugged, sitting back in the seat.

"Plus she's been pretty busy with everything going on with the twins these days. She doesn't have much time for herself anymore."

"Which also translated means less time for you?" Agent Hunter suggested, glancing back at her from the rearview mirror.

Scowling in admission, she nodded and confessed, "Well, I can't place full blame on her for that. We've been chasing down a lot of these possible sightings of Alexander Wells too, so that's been taking me out of town a lot."

"True," he gently reminded her. "We're not a nine to five operation."

"I'm not complaining, sir. I still love my job and can't imagine doing anything else," Piper vowed.

"I know you do, Agent Stirling. Life is all about balance. You'll find time to keep bonds with the people who matter most to you. Our job is demanding. There's no doubt about that. However, it also still allows you to have a personal life if you can find that balance," Agent Hunter assured.

"If you don't mind my asking, how long did it take you and your wife to find that balance, sir?" Piper asked.

"Well let's see," Agent Hunter paused, thinking back. "Miranda and I met through a mutual friend our third year of college. I was at the FBI Academy, and she was working toward her criminal justice degree at Stanford. We dated steadily until graduation; then she took another year to prepare for the bar exam, which she passed on the first try, thank goodness. Then I was assigned my first case with the FBI, she hired in as a prosecutor for the district attorney's office in D.C, then we got engaged. What is that, maybe three or four years up to that point?"

"Sounds like it," Piper agreed, understanding where he was leading.

"Miranda and I didn't move into a place of residence together until after we were married. So add another year for our engagement, making it five years. Then it took us a year or so to get used to being married, getting used to the demands we each had with our careers, typical newlywed behavior," Agent Hunter advised.

"Wow, six years. That's a long time," Piper admitted, her eyes flickering over to the seat where Riley was sitting.

Catching her glance, and seeing the concern on her face, Agent Hunter added, "Six years doesn't seem so long when you know it's for the right person. When you find that one person who accepts you for who you are and doesn't want to change you, you would wait forever if you had to."

"Amen to that!" Riley agreed, glancing back at Piper to give her a quick wink.

"True," Piper nodded, glancing down at the engagement ring on her finger. *"Then why can't shake this feeling I have that Riley and I are running out of time?"* she worried.

Chapter 21

"Hmm...that one's pretty close," Tori thought, pausing on one of the results of the facial recognition matches her program found that day. *"He has a similar facial structure and body size; it's just hard to tell from the ball cap he's wearing, covering part of his face. I better add it just in case,"* she told herself, entering a new location to the list Agent Hunter, Piper and Riley were using for sightings of Alexander Wells. *"Ravenswood, West Virginia. Huh, never heard of it,"* she thought then quickly dismissed it.

Momentarily distracted by a long drawn out yawn that escaped her, she glanced down at the time on her laptop and saw that it was almost two in the morning. "Yikes, I'm not getting as far as I hoped I would have tonight," she muttered, stretching out her neck. Yawning again, she selected the page advance for the next set of matches. "I'm just going to rest my eyes for a minute," she told herself sleepily while she waited for the page to load. Before the page results came back, her tiredness overpowered her and her mind began to replay familiar images in her head as she drifted off to sleep.

The old man with the vacant eyes sitting in an old wooden chair,

Alexander Wells watching her through the scope of his rifle,

Lightening striking darkened clouds in the sky above,

A winged angel falling slowly toward the earth,

The reverberating sound of the gunshot,

Goliath falling to the ground,

A baby crying,

Darkness,

Silence

"Too much silence," Tori thought warily, opening her eyes. *"Great,"* she sighed, finding herself lying on the red upholstered couch in Lucifer's favorite room. Turning toward the matching leather wingback chair across from her, she scowled when she saw Luc, elegantly dressed and perfectly manicured, quietly watching her. "What?" she complained, sitting upright.

"Well that's not a very nice way to greet an old friend," he chastised testily. "And here I am trying to be respectful allowing you to get some rest."

"Uh huh," Tori frowned, unconvinced. "If that were true, I wouldn't be here in your interrogation room; I would still be sleeping on my couch in my living room at home dreaming of something much more pleasant than this. What do you want?"

"Interrogation room," Luc laughed. "Well, now I am offended, especially when I always make a concerted effort to make things comfortable for you when you visit!"

Tori exhaled a frustrated sigh and stared at him quietly. *"Oh just get it over with and humor the big baby,"* she told herself, wearily.

Trying to make more of an effort to be pleasant, Tori gently cleared her throat and smiled at him politely. "All right," she agreed sweetly. "How are you doing, Luc? You look very handsome today. Is that a new suit?"

"Yes it is!" he grinned, slightly adjusting the knot on his tie. "I'm touched you noticed."

"Well your appearance seems to be very important to you," she noted, patiently.

"There's nothing wrong with caring about how you look," he remarked, dryly. "You only get one chance at a first impression. Besides, might I suggest you pay more attention to your appearance? That thick mass of auburn hair you've always been so fond has lost its shine. Not to mention your eyes are starting to look all baggy and bruised. It seems as though the role of the chosen one, slash working mother is starting to take its toll on you. You don't want some other woman turning your Ben's head in her direction and away from you do you?" he added, taunting her.

"Now who's being rude?" she asked, eyebrow raised.

"I'm the devil, deal with it. You should know me well enough by now to realize I'm not going to sugar coat the truth from you," he sighed, rolling his eyes at her.

"Perhaps you could try not being an insensitive jerk," Tori narrowed her eyes at him defensively. "Especially since you just called me 'an old friend,' I might also add. Besides, you do realize that vanity is a sin, right?"

"It's one of my favorites," he leered, laughingly.

Since her attempt at pleasantries was obviously not working, Tori sighed and raised her hands in surrender. "Okay, that's all I've got I'm too tired to play with you right now. What is it you wanted to talk about since obviously, you have something to tell me?"

"Oh, I don't know you may not think it's all that important," he sighed, feigning boredom.

"Well if it's nothing important then there's no reason for me to stay," she said, preparing to leave.

"They keep things from you, your little angels," he quickly alleged so she'd stay. "Did you know that?"

Recognizing a baited question, she paused a moment, deciding on the best answer to give him. "That's one of the beautiful things about free will, Luc. You have the power to choose the decisions you make. I trust my children. They know the Lord. I would be foolish to expect they would tell me everything."

"You're not even the least bit curious about what I mean?" he asked, mildly surprised by her calm response.

"Obviously you feel there's something I need to know so why don't you tell me?" she suggested.

"Oh, I don't know. Maybe it would be in my best interest to keep it to myself after all," Lucifer continued to taunt, dangling the carrot out a little further.

"Fine, if you think that's best," Tori shrugged, getting frustrated. "If that's all you wanted to say....,"

"He's curious about me, you know. Your RJ," Luc provoked, interrupting her.

Biting her tongue, Tori shrugged again and said, "Well if that's true, then I guess it was bound to happen eventually. If you think it's something I need to talk about with him, then I will."

Irked that his taunting didn't have the effect he was hoping for, Luc warned, "You know, someday he's going to get tired of playing second fiddle to his big sister, and he's going to want to take charge of his life and make his own decisions. Trust me; I've been there."

"Meaning what?" Tori almost growled, knowing full well what he meant.

"Perhaps I'll be able to help him, guide him, if you will. Like an uncle," he suggested, grinning wickedly.

Leaping off the couch, Tori stood over Luc menacingly and threatened, "Let's get something straight because believe me, I've already thought about what you just said and was just waiting for you to say something. You stay away from my children; you hear me? You may think you're funny and clever getting me to lose my cool but right now, you've seriously pissed me off, and I'm not going to play these games with you. You mess with my kids, and you're going to have to deal with me, with Remy and with the Lord God Almighty if that's what it takes! Do you hear me?"

Stunned into impressed silence, Luc regarded Tori calmly for a moment, expressionless. Then his face slowly broke out into a horrifically evil grin, and he replied, "Challenge accepted."

Before Tori could respond, she suddenly heard a loud popping sound, followed by the feeling of being pulled away and then immediately thrust forward. With one large gasp for breath, Tori's eyes fluttered open, and she found herself back on the sofa in her living room at home.

"What was that?" she mumbled as she regained her wits about her. Sensing the slightest movement from her peripheral vision, she turned her head and jumped when she saw Gemma and RJ standing beside her, with their palms pressed firmly against one another, quietly watching her. "What's going on?" she demanded, sitting up. "Are you both okay?" Then she smelled the hint of smoke in the air, and her eyes flickered over to the unlit candle on the coffee table. "Is something burning?" she asked.

"It was time for you to leave that place," Gemma replied quietly. "He was going to hurt you."

"What?" Tori blinked in confusion. "Who was going to hurt me, Gemma?"

Then the air in the room changed and an instant later, Remy was there with them. "What just happened?" he demanded, looking frantically around the room. "Was he here?" Then he saw Gemma and RJ standing beside Tori. "What are the two of you doing out of bed at this hour?"

"Mama had a bad dream. We brought her back," Gemma replied, quietly, watching her mother's face carefully.

Tori's confused eyes darted back and forth between her children. "What do you mean you both brought me back, sweetheart? Do you know where I was? Did you see it? Did you hear what we were saying?"

Both Gemma and RJ nodded their heads, solemnly and replied, "Yes, Mama."

"Was that man Uncle Luc?" RJ asked, curiously.

"What did you just say?" Remy demanded angrily. "Did you say, Uncle Luc?"

Tori quickly interrupted Remy so as not to scare the kids and replied, "That's what they heard him call himself in my dream. Right, sweetheart?" she asked, looking at RJ.

"Uh huh," RJ nodded.

"Uncle Luc. Now I've heard everything," Remy growled, his wings creating a current in the air as he paced the length of the room.

"We don't want you calling him Uncle Luc, RJ," Tori advised patiently. "You understand that Luc is Lucifer, right? You realize he's the devil?"

RJ nodded his head and replied, "But isn't he Remy's brother too, Mama? He used to be an angle like Remy, right?"

Briefly glancing up at Remy, Tori met his eyes, now filled with surprise and concern. "Yes, Lucifer used to be an angel and technically yes, he is Remy's brother. However, they're not siblings like you and Gemma," Tori explained.

"They're not?" RJ frowned. "Brothers are still siblings, aren't they?"

Seeing the confusion on RJ's face, Tori glanced back up at Remy and inclined her head in RJ's direction that he should step in.

Catching her meaning, Remy sat down on the edge of the coffee table, picked RJ up and set him on his knee. Not wanting to be left out, Gemma quickly climbed up and took the open spot on Remy's other knee.

"We're not supposed to sit on the coffee table," RJ observed, glancing over at Tori questioningly.

Remy looked over at Tori with almost an identical facial expression as RJ which made her laugh. "*I swear, some days he looks just like Ben, and other times like right now, he's the spitting image of Remy,*" she thought to herself, humorously. "Just this one time it's okay, sweetie," she permitted.

Nodding appreciatively at her, Remy turned back to the twins and smiled when he noticed they were staring up at him with wide, curious eyes. "You're mom's right. Lucifer and I are brothers. We also have many other brothers often referred to as Archangels. You've heard of them, right?"

Both Gemma and RJ nodded their heads and replied, "Uh huh."

"Good," Remy praised. "The Archangels were all created by God just like the two of you were, except we didn't have a mother, only our heavenly father. And together, we were a family like your mom, your dad and the two of you. You're each other's family."

"And Goliath, too," RJ innocently added.

"Yes, of course. And Goliath, too," Remy smiled. "So for a very long time, my family was very happy and content with the way things were. We loved each other, and we served God willingly without hesitation. Then one day, my brother Lucifer, decided he wasn't happy as an Archangel serving God anymore. He became bitter and angry and jealous of the power God had. He decided he wanted everyone to serve him instead of God."

As soon as Remy paused to take a breath, Gemma immediately raised her hand. "Yes, Gemma?" he asked.

"I read about that in one of the books Daddy let us check out from the library! It said that Lucifer convinced other angels to rebel against God and when they fought against God, He became angry and cast them out of heaven," Gemma recounted.

Impressed by her knowledge, Remy grinned and said, "That's right, sweetie."

Wanting to impress Remy as well, RJ's hand quickly shot up in the air. Laughing, lightly, Remy asked, "Yes, RJ?"

"We also read that Lucifer was given the gift of free will as we have. It said God left him free to choose good over evil, and he chose evil," RJ eagerly added.

"That is also correct, which brings up a good point," Remy nodded approvingly. "You understand what it means to have free will, right?"

RJ nodded and replied, "It's the decision you make to do the right thing without God having to help you."

Impressed again, Remy smiled and said, "That's exactly right. Well, the same applies for evil. When faced with a decision and you choose the wrong one that too is an example of free will without God helping you."

"Is it true He's always with us?" Gemma asked curiously. "Mama said that even though we can't see God, He's always there. Is that true?"

Remy nodded and affirmed, "Yes, that's true. Do you want to know what I think is the most amazing thing about God?"

"Yes!" Both Gemma and RJ exclaimed eagerly.

"Well," Remy paused, looking over at Tori to give her a quick wink.

"The most amazing thing about God is that He knows every single moment of our lives, long before we're even born. He always knows what you're thinking long before you think it. But the very best part of God's love is that even if at some point in your life you decide to turn away from Him, He will never turn His back on you or leave you. God loves you, and in return, He asks that we love Him back."

"Does it make Him sad when someone turns away from Him?" Gemma worried.

Remy turned to her and admitted, "Yes, it makes Him very sad. But He never gives up on us. He prays for our salvation every single day."

"Why don't you live in heaven with your brothers and God anymore? Did you stop loving God like Lucifer?" Gemma asked.

Remy exchanged another quick look with Tori, and then he addressed Gemma and RJ both directly. "No, I've never stopped loving God or my brothers. I hope someday I'll be able to return to them, but for right now, I'm meant to be here on earth with you."

"Did Lucifer try to convince you to come with him?" RJ asked curiously, abruptly changing the subject.

Having wondered this herself, Tori watched Remy's face carefully as she saw him deciding how he wanted to answer the question. Seeming to read her mind, he glanced over at her, meeting her eyes, unwaveringly.

"Yes he did," Remy finally replied, turning back to RJ, keeping his answer simple.

"Did he get angry with you when you told him no?" Gemma asked.

Recalling the intensity of their battle like it was yesterday, Remy nodded, sadly and said, "Yes, he was very angry with me."

"Did you two fight?" RJ asked, excitedly, raising his hands now clenched into fists.

"There was a battle, yes," Remy replied carefully, glancing over at Tori again, his eyes asking her how much he should tell them.

Understanding his hesitation, Tori gave him a quick nod and provided him with a subject change. "The fight isn't as important for you both to understand as is the reason why. What Remy and I want to make sure you understood is that Lucifer is still very powerful even though he's no longer in heaven. Mommy talks to Lucifer because, to be honest; I don't have a choice sometimes. As you saw in my dream, I didn't choose to go where you saw me; he brought me there. Lucifer will pretend to be very nice and clever and fun so he can trick you into doing things for him, but you shouldn't allow yourselves to get fooled by any of that okay? He is not a nice man, no matter what he says or does. Do you both understand?"

"We know. He's already tried to play with us once," RJ blurted out.

"RJ!" Gemma hissed, glaring at him angrily.

"What?" Tori exclaimed, surprised.

Pursing his lips together firmly, Remy exhaled an angry breath and as calmly as possible asked, "Was that the day the two of you were playing together in your room last week?"

Glancing up at him guiltily, Gemma nodded and whispered, "Yes, sir."

"Why didn't you tell us?" Tori cried out, fearfully. "Was that the only time he's done that?"

The twins nodded and replied, "Yes, Mama."

"Tell us everything, from the beginning!" Tori demanded, trying to keep her voice calm.

The twins looked at each other, communicating telepathically with one another, and then a few moments later, RJ nodded at Gemma in silent agreement.

Taking charge, Gemma looked at Tori and said, "It was last Tuesday when RJ and I were playing Candy Land. Remy had just checked in on us, and a few minutes later we felt a presence in the room we knew wasn't him so we suspected it was Luc."

"I don't want you calling him that," Tori interrupted sternly. "You will both call him by the name God gave him, Lucifer. Is that clear?"

"Why, Mama?" Gemma scowled, questioningly. "That's what you call him."

Silently cursing herself for reciting the phrase she vowed she would never say to her children, Tori quietly replied, "Because I said so."

Unable to suppress his reaction, Remy snorted a laugh and then quickly cleared his throat when Tori threw a daggered look in his direction.

"Now go on with your story," Tori instructed, ending that line of discussion.

"Okay," Gemma paused, thinking back. "We both felt the presence at the same time, and then RJ noticed his game piece had moved.

"Then we heard a scraping sound on the game board, and the red gingerbread man showed up at the starting spot."

"Figures he'd pick the red one," Remy muttered under his breath.

"So he hasn't said anything to you yet at this point?" Tori asked, ignoring Remy.

"He never spoke to us at all," RJ replied.

"But you knew it was him?" Remy asked.

Gemma nodded and admitted, "We knew right away when we felt him. His presence isn't like yours; it's different."

"Different how?" Remy asked, curiously.

Gemma looked at RJ again, silently conferring with him for a moment and then she turned back to Remy. "When you're with us, we feel warm and safe. When he was with us, the room felt cold and dark. Like when a cloud passes over the sun."

Touched by her clearly phrased analogy, Remy smiled and squeezed Gemma's shoulders gently. "I'm glad you both feel that way about me. I love you both very much; you know that right?"

Gemma smiled and nodded enthusiastically. "We know."

"Yep!" RJ grinned.

"Then what happened?" Tori interrupted, trying to be patient.

"Then Gemma said, 'We don't want to play with you,'" RJ exclaimed triumphantly.

"We agreed I would tell the story!" Gemma argued, glaring at RJ angrily.

"You always get to tell the stories!" RJ argued back.

"That's because I'm the oldest!" Gemma spat.

"That doesn't make you my boss!" RJ challenged angrily.

Recalling what Luc said in her dream, Tori placed one hand on Gemma's leg and her other hand on RJ's leg and advised, "Hey, if anyone is the boss here, it's me, got it? Gemma, just because you were born first, that doesn't make you RJ's boss, okay sweetie?"

"Fine," Gemma scowled, shooting another angry glance at RJ.

"What happened after you said you didn't want to play with him?" Remy encouraged, gently.

"RJ got scared when I said that so I told him we didn't have to be afraid and we could make Lucifer leave," Gemma confessed.

"Make him leave?" Tori exclaimed. "How exactly could you make him leave?"

Gemma shrugged and replied, "I told RJ to put his hand out like this," she demonstrated, holding out her hand with her palm facing her brother.

"And I did," RJ immediately replied, sticking out his hand toward his sister.

"And then we did this," Gemma advised, placing her palm against RJ's.

"Then what happened?" Tori prodded.

"Then we felt a tingling feeling in our hands, followed by a crackling pop sound," Gemma replied.

"Don't forget the smoke," RJ exclaimed excitedly.

"Smoke?" Tori asked, glancing at both of their faces.

"Oh right," Gemma agreed. "The room smelled like smoke afterward."

Tori's eyes flickered over to the unlit candle on the coffee table, recalling how she smelled smoke when she woke up earlier, and then looked back at Gemma. "How did you know that would work, Gemma? Did someone tell you to do that?"

"I don't know," Gemma shrugged. "I just knew."

Glancing up to see what Remy's expression looked like, Tori was relieved when she noticed he too seemed calmer having heard the children's explanation.

"Are you angry with us?" RJ worried, directing his question at both Tori and Remy.

Reaching up to tousle RJ's hair affectionately, Remy smiled and said, "No we're not mad at you. But I want you both to promise me and your mom that the next time Lucifer tries to contact you, you'll let us know right away, no matter what, okay?"

"Okay," RJ nodded.

"Yes, sir," Gemma agreed.

"Okay good. Now it's ridiculously beyond your bed time, so both of you go back to bed," Tori commanded sternly, pointing to their bedrooms. "Hopefully we can salvage what's left of the night, so you're not too tired in the morning."

"It's already morning, Mama," Gemma advised innocently.

"Yes, I know," Tori chuckled patiently.

"Good night, Mama," RJ said, kissing Tori on the cheek and giving her a hug.

"Goodnight, sweetheart," she murmured, hugging him tight.

"Good night, Mama," Gemma whispered, hugging Tori tightly. "I love you."

"Goodnight, baby girl, I love you too," Tori smiled, hugging Gemma back.

"Goodnight you two," Remy repeated.

As they turned to leave the room, Tori blurted out, "Thank you for what you did earlier, by the way, if I forgot to tell you."

"You're welcome, Mama," they sweetly replied before they left.

Getting up from his seat on the coffee table, Remy sat down on the couch next to Tori and waited with her a few moments until he heard the doors to the kid's rooms close and felt it was safe to say anything.

"Well, how do you think we handled that?" he asked in a hushed tone.

Exhaling a breath she felt like she'd been holding for the past half hour, she turned to him and quietly replied, "I have no idea, I hope well? I don't know what I'm terrified of more, to think he's already tried to make contact with them, or the fact that they didn't tell us."

"Well, knowing Lucifer the way we both do, it makes sense that he would start testing the waters when they're this young and impressionable," he admitted. "But I agree I don't like the fact that neither of them told us, Gemma, especially since she always seems to be the one who takes the lead between them."

"Which reminds me of something Luc said in my dream," Tori whispered. "I don't think he's as interested in Gemma as he is RJ. He said, 'someday he's going to get tired of playing second fiddle to his big sister, and he's going to want to take charge of his life and make his own decisions. Trust me; I've been there.' I'm scared for my son, Remy. I don't know what to do. I can't fight Luc. I don't have that kind of power."

Remy's expression darkened, angrily, realizing the war between he and Lucifer was inevitably going to get much worse, knowing he would need to focus more of his time protecting RJ. "I know. What's even more frustrating is that he's gotten much better at hiding from me lately. As soon as I get close, he just seems to vanish."

"That's an interesting analogy," she mused thoughtfully.

"What do you mean?" he asked.

"Luc and Zander are in the same situation," Tori noted.

"Zander? You mean the guy that shot you three years ago?" he recalled.

Tori nodded and replied, "Yes. Every time we think we've found him and start to move in, he disappears. Luc is doing the same thing with you. I find that ironic."

"Yeah well my brother has mastered the art of being a fugitive so unfortunately, your Zander is learning from the worst example possible," he growled.

"Plus he seems to be shielding him which isn't helping," she added.

"Yeah, why is that? This guy hasn't killed anyone since he shot you, and Luc is still protecting him. I don't get it. What's in it for him?" he argued.

"Well, here's my theory on that whole scenario. Since I've touched several items Zander has come in contact with, I have a strong memory of him in my mind. As much as I hate to admit it, he and I have a connection to one another. Maybe by still having control over Zander, Luc thinks he has some element of control over me," she suggested.

"Well I don't like the thought of that," he frowned. "If that were the case, wouldn't you be able to detect or feel things that this guy Zander does? If you two have a connection, shouldn't it work both ways?"

"Hmmm, I hadn't thought of that," Tori admitted. "Maybe Luc has him shielded from me."

"Your team seems to have become pretty fixated on finding this guy. Wouldn't you agree? Are you even working other cases?" he noted.

"Well, we may be a bit obsessive over this one case, but Zander is still a wanted man, aside from the fact that he shot me. We're not going to let him get away unpunished," Tori insisted.

"And yes we're working other cases! We're helping another team with a string of murders in Norfolk. AND I'm hoping to be able to start working on a new case involving the murder of Goliath's former family!"

"Ah, that's right. The lady Karla put you in contact with in your dream," he recalled.

"We can talk about that another time. We've gotten sidetracked. I'm sorry. I think that was my fault this time. Let's get back to the twins and what we're going to do," Tori insisted.

"I'm still thinking about that, don't worry," Remy admitted quietly.

"You've seen for yourself the combativeness the twins have with one another sometimes. I know they love each other and would protect one another to the end if need be, but Gemma is a force of nature to go up against at times, and she has the determination of a warrior. I can understand the frustration RJ feels. What I don't know is how to help them or what to do about it," she admitted.

"Agreed," he nodded. "The last thing we want is for RJ to become a pawn in Luc's game. The twins were created for a reason and are the most powerful when they're together. Putting a wedge between them would be the obvious thing he would try to do."

"Can you spend some time with RJ alone?" Tori suggested. "I can work with Gemma on softening her interactions with him a bit, but maybe having you play a bigger role in RJ's life will be a good influence on him. You know, like a Jedi and his Padawan?"

Remy chuckled and said, "Let me guess, we're giving Luc the role of Darth Vader?"

Tori's eyes widened in surprise realizing he knew what she meant. "You know Star Wars?"

"You'd be surprised what I know about this world," he grinned, wriggling his eyebrows at her.

"I don't think I want to know, do I?" she chuckled.

Remy shook his head and advised, "No, you most definitely do not want to know."

"So does that mean you'll do it?" she hoped.

"Will Ben have any issues with it?" he cautioned. "The reason I've kept my distance up until now is that I didn't want to interfere or confuse the boy or take away any of Ben's parental responsibilities. Ben has to be one hundred percent on board with this."

"I'll talk to him and explain everything. I'm sure he'll agree. Hey, maybe the three of you could do some things together. That would be good for RJ to experience I think. What do you think?" she suggested.

Remy nodded and admitted, "I like Ben. That might work."

"Okay great, I'll talk to him in the morning, and we'll start right away, deal?" Tori asked.

"Deal," Remy agreed.

Chapter 22

Zander released the trigger on the chainsaw once he saw the blade cleared the other side of the tree and set the saw down on the ground at his feet. "How about now?" he asked his companion on the other side of the trunk.

Pushing firmly with both hands, Pierce grunted as the log began to move off the path. "I think that one did the trick," he advised, rolling it into the brush safely out of the way. "Are we going to trim that down more and haul it away or leave it there?"

"Boss said to leave it. It's already half eaten through by termites, and the smaller animals will be able to use it as a refuge," Zander replied, rolling the other half of the tree to the opposite side of the path.

"That's too bad. It would be cool to watch it burn. Logs with holes in the center look like a volcano when you burn them," Pierce said, eyeing the wood wistfully.

"I'm sure there's plenty of seasoned wood in this neck of the forest you could take home and burn if you wanted to," Zander suggested. "Are you a fireplace or a backyard fire pit guy?"

"Fire pit," Pierce admitted. "Although we didn't use anything fancy like folks do today, we used a bunch of big stones from the creek and formed them into a huge circle. Then we'd build a bonfire inside of it. My dad and I used to have a fire every night in the summer when I was a kid. We'd walk the woods picking up sticks and dry pieces of wood during the day and then bring them back home with us for the next evening. It became our tradition, something we did together, just the two of us."

"That's cool. My dad and I did something along those lines too when we went camping. We'd roast hot dogs and marshmallows for smores. They're some of my favorite memories as a kid," Zander replied. "Do you still do that with your dad?" he asked as he set the chainsaw down in the bed of the pickup truck.

"No, my dad passed away when I was in high school," Pierce replied, tossing his work gloves onto the floorboard of the truck as he got inside.

"I'm sorry for your loss, man. That's rough losing your dad when you're that young. I bet it was hard for your mom too. How's she doing?" Zander empathized offering his condolences.

Looking out the window, Pierce quietly replied, "She's dead too. They died together."

"What happened if you don't mind my asking?" Zander asked.

"House fire," Pierce shrugged, pulling a pack of cigarettes from his pocket. Extracting one of the cigarettes from the pack, he placed cylindrical roll between his lips, slid the pack back into his pocket and retrieved a lighter. "I was out one night, and the house caught fire while they were sleeping," he explained. As Pierce talked, Zander noticed the lighter had a shiny metallic exterior with a face of a wolf embossed on the front casing.

"The Fire Marshal said it looked like my dad forgot to damper the fire in the fireplace and some of the embers sparked and caught the carpet on fire," he noted, pausing briefly to light the cigarette and take a deep drag into his lungs.

Exhaling a stream of smoke out the window, he added, "It probably didn't take long for the rest of the house to catch afterward. They found my parent's bodies in their bed." Flicking the flame on his lighter on and off as he spoke, he added, "They more than likely died from smoke inhalation before the fire got to them. I lived with my aunt and uncle for about a year afterward until I graduated high school, then I took off on my own."

Hearing the cold, detached manner in which Pierce recounted the story of his parent' death, made the hairs on the back of Zanders' neck stand up like a warning bell. "Well, like I said, I'm very sorry for your loss," Zander replied, uncomfortably. "That had to have been rough growing up on your own afterward."

"I've made do," Pierce shrugged again, pocketing his lighter. "So where are we going next?" he asked, deliberately changing the subject. "Want me to radio in and check with Zeke?"

"Yeah, that's a good idea," Zander agreed as he started the engine. Unable to shake the feeling that something about Pierce's story wasn't ringing true, he glanced at him out of the corner of his eye and thought to himself, *"Why would a guy who lost is parents in a house fire be interested in wanting to watch wood burn? That would be the last thing I would think about if I lost my parents like that."*

"Do you know where that is?" Zander suddenly heard Pierce ask him.

"What?" Zander muttered, realizing he didn't hear the first part of the question.

"Earth to Alex! Dude, where did your head just go?" Pierce teased sarcastically. "I asked you if you knew where Copper Ridge is. That's where Zeke wants us to go next."

"Oh yeah," Zander quickly replied. "It's just a couple miles north past that hill. But we need to stop back at the maintenance building before we go out that way. I need to get more gas for the saw."

"Well then we might as well grab some lunch while we're there then," Pierce suggested. "It's almost noon now. That will save us some time."

"Yeah, that sounds good," Zander agreed, turning the truck around. Eyeballing the remaining stump of the cigarette in Pierce's mouth, he added, "Make sure you keep your butt in the truck and use the ashtray. The woods are too dry right now. The last things we need is a forest fire."

"I agree. That would be horrible," Pierce acknowledged, crushing the burning stub of his cigarette in the ashtray. *"I can already envision it,"* he chuckled inwardly to himself.

Chapter 23

"Well that didn't take long for the twins to find the playground," Tori laughed as she removed the picnic basket from the trunk. "Geez Louise, Mom! What did you pack in this basket? It's really heavy! How can sandwiches and potato chips weigh this much?"

"I never said I packed just sandwiches and potato chips," Sarah teased.

"What else did you put in here?" Tori laughed, trying to peek inside.

"I guess you'll have to wait until lunch to find out!" Sarah teased again, taking the basket from Tori.

"Argh! You always were the queen of suspense when it came to stuff like this. It used to drive us crazy when we were kids," Tori complained.

"And just think, now you get to do it with your kids," Sarah laughed.

"Hardly, not when they're reading my mind the way they've been doing!" Tori exclaimed. "I can't get anything by them these days!"

"How's it going with your exercises on blocking your thoughts from them?" Sarah asked.

"Very slow and only rarely successfully," Tori admitted. "Goliath and I have been working on it too. The brain is a tricky thing to control. I guess it's something I'm going to have to work on over time."

"I'm here to help you if you want another person to practice with," Sarah offered. "Or even just to get away for a little girl time when you need a break."

"Thanks, Mom, I appreciate it," Tori smiled. "Speaking of getting away, how do you think the boys are doing?"

"Considering the number of years since your father went fishing, there's no telling!" Sarah admitted ruefully. "We may be going out for a fish dinner tonight. Let's put it that way."

"Mom!" Tori laughed, feigning surprise.

"I'm just teasing. That was very nice of Ben to ask Tanner to go with him." Sarah praised. "I hope your father doesn't slow him down too much."

"Are you kidding? Ben loves hanging out with Dad. Besides, I know how much Ben has been pining away wanting to get out on the water and try out his new pole I gave him for Christmas. The time outside will be good for them. We've just been so busy with work, then everything that's been going on with the kids. Time snuck by on us." Tori admitted.

"Well, the two of you need to make more of an effort to take a break and do things you enjoy," Sarah gently scolded. "It's good to recharge your batteries."

"Yeah, I know," Tori agreed.

"How long has it been since you took your kayak out on the water and just had some time for yourself?" Sarah asked.

"Since before I got pregnant with the twins," Tori confessed, hating how long ago that was.

"What?" Sarah exclaimed, stopping to stare at her daughter. "You love your kayak! Why haven't you gone out since then? Ben is certainly capable of watching the kids for a couple of hours."

Wincing, Tori replied, "There's no room in a kayak for a two-hundred-pound dog and asking Remy to come with me kind of defeats the purpose of alone time. It's too risky for me to be alone like that with Luc acting out the way he has been. One flip of my kayak and I could drown."

"Oh, that Luc, he gets me so angry sometimes," Sarah growled through her teeth.

"You might want to keep that anger of yours in check. I think Lucifer very much enjoys your frustration," Tori suggested.

"You're right, I know," Sarah admitted.

Glancing over at the playground area as they walked over to the picnic tables, Tori smiled watching Aubrey pushing the twins on the swings. To anyone else watching, it would appear as if the twins were propelling themselves. "Look at how much fun they're having. Just like two normal kids."

"Well, for the most part, they are two normal kids, honey," Sarah advised. "To an outsider, you, Ben and the kids look like a perfectly typical family."

Snorting a laugh, Tori rolled her eyes and snidely replied, "Yeah, of course, we are. Can you imagine the reality show ratings we would get if anyone knew how atypical we are?"

"Oh, I don't know. Here we are enjoying a beautiful day having a picnic lunch in a park while the kids are playing on the swings. That's pretty typical, don't you think?" Sarah tried to reason.

"Aside from the ghostly spirit pushing the swings and the telepathic dog by my side? Sure, why not!" Tori chuckled.

"You seemed excited about it earlier," Sarah frowned at her daughter's sarcasm.

"I am, Mom, this is fun!" Tori relented. "I think a picnic in the park will be a nice change and is something we don't do very often. Thank you again for suggesting it!"

"You're welcome," Sarah smiled happily. "How does this one look?" She suggested of a table beside them, positioned under a large shady oak tree.

"Perfect," Tori nodded. "Here, let me spread out the tablecloth then you can show me what you have packed in that basket!"

"Aren't you sneaky?" Sarah chuckled. "Besides the kids are having fun, we can wait to set things up for a little while."

"*Maybe you can but I can't,*" Tori thought, grinning wickedly at her mother. Focusing her thoughts on Gemma and RJ she called out in her mind, "*Kids, lunch is ready! And Grandma said she packed us something special!*"

"Yay! Lunch is ready!" Gemma cried out gleefully, releasing her hold on RJ's hand so she could jump off the swing mid-flight.

"Race you!" RJ challenged, his feet hitting the ground seconds before hers.

"What's the surprise, Grandma?" Gemma excitedly asked as she ran.

Sarah smiled and shook her head slowly, impressed by her daughter's ingenuity. "Clever girl," she admitted, glancing back at Tori. "You never could wait when a surprise was involved."

"Hey, I learned from the best," Tori winked. "Now, let's see what's in that basket!"

"Okay, okay, I give up," Sarah shrugged, opening the lid. "We have two peanut-butter and jelly sandwiches, one for Gemma and one for RJ," she began handing out the sandwiches. "Two roasted turkey sandwiches on multi-grain bread with sliced tomato, sprouts and a cranberry-orange relish for Tori and me."

"Yay, that sounds amazing!" Tori cheered.

"A snack sized bag of classic potato chips for Gemma," Sarah continued, handing Gemma the bag.

"Thank you, Grandma," Gemma politely replied, taking the bag.

"You're welcome sweetheart," Sarah smiled. "And a snack sized bag of sour cream and onion for RJ."

"Thank you, Grandma," RJ mumbled through a mouthful of sandwich.

"You're welcome, honey," Sarah replied, deciding not to correct him for talking with food in his mouth this one time. "And for the grown-ups, we have a red quinoa salad with crispy bacon; fresh herbs tossed in smoky balsamic vinaigrette dressing."

"When did you make that?" Tori demanded in surprise. "That sounds so good!"

"Aubrey and your father offered to watch the kids for a couple of hours yesterday while you and Ben were at the office, so I ran out to the store and picked up a few things to surprise you," Sarah admitted.

"Well, you sure did! This is the best picnic ever, don't you kids agree? Grandma rocked it out!" Tori praised happily.

"You knocked it out, Grandma," Gemma agreed.

"Yeah, out of the park!" RJ nodded emphatically.

"You two crack me up," Aubrey giggled, enjoying the conversation. "Everything looks great, Mom."

Sarah chuckled, bowing graciously and replied, "Thank you all for such praise! Enjoy!"

Sitting patiently on the ground beside the table, Goliath glanced at the basket anxiously. *"Goliath treat?"* Tori heard him ask.

"Umm, Mom is there anything else in that basket?" Tori asked, angling her head in Goliath's direction.

"Oh my, how could I forget you, Goliath?" Sarah exclaimed. Reaching into the basket, she removed an oblong object wrapped in butcher's paper. Goliath's tail instantly began to wag, recognizing the shape of the package. "Here you go, sweet boy," Sarah purred, unwrapping a large bone and handing it to him.

"Thank you," Goliath replied, hungrily. Taking the bone over to the ground by the base of the tree, he lay down and immediately began gnawing on one end.

"He said thank you," Tori advised.

"You're welcome, Goliath!" Sarah replied.

Quickly handing out juice boxes to the kids and spring water to Sarah, Tori sat down and scooped a large spoonful of the salad onto her plate. Then she took a bite and slowly chewed, closing her eyes blissfully. "Oh my goodness, this is amazing, Mom! What is in this dressing?"

"Just some extra-virgin olive oil, balsamic vinegar, spicy brown mustard, brown sugar, smoked paprika, ground chipotle, salt, and pepper. It's a very simple recipe," Sarah confessed.

"It may be, but the flavor is perfect for the bacon and the quinoa! I have to admit I've had quinoa in restaurants before but haven't made it at home. If it's that easy, I'm going to have to steal your recipe from you! Gemma, RJ, try some of this, it's really good!" Tori encouraged.

Eyeing the dish speculatively, Gemma and RJ both looked at one another debating. Then they looked back at Tori and Sarah. "Would it be okay if we didn't?" Gemma asked politely. "No offense, Grandma."

"No offense taken, sweetheart," Sarah smirked. "When you get older, you'll be more adventurous and try things like this."

"Yum. This sandwich is so good; it seriously tastes so much better when someone else makes them," Tori sighed in contentment.

"I'm glad you like everything sweetie," Sarah replied. "Now I didn't pack a dessert because as I was driving through town yesterday, I saw an ice cream shop a few blocks from here. Would anyone be interested in ice cream after lunch?"

"I would!" RJ's hand immediately shot up.

"Me too!" Gemma declared excitedly.

"Mmmm, I'm going to wait to give my answer after I've finished this sandwich and another helping of that salad!" Tori replied, taking another bite of her sandwich.

~~~~~~~~~~~

Once lunch was over, the twins played a bit longer on the swings while Tori and Sarah cleaned up and packed the picnic basket back into the car. "Okay gang, we're ready to roll," Tori called out.

"Coming!" the twins replied, quickly jumping off the swings and running toward the car.

"Okay little monkeys, in the back seat you go," Sarah directed, buckling them both into their car seats after they climbed in.

Tori waited until Sarah was safely buckled into the passenger seat and glanced back to make sure everyone was ready to go. "Everyone good to go?"

"Good back here," Aubrey confirmed.

"All right, then away we go," Tori replied, backing the car out of the parking spot onto the street.

As they were driving, Sarah, Aubrey, and RJ engaged in a lively discussion about what kind of ice cream was their favorite. When Tori realized Gemma wasn't chiming in, she glanced into the rearview mirror toward the back seat and saw Gemma staring out the window with a sad look on her face.

"Gemma, sweetie, are you okay?" Tori asked.

"Mama, can we stop?" Gemma asked, sniffing back tears.

Immediately pulling the car over to the side of the road, Tori looked back at Gemma and asked, "Sweetie, what's wrong? Are you feeling sick?"

"I'm okay, Mama," Gemma replied quietly. Then she pointed out the window beside her, "I don't think that little girl is, though," she added.

Tori looked out the window, and her breath caught in her throat when she realized she had stopped the car alongside a cemetery. Then she saw the spirit of a little girl, not much older than Gemma and RJ, standing just a few feet inside the wrought iron fence watching them.

"Where are we?" RJ frowned, straining in his seat to look out Gemma's window. "Why are all those rocks lined up like that?"

"That's a cemetery, sweetie," Tori replied.

"What's a cemetery?" RJ scowled.

"It's a place where families bury their loved ones when they die," Sarah explained.

Trying to understand, RJ looked over at Aubrey's spirit floating between his and Gemma's car seats and asked, "Is that where you buried Aunt Aubrey?"

"Have you not taken them to a cemetery before?" Sarah asked Tori curiously.

Shaking her head, Tori replied, "No, not yet. It's never come up before."

Turning in her seat to face RJ, Sarah said, "No, we haven't buried Aunt Aubrey in a cemetery, sweetie. Your Aunt Aubrey is special, so she stays with us. Like you and Gemma, she's one of Remy's children."

"But isn't she yours and Grandpa's child too?" RJ frowned.

Sarah nodded and said, "Yes she is. She and your mom are both my and Grandpa's daughters, as well as being Remy's daughters too. I realize that sounds a bit complicated."

RJ looked back at Aubrey and smiled. "You're special to us."

Aubrey grinned and replied, "Heck yeah I am! Don't you ever forget that, little man!"

"Can we help her, Mama?" Gemma whispered, hoping the little girl couldn't hear her. "I think she noticed I could see her. I don't want to look at her if we can't help her."

Sarah and Tori exchanged a look, asking each other the same unspoken question. *"Do you think they're ready for this?"* Silently, Sarah gave her daughter a slight nod indicating they should talk to the girl.

Looking back at Gemma, Tori replied, "Why don't we go talk to her and find out?"

Her face instantly breaking out into a big grin, Gemma nodded and replied, "Thank you, Mama!" Then she turned to look at the little girl and waved at her. Immediately the girls face registered surprise that Gemma could see her and she eagerly waved back.

"Well, there's no backing out now," Aubrey noted.

"Nope, definitely not," Tori agreed. "Let's go meet Gemma's new friend."

Chapter 24

"Come on RJ!" Gemma demanded, grabbing her brother by the hand and running in the direction of the little girl.

"Hang on guys!" Tori called out after them, trying to keep up. Sensing her anxiety, Goliath ran ahead of Tori to catch up with the twins until she got to them.

"Hi!" Gemma greeted the little girl excitedly. "I'm Gemma!"

"Hi," the girl replied, glancing back and forth between Gemma and RJ. "C-can you both see me?" she stammered.

"Yeah, I can see you too," RJ replied.

"I like your dog, he's huge!" the girl exclaimed.

"Thanks!" Gemma replied. "His name is Goliath."

Completely out of breath, both Tori and Sarah walked the last few paces toward the children. "Hey," Tori gasped. "The next time I tell you both to hang on, I expect you to listen, got it?"

"Yes, Mama," Gemma replied guiltily.

"Yes, Ma'am," RJ nodded.

Turning her attention to the little girl, Tori surmised from the style of the shirt and pants the girl was wearing; she hadn't been in the cemetery very long. "Hello, what's your name?" she asked the girl.

"Can you all see me?" the girl asked in surprise. As Sarah and Aubrey approached them, the girl's eyes widened further when she realized Aubrey was a spirit like she was. "Um, my name is Josie," the girl replied. "Are you a ghost too?" she asked Aubrey.

"We don't call her that," Gemma interrupted quickly. "My aunt Aubrey is an earthbound spirit like you are. We don't like the word ghost."

"Why not?" Josie frowned.

"Because when people hear the word ghost, they think of someone mean and scary. My aunt isn't mean or scary, she's nice and sweet," Gemma replied.

"Aw, thanks, Gemma," Aubrey smiled appreciatively.

"Josie, how old are you, honey?" Tori asked gently.

"I'm six," Josie replied, holding up her hands showing six fingers.

"Do you know how long you've been here?" Tori asked.

"Uh-uh," Josie replied shaking her head.

"Where's your rock?" RJ asked, looking around them.

Understanding his question, Josie looked behind her and pointed in the opposite direction. "It's over there," she replied. "Come on!"

Following her to her headstone, Tori, Sarah and Aubrey read the inscription, realizing Josie had only been there a few months. There were fresh flowers on the grave that couldn't have been more than a day old, and a weathered teddy bear resting up against the stone.

"Josie Kinsley, that's you?" Tori asked.

"Uh-huh," Josie nodded.

"Do you remember what happened to you, Josie?" Tori asked.

"We were driving home from my Grandma and Grandpa's house," Josie said, thinking back to that night. "It was dark outside, and I was watching the stars out my window. Daddy was driving; Mommy was in the seat next to him, and my brother Jack was in the back seat next to me."

"I like watching the stars too," Gemma admitted.

The girls smiled at one another, already forming a bond.

"Then what happened?" Tori prodded.

"Then there was a bright light shining in through the window, and I couldn't see the stars anymore. Daddy and Mommy started shouting and then everything went dark," Josie replied. Her voice wavered as she looked down at her headstone, filled with emotion as tears began to fall. "They come to visit me, my mom, dad, and my brother. Mommy has a cast on her arm, and she walks with a cane. I talk to them, but they can't hear me. All they do is cry and say how sorry they are and how much they miss me. I miss them too," she added, turning back to Gemma. "Can you talk to them for me?" she asked.

"What would you want me to say to them? Would you want them to know?" Gemma asked quietly.

"What do you mean?" Josie asked.

"Would you want them to know you're still here?" Gemma asked. "Even if that made them sadder than they are now?"

Glancing back at Aubrey, Josie furrowed her brow, trying to understand the question. "But your aunt is still with you, and you all talk to her. Why couldn't I do that too?"

"We are all from a unique family, sweetie," Tori tried to explain. "Do you know what unique means?"

"Yes," Josie nodded. "You're special, different."

"That's right!" Tori smiled. "Me and my sister, my mom, and my children, Gemma and RJ, all belong to a special family that's thousands of years old. We all have the gift of being able to see and talk to earthbound spirits who have died like you did."

"So that's why Aubrey is still here?" Josie asked.

Not wanting to confuse the girl, Tori nodded her head and replied, "That's one of the reasons, yes."

"So why am I still here?" Josie asked, her eyes filling with tears. "Did I do something wrong? Did my mommy and daddy do something wrong?"

"No, not at all sweetheart," Sarah quickly replied, sitting down on the ground beside Josie so she could look at her eye to eye. "When Aubrey died, we were all so sad. We cried like your parents are doing now, and we asked ourselves the same questions. You didn't do anything wrong, and neither did your parents. You were all part of a very unfortunate accident, by someone who made a very bad decision."

Josie's eyes returned to Sarah's, and she asked, "If you weren't part of your special family and you didn't know Aubrey was still here, would you want to know?"

Blinking back tears, Sarah hesitated, never having anyone ask her that question until now. "It's so hard to answer that question, Josie. For many years, we didn't know Aubrey was still here on earth. We thought she passed on and went to heaven like everyone else does. Then Tori found her, and we all had to accept what happened."

"We were very happy to have Aubrey with us, but it was still hard to come to the realization that she would never really be with us like before," Tori added.

Knowing Josie was looking for an answer, Sarah admitted, "If I didn't have the ability to see and talk to spirits, I wouldn't want to know Aubrey was still here. It would make me more sad knowing I couldn't help her."

"I feel the same," Tori agreed, taking her mother's hand.

"Can we send her to heaven, Mama?" Gemma asked innocently.

"You can do that too?" Josie exclaimed in surprise.

"Only if you're ready," Tori replied. "You have to be completely sure."

Glancing down again at her headstone, Josie sighed deeply and looked back at Sarah. "I'm ready to go now. I don't want to make my mommy sad."

"Okay," Sarah replied. Turning to Tori, she added, "You're up."

Preparing herself for the crossover, Tori knelt down in front of Josie and placed one hand around the amulet.

"Mama, may RJ and I do it?" Gemma quickly interrupted.

"Uh," Tori hesitated, exchanging a look with Sarah.

Sarah inclined her head that they should give it a try. "Why not?"

"Okay," Tori agreed. "But just remember, the amulet only responds to me. So don't be disappointed if it doesn't work."

"We don't need the amulet, remember, Mama?" Gemma asked. "Remy told us we didn't need the amulet or the statue."

"I do recall him saying that. I just want you both to be prepared," Tori stressed.

"We'll be fine," RJ assured her, reaching over to take Gemma's hand. "Ready Gemma?"

Taking RJ's hand in hers, Gemma looked over at Josie and reached out her hand to her. "Take our hands, Josie."

Tentatively taking both hands in hers, Josie looked over at Sarah again for her approval. "Will it hurt?" she asked.

"Not one bit," Sarah promised her.

"What do we say, Mama?" Gemma asked.

"Focus all of your attention on Josie and the path she'll need to take. So picture God and heaven's gates as we discussed. Then when you have that image in your mind, you say 'May your spirit be at peace, Josie, as you return to the Father.'"

Nodding in understanding, Gemma looked at RJ and asked, "Ready?"

"Ready!" RJ replied.

Then Gemma looked at Josie and asked, "Are you ready, Josie?"

Nodding confidently, Josie replied, "Yes, I'm ready."

Closing their eyes tightly, Gemma and RJ concentrated on Josie standing at the gates of heaven and loudly proclaimed in unison, "May your spirit be at peace, Josie, as you return to the Father."

When they opened their eyes, Josie was gone.

"Mama, look! We did it!" Gemma exclaimed excitedly.

"That was so cool!" RJ declared, jumping up and down.

"Yes you did," Tori smiled worriedly, still clutching the amulet in her hand.

Chapter 25

Logan rested the back of his head against the frame of the SUV and grinned when Scout poked he head out the opened window, taking advantage of the easy access to lick Logan sloppily on his face.

"Yeah, I love you too, buddy," Logan professed, reaching up to gently scratch Scout on his ear. "She shouldn't be too much longer."

Scout licked his face again in response.

"I hope she doesn't stand us up." Logan thought to himself.

Hearing the crunch of tires on the loose gravel behind him, he turned and grinned again when he saw Rebecca's vehicle pulling into the parking space beside them. "See? There she is!" he said more for his relief than anything else.

"Sorry, I'm late!" Rebecca winced, as she quickly got out of her car. "I forgot how long it took to get here from town."

"No worries!" Logan smiled. "We were just hanging out enjoying the scenery," he added, taking a moment to appreciate the colorful T-shirt and hiking shorts she was wearing. *"Talk about enjoying the scenery..."* he thought.

"Okay, great," Rebecca sighed in relief. "Hello sweet boy," she greeted Scout, walking up to Logan's car. "Thanks again for agreeing to meet me instead of driving together from the apartment complex. I hope you didn't think that was too weird."

"Not at all! I have a younger sister who tells me all the time how important it is for guys to realize women need to feel safe with a guy before she lets him too close. I totally get it," Logan replied. "That's why I picked this site. There are lots of other people around, so you don't think I'm some creep trying to get you alone in the woods."

Narrowing her eyes at him, she laughed and said, "That doesn't mean you still can't be a creep you know?"

Feigning a shot to the heart, Logan winced and groaned, "Ugh! And here I am trying to be so gallant and chivalrous!"

"No, you are, I'm just teasing you," she smiled. "So are you ready to head out?"

"Yep, just need to grab my gear! I've got extra water, a first aid kit, bug spray, sunscreen and our lunch for later," Logan advised, opening the hatch of the SUV. Maneuvering his pack onto his back, he adjusted the shoulder straps and added, "There! All set. Come on, Scout," he encouraged, taking the dog into his arms and then gently setting him on the ground.

"I brought extra water too. Let me grab my stuff real quick," Rebecca replied, opening her side door to retrieve her backpack. "That's a nice pack by the way!"

"Thanks! It's a National Park Service Traverse pack from REI. It had great online reviews, and part of the proceeds from my purchase went to the National Park Foundation which I thought was a pretty cool idea," Logan replied, turning around to show her.

"Very cool," Rebecca nodded. "Mine is an Osprey. I liked it because it's a light day pack for shorter hikes and doesn't have too many bells and whistles."

"Nice color. I like the deep shade of green," Logan noted.

"Thanks. Green is my favorite color, so I usually veer off and immediately go for the green," Rebecca admitted.

"Green is her favorite color," Logan thought, making a mental note. *"That's ironic, green is Tori's favorite color too. I'll store that little tidbit away for future reference."*

"What about you?" Rebecca asked curiously.

"What?" Logan faltered, distractedly.

"What's your favorite color?" she asked.

"Oh, uh I'm not sure," Logan quickly replied. "I guess I seem to gravitate toward purple."

"That's what I thought," Rebecca grinned, knowingly.

"You did?" Logan frowned, trying to think of how many things he had that were purple she would have seen.

Pointing to Scout's leash, she advised, "Purple."

Looking down at the leash in his hand, Logan raised his eyebrows in mild surprise, not remembering why he picked the color originally. "Will you look at that? I guess I didn't notice the color that much. He picked it out himself when we went to the store."

"Has your life lacked color and you don't know when to appreciate it, Logan?" Rebecca teased.

"Oh, quite the opposite, I have a few very colorful people in my life who quite literally live and breathe color," Logan admitted, as a fleeting vision of Piper entered his mind.

"Your little sister again?" Rebecca continued to tease.

Laughing nervously and wanting to change the subject, Logan replied, "Yeah, something like that. So, let's get going!"

"Sure, let's go," Rebecca motioned for him to lead, curious about his hasty reply. *"Hmm, if not his little sister, an ex-girlfriend maybe?"* she asked herself. *"It sounds a little mysterious to me."*

A few feet up the path, Logan was reprimanding himself loudly in his head. *"Something like that? What kind of a lame answer was that, you idiot! Yes! A simple yes would have been perfectly fine, and she wouldn't be looking at you the way she is now. You seriously are an idiot!"*

~~~~~~~~~~

Two hours later, both Logan and Rebecca were laboring to maintain their breathing as their hearts raced and the muscles in their legs began screaming out to them for a break. Even Scout, who started out scampering ahead on the path, investigating every smell and sound they encountered along the way, was now panting heavily and lagging behind on his leash.

"Okay, I say we take a lunch break," Logan conceded, looking for a shady spot under the trees. "What about that area under those trees?"

"Looks perfect!" Rebecca replied, thankful for the suggestion. "I don't think I could have held out much longer. I'm out of shape!"

"Are you kidding me? You're in great shape, look at you!" Logan exclaimed in surprise.

"You're sweet, thank you, but my cardio could be better," Rebecca replied, slightly embarrassed.

"How long has it been since you went hiking like this?" Logan asked, sliding the pack off his shoulder and resting on the ground in front of him.

Gazing off into the distance, Rebecca shrugged and admitted, "Six months maybe?"

"Well, there you go! I think you're doing great! This elevation is a lot steeper than I thought it would have been. I even have some muscle fatigue," Logan reasoned as he tugged on a section of a red and white checkered blanket he had stowed in one of the pack's many pockets.

"Here, let me help you with that," Rebecca offered, grabbing onto the pack so Logan could get a better grip. "What in the world did you manage to cram into that pack?"

Pulling the blanket free, Logan shook the folds open and gently laid it down on the ground under the trees. "You can't have a picnic without a picnic blanket!" he declared, triumphantly.

"Did you pack the basket too?" she smirked, narrowing her eyes at him suspiciously.

"Ha! Funny, and no, I did not smart aleck. I did, however, pack a fabulous lunch," Logan professed proudly. Reaching out his hand toward her, he offered, "Won't you have a seat, my lady?"

Rolling her eyes at him dramatically, Rebecca sighed, took his hand and insisted, "I am not calling you my liege."

"I believe you just did," he teased as they sat down on the blanket beside one another.

"Your confidence in yourself is overwhelming," she chided, humorously, watching him unzip another pocket from his pack.

"Life is all about perspective and appreciating what you have. I guess that makes me a glass-half-full kind of guy. Which reminds me," he added, producing two dog bowls from the pack. Setting the bowls down on the ground just beyond the edge of the blanket he opened a bottle of water and poured the cool liquid into one of them. "Hey Scout, would you like some water, buddy?"

Recognizing the bowls, Scout's interest in the nearby bushes was instantly redirected to what Logan was offering.

"Here you go, big guy," Logan encouraged, patting Scout gently on the top of his head as the dog thirstily attacked the water. Showing his appreciation, Scout paused long enough to give Logan a wet slobbery kiss on the mouth before returning to his bowl.

"Yech! A simple thank you would have sufficed, Scout," Logan complained, wiping his mouth with the sleeve of his t-shirt.

"I believe that's what he did," Rebecca giggled, enjoying Logan's expression of disgust.

"Yeah, well you'll get a smelly belch in the face followed by the slobbery kiss after he's done eating so prepare yourself and consider yourself warned," Logan advised.

"Good to know," Rebecca chuckled, keeping track of Scout's location out of the corner of her eye.

"Before we begin," Logan announced, handing her a small, square pouch that looked like a packet of sugar.

Taking a closer look, she found herself mildly impressed when she realized it was a pre-moistened towelette. *"Huh, this is a surprise."*

Noticing her expression, Logan shrugged and said, "I figured it would be more sanitary to eat our sandwiches with clean hands."

"No, this is great! I have to admit, I'm a bit surprised, that's all," Rebecca conceded, tearing open the pouch to retrieve the wipe.

"Why? I'm not some barbarian who eats food off the floor or out of garbage cans!" Logan challenged, good-naturedly. "That would be my spotted partner in crime over there behind you."

"It's just something unexpected, let's put it that way. Most guys don't think about clean hands on a hike," she replied.

"That goes back to our conversation earlier. I have had very strong female influences in my life who have taught me well," he admitted. "And I'm not ashamed to admit it."

"Very well," she agreed.

"Speaking of which, the inspiration for today's lunch came from one of my very best friends, who married my best friend out of college," Logan advised as he pulled several containers from his pack. "She said this is one of her new favorites and suggested I make it for our outing today."

"Really? That's cool that you're close with her too. What is this friend's name?" Rebecca asked, curious if this was the same woman he had eluded to earlier.

"Tori," Logan blurted out accidentally, forgetting to use a different name.

"*Dang it, you idiot! That's twice now! Stick to the plan, Logan. As long as you stick to the plan and don't tell her anything else, we can still make this work,*" he thought, trying to reason logic into his error.

"I've always liked that name. Is she a shortened version of Victoria I assume?" Rebecca asked curiously.

"*Don't do it….,*" he warned himself quietly. "Uh, yeah, I think so. Well, here we go! Roasted turkey sandwiches on multi-grain bread with sliced tomato, sprouts, and a cranberry-orange relish."

"Oh, that sounds really good," Rebecca replied, taking the sandwich from him.

"And on the side, I have a red quinoa salad with crispy bacon, fresh herbs tossed in smoky balsamic vinaigrette dressing," he offered in a smaller container.

"Are you kidding me? I love quinoa! I hardly ever meet anyone else who's heard of it much less cooks with it!" Rebecca exclaimed, happily. "How strange is that?"

"Really? That's quite the coincidence. I like it because it's really good and very healthy!" Logan agreed, preparing to take a bite of his sandwich.

"Same! Uh, I think you forgot someone," Rebecca grinned, looking just past Logan's shoulder behind him.

Sitting patiently on the edge of the blanket beside Logan, Scout eyed the sandwich in Logan's hands and licked his lips hungrily.

"I'm sorry buddy! I didn't mean to forget about you," Logan quickly apologized, putting his sandwich down. Opening a different container, Logan transferred the contents into Scout's food bowl and set it down beside the water bowl. "Here you go, Scout. Roasted turkey, sliced carrots and unseasoned quinoa for you."

Hungrily devouring the food, Scout's tail wagged as he ate.

"Does he always wag his tail when he eats?" Rebecca laughed, having never seen a dog do that before.

"Yep!" Logan grinned. "He's done that ever since the day I brought him home. He knows how to enjoy a good meal!"

"Well a protein filled lunch like that is perfect for him!" Rebecca approved.

"Yeah, I try not to give him too much human food and stick with the food my sister recommended. I figured all that protein would give him enough energy to be able to make the hike back down later," Logan admitted.

"Good thinking! And great sandwich I might add! Why do I only think about preparing a turkey for Thanksgiving? And paired with the cranberry-orange relish is amazing! Do you cook like this often?" Rebecca asked.

"Thanks! And yes, I enjoy cooking. It's not always fun cooking for just one person, but I try to experiment with new ingredients and recipes when something sounds interesting," Logan admitted.

"Well, you hit the nail on the head with the sandwich and this quinoa. The dressing is the star. I may have to get the recipe from you," she hinted coyly.

"Consider it done! Hopefully, you'll save some room for dessert," he tempted.

"Don't tell me what it is. I want to be surprised!" Rebecca insisted, taking another bite of the sandwich.

"Deal," he winked mischievously, finishing off the rest of his salad.

Convinced his bowl was now licked clean of any remaining traces of food, Scout sniffed the surrounding blanket area for any crumbs that may have fallen out. Finding none, as Logan had predicted, Scout belched loudly, yawned sleepily, and after spinning around in a circle three times, he lay down next to Logan for a nap.

"That's a good boy," Logan praised, gently petting Scout down his back while Scout drifted off to sleep.

Eyeing him curiously, Rebecca realized she liked being with Logan. He and Scout felt comfortable and unassuming. *"But you know very little about him,"* she warned herself. *"He's very handsome and has a great personality. But what if he turns out like…"* she thought, stopping herself from finishing the question.

Feeling her stare, Logan looked over guiltily and wiped his hand over his mouth. "What? Do I have food on my face?"

Laughing at him, Rebecca shook her head and said, "No. Sorry, I was thinking. I didn't realize I was staring."

"Thinking about what?" Logan urged, intrigued.

"I just thought this is nice. Then I realized I don't know that much about you," Rebecca admitted.

Turning his full attention to her, Logan sat back and rested his weight on his hands and asked, "What do you want to know?"

Debating on the best approach to ask her question, Rebecca took a deep breath and confessed, "I have a big problem with people who hide who they are from others."

Swallowing hard, wondering where this was going, Logan nodded and quietly said, "Okay."

"I've taken some pretty hard hits in the past from people I cared about who I trusted, so before we decide to become friends, I need you to know I have to be able to trust you," Rebecca replied firmly.

Cringing slightly inside, Logan knew he was walking a very, very thin line, and he needed to be extremely careful with not only what he said, but how he said it. They were both living under assumed identities so everything beyond this point would be a lie.

"Agreed," he replied.

"Earlier this morning when we were talking about the color of Scout's leash, you seemed uncomfortable talking about something from your past, someone from your past. Or I guess maybe still in the present?" she faltered.

"What are you asking me, Rebecca?" he challenged, sitting up so he could face her.

Looking around their picnic site, she sighed and admitted, "All of this today, has been wonderful. You put so much thought and effort into making this special, and I know that's not the typical behavior for a guy who just wants to be friends. I know I said from the very beginning that's all I wanted between us, and you've been great about not pushing the issue, but the bottom line is I like you, Logan.

"You're fun to be with, and I feel happy and comfortable when I'm with you, and that scares the heck out of me because I swore I never wanted to feel this way about anyone ever again. So before this goes any further, I need to know how you feel about all of this."

Looking back at this moment in time later, Logan knew he would be hitting himself on the head calling himself an idiot for the millionth time. But right now, this second, none of that mattered. Staring into her gorgeous hazel eyes, now filled with so many questions, all he could think about was how much he wanted to kiss her. So without saying a word, he leaned forward and pressed his lips tenderly to hers.

Thankfully she didn't pull away, or slap Logan across the face, which is what she should have done. Instead, much to his surprise, and his relief, she kissed him back.

Chapter 26

"Idiot!" his common sense screamed in his head, finally breaking through to his conscious thoughts. Sitting back, Logan searched her eyes carefully and whispered, "I'm sorry. I shouldn't have done that."

"Why are you apologizing?" Rebecca frowned, now totally confused.

Taking her hand, Logan felt his heart and his head battling it out, knowing he had just crossed a line he could never return. "I like you too, Rebecca, very much. I've been making a concerted effort to respect your decision to remain friends, and I agree that we should get to know each other before we take this any further. I just really wanted to kiss you, and if that was presumptuous of me, I'm sorry."

"I'm not sorry you kissed me," she whispered. "But you're totally right. We shouldn't have done that. Maybe we can do it again sometime in the not so distant future?"

"We'll see," he grinned, teasing her.

"Ouch!" she growled, punching him on the shoulder. "That was mean."

"I'm just teasing!" Logan laughed, holding up his hands to ward off her fists. Reaching beside him for one of the containers they hadn't opened yet, he quickly removed the lid and held it out to her. "Here, have a cookie."

"What? Do you think you can distract me with….wait, do I smell peanut butter?" she demanded, looking into the container. "Are those?"

"You said they were your favorite," Logan noted, hoping he remembered correctly.

"I did," she admitted, taking a cookie from the container. "Oh look, you even sprinkled sugar on top of them and pressed the forks in a cross like my mom used to."

"That's the only way to make them," he vowed, gazing upon the cookies lovingly.

"Your sister again?" she mumbled, taking a bite of the cookie. "Oh, this cookie is so much better than mine! They're perfect!"

"Thanks! Honestly, the credit goes beyond my sister and my mom; it belongs to my grandma. It's her recipe," Logan admitted, taking a bite of a cookie. "Every time I eat one of these, I swear if I close my eyes, I'm back in my grandma's kitchen waiting for her to pull the pan of fresh baked cookies from the oven. I used to sit at her kitchen table with a glass of milk, waiting for the sound of the bell on her oven to ring. Then she and I would sit at the table together and talk while we ate the cookies."

"Aw, that's a great memory to have," Rebecca replied, wistfully. "Is she?"

Nodding sadly, Logan replied, "Five years ago this past March."

"I'm so sorry for your loss, Logan," she empathized.

"Thanks," he smiled sadly. "My grandma lived a full life, died at home with her family by her side, and we buried her in the plot next to my grandpa. It was what she wanted. She missed him so much after he passed away. I've always hoped I would have a relationship with someone like that one day."

"But something happened, didn't it?" she asked quietly, watching his eyes.

Surprised, Logan frowned and asked, "How did you know that?"

Shrugging her shoulders, she admitted, "I see myself in you sometimes. The way you respond to questions and the guarded way you keep information about yourself close to your chest. You've been hurt by someone before and don't let people inside your inner circle easily."

"And here I thought I was mastering the male mystique of sullen and broody," Logan chided, gently. "I thought women dug that kind of thing."

Snorting derisively, she replied, "Well I don't know who those women are, but I can assure you I'm not one of them."

"Noted," he inclined his head in admission.

"So who's going to spill first?" she challenged.

"Spill what?" he frowned.

"The gory details of our horror story past relationships," she replied, wide-eyed.

"Ah, yeah that. Um, okay, I guess I'll go first. Unless you want to, you know, ladies first?" he invited.

Taking another cookie from the container, Rebecca shook her head and grinned. "I'm not a big feminist either so please, feel free."

Thanking Tori silently many times over for the make believe love story of Logan and Jade she created for this moment, Logan paused to formulate the character in his head.

"Remember, you need to make it convincing, Logan! Rebecca needs to be totally convinced, or she'll never open up to you and tell you her story," Tori had insisted.

"Ahem, okay," he began, clearing his throat nervously. "The woman's name was Jade. We dated three years, and lived together for two of those years." Glancing over at Rebecca, she was listening intently. When she didn't comment, he continued. "We lived in California at the time. I was working for Microsoft, and she was a firefighter for the Sacramento Fire Department."

"When was that?" Rebecca asked.

"Two thousand eight," Logan quickly replied. "That was one of the worst recorded years of forest fires in California. Over a million acres of land burned. By the peak of summer, there were more than thirty-five hundred distinct fires burning across the state."

"That's horrible," Rebecca murmured.

"It was," Logan replied, quietly. "Thirteen firefighters lost their lives that year; Jade was almost one of them."

"Oh my goodness, what happened?" Rebecca exclaimed.

"She and her team got caught in an area where several fires were burning around them. Jade lost sight of the barrier line, and she couldn't find the rest of her team. The communication device built into her helmet malfunctioned, and she couldn't call for help. As she was trying to leave, she stepped into a hole and twisted her ankle. She couldn't walk, and she knew her gear was too heavy and bulky for her to drag herself. She couldn't risk waiting around for someone to find her, so she removed most of her gear and crawled to safety."

Swallowing hard, Rebecca whispered, "How badly was she burned?"

"How did you know?" Logan asked in surprise.

"I could just tell by the way you're telling the story. Go on," she encouraged, taking his hand.

Feeling incredibly guilty for the lie he was telling her and her sincere reaction of concern for Jade, Logan added, "By the time she crawled to an area where other firefighters found her, she had burns over sixty percent of her body. She had kept her mask on which helped prevent damage to her head and her lungs from the smoke inhalation, but she lost several of her fingers because they were so badly damaged."

"Oh, that poor girl," Rebecca breathed. "How long was her recovery?"

"About eleven months," Logan replied quietly. "Her mom and I took turns taking care of her. We took Jade to all of her doctor appointments, her counseling sessions and support group meetings, praying she would be able to find peace with what happened to her. But she was never the same afterward. Her doctors diagnosed her with PTSD; do you know what that is?"

Frowning slightly, Rebecca nodded and admitted, "Yeah, unfortunately, I'm very familiar with the term."

'Well, part of Jade's treatment included a bunch of different medications. They were supposed to help her deal with her trauma, but I often wondered if they were helping her or not. When I looked at her, her eyes were vacant, like there was no one there. She wouldn't let me touch her, not even just a simple hug. I still thought she was beautiful, but she said when she looked at herself in the mirror, all she saw was a grotesque monster," Logan sighed.

"Who cut the cord?" Rebecca asked, watching him carefully.

"She did," Logan murmured, letting his eyes trail off in the distance as if in remembering. "She decided one day that I was no longer who she wanted by her side, and she didn't love me anymore. So honoring her wishes, I packed my things, and I moved out hoping maybe it was only temporary and she'd change her mind. Three days later I got a call from her mother telling me Jade was dead."

"What? What happened?" Rebecca gasped in surprise.

"It was an overdose. Jade swallowed every single pill from every container in the apartment," Logan mourned, surprised to feel tears on his cheeks. "Afterward, I kept thinking, what if I had refused to go? Would I have been able to stop her? Would she still be alive if I didn't walk out on her?"

Reaching out to pull Logan's body against hers in a tight embrace, Rebecca exclaimed, "Oh, Logan, I'm so sorry. You were doing what she asked you to do which was respecting her wishes. None of what happened was your fault!" Pulling back to look at him, she demanded, "You know that now, right? If she were truly determined to end her life, she would have found a way to do it whether you were there or not."

Wiping his eyes, Logan nodded and said, "Yeah, I know that now. It was a long time ago, so I've had some time to work through those feelings. I even went to see a counselor for a while. My therapist helped me realize none of what happened was in my control. So, deciding my life was in my control, I moved back to the east coast and lived with my friend and his wife for a while until I decided what I wanted to do. Then I started my software development company, hired myself out as a private contractor, and put all of my energy into my work."

"You haven't had a serious relationship since then?" Rebecca asked surprised at how much Logan's life sounded like hers.

Shaking his head, Logan replied, "Not anyone of importance like Jade no. Love is too complicated. Plus it's too risky giving your heart to someone who doesn't appreciate it. It's just easier alone."

Sitting back on her spot on the blanket, Rebecca stared at Logan silently, realizing how painful it must have been for him to tell her his story.

Hoping the ruse worked, Logan looked at Rebecca and asked, "So that's my past in a nutshell. Is it too messy and tragic for you?"

"Not at all," Rebecca murmured. "Surprisingly, it sounds all too familiar."

"Tell me about it," Logan urged quietly.

Exhaling a deep, anxiety filled breath; Rebecca nodded and took a drink from her bottle of water buying a few more seconds before she began. "His name is Alexander but he prefers to be called Zander," she began hesitantly, having not said her husband's name out loud for several years. *"That's strange, the sound of his name seems so foreign to hear coming from my lips now,"* she thought to herself.

Realizing his fists and his jaw were clenched tight just from the mere mention of her husband's name, Logan relaxed them before she noticed.

"We were high school sweethearts," she continued, with a small smile. "We got married shortly after graduation, and then I began my eight years of undergraduate and veterinary school. Zander followed in his father's footsteps by joining the Marine Corp. And in the beginning, it was good," she joked, attempting to add a bit of Biblical humor to her story before the rest came out. "I was excelling in my studies and Zander came home from his first tour in Afghanistan with a decoration of honor for saving his unit during an attack. Those were happy times," she lamented, thinking back. Then her eyes darkened, and her voice hardened, thinking about what happened next. "His second tour didn't go nearly as smoothly," she paused, remembering.

"What do you mean?" Logan asked, curious how much she would tell him.

"His second tour is when everything went wrong," she replied quietly. "His unit was stationed at a checkpoint in southern Afghan City. A suicide bomber drove up to the checkpoint, fully armed with explosive devices, and detonated his body right as he got to the gate. Zander was the only one from his unit who survived," she whispered, blinking back tears she feared would come when she got to this point.

Understanding how hard this must be for her to tell him, Logan took Rebecca's hand and waited until she was ready to continue.

"Very much like Jade, Zander was different after his accident. We went through the all of the doctor appointments, counseling sessions and support group meetings too. The number of prescription bottles lining the shelf of our bathroom cabinet worried me. I couldn't imagine all of those drugs being in a person's body at the same time without causing some after-effect. He was moody all the time, he hardly slept, and he couldn't hold down a job because he couldn't control his temper. Inevitably, someone would do something to make him angry, and he'd get into a fight, always over the smallest and seemingly insignificant things.

"The worst times were when we'd be talking, and he would be looking right at me, but I didn't think he ever really saw me. It was like he was a totally different person. He would say things during those times and then argue with me later, claiming he never said them. Heck, I even started doubting myself when he got that way. It was awful."

"What was the catalyst that split the two of you up?" Zander prodded gently.

Reflecting back on the nightmare that made her run, Rebecca hesitated having never told this story to anyone before today. She searched Logan's eyes for any sign of disbelief, but only saw patience and understanding. "That would be related to his support group," Rebecca admitted quietly.

"Here it comes," Logan thought, mentally preparing himself for the proper response. "What about it?"

"As I said, Zander was different afterward. On the nights he couldn't sleep, he started leaving the house. He didn't realize I knew he was leaving. At first, he would just go out in the backyard and sit in a chair, staring up at the sky. Then he would go out in the garage and putter around in there for a few hours. Then he began taking the truck out and drove to who knows where.

"Some nights he would only be gone a few hours, then it became early in the morning, then it became days later. I was frantic when it first started. I even called the police a few times when I was scared something happened to him. Then he would be angry at me when he got home to find police cars parked in the driveway. So after a while, I stopped calling the police and just waited for him to come home," Rebecca admitted.

"Sounds like a very lonely life," Logan noted.

"It was. I still had my dog at the time, so I had some company. But I missed my husband," Rebecca confessed.

"That was Domino, right?" Logan tested her.

"Y-yes, that was Domino," she lied. "He and I used to go for long walks together. There was a big park near our house that had a beautiful walking trail, so we went there a lot. One day I recognized one of the men from Zander's support group walking his dog there too. We waved and said hi to one another. After months of quick greetings and short conversations in passing, we started meeting at this one bench along the trail that overlooked the lake, and we would talk about whatever was going on in our lives at the time. We became friends. He was a very nice man and someone who understood Zander. The poor man was the sole survivor of an automobile accident that killed his wife and his son, so he knew some of what Zander was feeling. He caused the accident that killed his family and had to live the rest of his life knowing it. I can't imagine having to do that."

Realizing she was talking about Grant Albertson, who he and Agent Hunter's team believed to be her husband's first victim, Logan nodded and admitted, "Nor can I."

"So after Zander began disappearing, I mentioned it to Grant, the man from the support group, and told him I was afraid Zander was going to hurt himself. So he offered to talk to him for me," Rebecca said.

"She was the one who put Grant in her husband's path. No wonder…..," Logan thought quietly.

Blinking back tears, Rebecca admitted, "Not long after that, one of the nights Zander left, I had a strange feeling I couldn't shake. I felt certain something was wrong. So I checked his gun cabinet, fearing he was going to try hurting himself and saw his rifle was missing. I didn't know what to do! If I called the police again and it turned out to be a false alarm, Zander would be furious with me."

"So what did you do?" Logan asked gently.

"I didn't do anything," she mourned as tears began streaming down her face. "Just before dawn, I heard his truck pulling into the driveway. I was so relieved he was home! I pretended to be asleep when he came into the house so he wouldn't be angry with me for waiting up for him, but he didn't come to bed. So I crept downstairs and saw him lying on the couch sleeping. The TV was on so he must have fallen asleep while he was watching," she reasoned, wiping the tears from her cheeks. "When I went to turn off the television, the news was on, reporting a murder that happened overnight, near the park not too far from our house. Then I saw the name of the victim displayed on the screen. It was my friend Grant! He'd been shot while he and Brady were out for a walk the night before. I just stood there frozen, staring at the face of my friend on the screen! I wanted to scream, but I couldn't move."

"Did you suspect him right away?" Logan asked, curious how much Rebecca would admit to him.

"Zander?" she asked.

"Yes," Logan pressed.

"Yes," she whispered, brushing away more tears. "I checked the gun cabinet, and Zander's rifle was back in its slot. It smelled like gunpowder. I was terrified! I didn't know what to do; I had called the police so many times at this point; I was afraid they wouldn't take me seriously. I definitely couldn't confront Zander and ask him. I was so afraid of that look in his eyes when he was angry. What if he killed me too? I was the one who told Grant about Zander. It was my fault that he was dead!"

"No, it wasn't Rebecca!" Logan exclaimed, taking both of her hands in his. "Your friend made the decision to talk to your husband. He could have chosen not to. And just because he did that, it doesn't mean he deserved what happened to him. Neither you nor your friend was to blame for what happened. It was all Zander!"

"It didn't matter!" she cried out in frustration. "I couldn't stay with Zander after that. I could barely look at him. All I wanted to do was to run as far away from him as I could. So that's what I did. The next night, when he took off in his truck, I packed my clothes into our suitcases and put them back in the closet where they usually were so everything looked normal. The next day I stopped at the bank and withdrew all of our savings into cash. Then later that night when he left again, I packed up my car and Domino, and I drove away. And I've never looked back."

"How long ago did you leave him?" Logan asked.

"A little over six years ago," she admitted candidly.

Surprised by how much Rebecca had just revealed to him, Logan sat across from her, holding her hands, quietly watching her.

He didn't want to ask too many questions, preventing her from telling him anything else. *"You have her trust up to this point, Logan, but she still hasn't confessed to you that her real name is Veronica Wells,"* he reminded himself. *"You still need her to do that before you can be sure she's not even the slightest bit still connected to her husband."*

"What are you thinking?" Rebecca murmured, watching him. "Am I a coward for running away?"

Logan shook his head slowly and said, "No, I don't think you're a coward. Unless someone experiences the very same situation as you, that person could never truly know how they would react. Fear is a very strong motivator. You did what you felt you needed to do to stay safe. I think that's very brave."

"Has what I've told you changed how you feel about me?" she worried, thankful he was still holding her hands, and he hadn't pulled away.

"Maybe a little, but not enough to make me walk away," he admitted.

"Which part?" she asked.

"The part that you're still married," he confessed. "I like you a lot, Rebecca, and I want to continue seeing you. But at some point, if we stay together, you're going to have to address that part of your past, or I can't be part of your future."

"I know," she whispered, having thought of that reality herself many times. "I'm so scared of him, though, Logan. What if he did kill my friend? What if he killed other people? I'm so scared of what he would do if he found me."

Deciding it was time to end the Q&A session, for now, Logan pulled Rebecca into his arms and kissed her tenderly on the top of her head. "Don't worry. If he does, I'll protect you."

"My husband is a trained sniper, Logan. How could you protect me from someone like that?" she exclaimed.

"Just trust me when I say I can. I'm not going to let anything happen to you," Logan vowed.

Chapter 27

It was well after dark when Zander pulled into the parking spot in front of his motel room. Fortunately, the VA clinic in Parkersburg was only a half-hour away and had late hours on Wednesday's, so he had been able to make it out there to pick up the refill on his prescription before they closed. He had cut it too close this time with no pills remaining in the previous refill. Right now this drug was the only thing keeping the voice in his head quiet. Or at least that's what he told himself. The alternative was too scary to consider.

As he got out of the car, he caught the smell of smoke in the air. *"Someone must be having a campfire nearby,"* he thought. Then he heard the distant wail of a police siren and the horn of a fire truck heading toward him down the highway, and he knew it wasn't just a campfire. *"Well that can't be good,"* he thought, watching the vehicles as they raced down the road.

He debated whether he should just ignore it or get back in his car and see where the fire was. He had some volunteer fire management training, but that contradicted his intent to keep a low profile and not bring any unnecessary attention to himself. *"Stay out of it, Zander. Let the pros do their job,"* he told himself, preparing to go inside the room. Then he felt the vibration of his work pager against his hip. *"This can't be good either,"* he sighed, grabbing his phone and dialing his boss's number.

"Butler, is that you?" his boss's voice frantically screamed through the phone when the call connected.

"Yeah, it's me. What's up, Boss?" Zander asked, already unlocking the car door and getting back behind the wheel.

"We've got a fire just south of Copper Ridge. Some idiot apparently doesn't know how to damper a campfire. We need all hands on deck. Where are you?" Zeke demanded.

"Just pulled out of the motel parking lot and am headed your way. Do I need to pick up anything from home base on my way out or go directly to the fire?" Zander asked, speeding toward town.

"Go to the maintenance building and pick up a couple of chainsaws. And bring the big truck with the tow line. We may need it to move some of the heavier logs out of the way," Zeke instructed.

"Got it, on my way," Zander agreed, preparing to hang up.

"Do you know where Andrews is?" Zeke exclaimed angrily. I've been paging him but he hasn't dialed in yet."

Feeling the hair on the back of his neck rise uneasily, Zander admitted, "No sir, I haven't heard from him."

"Well if you do, you tell him to get his ass over to the site. I'll meet you there," Zeke demanded.

"Roger that," Zander replied, ending the call. "Well, that's most definitely not good," he murmured, thinking back to the conversation he had with Pierce a few weeks ago about how his parents died.

"What if?" he started thinking, then quickly admonished himself. "Don't start accusing someone of something like that until you have proof! He may be a creepy little dude at times, but so far, Pierce Andrews hasn't given you any reason to believe he's a fire bug. Just do your job and let the guys with the badges figure that part out."

~~~~~~~~~~~

By the time Zander made it to the fire's point of origin with the saws and the truck, the fire had spread to the surrounding area and several trees were burning. Glowing pieces of burning leaves were being picked up by the breeze as they fell from their charred branches, igniting the long, dry grass below. "Yeah, this most definitely isn't good," he growled.

Parking the truck out of the way, Zander got out of the vehicle and immediately began coughing as a thick, black cloud of hot smoke closed in around him, stinging his eyes and making it difficult to see where he was going. He could just barely pick up the voices of men and women shouting instructions at one another, yet he couldn't determine their origin through the roar of the fire.

As he stood there, watching and listening, a flashback of the aftermath in Afghanistan flooded into his mind. He stood frozen in place as his eyes tricked him into believing the smoldering embers of the charred tree trunks at his feet were the dismembered bodies of his former Marines. Next, the wave of guilt washed over him, having not been able to save them. Suddenly the smell of the smoke turned rancid, and the stench of burning human flesh filled his nostrils. Feeling the bile from his stomach starting to rise in his throat, he looked around frantically for a place to run.

"Butler!" His boss's voice barked at him from a few feet away. "Don't just stand there looking like a deer in the headlights, grab a chainsaw and get to work moving those trees out of the way!"

Feeling thrust forward into reality, the smell of smoke returned, and the bodies turned back into trees. Zander blinked and stared at his boss, dumbly, still unable to move.

"Do you need an invitation, Butler?" Zeke barked at him again.

"N-no, sir," Zander replied, suddenly springing into action. "I've got it."

"Good. Grab the other chainsaw for Andrews. He finally decided to grace us with his presence and help out. He's right over there to the right of that crooked oak," Zeke growled, pointing in the direction Zander needed to go.

"Got it, sir," Zander nodded, quickly putting on a ventilator hood and then running in the direction of the tree.

"Don't run with chainsaws in your hands for Pete's sake! The last thing we need is you slicing off part of your foot!" Zeke shouted angrily. "Sweet Lord, it's like having a bunch of kindergartener's working for me," he mumbled under his breath.

Feeling the sting of his boss's reprimand, Zander stopped running and briskly walked the rest of the way.

Recognizing Pierce's tall, lanky frame outlined in the smoke ahead of him, Zander noticed Pierce was staring at the fire, mesmerized with a fascinated, almost gleeful look on his face. Again, Zander felt the hair rise on the back of his neck. *"Okay, that's seriously not normal,"* he thought.

Thrusting one of the chainsaws into Pierce's hands, Zander shouted, "Here, the boss wants us to start clearing the unburned trees on the ground out of the path of the fire, so we remove its source of food. Put on your mask and let's get going!"

"After you!" Pierce shouted, reluctantly following Zander.

For the next several hours, Zander and Pierce cut the fallen trunks into manageable sections, while the second team of men and women followed behind them, and rolled the logs into unburned areas of the woods. A third team followed behind the second group, shoveling trenches in the dirt creating a barrier to contain the fire within the fire's ground radius.

By midnight, only smoldering embers remained. Exhausted beyond imagination, Zander set his saw down on the ground by his feet and stood up straight to stretch out the kinks in his aching back and shoulders. Looking at all the weary, soot-covered clothes and faces of the fire crew and volunteers around him, he decided they all looked like extras in a horror movie, waiting for the director to yell 'action.'

"Great job everyone!" the fire captain called out in a raspy, smoke drenched voice. "Thank you all for your hard work here tonight. We couldn't have done it without you. For the volunteers and non-fire crew, feel free to go home, we can take it from here. For the crew and any other folks who are staying, please meet over here by me for your next set of instructions."

Zander watched in disappointment as most of the people in the area began to leave, including Pierce and Roger, the manager of the general store in town. *"Way to represent, guys,"* he thought sadly. Knowing that more available able hands meant the rest of the crew could finish the job more quickly, Zander walked over to the group forming around the captain.

"You stickin' around a little longer, Alex?" Sheriff Ford greeted him as he approached.

Slightly surprised the sheriff knew him by name, Zander nodded and replied, "Yes, sir. I figured the more people able to help the quicker everyone could go home."

Inclining his head in acknowledgment, the sheriff said, "I couldn't agree with you more. I was watching you earlier. It looked like you knew what you were doing. Have you had experience with fighting fires in the past?"

"Yes, sir," Zander nodded. "Part of my Marine training involved fire management for incendiary devices and such. You never know what you're walking into so any kind of preparation for the worst possible scenario can save a life."

"Ah, that makes sense," the sheriff replied.

"All right, everyone, listen up," the fire captain croaked as his voice grew weaker. "For the time being, we're standing by until the arson investigator clears the area. If any of the hot spots flare back up again, we'll put them out, but that's all we're doing until then. Are there any questions?"

"An arson investigator," Zander thought. *"Do they already suspect this wasn't an accident? Zeke said something about a camper earlier."*

"All right, no questions mean everyone understands what I've said. I want you all to split off into teams of five, and then move to one of the locations marked on this map in my hand. One person from each team will wear one of these armbands," the chief instructed, holding up bright neon yellow bands. "That person is going to be designated as that team's leader. Any questions, observations or problems, you go to your team leader. Got it?"

"Yes sir," everyone shouted.

"All right, move out and form your teams. Then pick a leader and come get an armband!" the captain ordered.

"Looks like you're with us, Butler," Zeke advised, walking up beside Zander along with the sheriff's two deputies.

Glancing over at the sheriff, Zander noticed he was watching him carefully. "That works for me!" Zander grinned, hoping his voice didn't sound as nervous as it sounded in his head.

"You want to be the leader?" the sheriff invited.

Quickly shaking his head, Zander raised his hands in surrender and replied, "No, sir. I think you would be the best person for that job. I'm better at following orders, than giving them."

"Zeke?" Sheriff Ford offered.

"I agree with Butler," Zeke agreed. "You should do it, Sheriff."

"All right, just remember, I offered," the sheriff shrugged, walking over to the fire captain for an armband.

"Does anyone know how this fire started?" Zander casually asked while they waited for the sheriff. "This doesn't look like a good place for camping."

"No it doesn't," Zeke replied. "In fact, we didn't have any campers signed in this week. It's been too hot for most folks to sleep when it's this humid at night."

"Is that why the arson investigator is here?" one of the deputies asked.

"Most likely," Zeke answered gruffly.

"Okay, we've been assigned the area down the path about a hundred yards," the sheriff advised when he returned to the group. Pulling a crease free from his shirt under the neon armband, he said, "Let's start walking, men."

When they arrived at their designated spot, Zander noticed the fire chief and another man walking around the area off to the right of the path. *"That must be the arson investigator,"* he told himself. Immediately, Zander recognized where they were. "I know this spot," he blurted out before he caught himself.

Both Sheriff Ford and Zeke turned to look at him questioningly.

"You do?" the sheriff asked.

"Yes! Remember Zeke?" Zander quickly roped his boss in to confirm his statement.

"What are you talking about, Butler?" Zeke protested.

"That big dead tree with the hole in the center that fell during the storm a few weeks ago? You sent Pierce and me out here to clear it away. See? The sections we cut and rolled are right there on either side of the path," Zander exclaimed, pointing them out.

"That's interesting," the sheriff mused, glancing in the direction of the arson investigator.

"Why's that?" Zander asked, puzzled.

"That's where the arson investigator believes is the point of origin for the fire," the sheriff noted, watching Zander closely.

"Huh," Zander frowned. "You're right; that is interesting. I wonder what started it off."

"Or who," one of the deputies noted.

"Why would someone.....," Zander began to ask when the realization hit him. *"Careful how you react here, Zander. The sheriff is looking for someone to pin this on and right now he's looking directly at you."* Then another realization hit him. *"Andrews! Zeke said he couldn't find him earlier. Could he have done this?"*

"You were saying?" the sheriff encouraged quietly.

Looking directly at the sheriff, Zander shook his head in disbelief and said, "I don't understand why someone would intentionally start a fire like this! These woods are filled with wildlife and little kids play on the playground over there! There could have been lives lost here!"

"I agree," the sheriff replied, still watching Zander closely.

Their conversation was suddenly interrupted by a loud roll of thunder overhead, causing them all to look up at the sky.

"About time," one of the deputies remarked.

"Or ill-timed," the sheriff added, dryly. "I'm going to go talk to the chief. See how much longer they're going to be. You guys wait here."

Sheriff Ford barely made it across the path, when the clouds unleashed one final warning rumble and then proceeded to release a steady hard rain, quickly drenching anything beneath them. The teams scattered from their designated areas like roaches when the lights are turned on, trying to find refuge beneath the unburned trees.

"Well that will put out the rest of the hot spots," Zeke shouted over the rain, joining the others beneath the trees.

"Should we wait here? It may not be safe under these trees if lightning strikes," Zander shouted back.

Nodding in the direction of the sheriff, the chief and the arson investigator, who were all heading their way, Zeke replied, "Looks like they're going to call it."

Waiting until the three men joined them, the fire chief made the announcement. "We're not going to get anywhere with this rain. Sheriff, can you and your deputies stay here to secure the scene until we can get back out here in the morning?"

"Of course," Sheriff Ford replied. "We'll park the squad cars on either side of this area."

"Thank you," the fire chief replied. "Everyone else can leave. There's nothing more we can do tonight."

"You guys get dried off and changed into new uniforms," the sheriff instructed his men. "Then park the squads on either side of this area and stay put until you hear from me. I'll stay here until you get back."

"Yes, sir," both men nodded, running in the direction of the vehicles.

"I'll stay here with you until they get back," Zeke offered to his friend.

"Would you like me to stay as well, sir?" Zander asked.

"No, there's nothing more to do here for now. Go ahead and take the saws and the truck back to maintenance and go home and get some rest. I'll see you in the morning," Zeke replied.

"Very well, good night sir, Sheriff," Zander acknowledged both men before he walked away.

"Goodnight Alex," Sheriff Ford replied.

"So," Zeke murmured as they watched Zander load the chainsaws into the back of the truck, preparing to leave. "Between you and me, what's your gut telling you?"

"I don't think Butler's our guy," the sheriff admitted. "The way he helped out tonight and stuck around afterward doesn't scream arsonist to me. What about the other scrawny guy who high-tailed it out of here at the first opportunity?"

"Andrews?" Zeke asked gruffly. "I still don't know what I think about that guy. He took his sweet time responding to my page earlier. He said he had the pager on silent so he could take a nap."

"Hmmm... What about Butler? How quickly did he respond?" the sheriff asked.

"He dropped everything and came in as soon as I paged him," Zeke confirmed.

"Yeah, one of my deputies saw him driving into town from the direction of Parkersburg right before we got the call about the fire," the sheriff advised, pondering their situation in his head. "So we have two newcomers in town, possibly both without alibis, and a fire that mysteriously started out in an area of the woods both men are familiar with."

"Yep," Zeke shrugged.

"Well, then I guess I'll have to look into those alibis and find out what your boys have been up to," the sheriff suggested.

"Yep looks like it," Zeke agreed. "What do you want me to do in the meantime?"

"Nothing for now," the sheriff replied. "I'll let you know if I find anything."

Chapter 28

"Oh, this part of the state is so pretty!" Tori sighed happily as she stuck her hand out the passenger window so she could feel the waves of the air current as they drove. "Thank goodness for long holiday weekends and bosses who allow us to take them!"

"I agree," Ben grinned, enjoying the relaxed, carefree look on his wife's face. Glancing into the rearview mirror to check on the twins, Ben saw they were both still safely strapped in their car seats in the middle seat. "How's it going back there? Are you all good?"

"All good back here," RJ grinned, giving Ben the thumbs up.

"It's great, Daddy!" Gemma smiled. She glanced behind her to check on Goliath who was in the back third-row seat, and as usual he had his head sticking out the window enjoying the wind on his face. "I think Goliath would agree too!"

"Excellent!" Ben replied. "We're about an hour away so it won't be too much longer."

"This is so exciting. I've never been to an estate before. I can't believe Reagan hooked up with a guy who has a family estate!" Tori exclaimed.

"Agreed," Ben admitted. "And to think, it's all because she didn't know how to make fried chicken."

"I know!" Tori laughed, craning her head behind her to make sure Piper and Riley were still in the car behind them. "Good they're still back there. Riley's doing a good job keeping up with your lead foot. Well, that and he has Piper in the car with him. She hates driving slow."

"Hey! I'm still driving the speed limit," Ben argued, glancing down at the dashboard. "Well, I'm within ten miles of the speed limit," he added, grinning.

~~~~~~~~~~

"Look at you breaking the law," Piper teased, noticing how fast they were driving. "I do believe Ben is becoming a bad influence on you."

"Yeah, right," Riley grinned. "I hardly think a middle-aged man driving a mini-van could be a bad influence on me."

"I'm going to tell him you called him middle-aged!" Piper teased.

"You most certainly will not!" Riley laughed. "It's bad enough Reagan found some young, rich stud we're about to spend the day with, you could at least let me and Ben pretend that we're not a couple of old men."

"Ha!" Piper smiled, reaching over to rub his shoulder reassuringly. "I still love you, old man."

"Gee, thanks," he chuckled. "So has Reagan showed you any pictures of this guy? We know so little about him."

"No, she hasn't but she did describe him. You know the typical tall, dark and handsome, but no pictures. All I know is the name Brice Corbin, he works for the County West Fire Department, his parents are both deceased, and he inherited a huge estate out in the country of Virginia," Piper advised.

"You're sitting there telling me you and internet girl in the car ahead of us didn't dig up any dirt on the guy? Did you even visit the fire department's website and see if there are any pictures there?" Riley hinted.

"Oh my gosh, we didn't!" Piper admitted, pulling her phone from her pocket. "What's the matter with us? I can't believe either of us thought of that! I'm going to do that right now!"

"There you go!" Riley encouraged.

"All right," Piper murmured, opening a browser app on her phone. "County West Fire Department, and search," she said as she typed. "There we go. Click on about us, then meet the team and scroll down, and scroll down and there's his name, Brice Corbin. Click that link which brings me to.....whoa!"

"Is that a good whoa, or a bad whoa?" Riley asked, glancing over to look at her phone.

"Dang, nice catch, Reagan!" Piper praised, turning the phone for Riley to see.

"Hmm, okay. I'm a man who is very confident in his appearance, so I don't have a problem admitting, he's a nice-looking guy," Riley confided.

"I've got to send this to Tori," Piper insisted, sending the link to Tori's cell phone.

~~~~~~~~~~

"Hey, speaking of the she-devil, I just got a text from Piper," Tori announced, looking down at her phone.

"What's Piper up to now?" Ben asked, warily.

"I don't know. She sent me a link and said, 'click this link, I found a picture of Brice,'" Tori read from the screen.

"Who?" Ben asked.

"Brice. You know, Reagan's new boyfriend. The guy whose house we're on the way to see?" Tori reminded him.

"Oh, right, Brice. Why can't I seem to remember his name?" Ben shrugged.

"Beats me," Tori replied. "You're usually pretty good with names."

"I know, right? Maybe it will stick once I meet him," Ben suggested.

"I hope so," Tori agreed, pressing the link in Piper's text.

 "So what does he look like?" Ben asked.

"I'm waiting for the page to load from her link now," Tori replied. "Okay, here it comes. Holy cra...," she began to add when suddenly Ben interrupted her.

"Language," he cautioned, inclining his head toward the back seat.

"Whoops! Sorry," Tori winced apologetically.

"Mama thinks Brice is hot," Gemma giggled from her seat behind them.

"Eww," RJ groaned.

"See what you did!" Ben exclaimed shaking his head.

"I'm sorry, I can't always help it! You know me; sometimes my thoughts just pop into my head before I've had a chance to filter them!" Tori tried to reason.

"Mama still thinks you're hot too, Daddy," the little girl noted.

"Gemma stop," RJ complained loudly. "Can I change cars and ride with Aunt Piper and Uncle Riley?"

"Seriously, Tor!" Ben scolded, now embarrassed.

"I'm sorry!" Tori laughed, enjoying his flustered expression. "And no, RJ, you need to stay in the car with us. I promise I'll stop."

"Fine," RJ grumbled, unconvinced.

"Hey look at that covered bridge up ahead! Isn't it great?" Tori exclaimed, hoping to pique RJ's interest. "Do you guys know what a covered bridge is?"

"No," Gemma and RJ replied, looking out the windshield to see.

"They're made out of wood and have a roof on top to make the bridge last longer and give refuge when it's raining," Tori replied.

Tapping the brake gently so Riley would know to slow down, Ben advised. "It looks like the bridge only allows for a single car at a time."

As they approached the structure, Goliath got an uneasy feeling and began to whine. *"Something is wrong,"* Tori heard him call out to her.

Trusting Goliath's instincts, Tori braced her hands on the dashboard and yelled, "Ben, stop the car!"

Stepping down hard on the brake, Ben felt the van began to fishtail sideways. "Hang on everyone!" he said, trying to maintain control of the vehicle, praying that Riley and Piper didn't hit them.

"Kid's grab on tight to the armrests on your chairs! Goliath, get down to the floor, now!" Tori demanded, praying silently in her head.

Finally succumbing to Ben's command, the van screeched to a halt in the middle of the road, mere feet from the bridge's entrance. The second screech behind them indicated that Riley had been able to stop in time as well.

"Thank you, God, thank you, God," Tori breathed quietly, her eyes tightly closed.

"Is everybody all right?" Ben asked, turning around in his seat to check on Gemma and RJ.

"We're okay, Daddy," Gemma replied, her voice quivering with fear.

Reaching back to touch her hand, Ben smiled at Gemma and said, "It's okay, sweet-pea. We're all okay." Glancing further back to the back seat, he called out, "Goliath? Are you okay back there?"

Raising his head up above the seats, Goliath barked once in response. *"Goliath is okay!"*

"He said he's fine," Tori advised, quickly removing her seatbelt.

"Where are you going?" Ben demanded.

Pointing to the bridge, she replied, "To go look at the bridge! Goliath sensed something. I want to see what it was."

"Hey! What's going on? We nearly hit you!" Piper demanded as she and Riley ran up to the van.

"Goliath sensed something was wrong, so we stopped. I think it's the bridge," Tori replied, getting out of the van.

"You're not going out there alone!" Ben insisted, unbuckling his seatbelt and getting out of the van.

"Fine, then come with me!" Tori suggested. "Riley, Piper – will you stay with the kids for a minute?"

"Yeah, go ahead," Piper quickly replied, indicating they should go.

"We'll be right back," Tori advised, running toward the bridge.

"Thanks, guys!" Ben added, running after Tori.

"What do you think that's all about?" Piper asked.

"It was Luc," Gemma spoke up. "I mean Lucifer," she corrected herself quickly.

Alarmed, Piper looked at Gemma and asked, "Do you know that for sure, sweetie?"

"Uh huh," Gemma nodded. "I can feel him. He's still here."

Glancing at RJ, Piper asked, "Can you feel him too, RJ?"

RJ nodded quietly in response.

Quickly walking over to the back passenger door, Piper opened it up and said, "Goliath, you better to catch up to Tori, just in case. We'll stay here with the twins."

Understanding her concern, Goliath quickly jumped out of the van and ran to Tori.

~~~~~~~~~~

"So, what do you think?" Tori asked, gingerly stepping on the unbroken boards.

"I think this was intentional and recent," Ben frowned. "Look at the edges of these broken boards. The splintering is new and hasn't aged yet."

"Agreed," Tori sighed, looking down at the swift running river below. "This could have ended very badly had Goliath not sensed something. Thank you, Goliath," she praised, scratching him on the head.

"*Tori is my person to protect,*" Goliath vowed, pressing his body up against her affectionately.

"Yes, thank you, Goliath!" Ben agreed.

"Now what do we do?" Tori shrugged, glancing back at the cars. "We're obviously not able to keep going this direction now."

Pulling his cell phone from his pocket, Ben replied, "First of all I'm going to call this into the police, so they get someone out here to block the entrances to the bridge until it gets fixed. Then we'll check the GPS and see if there's an alternate route we can take."

"Good idea," Tori nodded.

"You probably should call Reagan and let her know what happened, so she doesn't' get worried when we're late. Maybe Brice can give some suggestions on an alternate route," Ben suggested.

"Hey, look at you! You remembered his name!" Tori exclaimed encouragingly.

"What? Oh, right! I guess I did. It must be because now I know what he looks like," Ben agreed.

"Yes, now we all know what Mr. Hottie looks like," she teased.

"Just make the call," Ben laughed.

Chapter 29

"Are you sure this is the right house?" Tori breathed, leaning forward to stare out the front windshield.

"This is the address on the GPS, so I'm going to say yes?" Ben replied, slowing the van to a stop in the middle of the driveway. "Geez Louise, will you look at this place! It's huge!"

"It's a castle," Gemma whispered, also awestruck by the beautiful home.

"You could fit ten of our house into that one!" RJ decided.

"Don't be silly, RJ," Ben argued. "You could maybe fit eight of our house in there; not ten."

"You're funny, Daddy," Gemma giggled.

"Oh, right on cue, there's Piper calling me," Tori replied reaching for her phone.

"She's in the car right behind us! Why doesn't she just come out and talk to you?" Ben asked.

"Shh!" Tori glared, engaging the call. "Hey! Are you seeing what I'm seeing?" Pausing for Piper's reply, she said, "That's what our GPS says too so I guess this is it. What?" She asked, looking up toward the front door. "Oh, I see her. Yep, this is the house. I'll meet you up there."   Ending the call, Tori pointed to the front door and said, "There's Reagan. It looks like we have the right place. Go ahead and pull the car up to the house. We'll ask her where we should park the cars, so we're not in the way."

"Not in the way of what?" Ben asked, snidely. "The horse-drawn chariot, which must be hidden out back somewhere?"

 Snorting a laugh, Tori nodded and agreed, "I know, right?"

"Does Reagan's boyfriend really have a horse-drawn chariot, Daddy?" Gemma asked with anticipation.

"You know, I'm not sure if he does or not, sweet-pea," Ben laughed. "Daddy was making a joke. But you can ask when we get inside, okay?"

"Ben! Don't tease her like that," Tori laughed, slapping him on the arm playfully. "We'll ask but don't be disappointed if he says no, okay honey?"

"Okay," Gemma agreed. "Maybe he has a pony!"

"You already have a dog the size of a pony, Peanut," Ben teased again.

"It's not the same, Daddy," Gemma argued.

"I know, I'm just teasing you, baby-girl," Ben smiled, parking the van. "Okay, everyone out. Let's go check out this castle!"

"I'll get Gemma and Goliath, you get RJ," Tori instructed, getting out of the van.

"Hi! You guys finally made it!" Reagan greeted as she approached them. "I can't believe the bridge was out. I just drove through there this morning!"

"Hi! Yeah, 'you know who' has been busy again," Tori greeted her friend with a quick hug. Looking directly behind Reagan, a tall well-muscled, handsome man with dark brown hair and gray eyes stood patiently waiting for introductions. "You must be, Brice," Tori smiled, extending her hand. "It's so nice to meet you!"

Brice smiled and shook her hand. "It's nice to meet you too! I've heard so much about everyone already; I feel like I already know you!"

"Oh, I'm sure there's still a lot you don't know," Tori grinned, looking back at Reagan with a wink.

"Ha!" Reagan laughed.

"This is my husband, Ben, and our son RJ," Tori advised. "I'll let him take over while I get the rest of our family out of the car."

"Hey! Nice to meet you," Ben greeted Brice warmly. "This is a great house!"

"What this old thing?" Brice grinned, returning the handshake. "It's nice to meet you too."

Reagan laughed and said, "He loves saying that about the house!"

"Hey!" Piper greeted, joining the group. "I'm Piper!"

"Nice to meet you, Piper, I'm Brice," Brice greeted her, recognizing her by Reagan's perfect description of a pixie with short, red spiked hair.

"Where should Riley park the car? He doesn't want it to be in anyone's way," Piper asked.

"He can pull it up beside the van. I'm not expecting any other visitors," Brice replied, waving Riley forward.

"Pull up beside the van," Piper yelled, motioning with her hands where he should park. "This place is amazing! I've never known anyone with a house this big!"

"It's not a house it's a castle!" RJ announced.

"You know what? It's not a castle, although I agree, it looks like one. It's actually called a manor. This house is known as Corbin Manor," Brice replied.

"What's the difference?" RJ frowned.

"Well," Brice, paused, thinking of a way to best describe the building to a child. "Manor's are smaller versions of a castle. A King and a Queen typically live in a castle, whereas a manor would be a house for a lord and a lady of royalty."

"Are you a lord of royalty?" RJ exclaimed in surprise.

Brice laughed and replied, "No, I'm not. But my great-great-grandfather was. He and my great-great-grandmother left the country of England when my great-grandfather was a very small boy. He wasn't much older than you. Apparently, my great-great-grandmother was so distraught having had to leave her beautiful home, my great-great-grandfather built her a new one, just like it right here."

"Wow! How long did it take him to do that?" RJ breathed, staring up at the immense structure.

"Didn't he get tired lifting all of that rock?" Gemma asked, joining them. "Hi, I'm Gemma," she added, extending her hand politely. "And this is Goliath," she added, pointing to the large dog beside her.

Brice shook her hand and replied, "It's very nice to meet you, Gemma and Goliath. My great-great-grandfather didn't build the house entirely on his own; he hired other people to help him."

"It must have taken forever," RJ insisted.

"Well, homes like this were often built in stages. For example, the original section of this house is the oldest part of the back of the building. It was what they called an apartment of rooms, usually only a kitchen with a small sitting area, a master bedroom, a small bathroom and room for the hired help. Then over the years, new sections were added."

"Sweetie, this is Riley," Reagan introduced as Riley joined them.

"Welcome!" Brice greeted warmly.

"Thanks for having us," Riley replied, shaking Brice's hand. "This place is beautiful."

"Thanks," Brice replied.

"Where do you keep your horses?" Gemma asked, still hoping to see a horse-drawn chariot.

"Well we do have a stable on the property, but we don't have any horses in it right now. I don't live in the house all the time, I have an apartment in town closer to where I work," Brice replied. "I mostly only come out here on weekends and my days off."

"Aw," Gemma groaned, disappointed.

"There are a lot of other cool things in the house you might like," Brice tempted. "Come on inside, and I'll show you."

"Like what?" Gemma asked curiously, her interest renewed.

As everyone made their way inside the front door, Brice replied, "For starters, this great hall has floors made entirely out of marble. See that big spiral staircase?"

"Yes," Gemma nodded.

"When I was younger, I used to sit on the banister at the top and ride it all the way down to the bottom," Brice exclaimed.

"Wow! Did you ever fall off?" RJ asked, eyeing the distance.

"Many times," Brice chuckled.

"What else is cool about your house?" Gemma asked, still wishing he had horses.

"Well," Brice paused looking up. "If you look up at the ceiling, you'll see a painting of angels flying around big fluffy clouds against a bright blue sky. My great-grandfather hired a famous artist to paint it."

Their eyes all drawn upward, RJ frowned slightly and said, "That's not what angels look like! At least not the ones we know."

Thinking RJ was just being imaginative, Brice chuckled and replied, "Well, those were the angels the artist knew when he was painting the picture. Your angels must not have been around back then."

"Of course they were!" Gemma argued. "Remy and Lucifer have been here since God created the earth!"

"What other cool things does your house have, Brice?" Tori quickly interrupted before the conversation became too intense. *"Brice doesn't know about Remy and Lucifer yet, kids. Let's give him time to get to know us before we tell him about them, okay?"* Tori spoke to the kids telepathically.

"Um, well we also have a huge library filled with hundreds of books from floor to ceiling, and a beautiful ballroom where the lords and ladies used to dance," Brice suggested.

"Wait. You have a ballroom?" Tori exclaimed, excitedly.

"Right through those doors," Brice grinned, nodding to the door at the end of the hall.

"I've got to see that," she informed everyone, walking briskly, almost running toward the end of the hall.

"Me too," Piper giggled, running after Tori.

"I want to see!" Gemma complained, rushing after them.

"Girls," RJ snorted in disgust as Reagan and the men slowly walked in the direction of the ballroom.

"I know, right?" Ben joked.

"Do you have a moat or a tower where the soldiers stood watch looking for robbers and thieves?" RJ asked Brice.

"No, although I agree that would be really cool! This place is basically a really big house with lots of rooms. Speaking of which, it's a great place to play hide and seek if you're interested and your mom and dad don't mind. My cousins and I used to spend hours looking for one another when we were kids," Brice replied.

"Daddy, can we?" RJ asked jumping up and down excitedly.

"May we," Ben corrected his son gently. "How about a little later once we've gotten used to it a bit, okay?"

"Okay," RJ agreed.

"Now this is a ballroom," Tori announced, quickly lowering her tone as the sound of her voice and her footsteps echoed throughout the huge dome-shaped room. Admiring the elaborately carved and richly stained wood pillars framing each window, she walked to the center of the room and spun around in a circle, envisioning women dressed in gowns of fine silk, gracefully floating over the polished marble floor to a waltz being played by a group of musicians. "It's beautiful," she said, dreamily.

Enjoying her delight, Brice reached over to a switch plate on the wall behind him and flipped on the row of switches, instantly filling the room with light. "Look up," he instructed Tori.

Glancing above her, Tori drew in a surprised breath as thousands of crystals suspended from the biggest chandelier she'd ever seen, reflected millions of tiny rainbows over the entire surface of the mirrored ceiling. "Oh it's lovely," she whispered. "Did your parents ever hold any formal dances here when they were still alive?" she asked, smiling as she watched Gemma twirl around in a circle so the skirt of her dress would fan out around her.

"Once when I was ten," he replied. "It was a Halloween masquerade party. My parents made it a theme party, and everyone was required to wear tuxedos and formal ball gowns like the men and women would have worn back in that time. They hired men to dress up like servants who walked around in black tuxedos and white gloves, carrying big silver trays filled with food and glasses of champagne."

"It sounds amazing," Tori replied, envisioning it.

"How cool would that have been to see?" Piper agreed, joining Tori in the center of the room. "Look at all those colors!" she laughed, looking up at the ceiling.

"It was pretty cool," Brice admitted. "Even at ten years old, I remember thinking how fun and full of life my parents were. People talked about that party for years afterward. Every once in a while, I'll run into one of the older folks in town who was there that night, and they talk about how much fun they had."

"Your parents only did it that one time?" Piper asked.

"Yeah, unfortunately, my dad had a heart attack a few years later and passed away. Mom didn't have the same spark in her after he was gone. She kept to herself a lot after that," Brice replied.

"I'm so sorry, I didn't know," Piper cringed, regretting her question.

"No, please don't apologize. It happens. My father was a great man, and he lived a happy life until his death. I only wish my mom's remaining years had been happier," Brice admitted. "She loved her garden and the orchard though so she still had things she enjoyed."

"And she still had you," Reagan smiled, taking hold of Brice's hand.

"My mama likes to garden too!" Gemma announced. "She's showing me and RJ how to grow herbs and hot peppers...."

"And pumpkins!' RJ interrupted excitedly.

"Big, fat, pumpkins!" Gemma grinned, stretching out her arms as big as she could.

"You get to grow your own pumpkins? That's really cool!" Brice grinned, enjoying how the twins interacted with each other.

"Do you still have the orchard?" Gemma asked hopefully.

"Yes, I do, right out there," Brice admitted, pointing outside the windows.

"May we see it? Are there apples on the trees right now?" RJ asked excitedly.

"Actually, yes there are!" Brice admitted. "We also have pears, peaches, cherries, and plums."

"Wow, that's quite a variety. I'm curious why you decided to keep the orchard productive after your mother passed?" Riley asked.

"I still maintain the orchard partly in honor of my mother but also because the local grocery stores pay me for my fruit, which helps me to be able to afford the maintenance on the house. I have a team of workers coming out here next weekend to harvest the apples and the pears, but there's plenty for everyone to pick some and take home with you," Brice offered.

"Wow! May we do it now?" RJ insisted.

"I'm okay with that as long as your parents are." Glancing at Tori and Ben, Brice asked, "Is that okay with you?"

"Sure!" Tori nodded. "That sounds like fun!"

"Let's do it," Ben agreed. "It will give us a chance to stretch our legs and let the kid's burn off some of their energy."

"I agree, that sounds like fun!" Piper exclaimed.

"I've never been to an orchard before so I would love to see it," Riley agreed.

"Okay, we'll go out through the kitchen so we can grab some baskets on the way out," Brice replied. "Follow me!"

Chapter 30

"I'm fascinated by the profitability of the sale of the fruit allowing you to cover the costs of maintaining the manor. How are you able to turn a profit each year? Don't you have to take things like weather, insects, deer and other things into consideration? If you don't mind all of my questions," Riley asked as they walked down a stone path toward the orchard.

"I don't mind at all! And yes, all those things, along with many others, factor into a productive growing season. Like I said, my mom's garden and orchard were her passions, so she put quite a bit of thought and design into them. For example, she found that planting dwarf trees were ideal for small acreage. They're more productive than standard sized trees, and you can tend and harvest yourself with minimum outside labor," Brice replied.

"What about pesticides? How do you keep the insects from eating the fruit?" Tori wondered.

"I use a homemade naturally organic mixture of olive oil, cinnamon oil, habanero pepper extract, garlic extract and liquid dish soap," Brice revealed.

"Are you serious? And you make that yourself?" Tori asked, admirably.

"Well it's my mom's recipe, but yeah, that's it," Brice shrugged.

"Told you he knows his way around a kitchen," Reagan grinned.

"I'm impressed that you chose to stay so close to your mom's methods," Piper admitted. "How often do you have to apply the mixture?"

"About every two weeks or after heavy rains during the growing season," Brice replied.

"Wow, no wonder you come out here so often," Ben noted. "That's a lot of work!"

"Well when you enjoy what you do, it doesn't feel like work. I think the whole process is interesting. We even have a row of beehives over there along the wall to help pollinate the trees in the spring. Which of course, means lots of honey to sell too," Brice replied.

"I've got to admit it. I'm totally in love with this whole concept you have here, Brice," Tori praised. "This is very cool."

"Thanks! It's a big part of my life. Fortunately, Reagan understands and seems to enjoy coming out here with me," Brice grinned, placing his arm around Reagan's waist and pulling her against him as they walked.

"I absolutely love it!" Reagan admitted. "Considering the sometimes gruesome work we do back in the city, coming out here is like a mini vacation for me."

"I bet!" Piper agreed. "That's yet another reason you've seemed so happy lately."

"Thanks for noticing!" Reagan grinned.

As they reached the top of a small hill, a shallow valley spread out before them revealing the orchard below, and a small cemetery off to the left, nestled under a grove of tall oak trees.

"There it is!" Brice announced proudly.

Giving a low whistle, Ben shook his head in disbelief and said, "And you tend to this whole orchard by yourself? That's crazy!"

"How many acres do you have?" Riley asked, equally impressed.

"The whole property is about a hundred acres, twenty of which are the orchard," Brice replied.

"That's a lot of trees!" RJ marveled, already hungrily eyeing the fruit. "How many are there?"

Brice paused briefly, calculating the numbers in his head and said, "Let's see. I have about a hundred and fifty trees per acre so that would calculate out to about three hundred trees."

"Three hundred trees, that's crazy! How many pieces of fruit do you get per tree?" Piper exclaimed.

"Each acre harvests about sixty-five bushels so roughly thirteen hundred pieces of fruit per acre," Brice replied.

"Wow, that's amazing," Tori declared. "This is me totally impressed."

"What's that over there?" Piper asked, pointing to another planted area on the other side of the stone wall.

"That's my neighbor's vineyard," Brice replied, his smile dimming.

"Oh, well that's kind of cool. Does the vineyard help cross-pollinate the trees too?" Piper wondered. "I bet that influences the flavors of the fruit. Is that something you both did together?"

"It does, and no we didn't. My neighbor and I aren't really on good terms," Brice frowned.

"That's too bad," Tori consoled. "What happened?"

"He pressured my mother for years into selling him some of our land after my father passed away," Brice replied. "My neighbor wanted to expand his vineyard, but my mom refused each time he asked. Then after she died, he came after me. Let's just say I wasn't as polite as my mom after he wouldn't take the hint that I wasn't interested in selling. He wasn't very nice about it, and I got the impression he doesn't like getting no for an answer. We don't talk anymore and do our best to stay out of each other's way."

"I understand, that sometimes happens," Tori admitted. "It's too bad it had to come to where it is now but sometimes conflict like that can't be avoided."

"Well, we don't have to worry about any of that today! How about we go pick some fruit?" Brice offered everyone excitedly.

"Yes!" RJ exclaimed eagerly.

"Let's go!" Gemma urged.

"Okay, grab a basket and go!" Brice grinned.

"I'm going to hang back here for a minute, Ben," Tori advised.

"I've got the kids, no worries," he replied, chasing after the twins. "Hey you two, wait up!"

While everyone quickly went off in the direction of the orchard, Tori turned to Brice and asked, "Would you mind showing me your cemetery? It looks beautiful from here."

"Sure! So you're not one of those women who is easily creeped out by old cemeteries?" Brice teased, redirecting their walk in that direction.

"Tori kind of has a thing for cemeteries, actually," Reagan winked at Tori mischievously.

"She does now, does she?" Brice grinned, glancing over at Tori.

"I find them interesting," Tori shrugged. "And often beautifully designed, especially small family cemeteries like yours."

As they approached the main gate, Tori glanced inside and saw a ghostly figure of an older woman, hovering between the headstones, watching them.

Noticing the style of the woman's hair and type of clothing she was wearing, Tori paused as they approached the gate and asked, "Do you mind my asking about your mother? Is she buried here?"

Looking over to one of the headstones where Tori saw the woman's spirit floating, Brice nodded and replied, "Yes. That's her headstone over there, the tall white one with the carved angel at the top."

Exchanging a knowing look with Reagan, Tori inclined her head in the direction of the cemetery and nodded her head slowly.

"Oh no," Reagan whispered, her expression immediately saddening. Taking Brice's hand in hers, she prepared herself for what she knew would come next.

"What?" Brice asked, confused by the women's exchange.

"How did she die?" Tori asked.

"Uh," Brice paused, exhaling a deep breath. "It was a car accident. She somehow lost control of her car and went off the road into an embankment. She had massive internal bleeding and died before they could get her to the hospital."

"I'm very sorry for your loss. There's a reason I asked how she died," Tori noted, sadly.

"I don't understand. What do you mean?" Brice frowned, glancing back and forth between Tori and Reagan. "What's going on?"

"Remember when I told you Tori can often look at certain pieces of evidence and determine how someone died?" Reagan asked Brice calmly.

"Yes. I don't know that I really ever understood what that meant, but I remember you telling me," Brice agreed.

"Well," Reagan paused, "She not only looks at the evidence she reads it."

"Reads it? Like a book?" he frowned.

"Not like a book," Tori admitted, quietly. "I can touch items and see what happened to the people associated with that item. But that's not all I can do," she added, hesitantly. "I can also see and communicate with people who've died of unnatural causes."

"Unnatural causes? What do you mean?" Brice asked.

"Meaning murdered by another human being," Tori advised, patiently.

"Murdered….," Brice murmured then stopped when he realized what Tori meant. Glancing over at his mother's headstone, he swallowed hard and asked, "Are you saying she's…," his voice trailed off.

"Was your mother a slender woman who had long hair and used to wrap it up in a bun?" Tori asked.

"Yes," Brice whispered, still not wanting to believe what Tori was saying.

"Did she used to wear a dusty rose colored embroidered silk shawl around her shoulders?" Tori continued, patiently.

"Yes," Brice swallowed again. "She'd wear it when it was cold outside."

"And did she used to call you her lucky charm?" Tori gently asked.

"Yes," Brice nodded, tears filling his eyes. "She used to call me that because whenever I was with her, good things would happen to her like finding money on the street or getting an extra fortune in her fortune cookie when we would get Chinese food."

Standing quietly beside him, Reagan held Brice's hand, supportively, having seen Tori have similar conversations with other people like this before.

Looking over at his mother's headstone again, Brice tried to reason, "Maybe if I had been with her in the car that day, she wouldn't have died."

"She wouldn't have wanted you in the car with her that day," Tori replied. "I think you know that already."

"Then what happened the day she died? If it wasn't an accident, then that means someone killed her. Who was it?" Brice demanded earnestly.

"Let's go talk to her and ask her," Tori suggested, indicating they should go inside the gate.

Stepping through the wrought iron entryway, Tori could see that Brice kept the cemetery grounds as well maintained as the rest of the property. The stone wall surrounding the area was in good condition, and each of his ancestor's headstones was upright and carefully manicured around the base. Very much to her relief, Brice's mother was the only spirit present.

As they approached, the woman reached out longingly toward Brice. Watching her hand pass through her son's body, she looked at Tori and asked, "Can you hear me?"

"Yes, I can hear you," Tori smiled at her. "My name is Tori."

"It's very nice to meet you, Tori. It's been so long since I've talked to anyone! My name is Rose," Brice's mother replied.

"It's a pleasure to meet you, Rose," Tori replied.

Hearing Tori use his mother's first name, Brice's head instantly turned, and he searched the air around them, trying desperately to see his mother. "Mom?" he whispered hopefully.

"My sweet, darling boy," Rose sighed wistfully, watching him. "He's grown into such a fine man."

"She knows you're here," Tori announced to Brice.

"She can hear me?" Brice hoped anxiously.

"I've always heard him," Rose admitted, sadly. "Every time he visits, he comes to talk to me and shares what's going on in his life before going out to work in the orchard. I especially like the times he brings his lunch and sits under that tree right there. It sounds like he's found his place in life. And someone to share it with," she added, looking at Reagan.

"She said she's always heard you when you've come out here. She's really enjoyed the times you've had your lunch under that tree, sharing what's going on in your life," Tori relayed back to Brice.

"Is it true?" he called out to his mother, fearfully. "Was your death not an accident after all?"

"Does it really matter what happened after all these years?" Rose asked Tori, painfully.

"It matters to him," Tori replied. "Don't you think he deserves to know the truth?"

"Please, Mom!" Brice begged. "I have to know what happened."

"There's nothing he can do about it now," Rose admitted. "Too much time has passed for justice to be served."

"I would have to argue with you there, Rose, respectfully of course," Tori replied. "I'm an FBI agent, as is the woman standing beside your son. Her name is Reagan Nichols. Our job is to investigate and solve murders, so families of the victims have justice and the guilty pay for the crimes they've committed. If you would allow us to help you, I promise I'll do everything I can to make sure whoever is responsible for your death, pays for what they've done."

"As will I," Reagan promised.

Rose hesitated, not wanting to anguish her already agonized son, but could see in his eyes, that he wouldn't rest until he knew the whole story. "Very well," she agreed. "Will you relay the story for me?" she asked Tori.

"Yes, whenever you're ready," Tori agreed.

"Okay," Rose nodded. "The accident wasn't a random incident; it actually went back a few weeks before that day. Victor, our neighbor, was becoming adamant about me selling him some of our land and was harassing me more than I ever let on to Brice."

"What is she saying?" Brice insisted.

"She said the incident started a few weeks before the accident. She mentioned your neighbor was harassing her more than she told you. Is his name Victor?" Tori asked Brice.

"Yes, his name is Victor Wilder," Brice confirmed, his jaw clenching angrily.

"Please continue," Tori encouraged Rose patiently.

"Property taxes were coming due that year, and his goal was to acquire the acreage before then, under the guise that it would help me with our financial situation. The irony of that was we were not in any financial constraint at all. In fact, the fruit production of the orchard was increasing as years went on, increasing our profitability. He had no idea what our financial situation was. All he saw was a widow who he thought wasn't smart enough to manage her household without a man around," Rose chuckled, remembering the conversation well.

Deciding she really liked and admired Brice's mom, Tori relayed the information back for Brice and Reagan to hear.

"Rose said the property taxes were coming due that year and Victor's goal was to acquire the acreage from her, telling your mom it would help her financial situation. Apparently, he didn't know how profitable the orchard was for her, and she was probably doing much better than he was. She thinks all he saw was a widow who wasn't smart enough to manage her household without a man around."

"So he's a murderer and a pig," Reagan snorted in disgust. "Nice."

Rose laughed at Reagan's blatant sarcasm and asked Tori, "She seems to have the right temperament for my son. Is she a good, honest woman?"

"One of the best," Tori assured Rose.

"What's one of the best?" Brice asked. "One of the best what?"

"Hold on; your mom is telling me," Tori lied, giving Rose a quick wink the other two couldn't see.

"He's going to have to be on his toes with you two," Rose smiled. "Okay, back to the story," she sighed, wishing she didn't need to go any further. "As I said Victor was becoming incessant, almost obsessed with getting our land. I was so fearful that he would find some legal way of going around me so I contacted a property attorney in town to find out what legal action I might need to take to ensure Victor couldn't get a hold of it. The attorney worked with a federal organization that secures rights and ownership to land owners and worked up a legal document, which I signed, preventing Victor from any access to our land as long as it remained in our family.

"Somehow Victor found out about the meeting and was enraged that I locked him out of any possible acquisitions. The day I signed the paperwork was the day of the accident."

"As I was driving home, when I rounded the curve in the road by the cliff, I saw one of Victor's work trucks coming from the opposite direction. He must have been watching, waiting for me because as I got closer, I saw his face and knew he knew what I had done. I tried to avoid him but he hit me head on, and I lost control of the car. The last thing I remember before I died was seeing the embankment in front of me. Then everything went dark."

"Before you go on, let me tell Brice and Reagan what you just said, okay?" Tori asked gently.

"Yes, go ahead," Rose agreed.

Turning to Brice, Tori relayed, "Victor was becoming obsessed with getting the land, and your mom got worried he would find some legal way of going around her. So she contacted a property attorney in town to find out what legal action she had, and he worked up a document which basically locked Victor out of any access to your property as long as there was a living relative owning the land. Somehow Victor found out and was pissed. The day she signed the paperwork was the day of the accident. As she was driving home, when she rounded the curve in the road by the cliff, she saw Victor driving one of work trucks coming from the opposite direction. She thinks he must have been watching for her. She tried to avoid him but she couldn't. He hit her car, and she lost control. Then she hit the embankment and everything went dark."

"I'm going to kill him," Brice threatened through gritted teeth.

"No, you're not," all three women instinctively replied at once.

"Brice, look at me," Tori demanded. "I can help your mother. I can send her to heaven to be with your father and finally give her peace. That's what any child should want for their parents.

"I can't, however, ever offer that to you if you kill another human being. Your soul will be dammed to hell for eternity. Is that what you want?"

"No, of course not, but I can't continue to let him get away with the fact that he murdered my mother!" Brice insisted angrily.

"Nor am I suggesting that trust me," Tori insisted.

"Then what am I supposed to do?" Brice argued. "Just sit here and pretend I don't know what happened?"

Reagan stepped in between Brice and Tori and announced, "You let me, Tori and the rest of our team take care of Victor. That's our job. That way you're not at risk for getting hurt and Victor stays alive, so he can stand trial."

Brice stared at Reagan angrily, debating if he could agree to those terms.

"Please, Brice," Reagan pleaded. "I really care about you. I don't want anything to happen to you."

"Nor do I," Tori agreed.

"Fine, but he better watch out. I would hate for his vineyards to get a sudden infestation of Grape Berry Moth's or something like that," Brice muttered under his breath.

"Provoking him won't do you any good either," Tori warned. "He needs to believe no one suspects him if we're going to find any proof of what he did."

"How are you going to be able to prove what he's done?" Brice argued, glaring at Tori. "No offense intended, but a woman who talks to ghosts isn't enough proof for any jury to convict someone of murder!"

"First of all," Tori replied, trying to maintain her patience, knowing how upset Brice was. "I never refer to the dead as ghosts. That word has a very serious negative connotation that I find incredibly disrespectful. They are either earthbound spirits or souls in limbo but never ghosts. Is that understood?"

"Yes," Brice reluctantly agreed. "I'm sorry. I know you're trying to help."

"Please don't apologize! I understand how upset you are right now. Anyone having just learned their mother didn't die of natural causes would be upset. I have an immense level of respect for those souls who don't cross over at the time of their death. It has to be horrible watching their loved ones move on with their lives, and they're trapped here. None of them deserve that kind of existence, especially your mother, who seems to be a genuinely lovely woman," Tori replied.

"Thank you, Tori," Rose smiled, comforted to know her son seemed to be surrounded by people who cared about him.

Tori smiled at Rose and replied, "You're welcome, Rose."

"What's the second thing?" Brice demanded.

"What?" Tori asked, confused.

"You said first of all when we were talking about getting proof of Victor's actions. What's the second thing?" Brice asked.

"Oh, right. We're going to need to look at all documents your mother had prepared during that time to see exactly what the terms of that document included. Also, if you have any physical evidence of the crime scene, I might be able to pick up some resonant images on the events that took place," Tori advised.

"Will the car do?" Brice offered.

"You still have the car from the accident?" Tori exclaimed in surprise.

"Yeah, it's in the carriage house behind the stables. I didn't know what to do with it so I just covered it with a tarp left it there," Brice winced. "Was that a bad thing to do?"

"Bad? It was brilliant!" Tori cheered. "We can definitely work with that!"

"Okay good. So what happens now?" Brice wondered. "You said you could help send my mother to heaven? How does a human have that kind of ability?"

"Well, actually I am not entirely human," Tori admitted.

"W-wait, what?" he stammered, looking at Reagan in surprise. "Is she serious?"

"Just let her explain," Reagan smirked, trying not to laugh at Brice's expression.

Turning his attention back to Tori, he hesitantly nodded and said, "I'm sorry, go ahead."

"When I say that I'm not entirely human, I mean that I'm part human and part supernatural. My ancestral lineage on my mother's side of the family was human, whereas my ancestral lineage on my heavenly Father's side was an Archangel by the name of Remeil," Tori began slowly.

Pulling up on the gold chain of a necklace she was wearing, she revealed a piece of carved turquoise suspended from the chain. Cradling the object gently in her hand, she said, "This is an amulet my ancestors have passed down through their daughters for generations. This is what we use as an anchor when guiding spirits. It gives me the power to help those in need cross over."

"How is that possible?" Brice shook his head in disbelief. "If that were true, wouldn't I have heard about you and others like you by now?"

"Tori's abilities are a secret we all keep, Brice," Reagan warned gently. "Throughout time, man has tried to use the power from the amulet for their own gain, so her ancestors learned to keep their abilities secret and only reveal them when they had no other choice. There used to be more people like Tori who could do what she does, but now she's the only one left," Reagan lied, not sure if she should reveal that the twins also had the same power.

"I've often wondered about the stories we were told as children about the Nephilim," Rose admitted. "But we were led to believe they were grotesque monsters, not humans with supernatural abilities."

"Your mom just mentioned she heard stories as a child about grotesque monsters called Nephilim who were thought to be offspring of fallen angels and humans," Tori advised.

"I grew up hearing those stories too," Brice admitted, still unsure what to think.

"As did I," Reagan noted. "Tori wasn't the first person I met with this power Brice, my first partner Karla had it too."

"Is that the same partner who was killed?" Brice frowned, turning to look at her.

"Yes," Reagan nodded. "She was killed because of the power she possessed."

Turning back to Tori, Brice stared at her, deciding if he believed her story could be true. "So that's why nobody on your team talks about what you can do? You help solve crimes and help the people you can, but no one else outside of the team knows?"

"A few people outside of our team know, but those people are highly trusted, and they have been brought in on a need to know basis," Tori admitted.

Contemplating a moment, Brice asked, "And Ben?"

"Totally human," Tori advised.

Contemplating a moment more, he asked, "And the twins?"

"They're hybrids like me and have their own special abilities. Because they're so young, we don't yet know what all of those abilities will be," Tori revealed, hoping she could trust him.

Furrowing his brow in concern, he asked, "You've taken a huge risk telling me that. Why?"

"Because I believe Reagan has good instincts and she wouldn't share her life with someone who wasn't a good person; and because I need you to believe in what I do for me to be able to help your mother. I'm a believer in the Lord God, and I believe this gift I've been given is a blessing. To deny it would be a sin."

Looking over at his mother's headstone, Brice asked, "Will it hurt her?"

"She will feel no pain at all what-so-ever," Tori promised.

"Okay," he nodded in agreement. "Whatever she decides, I'm okay with it."

"Is there anything you want to tell her before she goes?" Tori offered.

Brice shrugged and admitted, "I guess she's heard everything I've been telling her all these years, so she's caught up in my life up to this point." Searching the air around him, he asked, "Where is she right now?"

Walking over next to where Rose's spirit was hovering, Tori replied, "She's here to my right."

Fixing his eyes on that spot, Brice said, "I'm so sorry I didn't know you were here all these years, Mom. Had I know any of this before today, I promise I would have done something to try and help you."

"I know you would have, sweetheart," Rose replied.

"She knows you would have," Tori relayed back to Brice.

"I love you, Mom," Brice whispered, choking back a sob.

"I love you too, my sweet boy," Rose whispered.

"She said she loves you too," Tori repeated, brushing tears away from her cheeks. Without turning around to look, she could hear from Reagan's sniffling; she was doing the same.

"I promise Victor will pay for what he's done and that I won't go after him myself," Brice vowed.

"Thank you," Rose smiled.

"She said thank you," Tori relayed back.

Turning to Tori, Rose asked, "So what do I need to do? I'm ready to go."

Tori smiled and said, "You don't have to do a thing. It was a pleasure meeting you, Rose. I hope we meet again someday, under better circumstances of course!"

Rose laughed and agreed, "As do I. I was a pleasure meeting you too, Tori. Watch over my boy for me."

"I will," Tori promised. Closing her eyes tightly, she envisioned Rose standing at the gates of heaven and loudly proclaimed, "May your spirit be at peace, Rose, as you return to the Father." When she opened her eyes, Rose was gone.

"Is she....?" Brice whispered hesitantly.

"She's finally at peace," Tori nodded, slipping the amulet back inside her shirt.

"Thank you," he murmured, glancing back at his mother's headstone.

"You're welcome," Tori replied.

"To think all those years she was here listening to me and I never knew," Brice noted sadly.

"I believe she'll still be able to hear you. It will just be from a little further away," Tori suggested.

"I guess," he shrugged.

Gently rubbing her hand down Brice's back, Reagan asked, "Do you want to be alone here for a little while? I think I heard the rest of the gang head back up toward the house. Tori and I can join them if you need some time."

"No, I'm good, thanks. I honestly feel like I'm in a good place, thanks to you both," Brice smiled assuredly. "Let's go join the others."

Chapter 31

As Tori, Reagan and Brice approached the house; they could hear the muffled sounds of voices and the twins laughing somewhere nearby.

"It sounds like they're in the garden. Follow me," Brice instructed, directing them toward a very tall hedge of shrubbery manicured to resemble a wall. When they got closer, Tori noticed the hedge had a curved archway cut into one area revealing a secret passage into the main garden.

"Wow! I bet this wall takes a lot of work! It has to be at least ten feet tall!" Tori marveled, running her fingers through the leaves as she walked beneath the arch.

"Yes it does," Reagan advised. "I've seen Brice trimming it!"

"Here it is!" Brice presented proudly as they passed under the archway. "Welcome to Rose's secret garden."

"Oh my, it's lovely," Tori breathed as she emerged inside the wall. "I feel like Alice in Wonderland."

"I had that same feeling the first time I saw it!" Reagan laughed. "Isn't it great?"

"Yes, it is!" Tori agreed, staring wide-eyed as she looked around her.

As with the rest of the property, Rose's garden was pure magic. The center lawn was a lush, deep green carpet, beckoning you to take your shoes off to feel the soft, coolness of the grass between your toes. Where the grass stopped, massive flower beds lined with the same stone from the perimeter wall were filled with hundreds of various flowers and ornamental grasses, many of which Tori didn't recognize.

Even the air was filled with magic as dozens of hummingbirds, butterflies and honeybees hovered and fluttered as if they were dancing around her to music only they could hear. There were so many places of beauty to look Tori's eyes couldn't take it all in fast enough. Then she saw the herb bed and instantly fell in love.

"Oh my goodness, look at all of those herbs and edible flowers!" she marveled. "Did you do all of this?" she asked Brice excitedly.

Brice grinned, proudly and admitted, "I love to cook with fresh herbs whenever possible."

Grinning at Reagan, Tori shook her head and announced, "Okay Reagan, I've gotta say it, you found a unicorn. This guy's a keeper!"

"I know, right?" Reagan laughed. "He is pretty incredible."

"All right, that's enough," Brice waved them away, embarrassed.

"No, I'm serious! This place is amazing!" Tori exclaimed.

"Thanks," Brice grinned. "I have to give most of the credit to my mom. This place is all her. I just maintain it and make it look good."

"You're too modest," Tori argued. "I know how much work a garden takes. You have a garden, and an orchard, and a huge house and a full-time job in the city. I don't know how you do it!"

Brice shrugged and replied, "I guess that's why I've been single so long. But I don't mind hard work. That's how I was raised. Even though my ancestors came from old money, my parents never lived that way. Especially my mom, she worked until the day she died."

"Was that the lady in the cemetery? Did you help cross her over Mama?" Gemma called out as she rode Goliath like a pony around the lawn.

Surprised that Gemma had seen Rose but hadn't mentioned her until now, Tori turned to respond when suddenly had a feeling of déjà vu. *"I've been here before,"* she told herself decidedly. *"The frilly dress bouncing in a wavelike motion as Goliath gallops in a large circle in a wooded backyard with lush green grass,"* she recalled in her head. *"Did she pick that dress today or did I do it subconsciously?"* she wondered.

"Mama, help I'm slipping!" Gemma called out to her in a voice that sounded faint and far away.

Sensing the shift in Gemma's position on his back, Goliath quickly trotted over to Tori so she could safely help Gemma down.

"There you go, baby girl," Tori advised, setting the toddler on her feet.

"Look, Mama," Gemma giggled pointing in the direction across from them.

Glancing to her left, Tori saw the large water fountain with the stone cherub holding a cement seashell from her dream many years ago. As she remembered, RJ was standing outside the base, his denim jeans soaked from the knees down, indicating at some point he had been playing in the water. Knowing what came next, she reached out her hands toward him and screamed, "RJ, no!"

But it was too late.

He turned his mischievous face toward her, and made a slight motion with his hands, instantly freezing the water into a solid ribbon of ice that cascaded down into the large cement basin of the fountain.

"And there's that look that has Ben written all over it," she sighed inwardly regretting what would happen next.

"Hey! What's going on?" Brice demanded. "What happened to my fountain?"

Wincing apologetically, Tori replied, "I'm so sorry, Brice! I tried to stop him, but I wasn't fast enough. I promise the fountain is fine."

"What do you mean you tried to stop him? Who? Are you saying RJ did that?" Brice cried out in surprise.

Turning to RJ, Tori demanded, "RJ, change the water back this instant!"

Not understanding why she was so angry, the smile on RJ's face instantly disappeared. "Aw, come on. I wasn't hurting it, Mama!"

"RJ, right now!" Tori insisted.

"Fine," he grumbled. With a slight wave of his hand, the water was unfrozen, and the fountain was flowing again.

Standing motionless like the cherub statue, Brice stared at the fountain, completely dumbfounded, trying to comprehend what he had just witnessed.

Coming up beside him, Reagan touched Brice gently on the arm and asked, "Sweetie? Are you okay? You might want to breathe," she suggested. "And maybe sit down."

Turning to look at her, his eyes drifted past her, noticing Ben, Piper and Riley were quietly watching, their expressions pensive, yet unshaken.

"Is this normal for you guys?" he asked, curiously.

"Pretty much," Piper shrugged. "I'm surprised you didn't prepare him, Reagan!"

"Prepare him how exactly? I sometimes still find myself surprised by some of the things I see. How would you explain that to someone before they've experienced it themselves?" Reagan argued.

Inclining her head in agreement, Piper admitted, "Okay, you're right. I'm not sure how I would have approached this either."

Looking back and forth between Gemma and RJ, Brice asked, "So earlier when you said the twins have special powers of their own that were still evolving, what RJ just did, was that one of them?"

"Yes," Tori admitted, sitting down on one of the cement benches in the garden. "Here, come sit next to me, and I'll try to explain."

"Okay," he agreed, joining her.

"As we talked about earlier, the prophecy the twins and I are part of, allows us certain abilities other humans don't have. But before we go into that, I have to make sure I can trust that you won't use any of what I'm about to say against us. This is very important, Brice. The small circle of people who know about us would give their lives to protect us, and we would do the same for them. Do you understand?" Tori cautioned.

Looking up at Reagan with eyes filled with emotion, Brice turned back to Tori and said, "Look I'm not just some guy dating your friend. I really care about her and plan to do whatever it takes to keep her in my life. I understand you guys are close. I have no intention of changing any of that. So if that means being part of your lives means I have to keep secrets from other people, I can do that. Besides, after what I just saw you do for my mother, there's no amount of money in the world to show you how truly grateful I am for what you did!"

Reagan sat down next to Brice, took his hand and smiled warmly at him. "I'm really glad to hear you say that because everyone you see here is like family to me. As Tori said, I would give my life protecting them I love them that much. And I care a great deal about you too. Keeping secrets from other people is only part of it, though. I know you're a Christian based on previous conversations we've had, so you have to be prepared to keep secrets from beings other than humans as well if needed."

Frowning at Reagan in confusion, Brice turned to Tori and asked, "What does she mean beings other than humans? Are we talking about the earthbound spirits again?"

"In a sense yes," Tori admitted. "Let me back up to a place where I think might help clarify that a bit. You know about the battle in heaven for control which resulted in God casting certain angels from heaven, right?"

"Satan being one of them, yes," Brice nodded.

"Okay good, you know that part," Tori affirmed. "So you also know about Satan's army of angels who were cast out of heaven with him."

"Yes," Brice confirmed.

"Well, there was one other archangel pretending to be part of Satan's army, who was cast out of heaven by God intentionally."

"Why would an angel want to leave God's side? Isn't heaven the ultimate place of glory for all angels?" Brice argued.

"Yes, however, this one particular angel was on an assignment for God, so he willingly gave up his place in heaven," Tori replied.

"I'm not following you, I'm sorry," Brice frowned.

Pausing to re-think her explanation, Tori tried again. "Okay, maybe you don't need to know all about that for now, let's move on," she suggested, noticing Ben, Piper, Riley, and the twins had come to sit down on the grass next to them so they could hear the story again too.

"Tell him about Remy, Mama!" Gemma insisted excitedly.

Nodding in agreement, Tori admitted, "You're right, that's probably the best place to start, sweetie." Turning back to Brice, she said, "Remiel was the archangel who was with Satan's army under disguise. His mission here on earth was to find a way to bring Satan and the other angels back to heaven."

"God wanted them back even after what they did?" Brice asked in surprise.

"Of course He did!" Tori insisted. "It made God very sad that His creations turned against Him and left. I believe He would still welcome them back if they came to Him with an apologetic heart."

"Okay, I'm with you so far," Brice advised. "So this angel in disguise, Remiel, you call him Remy?"

"Yes," Tori replied.

"And is Remy the same angel you were talking about with my mom, who fell in love with a human female, and together they created children like you who have special abilities?" Brice noted.

"Also correct," Tori confirmed.

"So do all of your ancestors have that glowing necklace like you do? I don't see Gemma or RJ wearing one," Brice wondered.

"He's super perceptive. Not many people pick up on that right away," Tori thought, approvingly.

"RJ and I don't need the amulet or the statue to use our abilities. Remy says we're gifted and there are no other children of his like us. Isn't that right, Mama?" Gemma declared proudly.

"Statue?" Brice puzzled, looking at Tori. "What statue?"

"Oh, right, I forgot about the statue. Okay, I'm going to make this a crash course because there's a lot of information that will probably overwhelm you but it's helpful to know," Tori began organizing her thoughts.

"The first daughters of Remiel didn't have any special abilities however Remy still had some of his. So he decided to show God he still believed in the importance of saving lost souls here on earth and created two items for his children to use when crossing souls over into heaven. One was a turquoise statue carved into the shape of an angel with outspread wings reaching up toward heaven; the second was an amulet, carved very similarly. So originally, one daughter of Remiel possessed both items, which gave that daughter great power."

"You keep saying daughters, yet obviously RJ is male. Is he the only male offspring of Remiel?" Brice asked.

"I love how quick your mind is!" Tori praised. "I'll get to that in a minute. Okay, so original daughters had both items giving great power. Which was all well and good for a while, but you have to remember, Satan was also here on earth and he didn't like the fact that Remiel was saving souls. The earth was Satan's domain, so he decided to tempt the daughters into using their power against God, which as you can imagine, made Remy very angry."

"I would guess," Brice agreed.

"Unfortunately Satan was able to turn one of Remiel's daughters against him, and per the custom for that time, the earthly family of the daughter stoned her to death as punishment. Then they decided to separate the statue and amulet from one another and break their family into two separate families so no one would ever have that kind of power again.   The families moved far away from one another and never had contact with each other again," Tori revealed.

"That's a pretty harsh punishment for the girl. Where is her spirit now? Is she still here on earth?" Brice asked.

Impressed again by his questions, Tori laughed and said, "I'll get to that too, I promise! Okay, so fast forward hundreds of years, during which time, all offspring of Remiel is female, and each family passes the statue and the amulet down through history until we get to the Ramiel and Neviah families. Ramiel, with an 'a,' was my mother's maiden name. Neviah is Hebrew for prophetess, or seer into the future."

Knowing he had heard that name somewhere before, Brice turned to Reagan and asked, "Wait, didn't you say your former partner Karla's last name was Neviah or something like that? Was she one of Remy's daughters too?"

"Yes, she was," Reagan admitted. "Cosmic forces brought the two worlds together, and the families found their way back to one another."

"That's amazing!" Brice exclaimed, looking back at Tori. "And I would assume way too coincidental?"

"Yes, very well put," Tori nodded. "Because Karla was the last descendant of her family line able to bear a child, as I was on mine, I began having dreams about Karla which along with a few other dream details not important to this story, eventually brought me to Reagan and Agent Hunter. Then I met Meda, Karla's mother, who was such a lovely woman and we became friends. Then I introduced Meda to my mother and my sister, and that's when we learned about the amulet and the whole history behind the original family."

"I remember Reagan mentioning Karla's mother died of cancer a few years ago," Brice noted. "Since her death was natural, did she pass on like a normal human into heaven?"

"Yes, she did," Tori nodded. "Okay so going back to the story of the amulet and the statue...,"

"Wait," Brice interrupted her, giving her an odd look. "You just said you and Karla were the last descendants of your families yet you said you introduced Karla's mom to your sister. Was your sister not born with the Remiel abilities?"

"Sorry! Again, I wasn't sure how much to tell Brice before you met him. I didn't tell him about Aubrey," Reagan winced apologetically.

"No, that's okay. Don't worry about it," Tori assured her friend. Turning back to Brice, Tori gave him a sly look and admitted, "You really are sharp as a tack. I'm impressed! Yes, I did say I introduced my sister to Karla's mom. I have an older sister named Aubrey who is two years older than me." Pausing to re-think her phrasing she added, "At least she would be two years older than me if she was still alive."

"Oh, I'm so sorry! I had no idea!" Brice blubbered, feeling foolish for bringing up the subject.

"No, please don't be sorry! This is going to be a really strange part of the story, and our family has had time to become accustomed to the situation around my sister Bree," Tori assured him.

"What do you mean?" Brice frowned.

"Our Aunt Bree is a spirit!" Gemma announced excitedly. "She's so much fun! And she looks just like Mama but much younger!"

"She's a spirit?" Brice exclaimed in surprise. "Like my mother?"

"Yes," Tori nodded. "She was killed her senior year in high school by a man who lived in our town back in Cheyenne. It wasn't until about five or six years ago that we even knew her spirit was still here, very much like what happened to your mom. Again, my dreams led me to her body, and we brought her home. She stays with my parents most of the time."

"So she doesn't want to cross over yet?" Brice wondered.

"No, not yet," Tori replied. "It's been great having her home with us. Our family was pretty broken after her death so these past few years have been very healing for my parents, especially my mom who can communicate with her. My dad mainly converses with Bree through my mom. We love having her with us, so we're not ready for her to leave."

"I hope she never leaves," RJ sadly admitted.

"Me either, sweetie," Tori smiled.

"So after Karla and Meda passed, I guess you are now the sole possessor of both the statue and the amulet?" Brice asked.

"Yes I am," Tori confirmed. "For lack of a better explanation, I guess you could say the objects chose me. They stopped working for Meda, and my mom once that happened."

"But the twins don't need them?" Brice asked, getting lost again.

"We're getting close to that part, I promise," Tori assured him.

"Okay, so earlier when you mentioned Satan went after the last descendant possessing both objects that means you're a target now too, right?" Brice asked.

"That's an understatement," Ben snidely commented.

"I know, right?" Piper chuckled.

"He has become quite an inconvenience at times," Riley chimed in.

Baffled by everyone's casual responses, Brice gave Tori a look of complete confusion. "I don't understand. Why does everyone talk about the devil like he's just some guy with a really sour disposition?"

"Because that's basically who Luc is," Tori shrugged.

"Luc? Who's Luc?" Brice frowned.

"Luc is Tori's casual and shortened use of his other name, Lucifer," Ben replied.

"What does he mean? You seriously have conversations with Lucifer like we're having now?" Brice exclaimed in surprise. "Are you friends with him?"

"No, I wouldn't call him a friend. It's difficult to explain our relationship. I guess the easiest explanation would be for me to get to know the devil, I've had to get to know the devil if you catch my meaning," Tori admitted. "He continually tries to find ways of getting me to crack so he can coerce another one of Remy's daughters into doing his bidding. At the same time, I keep him close enough to me so I know what he's up to."

"Well, that's pretty horrific!" Brice declared. "I can't even begin to imagine what that's like for you. And you do this willingly on an ongoing basis? You seem to handle it well. You're happy and upbeat and willing to help someone at the drop of a hat. That has to seriously piss him off!"

Wiggling her eyebrows mischievously, Tori grinned and admitted, "Yes it does!"

"So the bridge issue earlier?" Brice asked.

"That was him," Tori confirmed.

"Dang, this is so hard to wrap your head around," Brice admitted.

"You'll get used to it after a while," Piper assured him calmly.

"Does he ever go after the rest of you?" Brice worried.

"Sometimes he does but between Tori, the daughters inside the amulet, the twins, Goliath, Piper and Remy, we have a pretty good alarm system in place when Lucifer decides to act out," Riley replied.

"Hold on," Brice paused, hands up in surrender. "What daughters in the amulet? Goliath as in the dog at Tori's feet? And what does Piper do? Is she related to Tori too? My head is spinning over here!"

Laughing apologetically, Tori placed her hand on Brice's arm and said, "I'm so sorry! Is this too much too fast? Do you want not to hear anymore and finish this another time?"

Exhaling a deep breath, Brice shook his head and confessed, "No, now my curiosity is piqued, so I have to know the rest."

"Okay, I promise I'll try not to delve into too many details unless you ask," Tori vowed. "We'll start with the amulet," she advised, retrieving the amulet again from around her neck. Holding it up so Brice could see it, she noticed the gentle pulsing blue-green light emulating from the stone seemed to relax him. *"I wonder if the ladies are doing any of that?"* she wondered.

"So this is the Remiel stone," Brice stated, examining it closely. "It's beautiful work."

"Yes, it is," Tori agreed. "Earlier you asked what happened to the first owner of the amulet, the one who was stoned to death. Her name is Elsbet. Upon her death, her spirit transferred into the amulet. No one knew for a very long time that she was trapped in there, not even Remy."

"That must have been pretty lonely," Brice replied.

As if in agreement, the stone pulsed brightly one time.

"Was that?" Brice exclaimed in amazement.

"That was Elsbet agreeing with you," Tori smiled, caressing the stone lovingly. "She and the spirits of my other sister's who have been murdered during their time here on earth, are all in the amulet with her."

"Does that include Karla?" Brice asked. "What's the purpose of their spirits being in the stone?"

"Yes Karla is with them," Tori nodded. "She and the other daughters have collective power they use through the amulet. As it turned out, the dreams and visions I was having for so many years were them trying to contact me. They're my guardians. They watch for signs of Luc and often have come to my aid when I've needed help."

"So if you ever are killed?" Brice wasn't sure if he should ask but wanted to know.

"My spirit would end up in there too," Tori finished his thought.

"Got it," Brice nodded. "That's a scary thing to think about."

Eyeing him carefully, Tori asked, "Very scary. Are you still good? Want me to keep going?"

Nodding enthusiastically, Brice said, "Yes, all good."

"All right, get ready," Tori advised mysteriously pointing to Piper. "The next part of the story is all about Piper!"

Chapter 32

"Hi there!" Piper waved at Brice, grinning.

Unable to help but smile back at her, Brice wondered what this pixie of a girl had in common with Tori. "Hi again," he grinned.

"Would you like to tell your story?" Tori offered Piper politely.

"Um, sure," Piper agreed, sitting up excitedly having been given the spotlight. "Tori and I met at the FBI Academy. We were roommates. That ended up not being a random thing it was arranged by Agent Hunter. He already knew about Tori's abilities and had suspicions about mine."

"So you're not related to Tori at all?" Brice asked.

"Nope," Piper shook her head. "But we're more like sisters than friends, so she feels like family to me."

"Same," Tori grinned happily.

"So what do you do?" Brice asked awkwardly. "I mean, what special things can you do? Sorry, this is still a bit weird for me."

Fluttering her hand in the air unconcerned, Piper assured him, "Don't worry; we're all friends here. You can ask whatever question you would like. We're used to it."

"Okay, thanks," Brice agreed. "How are you part of Tori's alarm system as Riley mentioned?"

Bowing gracefully, Piper dramatically announced, "I am an Auric. Do you know what that is?"

Darting his eyes around the group, Brice admitted, "Um, no?"

"That's okay, not many people do!" Piper assured him patiently. "An Auric is someone who can see people's auras. You know what an aura is, right?"

"Yes," Brice nodded. "I used to know a girl who said she could see them around people."

"More than likely she was saying that just to sound more interesting and mysterious. There are very few people who can see auras, and it's not something that's familial or passed down like Tori's abilities," Piper advised.

"So you see my aura right now?" Brice wondered, glancing down at his arms and hands.

"Since the moment we drove up in the car!" Piper grinned. "You have excellent color by the way. Would you like to know what your aura color means?"

"Uh, sure," Brice shrugged. "What color am I? Or colors? Do I have more than one?"

"You have three which is pretty uncommon but very good. I could tell the moment I saw you that you are an honest, kind man which made me very happy because Reagan deserves to be with someone like you," Piper confessed.

"Aw, thanks, Piper," Reagan smiled.

"I'm serious; I love you like a sister too!" Piper declared.

Shaking her head and laughing, Tori suggested, "Why don't you tell Brice what colors you see?"

"Oh, right!" Piper replied, turning her attention back to Brice. "Your dominant colors are a deep red, a bright orange like Riley has, and a dark green like Tori has. It's quite lovely."

"What do those colors mean typically?" Brice asked curiously.

"Deep Red represents someone who is grounded, realistic, and survival-oriented; orange means you're courageous and powerful, and that you're heedless of your own safety which makes sense since you're a firefighter. It takes a great deal of courage to run into a burning building."

"Yes it does," Reagan agreed.

"And finally we have green which means you have a peaceful spirit that's close to nature, and you communicate well with people. That color also makes sense since green usually represents someone in public services kind of careers which again, ties back to you being a firefighter," Piper suggested.

"Wow, that's pretty cool!" Brice grinned, enjoying this part of the story. "So how do your abilities help Tori?"

"There are two ways," Piper replied. "The first way is being able to see an aura around a person who has nefarious intentions and is planning to something harmful to someone. It gives me the advantage to alert the team or monitor that person until we have an opportunity to arrest them. The trick to that scenario is being patient and waiting for that person to attempt their action before we can arrest them. Otherwise, it won't hold up in court."

"That makes sense," Brice agreed.

"The second way is how I directly help Tori. When she's reading a piece of evidence from a crime scene or even sometimes while she's sleeping, her aura changes to a color indicating she's either in trouble or something is about to happen to her. When I see that, one or all of us step in and help her," Piper advised.

"That's impressive. And that's the ability that Agent Hunter saw would be a good fit for his team?" Brice asked.

"Exactly," Piper nodded.

Glancing around the rest of the group, Brice asked, "Do any of you have special abilities like Tori and Piper?"

"Nope, I'm just an ordinary human," Ben admitted.

"Same," Riley chimed in, raising his hand.

"Well, there is one other member of our team who's amazingly gifted, our four-legged team member!" Piper smiled. "Back to you, Tor," she announced, giving the imaginary spotlight back to Tori.

"Okay I guess next up, as Piper eluded, would be my sweet, boy, Goliath here," Tori advised, grinning when she noticed Goliath was already sitting beside the bench waiting for his turn.

Regarding the large dog thoughtfully, Brice asked, "Okay, what can Goliath do?"

"He saved Mama's life!" Gemma exclaimed excitedly.

"Yeah, he took a bullet for her trying to save her," RJ added enthusiastically.

"He did? When did that happen?" Brice exclaimed, impressively.

"It was the day we were born!" the twins replied in unison.

Chuckling lightly, Brice looked at Tori and asked, "Do they do that a lot?"

Nodding admittedly, Tori replied, "All the time. You get used to it."

"I'll try to remember that," Brice replied. "So tell me about Goliath and how he saved your life the day the twins were born. That sounds like an amazing story."

Petting Goliath affectionately on the head, Tori smiled and admitted, "That was quite a day, wasn't it, Goliath?"

"Yes!" she heard him agree.

"Goliath became a part of our lives through Remy," Tori began. "That would have been about a year before the twins were born. Luc was becoming more aggressive in his activities which concerned Remy, so he decided I needed another guardian who could be with me when he and the other's couldn't. At first, I didn't understand why Remy felt Goliath was a good choice then I got to know Goliath and realized he needed me as much as I needed him."

"What do you mean?" Brice asked.

"Remy gave Goliath the gift of telepathy and incredible strength," Tori replied.

"Telepathy? So you're saying you and he can hear each other's thoughts?" Brice exclaimed wide-eyed.

"Exactly," Tori confirmed. "He can sense my emotions so if I feel afraid or worried or scared, he tunes into that and begins to look for any danger around me. He also has a connection to Remy, so if I'm ever unable to call for help, Goliath calls for Remy."

"Wow," Brice breathed, eyeing Goliath with new appreciation. "That's how he knew to try and save you the day the twins were born?"

"Yep," Tori nodded. "We were on assignment looking for a serial killer who is a former Marine as well as a skilled marksman. Unfortunately, we got too close, and I became his target."

Glancing around the group, Brice asked, "Were you all there that day?"

"Yes," Ben replied, his jaw clenched, not enjoying this part of the story.

Reagan, Piper, and Riley nodded in agreement.

Reaching out to pet Goliath gently, Brice shook his head in disbelief. "I've never seen that kind of devoted loyalty and bravery in an animal before. Are Goliath's thoughts his own? Like a normal dog or did Remy enhance them too?"

"No, he has normal dog thoughts and emotions like any other dog," Tori admitted.

"I know when he's hungry; when he wants to go to the bathroom; when he sees a squirrel or rabbit in the yard that he wants to chase, and I completely understand his frustration with not being able to control his tail when he's happy. It's been interesting being able to hear his thoughts over the years. Dogs think very much like a human. They think, feel, reason, experience joy, mourn when someone dies, emotions just like us."

"Do you think people who kill animals for sport would change their ways if they knew that?" Brice wondered.

Shrugging her shoulders, Tori admitted, "I'm sure you've seen in your job how cruel people can be. We see people at their best as well as their worst. We're a violent race, capable of both horrible and amazing things. I can't imagine a hunter looking at the face of a doe through the scope of his rifle, pausing to consider what she's feeling at the exact moment he pulls the trigger. To him, she's just an animal."

Still petting Goliath, Brice shook his head and admitted, "I don't know if I'll ever be able to look at an animal again and not think about that."

"I would tell the entire world if it would mean making people think twice about how they treat animals, but doing that would expose what Goliath can do, and that's a risk I'm not willing to take," Tori confessed.

"I would probably feel the same way if it were me," Brice agreed. "So what did you mean earlier when you said he needed you as much as you needed him?"

Snapping her fingers at the reminder, Tori admitted, "That's right, I did say that. Boy, you're good at keeping up with details on a conversation!"

"It's part of my job too," Brice shrugged.

"No, it's much more than that. You are a very intuitive person; I like that!" Tori grinned. "So to answer your question about Goliath, ironically enough, Remy found Goliath in an animal shelter waiting to be adopted."

"What? That's horrible! A beautiful dog like this?" Brice frowned angrily.

"Thank you," Tori heard Goliath say to Brice.

"Goliath says thank you," Tori noted.

Not seeming to be surprised, Brice looked at Goliath and nodded in acknowledgment. "You're welcome, Goliath!"

"And yes, I would agree with you too," Tori admitted. "I'm sure people who visited the shelter also thought he was a beautiful dog. However, not many people would ever consider getting a dog this big. I'll be the first to admit; I wouldn't have."

"True, that is a consideration for a lot of people," Brice agreed.

"So when Remy came across him, he must have talked to Goliath and found out his story," Tori paused, looking at Goliath curiously. "You know what? I've never asked how that all came about. Do you remember Goliath?"

"Goliath told his story to everyone who came to his cage. Remy was the first one to listen." She heard him say.

Blinking back tears, Tori asked, "Do all dogs do that? Is that what they're doing when they rush forward in their cages excitedly when someone approaches? Are they telling the humans their stories to encourage them to pick them?"

"Yes!" Goliath barked.

"Oh, that's so sad," Tori whispered, reaching out to pull him into an embrace. "I'm so glad Remy found you when he did," she murmured, her voice muffled by his fur.

"Oh my gosh. I'm never going to be able to go into an animal shelter ever again," Piper vowed, sniffing back her tears.

"Same," Reagan agreed, sadly. "I never even considered the possibility of what they're trying to tell us."

"So what was Goliath's story before he found Remy?" Brice asked curiously.

"Goliath had a beautiful family with a father, a mother and an adorable little girl named Mandy. They were a happy family and loved each other very much," Tori replied.

"That's right!" Goliath barked again, nodding his head.

"Unfortunately Sam, the father, and one of his female colleagues discovered someone they worked with was an arsonist. While Sam and his colleague tried to obtain proof of the arsonist's activities, the man discovered what Sam and his colleague were doing, and killed them both. First, he tried to cover up murdering the woman by placing her body in her apartment and then setting the building on fire. When Sam found out, he confronted the man, so the man went after Sam and his family. The arsonist rigged the water heater in the basement while the family was inside sleeping."

"That's awful! I've been to scenes where water heaters have exploded, they cause a lot of damage and kill a lot of people," Brice said. "Where was Goliath in all of that? It doesn't sound like he was in the house."

Shaking her head, Tori confirmed, "As a matter of fact, he wasn't. They had a large kennel in the backyard where Goliath slept. He saw the man enter and leave the house, so we know it wasn't an accident."

"But of course, a telepathic dog as a witness isn't enough to convince anyone that it wasn't accidental, right? Even coming from an FBI agent," Brice scowled, knowing the system all too well.

"Exactly!" Tori exclaimed.

"And that's how Goliath ended up in a shelter. The relatives of the family didn't want him so off to the shelter he went," Brice surmised.

"That's what I believe happened, yes," Tori agreed.

"So were you ever able to give his family closure, like you did for my mom?" Brice wondered.

"Not yet, but that's on our list of things to do, isn't it Goliath?" Tori promised.

"*Yes!*" Goliath barked.

"So that's Goliath's story," Tori advised. "Like I said, Remy knew we would be good for one another in more ways than one. He's not just a dog to us; he's family."

"I get that," Brice agreed. "We used to have dogs growing up, and my parents always treated them like family too. When I'm more settled in my life, I would like to have dogs again. There's plenty of room to have several of them here. Of course, they won't be nearly as awesome as Goliath here," Brice chuckled, patting Goliath gently on the back. "Does he also communicate with Gemma and RJ like he does with you?"

"No, Goliath only communicates with me," Tori replied. "Gemma and RJ have already begun showing a whole new array of abilities no daughters of Remiel have ever had, so I'm not sure if there's a reason why they can't hear Goliath or not. I guess Goliath and I are old school. Gemma and RJ seem to be a new breed of guardian."

"So kind of like a changing of the guard," Brice suggested. "Which is why they don't need the statue or the amulet to use their powers?"

"I think so, yes," Tori admitted.

"Why is that? Did something happen when you were pregnant with them?" Brice asked.

Looking over at the twins, Tori could tell by their expressions they too were curious what she thought. "I believe it all started the day the twins were born," she admitted. "We had some signs of their emerging power when I was pregnant, but I feel it was their birth that set everything in motion."

"Which was also the day you were shot," Brice recalled. "Did the shooting cause you to go into labor?"

Blinking in surprise, Tori replied, "Yes, that's exactly what happened. How did you know? Did Reagan tell you?"

"No, she didn't. It just seemed logical that everything seemed to intersect on that same day," Brice shrugged.

"Like the Bermuda triangle," Piper snorted humorously. "That was such a horrible, wonderful day."

"Agreed," Reagan shuddered as the memory of Tori and Goliath falling to the ground after they were shot came back to her.

"Do you mind my asking what happened?" Brice asked Tori hesitantly. "I don't want to bring up a bunch of bad memories, but I'm really curious about the new abilities you mentioned the twins have, especially after seeing what RJ did to my fountain!"

"I guess I owe you that much," Tori inclined her head in agreement. "When we were shot," Tori paused, looking briefly at Goliath, "The bullet passed through Goliath into my shoulder right here," pointing to the scar near her shoulder. "Between the trauma of being shot and thinking Goliath was dead, I went into shock, my water broke, and I went into labor. The priority obviously was treating the gunshot wound then after I was stable I was given a drug to induce labor."

Hearing her voice start to tremble, Ben got up and walked over behind the bench where Tori was sitting and encouragingly placed his hands on her shoulders.

Smiling up at him appreciatively, she continued. "Labor was long and difficult, and I was weak from surgery, so it got a little scary during the actual delivery."

"A little scary?" Piper exclaimed. "I've never been so terrified in all my life!"

"Same," Ben murmured, squeezing Tori's shoulders gently.

"Okay so maybe it was a lot scary," Tori admitted with a small smile. "Gemma was born first; then my blood pressure dropped, and I began to lose consciousness. I was afraid we were going to lose RJ, so when I opened my eyes, I saw Gemma staring at me intently as if she was telling me to wake up, give her back her brother and finish what I started!"

"That's what I was saying to you, Mama," Gemma whispered with tear filled eyes.

In an unusual display of affection around strangers, RJ reached over and grabbed Gemma's hand tightly.

Brushing her tears away, Tori said, "I whispered to Gemma that I needed her help, so she and I both placed our hands on the amulet and one final push later, RJ was born."

"You forgot about the brilliant white light exploding out of the amulet that filled the entire room," Piper noted calmly. "She always forgets that part!"

"What was the brilliant white light?" Brice asked.

"I believe it was the combined power of all the daughters of Remiel transferring some of their power directly into Gemma and RJ," Tori admitted. "That's why I believe they don't need either the statue or the amulet to use their abilities. Some of their power is now part of Gemma and RJ's DNA."

"So what does that mean with regards to the legacy of the Remiel children?" Brice asked.

"I have no idea," Tori replied. "That remains a mystery to us all."

Chapter 33

"That's quite a testimony Mrs. Wells gave you, Agent Chase," Agent Hunter's voice emitted through the speaker on Logan's laptop. "We now have a witness who could corroborate the fact that Alexander Wells killed Grant Albertson."

"But we still don't know if it was pre-meditative or not," Ben pointed out.

"Good point, Ben. And I agree, that is excellent work on Agent Chase's part. However Mrs. Wells is still legally married to Alexander Wells which would prevent any of that testimony from being able to be used in court," Riley reminded everyone.

"I know," Logan sighed.

Picking up on the sound of Logan's frustration through the speaker, Tori said, "I think the more important thing we should focus on is the fact that Logan seems to have her trust now, which is a good thing. You've done a great job building that level of rapport with her, so she felt comfortable sharing her story, Logan."

"Thanks, Tori," Logan replied. "That stellar story you came up with of Jade, my ex-girlfriend, did the trick. She bought it hook line and sinker. You should write romance novels based on the reaction I got from that story."

Tori laughed and admitted, "Like I have time for that!"

"Well, as I said, excellent work, Agent Chase," Agent Hunter advised. "As always, keep us apprised of new details as they come up."

"Will do, sir," Logan agreed.

"Now that we're all back from our few days off, I hope everyone is recharged and ready to focus on our case," Agent Hunter announced. "Agent Cooper, I understand you and Agent Nichols obtained physical evidence tied to what may have been an unsolved murder. I trust you've gathered as many details as you could and passed that information along to the authorities?"

Tori nodded and replied, "Yes, sir. The details around the murder of Rose Corbin have been provided. We've already received word back that it was enough to open an investigation into the man who we believe committed the murder."

"Excellent, nice work as always," Agent Hunter praised. "Where are we on the search of men fitting our profile obtaining prescriptions of Quetiapine from VA hospitals?"

Suddenly Logan heard a soft knock at his door, and Scout began to bark. "Shh, Scout, quiet!" he whispered fiercely.

"Agent Chase, is everything all right?" Agent Hunter's asked, his voice carrying across the apartment.

Taking a quick peek out the peephole in his door, Logan was surprised to see Rebecca standing on the other side waiting. Quickly returning to the phone, Logan whispered into the microphone, "Sorry, sir, Rebecca is at my door, I'm going to have to hang up."

"Very well, Agent Chase, we'll catch up with you next week," Agent Hunter replied.

"Thank you, sir," Logan whispered, ending the call.

Quickly changing the display on his screen to the developer code screen Tori created for him, Logan walked over and opened the door. "Well, hi! This is a nice surprise!" he greeted Rebecca warmly while Scout danced around her feet happily.

"Hi! I'm sorry for showing up unannounced, is this a bad time? I thought I heard you talking to someone," Rebecca asked uncertainly.

"No, this is fine, come on in! I was just finishing up with a client, so your timing is fine. What do you have there?" Logan asked, noticing a large covered dish in Rebecca's hands.

Slightly embarrassed, Rebecca shrugged and said, "I decided to try out a new recipe, but it made more than I planned for. I remembered what you said about how it's not fun cooking for one so I was wondering if you would like to share it with me?"

"You brought me dinner?" Logan exclaimed, surprised. "That was so nice of you! Of course, I would love to share it with you! I haven't had dinner yet, so this is perfect. Come on in! What did you make?"

"It's a Vietnamese Pork and Noodle Salad. I was watching a cooking show a couple of weeks ago, and the guest chef made it. It looked really good, and I've had a craving for it since so I decided to try my hand at making it myself," Rebecca admitted. "I hope you like Vietnamese food."

"Are you kidding me? I love Vietnamese food! Now I'm intrigued. Here let me take that. Do we need to do anything with it?" Logan asked.

"No it's ready to eat whenever we're ready," Rebecca replied, pleased with Logan's willingness to try it. "Hi, Scout! How are you today, sweet boy?" she greeted the dog, squatting down to pet him.

"As luck would have it, I have a chilled bottle of Riesling which would go perfectly with this dish. Would you like a glass?" Logan offered.

"That would be nice, thank you," Rebecca replied, noticing the furnishings Logan had chosen were very similar to what she had in her apartment. *"That's funny. This looks just like my furniture. I wonder if he's renting his furniture too?"* she thought.

As he poured the wine, Logan watched Rebecca while her eyes traveled around his apartment. "So, did you do anything interesting today, other than experiment in your kitchen?"

Glancing at his computer screen, Rebecca replied, "No, not really. I caught up on some laundry and ran a few errands, nothing too exciting. How about you? Did you work all day inside again?"

"Yeah, I had a deadline to meet for the client I was talking to earlier," Logan lied. "Here you go!" he added, handing her a glass of wine.

"Thank you," Rebecca smiled. "Cheers!"

"Cheers!" Logan replied, gently tapping his glass against hers.

Taking a sip of the wine, Rebecca smiled and admitted, "Umm, this is really good."

"Good, I'm glad you like it! I like a lighter white wine with spicy food. Speaking of which, would you like to go ahead and have dinner now?" Logan suggested.

"Sure! I'm ready whenever you are," Rebecca replied.

Handing her his glass, Logan said, "Perfect, if you wouldn't mind taking my glass to the table, I'll go get the plates, silverware, and your delicious meal."

"May I help you?" Rebecca asked, taking the glasses over to the table.

"Nope, make yourself comfortable, and I'll be right there," Logan announced, disappearing momentarily into the kitchen.

"Can I at least feed Scout for you?" she offered.

"He's already had his dinner so he should be fine for a little while until I need to take him outside," Logan replied, returning to arrange his and Rebecca's place settings at the table.

"You're so good about keeping him on a schedule," she praised. "Not a lot of people do that."

"Well, I was raised in a very structured household. Lunch was at noon; dinner was at six and bedtime was at ten. If you missed a meal, you heated up any leftovers yourself. I guess a lot of that rubbed off on me and I still live by the clock," Logan admitted.

"Structure is good," Rebecca agreed.

Sitting down at the table across from her, Logan lifted the cover off of the serving bowl and breathed in as the fragrant aromas released into the air. "Wow! That looks and smells wonderful!"

"Thanks!" she beamed happily. "I snitched a piece of the cooked pork while I was making it. It is really good."

"Tell me about the recipe!" Logan asked, serving her first.

"Okay, first you slice a pork tenderloin roast into thin rounds, then you marinate it for two hours in a mixture of lime juice, olive oil, fish sauce, soy sauce, garlic, ginger, and sugar," she instructed.

"Do you partially freeze the meat first, so it's easier to cut?" Logan asked, placing a portion of the salad on his plate. "That always works best for me."

"I do! That's funny we both do that," Rebecca grinned. "The dressing has a lot of the same ingredients as the marinade, primarily olive oil, sugar, lime juice, fish sauce, soy sauce, garlic, ginger, jalapeno, crushed red pepper and black pepper."

"Jalapeno, nice, I love it!" Logan exclaimed, his mouth beginning to water in anticipation.

"Then you cook the rice noodles, chop some cilantro, red onion, radishes, and carrots and toss everything together with the lettuce, spinach and garnish it with some chopped peanuts," she summarized.

"Sounds easy enough," he admitted, taking his first bite. "Oh man. This is really good! It doesn't taste like a salad at all. It's hearty!" he exclaimed, looking down at his plate in surprise.

"Thanks," she grinned. *"This is nice,"* she thought. *"Just like before, it's comfortable and relaxing when I'm with him. It's been so long since I've felt this way."*

Looking at his face and body language, he seemed relaxed too. She had been worried just showing up as she did was a bad idea. *"I wonder what he's been thinking about since we talked the other day,"* she worried. *"Does he still feel the same about me knowing about my past?"*

Glancing up and catching her watching him, Logan paused, mid-bite and asked, "Is everything okay?"

"Fine!" she quickly replied, looking down at her plate.

"She's acting a little nervous," he thought, watching her. *"I hope everything is okay. Maybe she's been thinking about what we talked about on our hike. Maybe my story wasn't convincing enough! What if she's on to me? How do I ask without sounding obvious?"*

"Can I ask you a question?" they both said at the same time.

Laughing, Logan offered, "You go first."

"Thanks," she murmured anxiously. "Um, I've been thinking about what we talked about the day we went hiking."

"Here it comes," he warned himself. "Okay," he encouraged.

"We both have some baggage from our prior relationships, mine being the whole running away from my husband and all that," her voice trailed off nervously.

Reaching across the table, Logan took Rebecca's hand in his and asked, "What is it you want to know, Rebecca?"

Exhaling a shuddered breath, she looked into his eyes and asked, "Are you disappointed in me now that you know? I realize I could have handled that whole situation better than I did, but has it changed how you see me? It's been so long since I was able to trust someone enough to tell you the things I did so, please tell me honestly how you feel."

"Do you still love him?" Logan asked her.

"Not anymore, no," Rebecca admitted. "Not after what he did. He's not the man I thought I knew."

"Neither am I," Logan thought, wishing he could tell her the truth. *"This is all part of the plan, Logan. You knew going into this someone could get hurt. It's too late to walk away now."* Gazing intently into her eyes, Logan said, "Then nothing that you told me has changed how I feel about you."

"Really?" she smiled, relieved.

"Really, really," he nodded.

~~~~~~~~~~

After dinner was over, Logan carried the dishes into the kitchen and Rebecca covered the remaining salad and placed the bowl in the refrigerator. Like most apartments, the small galley kitchen was barely big enough for two people, much less one so as Rebecca turned away from the fridge; she ran directly into Logan as he turned away from the sink.

"Careful!" he laughed, grabbing her arms to keep them from colliding.

"Oh, sorry!" she laughed with him, holding on to his arms to regain her balance.

Locking eyes, the awkwardness dissolved as they stood motionless holding on to one another. Not used to having her stand this close to him, Logan could feel the toned muscles in her arms beneath his fingers and the heat radiating from her body. His pulse quickened as the delicate smell of her perfume lured him closer, teasing him into identifying the scent along the curve of her neck. He wasn't exactly sure what set off the chain of events that followed, or who kissed who first, all he knew was suddenly he had the taste of the wine from her lips on his tongue and the feeling of her body pressed up against his. It was a desperate, passionate kiss between two lonely people unwilling and unable to be apart a moment longer.

Pushing her forward against the counter, Logan ran his hands down to Rebecca's hips and lifted her up to the countertop. Willingly parting her legs for him, he pressed his body against hers, moaning deep in his throat when she wrapped her legs around him, pressing him more firmly against her. He didn't care that what he was doing was wrong, or how much trouble he would be in with Agent Hunter afterward, all he knew is he wanted, no needed, to feel her skin against his. Pushing all logic willfully from his mind, he lifted her lithe body off the counter and carried her into his bedroom.

~~~~~~~~~~~

Logan squeezed his eyes tightly shut as the first rays of morning sun filtered in through the window blinds onto the bed. Moving his head until the light disappeared he opened his eyes and was quickly greeted by a wet tongue across his mouth.

"Scout, no," Logan grumbled, wiping the back of his hand over his mouth. Lifting his head up, he saw that during the night, Scout had crawled into bed, wormed his way in between Logan and Rebecca and stretched out between them.

Logan grinned, seeing Rebecca's arm draped over Scout's body, spooning him like a large stuffed animal. Gently nuzzling Logan's cheek with his cold, wet nose, Scout gave Logan a look of intense struggle which Logan recognized as the signal Scout needed to relieve his bladder. "Okay, buddy, I hear you. Let's go outside," Logan whispered, trying to ease slowly out of bed, so he didn't wake Rebecca.

Not accustomed to having another sleeping companion, the mention of the word, 'outside' set Scout's mind in motion and he scrambled up from the bed, pulling the sheets with him as he jumped down to the floor.

"Scout!" Logan whispered fiercely.

Feeling the sudden exposure of the cool air against her naked body, Rebecca slowly opened her eyes. "Good morning," she murmured, stretching out her lean body like a cat.

Logan, who was in the process of pulling on his jeans, paused to admire the view, still in awe of how truly beautiful she was. As his eyes traveled up her body, he felt his arousal for her return. When their eyes met, he knew hers never left.

"Good morning. Sorry about that," Logan greeted her, leaning across the bed to kiss her on the lips. "I have to go take Scout outside. I'll be back in five minutes."

"I'll be here when you get back," she purred, pulling him back toward her for another kiss.

Reminding Logan of his mission, Scout barked from the entrance to the living room.

"Hold that thought," Logan whispered, grabbing his shirt from the pile of clothing on the floor. Rushing toward the front door, he said, "I heard you, buddy, hold on." Slipping his feet into his sneakers, Logan pocketed his cell phone and his apartment key, snapped Scout's leash on to his collar and headed outside.

While they walked the perimeter of the apartment complex lawn, Logan silently willed Scout into finding the perfect patch of grass to relieve his bladder, yet it seemed to elude him continually. Scout, on the other hand, seemed content to explore each new smell since the last time he visited.

Considering the possibility of forcing Scout back inside and trying again later, Logan felt the vibration of his cell phone in his pocket, indicating an incoming call. Pulling the phone from his pocket, Logan looked at the screen and saw it was Tori calling. *"Hmm answer it or let it go to voice-mail?"* he debated silently. "Ugh, you know she'll keep calling until you talk to her," he groaned, engaging the call. "Hey, Red! What up?"

"Hi, Logan!" Tori greeted him happily. "I've been thinking about you since you had to drop off the call yesterday. Is everything okay?"

"Y-yeah," Logan stammered, wondering why she seemed concerned. "I'm just outside with Scout trying to get him to go to the bathroom."

"So Rebecca's unannounced visit wasn't something bad?" Tori asked.

"Nope, everything's fine," Logan assured his friend. "She brought dinner over; that's all." Not getting an immediate response from Tori, he nervously asked, "What? It was just dinner."

Drawing in a surprised breath, Tori exclaimed, "It was more than just dinner, Logan! Did you two…" Not getting an immediate response from Logan, she exhaled a frustrated sigh, "Oh Logan. Are you in love with her?"

"I don't know. I haven't had time to think about that yet," he admitted quietly. "How did you know something happened?"

"I just had a feeling," she admitted.

"Please don't say anything to anyone yet, especially Piper or Ben," he begged. "This has all happened so fast, and I haven't had a chance to think about it really. Please, Tori."

"I won't say anything, I promise, that's your story to tell," Tori agreed. "I just don't want you to get hurt, Logan. She's a married woman who still hasn't told you the whole truth about who she is."

"Neither have I," Logan tried to argue.

"You know what I mean," Tori argued back.

Saying a silent prayer of thanks watching Scout, finally squat and pee, Logan said, "Look, I've got to go, Tor. Thanks for checking on me, I'm okay."

"All right, if you say so," Tori relented. "But if you need help, please promise me you'll call me, okay?"

"I will," Logan agreed. "I'll talk to you later."

"Okay, bye," Tori replied, ending the call.

Slipping his phone back in his pocket, he glanced up at his bedroom window, envisioning Rebecca stretched out naked on his bed.

Feeling his desire for her return, he looked down at Scout and began walking back toward the apartment. "Come on, Scout. Let's go spend some more time with our girl."

Chapter 34

"Quetiapine," Sheriff Ford scowled, tucking the phone receiver under his chin so he could enter a search on his computer. "What does that drug do? And how do you spell that?"

"Q-u-e-t-i-a-p-i-n-e," the pharmacist slowly spelled out on the other end of the call.

"Was that an 'n' like Nancy or a 'm' like macaroni?" Sheriff Ford asked.

"Nancy," the pharmacist replied. "The drug is mainly prescribed to people suffering PTSD. Since your guy is filling a prescription from a VA hospital that makes sense."

"What does the drug do specifically?" Sheriff Ford asked again.

"It decreases hallucinations, improves concentration, provides a better quality of sleep and can help prevent severe mood swings or decrease how often mood swings occur," the pharmacist advised.

"Yeah, I'm reading about it now," Sheriff Ford admitted, scrolling through the page on his screen. "Thanks, Chuck. I think I have what I need. I appreciate your help."

"Anytime, Sheriff, have a good day," the pharmacist replied.

"You too," the sheriff answered, ending the call.

"Okay, I've got a former Marine checking in regularly with the VA hospital in Parkersburg, using a drug to treat severe PTSD, which may or may not include hallucinations and severe mood swings. Could a mood swing trigger an act of arson?" Sheriff Ford began to reason in his head.

"His name and social security number check out, but I haven't been able to find a record of a Kentucky-based landscaping business under the name of Butler that went insolvent in the last ten years. At the same time, I can't overlook how much help he was putting out the fire and his willingness to stay afterward that night."

"Excuse me, Sheriff?" his deputy, Bill, interrupted, quietly from the open doorway of the sheriff's office.

Looking up, Sheriff Ford saw his colleague holding several copies of printed newspaper articles in his hands. "Are those the articles I asked for?" he hoped, reaching for them.

Stepping into the office, Bill handed the stack of papers to the sheriff and said, "Yes, sir. They're all the unsolved arson investigations in a five state area in the past ten years. It's not much, fortunately, or unfortunately depending on how you look at it."

"Good point," the sheriff admitted, glancing briefly at the headlines as he shuffled through them.

"Is there anything else I can get you?" Bill asked.

Glancing at the clock, the sheriff nodded and asked, "This will probably take me a while to get through. Would you mind calling over to the general store and ask Betty or Mae to send lunch over in about an hour?"

"Sure thing," his deputy replied. "I'll bring it in when it arrives."

"Thanks, Bill," Sheriff Ford replied, appreciatively. "Please close my door on your way out."

"Yes, sir," Bill agreed, pulling the door gently closed as he left the room.

Re-reading the notes he collected on Pierce Andrews thus far, Sheriff Ford continued to reason what he knew in his head. *"On the flip side, I have a second guy who I know very little about other than his name, social security number and a suspicious lack of response when Zeke tried to reach him about the fire. I need to know more about Mr. Andrews,"* he decided, opening a new browser page.

Typing in the name 'Pierce Andrews,' he executed his search and frowned when he saw the results. "Hmm, over ten thousand matches. I need to narrow that down somehow." Looking over at the stack of arson articles on the desk next to him, he entered 'arson' as an additional filter. "Just over six thousand matches. That's better but still too many," he frowned again.

On a whim, he changed his filter from 'arson' to 'fire,' and got a more reasonable list. "Three thousand matches, still too many." When he changed the filter again from 'fire' to 'house fire,' he got the match he was looking for.

Son Survives Suspicious House Fire that Kills Parents

"Well, I'll be damned," the sheriff whistled, clicking the hyperlink to the rest of the story. Scanning the article, he picked up his phone and dialed Bill's extension. "Bill, I do need one more thing, please. Would you also pull any articles you find for fires that were suspicious in nature yet not ruled as arson?"

"Yes, sir, same state pattern and dates as before?" Bill asked.

Looking back at the article pulled up on his screen, the sheriff replied, "Let's broaden the search a bit. Let's try the entire southern region of the United States for the past twenty years."

"That's going to pull back a lot of results, sir. Is there something, in particular, you're looking for?" Bill warned.

"Just let me know what you find, Bill," the sheriff replied.

"Yes, sir," Bill agreed.

~~~~~~~~~~

Later that evening as the clock struck midnight, Sheriff Ford sat back in his chair wearily and rubbed his hands across his dry, overused eyes. Reviewing his work for the day, he was convinced he now had five separate cases under suspicious circumstances he needed to focus on more closely.

The first case was a gas station explosion in Harrisonburg, Virginia with no deaths reported; next was an apartment complex fire in Pikeville, Kentucky with one death reported; the third was a residential water heater explosion killing a family of three, also in Pikeville, which the sheriff found too coincidental; the fourth was a warehouse fire in Wilkesboro, North Carolina with one death reported and finally the fifth was the forest fire in Ravenswood.

Unable to shake a feeling he got when he read through the details of the two cases in Pikeville, Kentucky, he decided to try his luck and call their local police department to see if anyone was still there he could talk to.

"This is the non-emergency line for the Pikeville Police Department, how may I help you?" a pleasant female voice on the other end of the line asked.

"Hello, this is Sheriff Jethrow Ford from the Ravenswood, West Virginia Sheriff's Department," he formally advised.

"Good evening, Sheriff. What can I do for you?" the woman asked.

"Is this dispatch?" he checked before explaining the reason for his call.

"Yes, sir, this is Officer Truman on dispatch. How may I help you?" she replied.

"Good evening, Officer Truman. I'm investigating a possible arson incident we recently experienced in Ravenswood. I was wondering if the Chief or one of his officers might be available to talk to me about two arson incidents your town experienced several years ago," the sheriff replied. "I realize it's very late so perhaps I could leave a message for someone to call me later on this morning?"

"One moment, Sheriff Ford," the dispatcher advised politely. "I believe the detective who worked both of those cases is still here this evening. Let me check. Hold please."

Before he could thank her, the sheriff heard the click of his call being placed on hold. *"What are the odds the very person I want to talk to is still there at this hour? Please still be there,"* he prayed silently.

"This is Detective Drew Daniels, how may I help you?" a male voice returned to the line.

"Good evening, Detective. This is Sheriff Jethrow Ford from the Ravenswood, West Virginia Sheriff's Department," the sheriff replied.

"What's keeping you in the office at this late hour, Sheriff?" Detective Daniels asked good-naturedly.

"Well, I'm investigating a possible arson incident we recently experience here in Ravenswood," the sheriff admitted.

"I'm very sorry to hear that, Sheriff. How is your fire connected to Pikeville?" Detective Daniels asked curiously.

"It's not so much a 'how' as it is a 'who,' Detective," Sheriff Ford replied.

"I'm sorry, I'm not following you, sir," Detective Daniels readily admitted.

Chuckling lightly, the sheriff admitted, "I'm sorry Detective, it's been a long day. I understand from Officer Truman that you were the investigating detective on two arson cases in Pikeville several years ago. I believe our cases could be related to the same man."

Suddenly feeling goose bumps rise along both of his arms, Detective Daniels swallowed hard and sat down in the chair beside him. "Okay, now you've got my attention," Detective Daniels advised. "I've been waiting a long time for that scumbag to slip up so he can be put behind bars. What is it you need, Sheriff?"

Surprised by the vehemence in the detective's voice, Sheriff Ford replied, "You seem to know already who I'm talking about."

"If you're about to tell me your suspects name is Pierce Andrews, then yes, I already know," the detective growled, angrily.

Feeling a growing uneasiness inside him, Sheriff Ford admitted, "As a matter of fact, that is the name of the man in question. He's one of the suspects in our investigation, and I spent the better part of the day researching suspicious fires in our extended area to see if Mr. Andrews was ever a suspect in other fires. I was surprised to find two cases in your town within weeks of one another, both with fatalities. Mr. Andrews was a suspect in one of the cases. Were the victims related? What can you tell me about them?"

"So you know about the details for both Gretchen Mallory's case as well as the Cutler family?" Detective Daniels asked, warily.

Running his hand through his hair disheveling it, Sheriff Ford replied, "I only know what I read through articles online and the case information you have uploaded in the online police files. What I'd like to know is your take on what you think happened."

"How far are you from Pikeville, Sheriff? It would be better to have this conversation face to face," the detective asked.

"We're only about two and a half hours away," Sheriff Ford advised.

"Would you be willing to come out here tomorrow so we can compare theories?" Detective Daniels asked. "I would come to you but don't want to risk Andrew's seeing me and spooking him. Would you agree?"

Appreciating the detective's forethought, Sheriff Ford nodded and said, "I agree that would be risky having you come here. I don't mind heading out your way. It's been a while since I visited that part of Kentucky. What does your day look like later today?"

"Well, I was just about to head home and catch a few hours of sleep. It sounds like you could use some too. How about we plan for three o'clock here at the station?" Detective Daniels offered.

"That will work for me," Sheriff Ford agreed, preparing to hang up the phone.

"Oh, hang on, I almost forgot. There's one other person we should have join us for this discussion. It's an FBI agent who I've spoken with a few times regarding the Cutler family murder. She's been trying to work the case from her angle as well. Would you mind if I call her and see if she's available?" Detective Daniels asked.

"An FBI agent," Sheriff Ford paused, caught slightly off guard. "Well, I guess if Mr. Andrews is our man, his crimes have crossed state lines which would make it jurisdictional for the FBI. Sure, go ahead and see if she's available."

"Great, I do think having her join us would be beneficial. Like I said, she's got as much time invested in this as I do. Having another branch of law enforcement helping us would be good here," Detective Daniels admitted.

"I'll take your word for it," Sheriff Ford agreed. "See you at three o'clock."

"Great. Looking forward to meeting you, Sheriff," Detective Daniels advised.

"Likewise, Detective, goodbye," Sheriff Ford replied.

As he hung up the phone, Drew couldn't help but feel the anticipation building inside him, with the hope of finally being able to solve both cases which had plagued him for far too long.

Recalling Agent Cooper had left a voicemail for him earlier in the week that he forgot to return, he scrolled through the voicemail messages on his cell phone and pressed the redial button on Tori's message. Somewhat relieved, the call went to voicemail.

"Hi, Agent Cooper. This is Detective Daniels from the Pikeville Police Department. I'm sorry I forgot to call you back. It's been a little crazy this week. Listen, we may have some new information in the Cutler family case so when you get this message would you give me a call? Actually, I'm about to go home and try and catch a few hours of sleep before I have to come back so maybe call me later this morning about nine o'clock? I look forward to hearing from you."

Chapter 35

Mesmerized by the beautiful waves of orange, yellow and white dancing in between the pieces of burning wood, Tori felt the tension in her body relax, enjoying the rare opportunity to sit outside by the fire pit and clear her mind. As she mentally filed conversations, observations and random moments away, one thing remained in question that she hadn't been able to reason out in her head, the admission from Remy that the twins didn't need the statue or the amulet to use their abilities.

"What does that mean for my sisters inside the stone?" she worried. *"Who will take care of them after I'm gone? Who will release them and finally give them peace? Will they still be able to communicate with Gemma and RJ without me?"*

Gently cradling the amulet in her hand, she closed her eyes and called out to her eldest sister. *"Elsbet, are you there?"*

"I'm here, Tori," she heard Elsbet reply. "Open your eyes."

When Tori opened her eyes, she found herself standing beside Elsbet in the large white room. Embracing Elsbet in a warm hug, Tori greeted her fondly. "It's so good to see you!"

"It's good to see you too," Elsbet smiled, returning the embrace. "You should visit us more often!"

"I know, I need to be better about that," Tori admitted. Glancing around her she asked, "How do you exist in this white cloudy mist all the time? Don't you get bored not being able to see any colors?"

Elsbet laughed lightly and replied, "I was wondering when you were going to ask that question! It only looks like that to you. Our sisters and I see beautiful green trees, colorful flowers and gardens, and all sorts of birds and wildlife."

Tori's eyes widened in surprise, and she exclaimed, "Are you serious? Why can't I see all of that?"

"You can't see it because you still exist on your earthly plane, we don't," Elsbet advised.

"Well, that's just crazy!" Tori declared, unable to imagine seeing any of those things Elsbet described. "So you can see and hear birds singing right now?"

Glancing above her head, Elsbet smiled and nodded. "Yes."

"There are so many things I still don't understand about our existence," Tori sighed.

"You didn't come here to talk about the mist. What's on your mind?" Elsbet asked, knowing Tori's visits weren't usually very long.

"I'm worried about the twins not needing the statue or the amulet to use their abilities. Remy hasn't really told me much. Do you know why or what that means?" Tori asked.

"It's a good thing they can function on their own, don't you think? Why are you worried?" Elsbet asked.

"I'm not so much worried about the twins I'm worried about what that means for you and the others!" Tori explained. "If the twins don't need you, who will take care of you all when I'm gone? Who will become the rightful owner of the Remiel legacy?" Tori fretted.

Elsbet smiled at Tori and touched her arm reassuringly. "None of us knows what will happen, Tori. For reasons that only God understands, He doesn't want us to know. We have to trust that everything is in His control."

"So you're not even the slightest bit worried? What if you all go back to living in the amulet without having contact with anyone anymore? Doesn't that scare you?" Tori asked with concern.

Shaking her head slowly, Elsbet smiled again and admitted, "No, not even in the slightest. Remember none of this is in our control it's all up to God. Just focus on what we can do now while we're all still together. Worrying about it only distracts you from where your mind should be which is always looking up toward heaven."

"There you go sounding like a greeting card verse again," Tori grinned, unwillingly.

"You know I still don't get that joke no matter how many times you explain it to me," Elsbet frowned.

"Yeah, I know, you've told me," Tori noted, rolling her eyes.

"Is there anything else on your mind?" Elsbet asked.

Tori hesitated, not sure how Elsbet would react to her question. "You've mentioned before that you can see and hear everything that goes on around me. Does that include the conversations I have with Luc?"

"Yes," Elsbet readily admitted.

"So you know that we've formed a sort of....," Tori paused, knowing 'friendship' wasn't the word she meant but that's the only word that came to mind.

Seeming to understand her hesitation, Elsbet suggested, "A mutual respect for one another?"

Grimacing at the thought, Tori shrugged and admitted, "I honestly have no idea what would be the proper response there. I'm not sure respect is the right word either."

"I understand the meaning, what's your question?" Elsbet prompted gently.

"Symbiosis!" Tori declared victoriously. "That's the word I was looking for!"

Nodding in approval, Elsbet conceded and replied, "Agreed, that one is much better."

Tori laughed and said, "Sorry! I started going off on one of my tangents. Anyway, my question is when you were in possession of the statue and the amulet, did you have a similar relationship with Luc as he and I do?"

"It was much the same as it was different," Elsbet replied. "There was more mystery around Lucifer at the time when I was alive on earth. I'm not sure he felt as comfortable there as he does now. The two of you have a level of respect for one another, whether you want to admit to it or not. He would cringe to hear me say this but I actually think he enjoys your company. I think he misses you when you don't see him which is usually when he tends to act out."

Blinking in surprise, Tori asked, "So basically what you're saying is when Luc acts out, it's like a toddler having a temper tantrum?"

"Pretty much," Elsbet shrugged. "Can you think of a better description?"

Chuckling at the image in her mind Tori shook her head and said, "No, I think yours is perfect. Thanks. I'm going to recall that visual in my head every time from now on."

"Oh, he would hate it if he knew what we say about him," Elsbet laughed.

"Yes, he would," Tori agreed.

"Did that answer your question?" Elsbet hoped.

"Yes, thank you. I was just curious, and you're the only person who would understand," Tori confessed.

"I do understand," Elsbet assured her friend. "Is there anything else on your mind?"

"Not that you can help with no, but thanks for asking. I guess that's it. It really was good to see you again. Would you mind telling the others I said hello?" Tori asked, embracing Elsbet again.

"I will. Until next time," Elsbet agreed.

"Until next time," Tori replied closing her eyes. Suddenly a pocket of steam within one of the piece of wood on the fire erupted, making a loud popping sound. "Oh!" she jumped, caught off guard.

Immediately Goliath sat up and looked at her with eyes filled with concern. *"Is Tori okay?"* she heard him ask.

Gently rubbing his ears, Tori smiled and assured him, "I'm okay, thank you, Goliath. The popping sound from the fire startled me that's all."

"Hey, you had a call a few minutes ago. Here's your phone." Ben informed as he joined her. "And I saw you were running low, so I brought out the bottle," he added, refilling her wine glass as he sat in the chair beside her.

"That was sweet, thanks!" Tori smiled, setting her glass down on the table. Swiping the screen on the phone, she saw it was a call from Detective Daniels.

"Was it a call you were waiting for?" Ben asked.

"Yes, it's from Detective Daniels in Pikeville. Remember, the detective who's been working the Mallory and Cutler deaths?" Tori asked.

"Yeah, I remember him," Ben nodded.

"I left him a message yesterday so I could bring him up to speed on what we found after the exhumation of Gretchen Mallory's body," Tori replied. "I'll call him back in the morning," she dismissed, setting the phone down.

"He called after midnight, maybe he's still at the office," Ben suggested.

"He's called me after midnight before. The guy's a night owl. I swear he never sleeps," Tori shrugged. "Besides, one more day won't change anything. We have a rare night of being alone without the kids, let's not ruin it!"

"Agreed," Ben grinned, tapping his wine glass on hers. "I don't know how you convinced your parents to take the kids back to Cheyenne for a few weeks, but I am so glad they did! Have you heard from them yet?"

Tori grinned and replied, "Mom called about a half hour ago. The kids are fine; they're having a blast with their Aunt Aubrey, and most importantly, they're behaving themselves."

"What will be most impressive is if RJ can help your dad with all that water from the broken sprinkler pipe. It's a good thing their neighbor saw the water pooling in the backyard and called your dad. That could have caused some serious foundation issues," Ben noted.

"I agree. We need to meet some neighbors like that," Tori replied then laughed when she thought about it more. "On second thought, having neighbors see some of the things that go on around here probably wouldn't be a very good idea."

"I know, right?" Ben chuckled. "So what else is going on? How was your day?"

"Well, I heard from Agent Sullivan earlier today," Tori admitted.

"You did? How's he doing? Is he still in Italy?" Ben asked.

"Yes, he and his colleague are still researching the missing part of that parchment he showed me. He said he's getting fat with all the pasta he's eating, but otherwise, he sounded good," Tori smiled.

Knowing his wife too well, Ben asked, "That's good. How envious were you hearing him talk about all that authentic Italian food?"

"SO jealous!" Tori laughed, rolling her eyes dramatically. "I was totally craving carbs afterward. What about you? When do you leave for DC tomorrow?"

"My deposition is at eleven, so I have to catch the early flight at seven tomorrow morning," Ben grimaced. "I'm sorry how that worked out. I didn't have a choice on this one. They called me in as a material witness."

"I know," Tori frowned. "It will only be one overnight, so we'll spend more time together this weekend."

"Thanks for always understanding. Are you sure you're going to be okay by yourself?" Ben worried.

"Woof!" Goliath objected firmly.

Reaching down to pet Goliath, Ben laughed and said, "I'm sorry, Goliath. I promise I didn't forget about you, buddy."

"Goliath and I will be fine," Tori advised calmly.

"Well, you know who better be on his best behavior, that's all I'm saying," Ben warned.

"I might just surprise Luc and pay him a visit," Tori shrugged, thinking back on her conversation with Elsbet.

"Really?" Ben asked in surprise. "Isn't that like poking a bear with a stick?"

"I don't know. Elsbet and I have a theory I might decide to test out. We'll see," Tori shrugged, taking a sip of her wine.

"Well I have a theory of my own that I wanted to test out on you tonight," Ben suggested, wiggling his eyebrows at her.

Narrowing her eyes back at him, she coyly asked, "You do, do you? And what theory would that be?"

Getting up from his chair, Ben placed the lid on the fire pit. Then he turned to face her and held his hand out to help her from her chair. "Come inside the house with me, Madam, and I'll show you."

Smiling at how unbelievably cute she still thought he was after all these years; she took his hand. "Okay, buddy, let's see what you've got!" she agreed.

Chapter 36

Zander choked, covering his mouth with his arm as a pillar of hot, ash infused smoke billowed up from the charred remains of a large oak he was trying to extinguish. Glancing over at the other volunteers fighting the fire with him, he could see they too were beginning to struggle with the intense heat and limited visibility.

Wiping his stinging, bloodshot eyes with the back of his hands, he leaned against the handle of his shovel, feeling defeated and exhausted. Looking down, he noticed something shiny and reflective on the ground a few feet away. Curious, he walked over and reached down to clear the debris around it. When he turned the object over, he drew in a surprised breath, recognizing the silver lighter with the face of a wolf embossed on the front. "This is Pierce's lighter," he exclaimed in surprise.

Suddenly a voice filled with panic cried out behind him. *"Retreat, retreat, that tree is about to fall! Everybody get back!"*

Hypnotized by the fire reflecting off the silver image of the wolf's face, Zander stared at the eyes of the wolf, glowing like pools of molten lava. Unable to look away, a hauntingly familiar voice called out the same warning from another place in time where flames and devastation were all too familiar to him.

"*Retreat, retreat, the guy's wired! Come on, move, move, move,*" Corporal Davies cried out, backing away from the window of the vehicle stopped at the checkpoint. The sound of the explosion, followed by the screams of the men as the impact tore the limbs from their bodies, woke Zander from the horrific nightmare of his past, thrusting him into the present with a violent jolt.

Lying in the dark covered in sweat while his heart pounded in his chest, he felt a dull throbbing in his head as the sounds of the screams from his fallen comrades began to fade. "Not tonight," he moaned.

"*Why not tonight, dear boy?*" the voice in his head hissed.

Feeling his heart skip a beat, Zander held his breath, hoping his ears were playing tricks on him.

"*Hello? Is this thing on?*" Lucifer mocked Zander annoyingly. "*Testing, one, two…,*"

"I hear you, shut up," Zander growled rolling over in bed, not in the mood to play games with the devil tonight.

"*Aw, come on, Zander.*" Lucifer taunted. "*Haven't you missed me?*"

"No," Zander whispered, covering his ears with his hands.

"*Don't be silly, you know very well that won't work,*" Lucifer admonished with a sigh.

Convicted not to give in, Zander grabbed one of the pillows and placed it over his head.

"*Aww….are you having a rough night, buddy? Those bad dreams are a drag, aren't they?*" Lucifer pretended to pout. When Zander still refused to respond, Lucifer began to sing. *"Someday, when I'm awfully low, when the world is cold, I will feel a glow just thinking of you....."*

"ARGH! I said shut up!" Zander shouted, getting up from the bed and stomping toward the bathroom.

"Well there's no reason for you to be rude," Lucifer declared, watching Zander pick up the bottle containing his prescription. *"Uh, uh, uh, it's not time yet for that, remember? You need to wait until morning."*

"Screw that, I need to get rid of you now," Zander spat angrily. Popping the top off the pill container, he shook one of the tiny pills into the palm of his hand, shoved the pill into his mouth, turned the handle on the cold water faucet and scooped a palm full of water into his mouth. Forcing the pill down his throat, he braced his hands on the edge of the sink and closed his eyes, praying silently for the drug to take effect speedily.

"Geez, what is it with everyone? All I want to do is talk, and people keep ignoring me!" Lucifer alleged testily.

"Yeah, well you're not a very nice person to be around, think about that," Zander argued, feeling the lightheaded drowsiness of the drug starting to kick in. When he no longer heard any further commentary from Lucifer, Zander heaved a deep thankful sigh, shuffled his feet wearily back to bed, climbed under the covers and drifted off to sleep.

~~~~~~~~~~

The click of the alarm clock on the nightstand, followed by the sound of music, alerted Zander's subconscious morning had arrived, and it was time to get up. It took a few seconds for his brain to recognize the song on the radio, 'Runnin With The Devil' by Van Halen.

"Oh, you've got to be kidding me!" Zander groaned, quickly reaching over to turn off the music. Rolling onto his back, he lay motionless, waiting for Lucifer to come back with one of his snide comments. Hearing only the sound of birds singing outside his window and the thud of a door slamming somewhere in the complex nearby, Zander reluctantly decided the song choice must have been coincidental. Exhaling a relieved sigh, he stared at the yellowed, water-stained ceiling above him, thinking back to his dream from the night before.

"Would Pierce be dumb enough to leave something so easily recognizable at the scene of a crime like that?" Zander mused in his head. *"Maybe he didn't know he dropped it, maybe it fell out of his pocket,"* he further reasoned. *"You need to go back to the scene and look for it,"* he told himself firmly. *"What will you do with it if you find it?"* he pondered.

Glancing over at the clock, he barely had time to shower, grab a quick breakfast at the diner and still make it to work on time, so he decided he would have to find a reason to go out to the fire site during work hours. As he sat up to get out of bed, a slight wooziness in his head made him pause until his vision came back into focus.

"Well that's not good," he frowned, realizing the extra pill in his bloodstream was still pretty strong. He slowly stood, again having to wait a moment for the dizzy feeling to pass and walked into the bathroom to read the warning label on the pill container.

"Dizziness, headache, weakness and drowsiness," he read out loud. "Well, I guess there's nothing I can do about it now other than holding off from taking another pill until tonight. Some food in my stomach might help." Setting the container back on the shelf, he reached into the tub and turned on the hot water faucet, which he knew would take several minutes to deliver slightly more than room temperature water.

Quickly showering, shaving and brushing his teeth; Zander fingered a dollop of gel through his hair and went back to the bedroom to get dressed. Appreciating the convenience of a work uniform, he got dressed, made his bed, and picked up his phone, wallet, and keys from the table. Taking one final look around to make sure he hadn't forgotten anything, he locked the door behind him, reset the booby trap string above the doorframe to let him know if someone entered his room while he was gone, and headed for the diner on the other side of the parking lot.

"Good morning, Alex!" one of the waitresses greeted him as he came in.

"Good morning, Pearl," Zander nodded.

"Go ahead and pick a table. Do you want your usual today?" Pearl asked, already following Zander with a fresh pot of coffee.

"Yes, please," Zander replied.

"No problem, I'll have that out to you in a few minutes. Here's your coffee darlin'," Pearl drawled filling the cup.

"Thank you, Pearl," Zander smiled.

"Are you feeling okay today?" Pearl asked with concern. "You're eyes look a little bloodshot."

"Ah, allergies," Zander lied. "I'll be fine, thanks for asking."

"All right, if you say so. I'll go get your order in," Pearl replied walking away.

"Thanks," Zander called out after her. As he turned his head back toward his table, he saw Sheriff Ford a few tables over, watching him. "Morning, Sheriff!" Zander greeted.

"Mornin' Alex," the sheriff nodded in reply.

Focusing his attention forward, Zander took a sip of the steaming coffee and tried to appear as inconspicuous as possible.

A few minutes later, Pearl returned with a heaping plate of scrambled eggs, hash browns, bacon, and toast. "Here you are, Alex. Can I get you anything else?" she asked, setting the plate down in front of him.

"No, thanks, Pearl, this looks great as usual," Zander smiled.

"Well eat up. You don't want to be late for work," Pearl noted, pointing at the clock above the register.

"You're right, I don't," Zander agreed, picking up his fork and quickly shoveling a small mound of eggs into his mouth.

"I like to see a man enjoying a meal," Pearl announce to no one in particular as she returned to the counter.

Finding the food more satisfying than usual, Zander quickly finished his breakfast and took one final sip of the dark, soothing liquid. Then he pulled a ten dollar bill from his pocket and placed it beside the edge of his plate. Catching Pearl's attention as he walked out the door, he motioned that his money was on the table. "Thanks again, Pearl!"

"You're welcome, darlin'. See you tonight for dinner!" Pearl waved.

One left turn, five stoplights, and two right turns later, Zander parked beside the city parks and recreation maintenance building and went inside. As he about to clock in, he saw Zeke in one of the maintenance bays, struggling to move a large crate.

"Here, let me help you with that, boss," Zander quickly rushed forward, pushing on the other end. "Where do you want this?"

"Thanks, Butler," Zeke grunted as he pushed. "Against that wall there," he motioned with his head.

"There you go," Zander replied, sliding the wooden crate across the cement floor to the wall.

"Thanks," Zeke gruffly replied, annoyed he was no longer strong enough to have been able to move the crate on his own.

"What's in the crate?" Zander asked trying to read the lettering stamped on the side.

"I don't know, some statue the mayor decided he wanted in the center of town during next month's anniversary celebration," Zeke growled. "It's not enough that I have to get the flower beds replanted, the lamp posts repainted, potholes in the streets filled, and power wash the town hall; now I have to deal with a friggin' statue too!"

"We should be able to get everything ready in time, Zeke. What do you want me to work on today?" Zander offered.

"I'm going to put some of your former landscaping experience to good use and put you in charge of getting all the flower beds in town weeded and replanted. That also includes working with

Walter's team to hang the flower pots from the lamp posts once they've finished painting them. Do you think you can handle that?" Zeke challenged.

Zander envisioned what his tasks would entail and felt confident in his ability to wing it. *"How hard could it be?"* He thought to himself. "Absolutely," he nodded, accepting the challenge.

"Good. Go clock in and take the truck to maintenance building two. That's where you'll find all the equipment you'll need. The mayor's wife already picked out the flowers she wants so you'll also need to contact Petals Nursery on Highway K to arrange for delivery once you've prepared the beds. Any questions?"

"Nope," Zander shook his head assuredly, pleased that maintenance building two would take him near the point of origin of the fire. "I'll get to work! Am I working alone or is Pierce doing this with me?"

"You get to fly this one solo," Zeke advised. "I put Andrews on Walter's team this week. Evans is on vacation, so I needed to move a few folks around."

"Got it," Zander replied, thrilled that he didn't have to work with Pierce for a few days.

Sliding his timecard into the slot, he waited for the machine to register his time and then returned the card to his spot in the rack. Curious, he glanced at Pierce's card and noticed he hadn't clocked in yet. *"I wonder if that's contributing to Zeke's foul mood?"* he thought.

Not wanting to also contribute to his boss's unpleasant demeanor, Zander briskly walked over to the drive bay, plucked the keys for one of the trucks off the hook, climbed inside the vehicle and started it up. Frowning at the gas gauge, which was almost on empty, he shook his head, annoyed. *"Great, is it so hard to fill it back up when you return it?"* he silently cursed to whoever drove the truck last.

Carefully exiting the drive bay, he parked the truck beside the gas pump behind the building, unscrewed the cap from the tank on the truck and reached for the pump nozzle. Just as his fingers were about to close over the handle, he saw a light dusting of blue powder setting off an alarm in his head. Quickly drawing his hand back, he thought, *"Someone recently dusted this handle for prints."* Then another realization came to him. *"Your prints are in the system, dude and they're not going to match Alex Butler."*

"Crap," he muttered under his breath, grabbing the nozzle and shoving it into the opening of the tank. *"It's too late now they've already collected the prints and are probably running them through AFIS now. I wonder how long it will take until they find my prints in the system. Is that why Sheriff Ford was in the diner this morning? Is he watching me? Are they going to try and pin this arson crap on me?"*

Feeling his anxiety beginning to rise, he started taking long, drawn out breaths to prevent his pulse from rising. *"Okay, just calm down and think."* He told himself firmly. *"Until you have a better idea, right now you need to do your job and try not to do anything to bring attention to yourself. If they're looking at you, they're probably looking at Pierce too. Maybe he'll do something stupid and incriminate himself."* Suddenly feeling exposed, he looked around for signs of anyone watching him. *"Just because you can't see something, doesn't mean someone isn't watching,"* he warned himself.

Topping off the tank, he returned the handle to the pump, secured the gas cap and got back behind the wheel. "Okay, be cool," he told himself as he started the engine and began driving toward the maintenance building on the other side of the park.

As he approached the spot on the trail where he and Pierce cleared the path a few weeks earlier, he slowed the truck and frowned when he saw the blackened wound of charred wood and scarred earth amidst the green grass and unscathed trees surrounding it. *"This should never have happened,"* he thought angrily.

Parking off to the side of the trail, he turned off the ignition and got out of the truck. Placing his hands on his hips, he surveyed the area, trying to remember the location where he was standing in his dream. *"The voice yelled out behind me that the tree was going to fall so look for a large tree on the ground,"* he decided.

Spotting what looked like as the possible tree, he picked his way carefully through the debris, scanning the ground for anything reflective. Then he completed three perimeter circles, widening each one a few feet as he walked, scowling in frustration when he didn't find anything.

"Looking for anything in particular?" the sound of Sheriff Ford's voice called out behind him.

"Crap," Zander cursed in his head, *"so much for you not doing anything to make you look conspicuous!"*

Standing upright, Zander turned around slowly to face the sheriff, who was standing directly behind him. "Just clues as to what could have started the fire, sir," he lied.

"So you're a firefighter as well as an arson investigator now?" Sheriff Ford asked, rolling a wooden toothpick around in his mouth.

"No, sir, but I have had some experience looking for incendiary devices or detonating materials used to build them," Zander admitted, his eyes glancing down to watch the toothpick dance in the sheriff's mouth while he talked.

"Did you find anything like that?" the sheriff asked, catching Zander's gaze.

"No, sir," Zander replied as the toothpick flipped to the other side of the sheriff's mouth.

"I saw you at the gas pump filling the tank on the truck earlier," Sheriff Ford advised, playing a card from his hand.

"He knows you saw the powder," Zander quickly realized. "I saw the layer of dusting powder on the handle," he replied, playing one of his cards as well.

Grinning appreciatively, Sheriff chuckled quietly, removed the toothpick from his mouth and confessed, "I was wondering how you were going to play this. Am I going to have any surprises when the results of those prints come back?"

"I don't know. I'm sure there are a lot of prints on that handle," Zander shrugged.

"Including yours," Sheriff Ford advised.

"Yes, among others," Zander agreed.

"Any other set of prints in particular?" Sheriff Ford asked curiously.

"It's just a gut feeling I have. Nothing I can prove," Zander replied.

"If you have information about what happened here, now's your chance, son," the sheriff suggested, laying the trap.

Unsure which card to play next, Zander hesitated and thought. *"Anything you say from this point forward is going to either incriminate you or incriminate someone else. Are you ready to do that?"*

"What do you think happened here? Was this an accident?" Sheriff Ford continued to press.

Noticing that the sheriff intentionally didn't use the word arson in his question, Zander met the sheriff's eyes steadily and decided it was best for him to lay his cards out on the table. "I believe this was intentional, sir. I have my suspicions about who may have done it, but I don't have any proof to give you," Zander replied. "That's what I was looking for."

"That's interesting. Someone else is saying the same thing about you," Sheriff Ford advised, laying the bait.

Clenching his jaw tightly, Zander exhaled a deep breath trying to maintain his anger. "That is interesting," he agreed.

"You don't seem surprised," Sheriff Ford replied.

"Very little surprises me anymore, sir," Zander growled, clenching his fists.

"You're far too young to have such a cynical outlook on life like that," Sheriff Ford admitted, noticing Zander trying to maintain his anger. "When you're old like I am, then you can see the world through those rose colored glasses you have on."

"Age has no bearing on experience, sir," Zander replied respectfully. "I've experienced more in the few years I've lived than many do in an entire lifetime."

"Who does your gut tell you started this fire?" the sheriff bluntly asked.

"I would assume it's the same man who's pointing his finger at me, sir," Zander suggested.

"Meaning?" Sheriff Ford prompted.

"Pierce Andrews, sir," Zander stated firmly.

Nodding his head, Sheriff Ford sighed and admitted, "As of right now, he hasn't been able to give me any solid proof of your involvement. What makes you think Pierce is our guy?"

"Well for starters, he told me his parents died in a fire in their home when he was young. He gave the details of their death with such cold detachment it gave me the chills. And, he was completely fascinated with a large tree we cleared away from this area. He said it would fun to watch it burn. Next thing I know, this whole area is engulfed in flames," Zander exclaimed.

Already familiar with the story of Pierce's parent's deaths, Sheriff regarded Zander carefully, still unsure which of the two men was telling the truth. "Anything else?" he asked.

"Like I said, that's why I was here, I was looking for proof," Zander admitted. "I had a dream last night about the fire and in my dream I saw a silver lighter with the face of a wolf embossed on the front of it. The same day I was out here with Pierce clearing the path, he lit a cigarette using a lighter that looked just like it."

"So you saw Andrews with the lighter?" Sheriff Ford asked, mildly surprised since the arson investigator had found a silver lighter in the debris, matching that description, now tagged as evidence in the case.

"Yes sir," Zander confirmed.

Flicking the toothpick into the grass, Sheriff Ford looked up into the trees and then surveyed the ground around him. "It is a shame how much destruction happened here. We've never had a fire like this in Ravenswood before."

Zander stood silently watching the sheriff, waiting to see what he would say next.

Returning his gaze to Zander, the sheriff tipped his hat and said, "I appreciate what you've told me today, Alex. I would prefer you didn't repeat what you said to anyone else. I'm sure you've got a lot of work to do here, so I'll let you get back to it."

"Yes, sir, thank you, sir," Zander replied, immediately walking back in the direction of the truck.

Just as Zander started the ignition and was about to pull away, the sheriff called out, "Alex?"

"Yes, sir?" Zander asked.

"Don't leave town," Sheriff Ford advised.

Giving the sheriff a brief nod, Zander said, "Yes sir."

Pulling the truck back onto the road, Zander looked into the rearview mirror and noticed Sheriff Ford watching him as he drove away.

"Well that wasn't fun," he declared, exhaling a deep breath. "Damn Pierce," he muttered under his breath. "There's no way he's going to pin this on me. The question is how am I going to be able to prove he did it?"

Pondering the question as he drove, he heard the sound of his father's voice offering him his favorite piece of advice. *"Keep your friends close and your enemies closer, son. That way you always know what they're up to."*

Smiling at the memory, Zander nodded and replied, "Thanks, Dad. As usual, you're right. Since I've somehow become acquainted with the devil, I guess it's time to make friends with an arsonist too."

Chapter 37

Tori stepped across the marble threshold from the front hallway into a large open living area which was possibly the most beautifully decorated room she'd ever seen. *"Whoa! Now this is how I would decorate a home if I had a million dollars,"* she thought admiringly.

"This is crazy," she whispered, noticing four arched windows along the far end of the room overlooking a beautiful, lush back yard. Dividing the windows in two on either side was a massive stone fireplace with smooth rounded rocks cemented into a tall pillar that led all the way up to the ceiling.

"Why is it so cold in here?" she shivered, wishing the wood in the fireplace was lit.

Instantly flames sprang to life lighting the wood. "Well that was weird," she murmured, thinking, *"If wishes were horses, beggars would ride."* Checking her pockets, she sighed and added, "No million dollars. Oh well, beggars can't be choosers either."

As she walked, the sound of her heels on the hardwood floor echoed throughout the room, which she assumed would announce her presence to anyone nearby.

"Hello?" she called out quietly.

Not hearing a response, she walked toward an open doorway at the other end of the room, pausing to run her fingers along the top of a shiny black baby grand piano as she passed by. *"Not even a speck of dust in this place either,"* she noticed, glancing at her fingertips.

Reaching the doorway, she heard the faint sounds of Mozart's opera, 'The Marriage of Figaro.' Following the sound, as she got closer she heard someone humming along with the tune. When she reached the doorway to a large room at the end of the hall, she paused, briefly peeking through the entryway before going inside.

The room was slightly smaller than the formal living room, yet still beautifully decorated with rich tones and lush fabric on the furniture and windows. While she soaked in all the lavish décor, her gaze stopped on the one thing in the room which should have looked completely out of place, yet she had to admit, it didn't at all.

Lucifer was standing in front of a large wooden easel, holding a paint filled palette in one hand, mixing colors with a paintbrush in the other. He was humming happily along to the music, masterfully blending colors onto a large canvas. He still wore one of his typical fancy suits, however today, the suit coat and tie were draped over a chair, and the shirt sleeves were rolled up to his elbows.

"Well, I certainly wasn't expecting this," Tori admitted, mirthfully watching him. Taking a closer look at the canvas and the striking abstract design he was painting, she shook her head in disbelief, *"Yeah, I could never have even begun to imagine something like this coming from him."*

"So what do you think? Do you like it?" he asked, not turning around.

Surprised he knew she was there, Tori stepped into the room, crossed her arms over her chest and pretended to scrutinize the painting critically. "Hmmm..., I don't know. It seems a little light-hearted and whimsical, not like you at all."

Turning his head to look at her, he roguishly grinned, and asked, "How about now?"

Glancing at the image of the painting the canvas now showed Tori lying stretched out on a red velvet chaise lounge, completely naked.

Unfazed by his brazenness, she inclined her head to the side and narrowed her eyes contemplatively. "Hmm, closer but it still needs work."

Turning back to his masterpiece, he frowned and asked, "What? It's perfect! What's missing?"

"Uh, my clothes for starters," Tori pointed out dramatically.

"Oh well, art is a matter of interpretation, and the human form is a beautifully elegant subject matter. I find it interesting how obsessed humans are with covering their bodies. I think you look lovely au natural," he advised, setting the palette and brush down on a small table beside him. "Other than that, do you like my work?" he asked, turning to face her.

"Honestly yes, it's lovely. Although I liked the first picture you were painting much better," Tori admitted. Suddenly the picture changed back to what it was before. "Lovely!" she smiled.

"You seem surprised that I could create something beautiful," Luc noted, picking up a small white rag and wiping paint from his fingers.

"You know what, I was, and that was totally unfair of me. I just never envisioned you painting something so completely stunning while listening to one of Mozart's finest works," she admitted.

"What? Can't I have a hobby? I'm not a total barbarian, Tori," Luc chastised. "Besides, I've had many years of practice. My earlier works were much less civilized. I called it my dark, brooding, angry period. You wouldn't have liked it."

Deciding it was best not to ask him to elaborate what that meant, she asked, "So, is this where you live? I mean when you're not, uh bargaining for someone's soul?" she winced, not knowing how else to phrase her question.

"Why are you here?" he asked, ignoring her comment. "You never come to visit me in this civilized manner. Usually, you barge in furiously, accuse me of every wrong doing going on in your life and then disappear. What's up?"

Tori shrugged, innocently and replied, "Nothing's up. I just thought I would pay you a visit for a change. You know, have a normal conversation."

Eyeing the glowing amulet around her neck, he asked, "You're not one to shoot the breeze with the devil. Did she put you up to this?"

"Did who put me up to what?" Tori feigned ignorance.

Luc scowled at her, trying to remain patient. "If you're going to stand there and play games with me, you can leave. This home is my sanctuary. It's the one place I have to myself. I don't even know how you found it! No one has ever been here but me. So if you don't mind, I have better things to do with my time than to be subjected to your intrusive cruelty."

Tori blinked in surprise at his choice of words. "Subjected to my cruelty?" she exclaimed.

"That's what I said," he accused.

Realizing he was acting difficult intentionally to rile her, Tori exhaled a calming breath and asked, "When have I ever subjected you to any form of cruelty?"

"I can't think of an example off the top of my head," he admitted. "Invading my home comes pretty close."

"Invading your home? Oh no, that's not it. There's more than that going on here. Do you want to know what I think it is?" Tori asked.

"I can promise you I don't," Luc glared at her.

"Tough! I'm still going to tell you. I don't think you like someone showing up here unannounced because that's your thing, right? Catching someone off guard the way you do? Disturbing their lives no matter what they're doing?" Tori accused.

Raising his chin defiantly, Lucifer advised, "I believe it's time for you to go."

"Seriously? You don't like someone else's rules, so you quit?" Tori exclaimed in surprise. "Just like that, you're done?"

"Just like that," Luc replied firmly.

"Fine, I was trying to be friendly, but I guess that's not possible with you." Tori fumed.

"I can't imagine how that could surprise you. If it has then you truly don't know me at all," Lucifer quipped.

"I guess I don't," Tori admitted.

"Then I don't think there's anything more for us to discuss," he dismissed her, turning back to his painting.

"I agree. Goodbye, Luc," Tori replied, leaving him.

Opening her eyes, Tori lay in bed staring up at the ceiling, frustrated that her idea had backfired on her.

"Welcome back," Remy greeted her quietly.

Looking down at the end of the bed, she saw Remy sitting on the edge beside her, leaning against the footboard pedestal.

"What are you doing here?" she whispered fiercely, glancing beside her where Ben usually slept. "Where's Ben? Does he know you're here?"

"No, he doesn't. He's in the shower getting ready for his trip out to DC," Remy replied. "And I don't think the question of the hour should be what am I doing here; it should be what were you doing there? Why would you go there alone unprotected? Do you suddenly have a death wish you want to share with me? Even more importantly, how did you find him so easily? He's still masking himself from me. I can't see him I can only feel him when he's near you."

"Well, then next time I'll take you with me," Tori sighed in frustration. "It doesn't matter either way. He clearly didn't want me there, so I left."

"Answer my question. What were you doing there?" Remy insisted.

"I was just something me and Elsbet talked about recently. We thought maybe the reason Luc is always acting out is because he's lonely. I thought visiting him for a change would, I don't know, make him less hostile?" she shrugged.

"You need to stop trying to find common ground with him," Remy warned. "You're darn lucky he didn't lash out at you right there. Do you realize what would have happened if he had? There was no one with you to protect you!"

Objecting to Remy's comment, the amulet suddenly pulsed a brilliantly bright turquoise light.

"I believe someone disagrees with you," Tori noted defiantly.

Remy sighed in defeat, knowing the collective power and stubbornness of his daughters were powerful forces even he couldn't fight. "All right, Elsbet, I hear you." Looking intently into Tori's eyes he asked, "Just promise me you'll never do anything like that again, okay?"

"I promise I won't," Tori vowed.

"Thank you," Remy replied. Hearing the sound of the shower turn off, he added, "I guess that's my queue to leave. I'll check in on the twins to make sure they're still behaving for your folks. You stay out of trouble!"

"I'll try," Tori grinned, wryly.

"No, I mean it," Remy frowned. "That little visit to Luc's might set him off once he's had a chance to fume about it. Be carefully today and keep Goliath with you at all times!"

Tori glanced down at the spot on the floor beside the bed where Goliath lay sleeping and whispered, "I promise I will. Thanks, Remy."

Reaching out to take her hand in his, he patted it gently and smiled fondly at her. "You're welcome." A moment later he was gone.

"Oh, you're up! I'm sorry did I wake you?" Ben asked as he emerged from the bathroom, partially dressed and his hair still damp. "I was trying to be quiet."

"No, you didn't wake me, I just had a bad dream, and it woke me up," Tori partially lied.

Frowning in concern, Ben came over to sit beside her and asked, "I don't like the sound of that. Was it a dream I need to be worried about?"

"No, it's fine, I promise," she smiled leaning forward to kiss him on the lips. "Last night was fun."

"Yes, it was," he grinned wickedly, thinking about repeating some of it again now. Glancing at the clock on the nightstand, he grimaced and said, "Too bad we don't have time to do it again. I've got to get going."

Tori smiled and replied, "That's okay. We'll have all weekend together to ravish each other's bodies."

"Hmmm, I like the sound of that," he grinned, kissing her passionately on the lips. Reluctantly releasing her, he got up from the bed and began gathering his things. "Okay, I'm out of here. You have a good day and stay out of trouble."

"Geez! Why does everyone keep saying that to me?" she scowled.

"What? Who else said that to you recently?" Ben asked, pausing at the doorway.

"No one, it was just an expression," she lied. "Go! Have a good flight. Text me when you land."

"I will. I love you," Ben proclaimed.

"I love you too," she replied.

Once she heard the sound of the garage door closing, she lay back against the pillows, deliberating what she should do that day. *"Ben is on his way to DC, Agent Hunter, Piper, and Riley are checking out more of those pharmacy leads, and Reagan is helping the police catalog all the evidence from Brice's mother's murder. It looks like I have the day to myself today. I guess I could check the message from Detective Daniels,"* she mused, glancing over at her phone on the nightstand. Groaning as she reached over to pick it up, she unlocked the screen and pressed the voicemail icon to hear the message.

"Hi, Agent Cooper. This is Detective Daniels from the Pikeville Police Department. I'm sorry I forgot to call you back. It's been a little crazy this week. Listen, we may have some new information in the Cutler family case so when you get this message would you give me a call? Actually, I'm about to go home and try and catch a few hours of sleep before I have to come back so maybe call me later this morning about nine o'clock? I look forward to hearing from you."

"Huh. That's interesting. I wonder what new information the detective has found?" Tori puzzled. "It's still too early for me to call him," she continued to muse, glancing at the time on the clock.

Uncurling from his spot on the floor, Goliath stood up, stretched out his body and yawned. Then he looked at Tori, cocked his head to one side and began slowly wagging his tail. *"Goliath outside?"* she heard him ask politely.

Grinning at his adorable expression, Tori sat up and leaned over to rub his ears. Kissing him on the bridge of his nose, she got out of bed and replied, "I agree, that's the first thing I should do, Goliath. Come on!"

Obediently following her down the hallway to the living room, as soon as Tori opened the back patio door, he bounded through the open doorway toward the grass.

"Okay, coffee or shower?" she debated closing the door. Thinking it through, she decided, "Shower first, then coffee in a travel cup. It looks like Goliath and I are heading out to Pikeville today."

~~~~~~~~~

A few hours later, after having spoken to Detective Daniels and agreeing to talk with him and the sheriff from Ravenswood, Tori and Goliath were in a rental car leaving the Pike County Airport on their way into town. She had all four windows rolled down, taking advantage of the unexpectedly cool sunny day for the month of August so, in true Goliath fashion, he had his head out the back passenger window, grinning happily with his tongue hanging out, leaving a trail of saliva in their wake. Tori had the radio cranked up high, happily singing along with Little River Band's 'Take It Easy On Me' as she drove.

Just a few miles outside of Pikeville, without warning, Tori heard the shotgun blast noise of a tire blowout and felt the car start to veer off to the right. "Oh my gosh!" she exclaimed in surprise.

Remembering her father's lessons when she was a teenager learning to drive, she gently pressed the accelerator for a moment to regain control of the vehicle then held the steering wheel firmly and steered in a straight line, letting the car coast down to a slower speed. When she felt the speed was slow enough, she pulled over to the shoulder and parked. Resting her forehead against the steering wheel, she slowly released the death grip she had on it and exhaled a sigh of relief.

"Well that was terrifying," she exclaimed, sitting back against her seat. Looking back at Goliath, who now had his head back in the car, she asked, "Sorry about that big guy. Are you okay?"

"Goliath is fine," she heard him reply.

"Good boy," she smiled, reaching back to pet him.

Suddenly Goliath's head whipped around, and the hair on the back of his neck rose up. Growling lowly in his throat, he searched the area around him, sensing something.

"What's wrong, Goliath?" she asked, glancing up the road for something or someone to make him act like that.

"Lucifer is near," he warned her, growling again.

"He is huh? Well, that explains the tire. What a big baby he can be! It's a good thing we have a spare in the trunk," she sighed.

Then she heard the popping sound three more times and felt the car slowly drop lower to the ground. "Great," she fumed knowing Luc was retaliating from her visit earlier that morning.

"Unfortunately, I do not have four spare tires." Refusing to let Luc's antics upset her, she reached for her purse and pulled out her wallet. "What I do have, however, is excellent insurance and the ability to call for a tow truck."

As she was searching for her insurance card, Goliath barked, alerting her that someone was approaching. *"Stranger outside,"* he advised, sticking his head out the window behind her.

Looking into the side mirror outside her window, Tori saw a man in a law enforcement uniform exiting a vehicle now parked behind them. As he approached, she knew from the khaki hat and shirt and the olive green trousers that he was likely from the sheriff's department or highway patrol. She could also tell by the whitening of his hair and the slight paunch of his belly that he was probably somewhere in his mid to late sixties. Not yet knowing the situation she was in, she placed her wallet on her lap, and her hands on the steering wheel. Both her badge and her gun were in her purse on the passenger's seat.

"Good afternoon," he greeted her amicably. "It looks like your day isn't going so well."

"Good afternoon," she replied, looking up at him through the window. "No, it isn't."

Glancing down at the tires, he whistled lowly and said, "How on earth did you manage to blow three of your tires?"

Tori winced and replied, "Actually it's all four of them, and I have no idea. I just left the airport less than an hour ago, and this is a rental car. Obviously, someone didn't check the tires before they put it out on the lot."

"Are you sure you didn't drive over one of those spike guards they have at the exit of the lot?" he asked.

"No, sir, no spikes," Tori assured him. "I was just about to call a tow truck, so I'll make sure the vehicle gets removed from the road soon."

"I'm not as concerned with the car being on the road; you've pulled it safely out of the way. I don't like the thought of you stranded out here by yourself." Taking a quick look at Goliath, who still had his head out the window behind Tori, the man admitted, "Well, it looks like you have some protection with you. He's a beautiful dog, is he friendly?"

"Very," Tori smiled. "His name is Goliath."

The man smiled and held out his hand for Goliath to smell before petting him. "Well that's a perfect name for you, isn't that right, Goliath?"

"Man is good," Tori heard Goliath inform her as the man gently rubbed Goliath's ears.

"Tell you what," the man seemed to decide suddenly. "I'll give you and Goliath here a ride into town, and you can call for a tow truck on the way. Would you be willing to consider that? I wouldn't feel right leaving you both out here."

Considering Goliath had already given the man the green light, Tori decided it was safe to accept his offer. "Are you sure you're okay having him in your car? He tends to slobber."

"Of course I don't mind! I love dogs. Besides, considering some of the other things that happen in the back of my car a little dog slobber is nothing," the man grinned.

"Okay then, thank you. I accept. I just need a few minutes to gather my things and lock up the car." Tori replied.

"No problem. I'll meet you back at the squad car," the man replied.

"Okay," Tori agreed, quickly returning her wallet to her purse. "Head inside, Goliath," she instructed as she began pushing the buttons to close the windows.

Obediently pulling his head back in the car, Goliath waited for Tori to open his door, then remained close by her side as she removed her suitcase from the trunk, locked the car and began walking to the squad car.

"Here, let me take your bag for you," the man offered to take her suitcase to place it in his trunk.

"Thank you," Tori replied, noticing he had already lowered both back windows for Goliath. Opening the back passenger door, Tori instructed, "Goliath, inside."

Used to a bigger vehicle, Goliath clumsily climbed into the back seat, spun around once trying to find his footing and attempted to sit, most of his body overflowing off the edge of the seat. Fortunately, he was able to stick his head out the window, allowing him a bit more head room. *"Car too small for Goliath,"* she heard him complain.

"It will be okay for the short drive into town," she silently communicated back to him.

Hesitating before opening the passenger door, Tori looked at the man and asked, "Is it okay for me to sit in the front?"

"Well of course! You're not an armed criminal are you?" he teased, getting into the driver's seat.

Opening the door and sitting on the seat beside him, Tori replied, "A criminal no, but I do have to tell you that I am armed. I have a service weapon in my purse."

Slightly surprised, the man turned to her and asked, "A service weapon? Are you law enforcement?"

"FBI," Tori replied extending her hand to him. "My name is Agent Tori Cooper. I'm a consultant for the FBI Behavioral Analysis Unit Division Two out of DC."

"Well I'll be," the man chuckled shaking her hand. "I'm Sheriff Jethrow Ford from the Ravenswood West Virginia Sheriff's Department. I believe we have a meeting in less than an hour. It's very nice to meet you, Agent Cooper."

Laughing with him, Tori shook her head at the irony and replied, "It's very nice to meet you too, Sheriff Ford."

Starting the car, Sheriff Ford joked, "Well I guess I don't need to ask you where you're going, do I?"

"No, I guess you don't," Tori agreed.

Chapter 38

"I still can't get over the irony of your car breaking down and you being the one to rescue her," Detective Daniels exclaimed in disbelief as they all sat down together in the interrogation room. "Sorry again about the accommodations. We don't have a conference room, so this was the next best thing."

"No, it's fine," Tori grinned, setting her satchel on the floor beside her chair. "I've never been on this side of the table in an interrogation room before."

"Me either!" Sheriff Ford winked at her from the chair beside her.

"You're sure you have the arrangements taken care of for your rental car?" Detective Daniels asked.

"Yes, my insurance company has already arranged for a tow truck," Tori assured him. "There will be a replacement vehicle parked in your parking lot in the next couple of hours."

"Okay good," Detective Daniel's replied. "So, now that we've gotten to know each other a bit, how about we share what we know about Mr. Pierce Andrews?"

"Well, I think..," Tori started to reply when suddenly a knock on the door interrupted them.

"Hold that thought," Detective Daniels broke in, getting up to open the door.

"Hi, I'm sorry for the interruption. I brought you all some coffee and water," the receptionist announced, entering the room. Tori smiled when she noticed a bowl of water for Goliath included on the tray.

"That was very thoughtful of you, Joyce, thank you," Tori said, acknowledging the gesture.

"You're welcome Agent Cooper," the woman smiled, setting the bowl on the floor for Goliath.

"Goliath thirsty," Tori heard Goliath announce as he immediately came over to lap up some of the cool water.

"Thanks, Joyce," Detective Daniels nodded to the young woman as she closed the door behind her. "I'm sorry for the interruption."

"No, worries, I appreciate the hospitality," Tori assured him, reaching for one of the cups filled with coffee. As the aroma of the coffee beans drifted past her nose, she suddenly felt her stomach turn, and a wave of nausea wash over her. Swallowing carefully, she opted for one of the bottles of water instead. *"That incident with the tires blowing out earlier must still have me a little off balance,"* she thought to herself.

"What were you starting to say a moment ago, Agent Cooper?" Sheriff Ford asked.

Taking a quick sip of water to settle her stomach, she replied, "I was about to say that I thought it would be a good idea for Detective Daniels and me to share what we know first. Then Sheriff Ford can add what he's learned so we can talk through some of the holes in each other's stories."

Nodding in agreement, Sheriff Ford replied, "Okay, I think that sounds fine."

"Mine and Agent Cooper's investigations have become a bit intertwined over the past few years, so I'll start with the case related to Gretchen Mallory," Detective Daniels advised, handing Tori and Sheriff Ford copies of the police report. "Ms. Mallory was a thirty-year-old Caucasian woman who worked as an insurance adjuster at Wells Brother's Insurance here in Pikeville. She was employed there for just over ten years and was both liked and well respected by her fellow employees. The fire crew discovered Ms. Mallory's remains in her apartment, and the cause of death determined to be accidental due to smoke inhalation."

"Were there any other deaths from the fire?" Sheriff Ford asked.

"No, all of the other tenants were able to get out in time, Ms. Mallory was the only victim," Detective Daniel's advised. "The fire department was able to contain the fire, so the damage was limited to the floor above and directly below Ms. Mallory."

"Was Mr. Andrews immediately suspected of the fire or was that discovered later?" Sheriff Ford asked.

"Initial findings did not point to arson; the Fire Marshall found poorly conducted wiring in one of the laundry rooms which was thought to be the original cause of the fire," Detective Daniels replied. "It wasn't until one of the victims from our second case brought to our attention that the wiring appeared to have been tampered with."

"And that would be Mr. Samuel Cutler?" Sheriff Ford asked.

"Yes. Before we go there, I would like to add a few things that the FBI has found while investigating Ms. Mallory's case," Tori interjected. "If that's okay with you?" she asked Detective Daniels.

"Of course, please feel free to add any supplemental information you've found," Detective Daniels encouraged.

"Thank you," Tori replied reaching for her satchel. Retrieving a small stack of papers from inside, she handed both men a copy of the FBI report for Gretchen Mallory. "As Detective Daniel's said, the initial cause of the fire was thought to be accidental and Ms. Mallory's cause of death due to smoke inhalation. There was no official autopsy done by the coroner, so the body was released to the family for burial. Later, when the ruling was changed to arson, the police asked Ms. Mallory's parents for permission to exhume their daughter's body to confirm if her death was accidental, but they were too distraught at the time to even consider it."

"I remember that day. I felt horrible having to ask them. I understood why they didn't want to go through that," Detective Daniels reminisced sadly.

"Well, they've since changed their mind. I contacted Gretchen's parents a few weeks ago and explained that we have a possible person of interest we feel may be responsible for their daughter's death, and we needed to prove Gretchen's cause of death to arrest him," Tori replied.

"What? How in the world did you convince them?" Detective Daniels stared at her wide-eyed.

"I think they've had time to mourn for their daughter and the thought of having closure was something they were willing to consider," Tori suggested.

"When were you going to tell me about this? I thought we agreed we would keep each other apprised of new information if either of us had any!" Detective Daniels demanded angrily.

"Take a look at the date on the report," Tori pointed out calmly.

"Oh, two days ago," he noted, embarrassed. "Which is the day you tried to call me. I'm sorry for getting upset."

"No worries, Detective. Take a look at the second page under the coroner's finding," Tori urged excitedly.

Flipping the page, Detective Daniels read through the document and drew in a surprised breath when he read the true cause of death. "It was blunt force trauma? So it wasn't an accident?"

"Nope," Tori confirmed. "Sam Cutler was right. It wasn't an accident. Her lungs were clear of any smoke which means she was already dead when the fire started. There was a crack on the right orbital surface of the frontal bone on her skull and the right parietal bone, indicating she either hit her head on something or someone hit her with something hard enough to crack the bone. The location of the injury would have killed her instantly."

"Damn, all this time I had it wrong," Detective Daniels sighed, sitting back in his chair.

"It doesn't sound like you were the only one who had it wrong. I wouldn't be too hard on yourself, son," Sheriff Ford assured him. "Tell me what you know about Sam Cutler."

Handing out copies of the case for the Cutler family to Tori and Sheriff Ford, Detective Daniels admitted, "Sam Cutler was a nice guy. I was pretty upset when I heard about the accident that killed him and his family. He also worked at the same insurance company where Gretchen Mallory worked. They were friends. He was the one who asked me to reopen the investigation of Ms. Mallory's death because he suspected a guy at his office was involved."

"Was the guy Pierce Andrews?" Sheriff Ford asked.

"Yes. Mr. Cutler said that Mr. Andrews was an arson investigator who had only been with the agency less than a year. Apparently, he was a loner and didn't make much of an effort to get to know any of his colleagues. Mr. Cutler said he and Ms. Mallory became suspicious of Mr. Andrews when the fire chief mentioned Mr. Andrews seemed to always be one of the first people at the scene of several fires in the area. So Mr. Cutler and Ms. Mallory began to work together to monitor Mr. Andrews' movements."

"Did they tell anyone else they were doing that?" Sheriff Ford asked.

"Not that I'm aware of. The day after Ms. Mallory's death, Mr. Cutler came to my office, convinced Ms. Mallory's death was not accidental and the fire was caused by Mr. Andrews. I tried to explain that I needed proof to get my chief to consider pursuing Mr. Andrews as a suspect but Mr. Cutler didn't have anything concrete," Detective Daniels advised. "Next thing I know, we received a 9-1-1 call about a home explosion, killing three people, which turned out to be Sam Cutler and his family. Unfortunately like the fire in Ms. Mallory's building, the cause of the explosion was determined to be a faulty water heater and was ruled accidental."

"I have a bit more information to add here as well if you don't mind," Tori interrupted.

"Sure, what have you found?" Detective Daniels asked.

"We have a witness," Tori eluded, dividing the remaining sheets of paper in her hands between Detective Daniels and the sheriff.

"A witness, since when has there been a witness? We never had anyone step forward claiming they saw anything," Detective Daniel's insisted.

"Remember the house to the right of the Cutler home?" she asked. "I believe you talked to them that night, the Wynn family?"

"Vaguely," he agreed, flipping through his report. "Yes, here it is. The husband's name was Charles, the wife's name was Brenna and they had two kids, Matthew and Meagan."

Carefully reciting the story she and Agent Hunter fabricated for this discussion since the true witness was Goliath, but she couldn't tell anyone, Tori replied, "Well as it turns out, Matthew snuck out of the house that night to visit the Cutler's dog. Matthew saw a man dressed in dark clothing crawl out of the lower basement window a few minutes before the explosion. Which means the explosion wasn't an accident."

"Which means it was murder," Sheriff Ford murmured, sitting back in his chair, wondering if his town was in danger having Pierce Andrews there roaming free. "Was Matthew able to positively ID the man?"

Tori shook her head and admitted, "No, only that he saw a man come out the window and leave."

"Hang on," Detective Daniels exclaimed. "Why didn't Matthew tell anyone about seeing the man? How credible is his testimony?"

"Apparently he was afraid to tell what he saw because he wasn't supposed to leave the house at night. He was afraid of what his parents would do if they knew so he didn't tell anyone."

"Now that I think about it, I do remember seeing Matthew in the Cutler's backyard when we arrived. I think he was trying to comfort the dog who was barking frantically, trying to get out of the pen……"

his voice trailed off, wrapped up in the memory. Then he looked at Goliath with a curious expression and added, "As a matter of fact, the dog looked a lot like Goliath. He had the same coloring and was about the same size which is unusual because Goliath is a huge dog. How crazy is that to have two dogs so identical?"

"*He knows,*" Tori heard Goliath warn.

"*He's not sure. Just relax,*" Tori communicated back to him.

"That would be a very strange coincidence," Sheriff Ford agreed.

"Let's not concern ourselves with the dog," Tori interrupted quickly taking the attention away from Goliath. "Before the police could ask Pierce Andrews about his involvement, in either event, he disappeared, right Detective Daniels?"

"Y-yes," he stuttered, drawing his attention back to Tori and Sheriff Ford. "He was and remains a person of interest in both cases. Unfortunately, up until the call from Sheriff Ford, Pierce Andrews' whereabouts have remained unknown."

"So what brought Mr. Andrews' actions to your attention, Sheriff?" Tori asked curiously.

"Well, I didn't suspect him originally. We had a small forest fire in our town a few weeks ago, and once our Fire Marshall deemed it as arson, I began looking at the possible suspects in town and only came up with two. One of them is a former Marine who's a bit of a wanderer but seems like a decent enough fellow. The other guy was Pierce Andrews who was like the Goofus side of the Highlights 'Goofus and Gallant' cartoon I read as a kid. Did either one of you ever read that magazine?"

Both Tori and Detective Daniels shook their heads, having no clue what the sheriff was referencing.

"Never mind, the point I was trying to make is Mr. Andrews is the direct opposite of the other guy I mentioned. He shows up late, leaves early, doesn't respond when his boss tries to reach him and to be honest he gives me the creeps. But since being creepy isn't a crime, and we don't have any proof he started the fire, my hands are tied," the sheriff shrugged.

"But what made you start looking at him as a possible suspect?" Tori asked.

"It started with researching all the fires in the area in the past several years where either arson was suspected or the origin of the fire was suspicious in nature. I ended up with five cases my gut told me were ones I needed to look at more closely. The first one was a fire in Harrisonburg, Virginia. That one was a large pump explosion at a gas station. There was extensive damage and fortunately no deaths, but also no witnesses or suspects.

"The next case was the death of Gretchen Mallory. Then when I saw only a few weeks later you had another fire, this time killing a family of three, I got a strange feeling. Then there was a fire in Wilkesboro, North Carolina. That one was a Warehouse fire.

"It was a big one and needed four of the surrounding town's fire departments to assist putting it out. There was one fatality, a security guard. The police believe the guard may have seen who started the fire and tried to stop them," Sheriff Ford replied.

"So at that point, you had a feeling all of those fires were connected, but you had no proof," Tori summarized.

"That is correct. But what got me was the last case I found which pretty much made up my mind," the sheriff confessed.

"What was that case?" Detective Daniels asked, leaning in with interest.

Sheriff Ford took a sip of his coffee and sat back in his chair, looking alternately between Detective Daniels and Tori. "Did either of you know that Pierce Andrews' parents died in a house fire when he was a boy?"

"What?" Tori breathed in surprise.

"Are you serious?" Detective Daniels exclaimed.

"Both his mother and his father died during the fire. The report I found indicated the house caught fire while the parents were asleep and moved quickly through the home. By the time the fire department arrived, the house was engulfed in flames. The police didn't know there was anyone inside the structure until they found the bodies the next day," Sheriff Ford declared. "They found evidence of an accelerant used in different parts of the home and ruled it as arson."

"Where was Pierce during the fire?" Tori frowned, her dislike for Pierce growing by the minute.

"He told the police he was with friends at the time which gave him an alibi. Afterward, rather than him becoming a ward of the state, the mother's sister and her husband took custody of the boy, and he lived with them until he was old enough to be on his own," Sheriff Ford stated.

"How old was he when that happened?" Detective Daniels asked.

"He was sixteen years old," Sheriff Ford replied.

"And still a minor," Tori sighed. "If only someone had looked at him more closely at the time. Maybe none of the events that followed would have happened, and all of those victims would still be alive."

"Amen," Sheriff Ford agreed.

"Do you have any proof at all to begin building a case, Sheriff?" Detective Daniel's asked.

The sheriff nodded and admitted, "I have a piece of evidence found at the scene, and a witness claiming the item belongs to Pierce Andrews. Unfortunately, the fire destroyed any DNA or fingerprints on the item, so all I have is associated possession. The witness also freely communicated that Mr. Andrews told him about his parent's deaths and how they died."

"So what's the problem?" Tori frowned. "Is this not a credible witness?"

"My problem is that Mr. Andrews is pointing the finger at the other guy claiming he was the one who started the fire." Sheriff Ford exclaimed.

"That is a problem," Detective Daniels nodded in agreement.

"So this other guy, the former Marine," Tori prompted.

"I haven't been able to find much about him other than confirming his name and social security number seem to match. I dusted a few items he's touched for fingerprints to see if they're on file in AFIS but haven't heard back from my officer if he's found a match yet," Sheriff Ford replied. "But like I said, so far, he hasn't done anything to make me suspect him, quite the contrary. He even helped put out the fire and stayed after most people left to make sure none of the hot spots flared back up. I'm not sure an arsonist would do something like that."

"Unfortunately you never know, though. People are just as predictable as they are unpredictable." Tori stated.

"Amen to that too," Detective Daniels agreed.

"Maybe I can help do some digging for you using the FBI database," Tori offered. "What's his name?"

"His name is Alex Butler," Sheriff Ford replied.

Suddenly a warning bell went off in Tori's head. *"Why does that name sound so familiar? Do I know anyone named Alex Butler?"* she thought curiously. "Well, email me what you have and when I get back to Virginia, I'll poke around a bit and see if I can find anything."

"Thank you," Sheriff Ford smiled appreciatively. "I was hoping between the three of us we could come up with some way of helping one another."

"Sheriff, I believe we can!" Tori agreed.

Chapter 39

The Pikeville Cemetery was a short distance outside of town, nestled in a patch of woods beside a small white church with a tall louvered spire. As with many traditional churches, Tori could see this one had a belfry, housing a large bronze bell inside. The idyllic scene looked like something out of a Norman Rockwell painting and was a striking image against the clear blue sky.

Parking the car in one of the parking spaces facing the cemetery, Tori counted fifty headstones, and fortunately only three spirits. She turned to look in the back seat where Goliath sat and noticed he already had his head out the back window, anxiously searching for his former family, and could tell from his expression that he was unable to see them. Reaching back to pet him gently, she asked, "Are you ready to say goodbye to Mandy?"

"Goliath can't see her!" she heard his anguished reply.

"I see her," Tori assured him. "I see all three of them. They're here."

"Open the door!" he demanded excitedly, his paws dancing on the seat cushion.

"Okay," she agreed. Not sure what Goliath was expecting to happen, Tori got out of the car and walked around to the back passenger door. As soon as she released the handle, Goliath pushed his way out of the car and began galloping toward the cemetery.

"Goliath, wait up!" she called out quickly locking the car and running after him.

Then she heard the gleeful shriek of a little girl's voice calling out, "Bear! Come here Bear! Mommy, Daddy, look it's Bear!"

Not having any idea where the Cutler family was buried, Goliath ran frantically through the cemetery, looking for them. Meanwhile, unbeknownst to him, Mandy, the spirit of the little girl, chased after him calling out to him.

As Tori reached the large family headstone bearing the names of Samuel, Ashlyn, and Miranda Cutler, she cleared her throat gently, bringing Sam and Ashlyn's attention away from Mandy and Goliath.

"Good afternoon, Mr. and Mrs. Cutler," Tori greeted them quietly. "My name is Agent Tori Cooper. I'm a consultant for the FBI Behavioral Analysis Unit Division Two out of Washington, DC."

Both visibly surprised, Sam approached Tori and hovered directly in front of her. As he did, the familiar chill of being close to an earthbound spirit washed over her like a cold breeze.

"You can see us?" Sam exclaimed. "How can you see us? How do you know our names?"

Distracted by Goliath's erratic movements, Tori called out, "Goliath, come here!" Turning back to Sam, she replied, "I have a gift. I can communicate with victims of violent death. I know your names because Goliath told me all about you, your wife, Ashlyn and your daughter Mandy."

"Why are you calling him Goliath? His name is Bear!" Mandy insisted, returning to the spot beside her parents.

Tori smiled at the little girl and replied, "Well, Goliath was a gift that someone very special gave to me. When I met him, I didn't know his name was Bear; it had been changed to Goliath. I think both names fit him pretty well, don't you?"

"I like my name for him better," Mandy pouted. "Why can he see me as you can?" she frowned, trying to get Goliath's attention.

"Well, his gifts are limited. He's very strong; he can sense when evil spirits are nearby, and he can talk to me telepathically. Do you know what that means?" Tori asked.

"Do you mean he can read your mind?" Mandy exclaimed excitedly.

"Close, he can hear my thoughts, and I can hear his. We talk to one another without anyone else being able to hear," Tori replied.

"Anyone except for God, he hears everything," Mandy corrected Tori firmly. "Isn't that right, Mom?"

"Yes," Ashlyn smiled. "God hears everything."

"What kind of evil spirits can he see?" Mandy asked curiously. "Are they spirits like us only they're bad?"

"Something like that yes," Tori agreed.

"Why are you here Agent Cooper?" Sam interrupted.

"Please, call me Tori," she replied. "I'm here to give all of you the closure you need to pass through to heaven. I know it would make Goliath feel better too, not having to worry about you being here anymore."

"Why didn't we go directly to heaven when we died?" Ashlyn asked, her eyes glistening with tears. "I've been praying to God every single day since we arrived here and he's never replied. I know he's heard me. Why are we being punished?"

"You're not being punished, I promise you," Tori assured her. "When a human life is taken by another human, I believe they remain here on earth, so people like me can help solve their murders and finally give them peace before they ascend."

"So there are many people on the earth like you, traveling to cemeteries and helping people like us?" Sam asked.

"Unfortunately, no, I'm the last one. Well, actually my two young children will be the last ones once I'm gone. There used to be more of us with the gift, however as I mentioned, evil spirits sometimes take the lives of the other gifted because they don't want souls like you to have peace," Tori replied.

"So Goliath is like your guardian angel?" Mandy asked innocently.

Tori smiled down at Mandy and admitted, "That's exactly what he is." Then she looked at Sam and Ashlyn with a fierce intensity and added, "And Goliath told me everything about what happened the night of the explosion in your home. I know it wasn't an accident, I know who is responsible, and I promise you right now that I will make sure Pierce Andrews pays for what he's done."

"What about my friend Gretchen Mallory?" Sam worried. "He killed her too and tried to cover it up in an apartment fire."

"I know all about that too," Tori assured him. "Don't worry I'll make sure Gretchen crosses over safely as well."

"Thank you," Sam breathed in relief. "She didn't deserve to die the way she did."

"No, she didn't," Tori agreed.

"Has he killed any other people, the man who killed us?" Ashlyn asked.

"Seven people that we know of, including his parents when he was a teenager," Tori replied. "They both died in an apparent house fire I believe was caused by their son."

"Seven people! How does someone go through life like that unnoticed? Don't they act differently than other people, so they stick out somehow?" Ashlyn insisted.

"Often, murderers look and act just like we do. Sometimes their actions are pre-meditated, other times it's an act of passion at the spur of the moment," Tori admitted.

"He burned his parents to death!" Ashlyn exclaimed angrily. "He's a monster!"

"What was Pierce like to work with, Sam?" Tori wondered.

"Other than being a bit socially awkward and totally uncomfortable around women, he seemed just like any other guy in the office," Sam admitted.

"His parents, do you know why he killed them?" Ashlyn asked.

Shaking her head slowly, Tori admitted, "No, we don't know why however we do believe it was his first act of arson."

"How sad for them," Ashlyn murmured.

"Will you kill him when you catch him?" Mandy asked quietly.

"Our goal is not to kill someone when we're trying to catch them. Sometimes, a suspect will try to hurt us first, and we have no choice, but our intention is first to arrest the bad guy, so he or she can stand trial and be judged for his or her crimes," Tori advised.

"But I thought only God could judge us," Mandy replied, looking up at her mother. "Isn't that what you told me, Mom?"

Tori smiled and said, "You are exactly right! God judges our time on earth when we get to heaven; our judicial system judges people while they're here on earth. I believe that in the end, God takes care of everything and what is meant to happen is what happens."

"I call it Karma," Sam growled angrily.

"Tell Mandy, Bear loves her and is sorry he couldn't protect her," Goliath asked Tori, sorrowfully.

"I wish he could tell her himself," Tori thought. Suddenly a memory flashed in Tori's mind of the day of the shooting when she and Goliath touched, creating a bond with Elsbet and the others. *"I wonder...,"* she thought further as an idea came to her.

Enclosing the amulet in her left hand, she crouched down, put her right hand on Goliath's back and asked, "Elsbet, can we give Goliath the ability to communicate with them?"

Tori felt the amulet warm in her hand as a bright white light pulsed from the stone and a shower of glowing powder, like fairy dust, cascaded over them. A moment later, Tori saw Goliath react in surprise, seeing Mandy standing there in front of him.

"Goliath can see Mandy!" he exclaimed, excitedly, his tail wagging furiously.

"Did you hear what he just said, Mandy?" Tori asked.

"No, what did he say?" Mandy replied curiously.

"He can only see them," Tori, though, slightly disappointed that he couldn't hear them as well.

"He said to tell you Bear loves you and is sorry he couldn't protect you that night," Tori relayed.

Tentatively reaching her hand out toward Goliath, tears began to fall from the little girl's cheeks when her hand passed through him. "I love you too! I've missed you so much, Bear!"

"He's missed you too, sweetie," Tori replied.

"So how do you help cross spirits over, Tori?" Ashlyn asked.

"I use the power from this amulet to help guide them from this earthly plane to heaven," Tori replied.

"Can you cross us over together as a family? I don't want us to get separated after all this time," Sam asked urgently.

Pausing to consider his question, Tori admitted, "Honestly, I've never crossed a family over at the same time before, but I would be willing to give it a try."

"I would prefer that if you could," Sam admitted.

"So would I," Ashlyn agreed.

"Can Bear come with us?" Mandy hoped.

Cringing inside at the thought of Goliath leaving her, Tori shook her head and said, "I'm sorry, sweetie. He'll have to stay here with me and hopefully live out a very long life here on earth."

"Will I ever see him again?" Mandy asked.

"I don't know, honey. That's one of those questions you can ask God when you meet Him," Tori suggested.

Satisfied with Tori's response, Mandy nodded and agreed. "Okay."

"What do we need to do?" Ashlyn asked eager to end her ghostly existence.

"Stand together just like that, and I'll do the rest," Tori replied.

"Should we hold hands?" Ashlyn asked.

"If that would make you feel better, sure, go ahead," Tori agreed.

As Sam, Ashlyn and Mandy moved closer together, they clasped hands and smiled excitedly at one another.

"I love you both so much," Sam told his wife and daughter.

"I love you too," Ashlyn told him. Glancing down at Mandy, she said, "And I love you too, baby."

"I love you both too," Mandy replied. Looking back at Goliath, she said, "Goodbye, Bear. Be a good boy."

Blinking back the tears forming in her eyes, Tori kept her hand enclosed over the amulet and her hand on Goliath's back. "Okay, here we go."

"Thank you, Tori. Thank you for everything," Sam said.

"You're welcome, Sam," Tori replied. Closing her eyes, Tori focused her thoughts on Sam, Ashlyn and Mandy standing at the gates of heaven and loudly proclaimed, "May your spirits be at peace, Samuel Cutler, Ashlyn Cutler and Miranda Cutler, as you return to the Father."

When she opened her eyes, they were gone. Having seen them disappear, Goliath, whined sadly, watching his family leave.

"I believe you'll see them again someday, Goliath," Tori told him quietly.

Releasing her grip on the amulet, she pushed herself up from the ground and instantly felt the earth sway around her, making her feel dizzy and a little nauseated as she stood. Bracing her hand against the Cutler headstone, she took a deep breath and waited for the feeling to pass. "Okay maybe crossing three people over at the same time packs more of a wallop than I thought it would."

"*Is Tori okay?*" Goliath worried, remaining close by her side.

Exhaling another deep breath, Tori felt her head begin to clear and the turning in her stomach settle. "I'll be okay, thank you, sweetie. Are you ready to leave?"

Looking up at her with his beautiful gold eyes filled with sorrow, he told her, "*There's nothing here for Goliath anymore.*"

Frowning slightly, Tori asked, "You mean there's nothing here at the cemetery right? You still have me, Ben, the twins, Piper, Riley, Reagan, Sarah, Tanner and Aubrey and we all love you very much. You've been blessed to have two loving families during your lifetime."

Rubbing his face against her leg affectionately, she heard him reply, *"Goliath knows. Goliath loves you all too."*

"Okay, good. Let's go, sweet boy," she suggested, walking toward the car.

Hearing a loud screech from overhead, Tori looked up and saw a six large crows sitting on the branches of one of the trees, watching her. *"That's creepy. Have they been there the whole time and I didn't notice them?"* she thought as a chill went through her.

As she and Goliath continued walking, more of the large carrion began to arrive and land in the trees above them. Feeling her uneasiness growing, Tori began walking more quickly. *"Come on, Goliath,"* she urged him silently.

"Goliath feels it too. Evil is here," he warned her.

Passing the final row of headstones to the open grass by the parking lot, Tori breathed a sigh of relief, seeing the car only a few yards away. *"If we can just make it to the car, everything will be fine,"* she told Goliath telepathically.

Suddenly the flurry of birds erupted from the trees forming a large black cloud overhead. Instinctively clasping the amulet in her hand, Tori crouched down and wrapped her arms around Goliath's neck. "Elsbet we need you!" she cried out fearfully as the blackened cloak descended upon them.

Instantly a blast of light flashed from the stone, forming an iridescent shield around Tori and Goliath. When the birds made contact with the shield, Tori could feel a jolt of electricity flow across the surface of the sphere, which somehow didn't affect her or Goliath.

Closing her eyes tightly, she held her breath as the sound of the large birds hitting the shield, followed by their shrieks of pain filled her ears. When the sounds finally ceased, she opened her eyes and nearly vomited in revulsion at the sight of hundreds of birds lying motionless at her feet.

"What is wrong with you, Lucifer?" she screamed angrily as the shield dissolved. "Why would you do something like this?"

"It's okay Tori, they're not dead, merely stunned," Elsbet called out to her from within the amulet.

"They're not?" Tori murmured, wiping tears from her eyes.

"No, they're fine, but they are still cursed. You and Goliath need to get out of there before they wake up," Elsbet warned.

Not needing to be told twice, Tori got up and began stepping carefully around the birds, walking quickly toward the car. "Come on Goliath," she urged, making sure he was behind her. "We need to get out of here fast!"

~~~~~~~~~~

Without any further rebellious acts from Lucifer on their drive back to the airport, Tori and Goliath arrived earlier than expected before their flight was scheduled to depart.

Stopping at a convenience mart to refill the gas tank on the rental car, as Tori waited for the tank to fill, she realized she hadn't heard back from Logan regarding her last email to him.   Dialing his work number first, she waited for him to pick up, frowning when after several rings the call went to voicemail. "Logan, it's Tori. Give me a call when you get a chance okay? Bye."

Undaunted, she immediately dialed his undercover phone number at the apartment, frowning again when it went to voicemail. Realizing a possible risk that Rebecca might overhear, Tori left a safe message she hoped Logan would return. "Logan, it's Tori. Hey, Ben and I were talking about having a barbecue this weekend and were wondering if you wanted to drive in. You can bring Scout too. The kids would love to meet him. Give me a call."

Screwing the gas cap back on the tank, she took the receipt from the slot on the gas pump and got back behind the wheel of the car. Uncertain as to what she should do, she couldn't shake the feeling that something was wrong. Opening a map application on her phone, she entered Logan's address into the destination field and estimated how long it would take her to drive to Blacksburg from where she was. *"Just over three hours, that's not too bad,"* she mused, debating what she should do.

"Is Logan in trouble?" Goliath asked her.

"I don't know, Goliath," Tori replied. "My gut is telling me something's off, and we need to check it out."

"Goliath feels it too," he admitted, which was uncommon for him to perceive danger for anyone but Tori. *"Logan needs Tori."*

Realizing she couldn't ignore both hers and Goliath's instincts, she got back on the road and headed toward Blacksburg.

"All right, let's go!" she agreed.

Chapter 40

"And here I thought I got the crap job," Pierce chuckled heartily watching Zander shovel composted manure from the bed of a truck into one of the large planting beds outside the town hall.

Standing erect, Zander leaned against the handle of his shovel, glared down at Pierce and snidely replied, "That's funny, the only thing I think stinks around here is you."

"Ha! I would argue that point," Pierce laughed as he tapped a cigarette out of the paper pack and placed the diffused end between his lips. Producing a lighter from his other hand, he flicked the metal wheel, creating a small flame, lit the cigarette and sucked in until the tip radiated a bright orange glow.

Never understanding the lure of the disgusting habit, Zander's eyes traveled down to Pierce's hand, and noticed the lighter Pierce was using was a small plastic disposable lighter, not the same one he had used a few weeks ago. *"What happened to your shiny silver lighter with the embossed wolf on it, buddy?"* Zander thought curiously.

Catching the look, Pierce quickly dropped the lighter into his pocket. "Walters wants to know when you'll have the flower baskets ready," he demanded.

"They'll be ready when I'm finished with them," Zander challenged testily. "You guys haven't even finished painting the lamp posts yet, plus the paint still needs to dry a few days before I can hang the baskets. I would suggest you get to work, buddy and stop wasting time!"

"And I would suggest you watch your back," Pierce hissed in reply. "You've got eyes on you, buddy," spitting the last word angrily.

"So do you, buddy," Zander warned, holding his ground.

Pierce glared at Zander, flicked his cigarette butt into the bed of the truck, narrowly missing Zander's head by a few inches, and quickly walked away.

"What a prick," Zander muttered, retrieving the cigarette butt with the blade of the shovel and then extinguishing it with the toe of his boot. "So much for trying to be friendly with him," he added.

After he was finished preparing the remaining planting beds in the center of town, Zander drove over to the entrance of the city park to start working on two planting areas on either side of the cement path. As he was pulling out the old plants and the weeds inside one of the beds, he heard the familiar sound of a dog barking. When Zander looked up, he was shocked to see a dog, bearing a striking resemblance to his old dog, Butler, playing with a young girl. Quickly standing up, Zander brushed the dirt from his hands and began walking toward them.

"Butler!" he called out hopefully as he approached.

When the dog heard the sound of his former master's voice calling out to him, he froze and then turned in the direction of the source of the voice. Instantly recognizing Zander, Butler raced toward him, barking excitedly.

"Butler stop!" The girl cried out with no effect. "Mom, Dad, Butler is running away!"

A man and a woman sitting at a picnic table nearby immediately got up and began walking in Zander's direction. Butler meanwhile, covered the distance across the grass in record time, vaulting his body upward into Zander's open arms.

"Come here, good boy!" Zander praised, laughing as Butler covered his face with happy kisses.

"Excuse me," the man interrupted the reunion as he caught up to them. "That's our dog."

Surprised by the man's comment, Zander pet Butler affectionately as the dog squirmed excitedly, pressing his body against Zander's legs. "I'm sorry. I know this dog. He ah, belonged to a friend of mine a long time ago," he lied.

"You know him?" the woman asked as she and the little girl joined the men. "How do you know him?"

"Yes, his name is Butler right?" Zander asked, still petting his dog.

"That's right," the woman admitted cautiously.

"My name is Alex Butler, ironically enough," Zander announced, extending his hand to the man first. "One of my former Marine buddies and his wife owned this dog. They lived just outside of Lexington, Kentucky."

"It's nice to meet you, Alex, I'm Don, this is my wife Margaret and our daughter, Ramona," the man replied.

"How did you come into possession of Butler?" Zander asked curiously. "My friend's wife loved this dog more than anything, so I know she wouldn't just give him up. Unfortunately, I lost touch with them. I hope they're okay."

"I'm sorry, Alex, we don't know anything about what may have happened to your friends. We adopted Butler a little over six years ago from an animal shelter in Huntington," Margaret replied.

"We live in Blacksburg now! We're just visiting my Aunt Susan this weekend," Ramona revealed innocently. "She lives a few miles from here, but we have to wait until she gets off work until we can go to her house."

Irritated with her daughter for telling a stranger more details than she cared he know, Margaret quickly clipped Butler's leash onto his collar and said, "Well, It's time for us to get going. It was nice to meet you, Alex. Come on, Butler, Ramona."

Butler whined, reluctantly following his new master, and he looked back at Zander anxiously.

"It's okay, Butler," Zander assured the dog, knowing there was nothing he could do.

"Thank you for your service," Don quickly added, recognizing the lower portion of a marine corps devil dog tattoo beneath the shirt sleeve on Zander's arm. "I hope your friends are okay."

"Uh, thanks," Zander murmured, still watching Butler leave.

"Don!" Margaret said sternly, noticing Don was still talking to Zander.

"Coming, dear!" Don instantly jumped, hurrying to catch up with his family.

Completely baffled by what just happened, Zander stood frozen in place, watching his dog disappear into the back of an SUV and driven away.

"Rhea would never leave that dog," he told himself silently. *"I know her. Either something happened to her, or she's not far away from him. Even if that means someone else owns him, she has to be somewhere close,"* he continued to reason. *"Where did the little girl say they lived, Blacksburg? I have no idea where that is, but I'm going to find out. I think I need to pay Rhea a little visit."*

Zander worked hard the rest of the afternoon in an attempt to get far enough ahead on the list of things Zeke wanted him to do where he could take a couple of days off and drive out to Blacksburg. It was almost dark when he finally stopped no longer having any light from the sun to guide his way. Once he secured and locked all the vehicles and equipment into maintenance building two, he drove over to building one to talk to Zeke.

The stars must have been aligned at just the right angle because when he got there, Zeke was in an unusually good mood. Then Zander noticed the open bottle of bourbon on Zeke's desk.

"Hmm, this could work to my advantage," Zander thought optimistically.

"Hey, Butler, are you wrapping up for the day?" Zeke greeted Zander through the open door of his office.

"Ah, yes, sir. I ran out of daylight," Zander admitted pausing in the doorway.

"Oh, that's too bad. Do you want to come in and have a drink?" Zeke offered, motioning to the empty metal chair on the other side of his desk.

"Uh, sure, thanks," Zander replied, unfamiliar with Zeke's jovial behavior. "Are we celebrating something, sir?" he asked, sitting down in the chair.

Pouring Zander a sloppy drink into a plastic cup, Zeke reached across the desk and handed the cup to Zander. "We're celebrating life!" Zeke announced holding his glass up in the air. "The results of my prostate exam came back, and I am cancer free!"

Realizing by the level of the bourbon missing from the bottle that Zeke seemed to have been celebrating long before he showed up, Zander held his cup in the air as well and replied, "Congratulations, to life!"

"To life!" Zeke repeated gulping down a large sip of the strong golden liquid. Setting his glass down a little too firmly on the desk, he smiled at Zander and asked, "So, what's on your mind?"

"Give it a shot and see how it goes," Zander told himself. "Well sir, a friend of mine just moved to Blacksburg, and she asked if I could come help her unload her furniture this weekend. I'm all caught up on all the beds in town and have the soil prepared for the hanging baskets, but I have to wait for Walter's team to finish painting the posts before I can hang them. That won't be for three maybe four more days. Would it be okay for me to take a couple of days off so I can help my friend?"

"Is she your girlfriend?" Zeke grinned lewdly.

"Uh no sir, she's the younger sister of one of my former Marine troop-mates who was killed in combat. I promised I would keep an eye on her for him. She and I are just friends, sir," Zander lied.

"That's a very nice thing for you to do Alex," Zeke pointed out. "You know, you're an admirable young man, Alex Butler. Much more than I gave you credit for in the beginning."

"He's going to wish he didn't remember saying any of this in the morning," Zander laughed inwardly. "Thank you, sir. No offense taken. I understand that respect needs to be earned," he continued to wheedle his boss. "So is that a yes? May I have tomorrow and Friday off, sir?"

"Sure, go ahead, if you're all caught up," Zeke agreed. "But you better be on time first thing Monday morning!"

"I will, sir," Zander agreed, getting up from his chair. "Thank you, sir. And thanks for the drink!"

~~~~~~~~~~

Two hours later, an incessant sound of someone pounding on the door and a ringing in his head woke Zeke from an alcohol induced sleep.

"What...," he groaned, opening his eyes blearily. Recognizing the familiar surroundings of his office, he further realized the ringing was from the telephone, and the pounding was coming from his head. "Hel...hello?" he mumbled into the mouthpiece.

"Zeke, is that you?" Sheriff Ford's voice barked through the receiver.

"Yeah," Zeke croaked. "Who else would be answering my phone? And why are you yelling?" he asked, resting his head in the palm of his hand.

"What are you still doing at work at this hour?" Sheriff Ford demanded.

"Why are you calling me at work at this hour?" Zeke demanded in return.

"Because you didn't answer your phone at home," Sheriff Ford replied.

"Well, that doesn't mean anything. I could have been out for dinner or taking a walk or buying groceries," Zeke continued to plead his case.

"Were you doing any of those things?" Sheriff Ford continued to argue.

"No," Zeke groaned. "What do you want?"

"I'm on my way back from Pikeville and learned a lot about our friend Pierce Andrews from the local authorities and the FBI," Sheriff Ford revealed.

"The FBI, what in the Sam Hill has he done to get on their radar?" Zeke asked.

"I can't tell you anything over the phone," The sheriff admitted.

"Gee thanks," Zeke scowled.

"I need you to keep a close eye on him until I get back in town. In fact, try to keep a close eye on both Pierce Andrews and Alex Butler. I'm still not thoroughly convinced either one of them are innocent at this point," Sheriff Ford instructed.

Regretfully recalling the conversation he had with Alex a few hours earlier, Zeke winced and admitted, "Well sheriff I'm afraid I'm only going to be able to accommodate one of your requests."

"What are you talking about? Which one?" the sheriff exclaimed.

"The one about Andrews," Zeke admitted. "I gave Butler permission to take off the next two days to help a friend who just moved to Blacksburg."

"Blacksburg! I told him not to leave town!" Sheriff Ford advised angrily.

"I'm sorry, Sheriff I didn't know that," Zeke apologized.

"It's alright, Zeke. I didn't mean to bark at you," Sheriff Ford grumbled. "Dang kids don't know how to follow orders anymore! Just keep an eye on Andrews until I get back. Can you do that?"

"Sure thing, Sheriff," Zeke agreed. "What are you going to do about Butler?"

"Well, Blacksburg is only a few hours from here. I guess I'll head out that way and check out his story. Make sure he's not getting himself into any trouble," Sheriff Ford replied.

"Okay. I'll let you know if I see Andrews doing anything suspicious," Zeke confirmed.

"Good man, oh and Zeke?" Sheriff Ford hesitated before hanging up.

"What?" Zeke asked.

"Be careful," Sheriff warned his friend.

Chapter 41

Logan reached across the table and took Rebecca's hand in his enjoying how the soft glow of the candle on the table, cast flecks of light throughout her hazel eyes. "Hi," he smiled when he saw that special look she sometimes gave him that always made his heart skip a beat.

"Hey you," she smiled coyly back at him. "You're not at all squeamish about PDA are you?"

"Nope," Logan replied softly, his eyes traveling down to her lips. "I believe if you care about someone, you shouldn't hide it or be afraid to show it. Was your ex not big on showing affection in public?"

"Oh, he hated it. He wouldn't even let me hold his hand like this if we were walking together," Rebecca admitted. "Sitting at a table like this in front of a big glass window where anyone could see is something he would never do."

"Well, I don't mind holding your hand, or anyone seeing how much I care about you," Logan assured her, bringing her hand to his lips and gently kissing her knuckles one by one.

"Hmm, you keep doing that, and I'm going to say we skip dinner and go back to your place," she teased.

"We could eat pizza naked in bed if you want to," he teased back. "Do you want to order dinner to go?"

"Hmm... actually no, not tonight," she decided. "As much as I enjoy our intimate times together, we've been spending too much time indoors the past few weeks. I think it's important we go out on more dates like this so we can continue to get to know each other better."

"I agree. Besides neither one of us has any edible food left in our apartments. We've pretty much cleaned the cupboards bare. Maybe we should stop at the store on the way home and pick up a few things for tomorrow," Logan suggested.

"So are you saying tomorrow is another indoor day?" She proposed, stroking his fingers seductively.

"Most definitely," he agreed.

~~~~~~~~~~

Zander arrived in Blacksburg shortly before seven o'clock and spent the first half hour driving through town familiarizing himself with his surroundings. *"So far I've only seen two veterinary clinics, so I'll probably check those out in the morning,"* he thought to himself. *"I can't see her shampooing poodles, so I won't waste my time with pet shops or groomers."*

Having skipped dinner to make better time, he decided he would grab something quick to eat before finding a place to stay for the night. *"What am I in the mood for?"* he pondered, stopping behind a row of cars waiting at a traffic light.

Glancing over to a building on his left, he saw a glowing red, white and green fluorescent sign inviting him in for authentic Italian food. *"Hmm, pizza sounds really good,"* he thought.

Looking for an open parking spot in front of the building, he noticed a couple sitting at a small table in the front window holding hands across the table. He shook his head disapprovingly at their indecent behavior and thought, *"Look at those two, they're practically doing it right there at the table."*

Then he realized the woman looked very familiar. *"Wait, is that…, no way, that's not her. That woman's hair is too short. Rhea likes to wear her hair long. My eyes are playing tricks on me,"* he told himself. Then he saw the woman laugh at something the man across the table from her said, and the tilt of her head and the expression on her face convinced Zander it was her.

"What the hell…," he began to growl when suddenly he was interrupted by the persistent blare of several car horns honking behind him. Glancing forward, he realized the light had turned green, and the cars ahead of him were gone.

"Crap!" he exclaimed, quickly pulling forward before Rhea looked out the window and saw him. *"What do I do?"* he thought as he drove. *"Do I go back there and confront her? Ask her where the heck she's been the past three years? And who's that blonde guy she's obviously screwing? Does he even know she's married?"* Then he felt the familiar pang of pain begin behind his temples.

"I have an idea. You could just kill them both and save yourself the agony of all these questions," the voice in Zander's head suggested.

"Not now," Zander groaned inwardly.

*"She doesn't deserve you, Zander! Obviously, she doesn't care about you anymore; she's moved on. Maybe it's time you did too. If

you plan it right, you could even use one bullet and kill them both at the same time. Of course, I'll have to find you a new gun since you buried the last one in the woods..,." Lucifer reminded him.

"Shut up, Lucifer! You are not the voice of logic I need in my head right now!" Zander demanded as a spear of pain pierced behind his eyes.

"Are you sure?" Lucifer offered. "I could make all of this go away for you, just like I've done before."

"No!" Zander insisted. "I need to figure this out by myself!"

"You know you can't do this on your own; you're not convicted to our cause anymore!" Lucifer argued again.

"I said no, now leave me alone!" Zander shouted angrily.

"Fine, suit yourself, just say the word. I'll be waiting," Lucifer reluctantly agreed.

~~~~~~~~~~

Tori checked her phone again, sighing in frustration when she saw Logan still hadn't returned any of her messages. "I hope he's okay," she murmured as she drove down the main street in Blacksburg. "I don't want to blow his cover so it's not like I can just go knock on his front door," she mused silently.

Stopping at a red traffic light, she noticed all the restaurants and pubs lining both sides of the street. "So far Blacksburg seems like a pretty cool place," she thought. "I can see why Logan likes it."

As the light changed to green and the cars ahead of her began moving, she slowly accelerated forward. Then she heard several car horns blaring followed by the low growl from Goliath in the back seat causing goose bumps to rise up on both of her arms.

"Goliath, what's wrong?" she asked, fearing it was Luc again.

"I feel the man. He is near," she heard Goliath warn.

"What? Do you mean Zander? He's here?" Tori exclaimed, quickly glancing around her.

"Yes, he's close!" Goliath growled.

As she passed the row of cars from the opposing lane of traffic, her eyes stopped on a familiar face behind the wheel of one of the vehicles. "Oh, there he is!" she cried out in surprise. Quickly averting her eyes, she continued driving forward, watching the car Zander was in from her rear view mirror.

"I need to turn around and see where he's going," she decided, looking ahead for an opening in traffic. "Come on, come on!" she urged the other cars out of her way. When finally a break in the cars opened up, she pulled her car into a parking lot, turned around and pulled back onto the street, heading in the direction Zander was driving. "I don't see his car anymore, do you, Goliath?" she asked.

"Goliath doesn't see him," she heard him reply, anxiously, sticking his head out the back window trying to catch the scent. *"Goliath doesn't smell him either,"* he told her.

"Well, shoot," she sighed, straining her head around the other vehicles for a better view.

After a couple of blocks without any further sightings, Tori drove back to the intersection where she first saw him, pulled the car into the parking lot of a gas station and dialed Logan's number.

Groaning in frustration when her call went directly to voicemail, she hung up. "Dang it Logan!" she sighed, switching to a text conversation on her phone. Quickly typing him a message, she hit the send button, hoping he would at least feel the vibration of his phone in his pocket and call her.

Tori: Logan, it's Tori. Call me immediately. 9-1-1!

~~~~~~~~~~

Sheriff Ford took a large bite from the toasted hoagie roll, sighing in contentment as he tasted the tangy sauce and warm, gooey cheese melted on top of the row of Italian meatballs nestled in the bread. It was a rare opportunity he allowed himself such an unhealthy dinner, but he decided tonight he deserved it.

Barely a third of the way through his meal, his phone began to ring. Gazing at his sandwich wistfully, he groaned sadly, having to wait for his next bite. Fortunately, the dispatcher at his office back in Ravenswood had insisted on installing Bluetooth devices in all of their vehicles, so he didn't have to put the sandwich down. Taking a quick sip of his cola, he engaged the communication device on the steering wheel and said, "This is Sheriff Ford."

"Sheriff, this is Officer Poag at the Blacksburg Police Department," the voice on the other end replied.

"Good evening, Officer Poag. Have you been able to locate the vehicle I asked you about?" Sheriff Ford asked.

"Yes, sir," Officer Poag confirmed. "I have a white male driving a tan Mercury Marquis with a West Virginia license plate in my sight. He's headed north on Main Street just passed the intersection of Maple and Main. What would you like me to do, sir?"

"Nothing for the moment, I'm about a block away from your position," Sheriff Ford advised. "Are you in an unmarked vehicle?"

"Yes, sir, I'm in a black Ford Crown Victoria," Officer Poag replied.

"I see you. I'm two cars back. I also see the tan Marquis. Thank you, Officer Poag, I'll take it from here," Sheriff Ford replied.

"You're welcome, sir. Would you like me to hang back behind you, just in case you need me?" Officer Poag offered.

"No, I don't want to risk drawing any unnecessary attention," Sheriff Ford admitted.

"Roger that. I'm on duty until midnight tonight so feel free to call dispatch if you need assistance. They'll send me out your way," Officer Poag agreed.

"Will do, thank you again for your help," Sherriff Ford said.

"Any time, sir," Officer Poag replied, ending the call.

"All right Mr. Butler, let's see what you're up to tonight," Sheriff Ford declared, taking a bite from his sandwich.

Passing a row of cars on his left crossing the intersection opposite him, he saw a woman with dark auburn hair behind the wheel of one of the cars and glanced in her direction. *"Who wants a blonde when you can have a red-head,"* he thought when suddenly he recognized the red-headed woman in question.

"That's Agent Cooper! What is she doing in Blacksburg? She should be on her way back home by now!" Thinking about it more, he decided, "There's more than just coincidence going on here, something is up. Andrew's is still back in Ravenswood, what would she be doing here?" Then another thought occurred to him, "Could she be here looking for Alex Butler too? Why?"

Sticking with his current plan, he decided, "Well, I guess I'll have to worry about that later."

Then he noticed Alex engage the turn signal on his car, indicating his intent to turn into a grocery store parking lot. Afterward, Alex quickly pulled his car in a spot facing the street.

"What are you up to now, Alex?" Sheriff Ford wondered, turning his car into a strip mall parking lot just beyond the grocery store.

Parking his vehicle in a parking spot where he could watch Alex, the sheriff thought, "Who are you watching for, Alex? Agent Cooper maybe?" Trying to put the puzzle pieces into place, he sat back in his seat and finished the rest of his dinner while he waited.

~~~~~~~~~~~

"I'm going to make a quick trip to the ladies room while we wait for our food to arrive," Rebecca advised, getting up from her chair. "I'll be right back."

"I'll be right here, waiting for you," Logan promised, feeling the vibration of his phone against his leg. Waiting until he saw Rhea enter the bathroom and for the door to close behind her, he pulled his phone from his pocket and glanced at the screen. Frowning when he saw Tori's message, he immediately dialed her number, glancing around the crowded dining room. "Hey, Tor, what's up?" he whispered, getting up from the table so he could talk more privately outside on the sidewalk.

"Why haven't you returned any of my calls?" Tori demanded angrily.

"I've been busy!" Logan argued. "Why?"

"Where are you?" she asked.

"Rebecca and I are out having dinner, why? What's going on?" he asked, getting annoyed.

"What's going on is her husband is in town looking for her and possibly you too!" she insisted.

"What? How do you know that?" Logan scowled, thinking she was acting a bit overly dramatic.

"Because I'm in Blacksburg too and I just saw him drive by me!" she exclaimed.

"What? Why are you here?" he frowned.

"Because you weren't returning my calls and I was worried!" Tori insisted.

"Well, crap, where are you now?" Logan asked, his mind already beginning to think.

"I'm at a gas station called the Chug Hub on Main Street," Tori replied. "Do you know where that is?"

Surprised by her response, Logan looked up the street to his left and asked, "Are you in the silver Taurus or the white Pathfinder?"

"The white...wait, how do you know what car I'm driving?" Tori asked.

"Because I can see you from here," Logan replied. "And I see Goliath too. You realize you don't exactly blend in with him sticking his head out the window like that. Is there anybody else in there with you?"

Knowing he meant the twins, Tori replied, "No, It's just us." Turning in her seat to look down the road, she saw Logan standing on the sidewalk outside of a restaurant. "I see you. Where's Rhea?"

"She's inside in the ladies room. Speaking of which I better get back in there before she suspects anything," Logan advised.

"Logan you don't have time, you have to tell her what's going on. Zander is here in town, and it's only a matter of time until he finds her. He may already know where she lives," Tori warned.

"What do you suggest I go back in there and tell her, 'Hey, so guess what, I'm not a computer programmer, I'm an undercover FBI agent, and your life is in danger?'" he presented angrily.

"Yes, that's exactly what you need to do! I'm serious Logan! You need to tell her right now, tonight. If you don't, she'll innocently go off to work in the morning, and he'll be somewhere nearby watching for her, maybe even planning to kill her. Do you want to take that risk?" Tori demanded.

Hating the fact that she was right, he sighed in frustration and replied, "No, I don't."

"Good now get back in there, get your food and get out of there," Tori instructed firmly.

"Where should I take her, back to my place?" he asked.

"For now yes. Your building is on the other end of the complex from hers, so Goliath and I will drive over to your apartment now and make sure we don't see Zander nearby. I'll text you when I think it's safe to bring her in. Do not under any circumstances go to her apartment, understand? You keep her with you, don't let her go," Tori insisted.

"I'll try, but once she hears what I have to say, she's not going to want to have anything to do with me. I won't be able to make her stay," Logan replied.

"You most certainly will! She's a material witness in a murder investigation, and you're an officer of the law," she reminded him. "Heck put her in handcuffs if you have to! And before you say anything, I don't want to know if you've already done that."

"Funny," Logan quipped, trying to think of a way out of this situation. "Argh, I hate it when you're right," he groaned, heading back inside the restaurant. "Fine, I'll do it. I'm hanging up now."

"Remember, I'll text you if the coast is clear," Tori told him.

"I heard you," he snapped angrily, ending the call.

"Hey, I was beginning to worry!" Rebecca greeted him as he returned to the table. "Is everything okay? You look agitated."

Sitting down at the table with her, Logan replied, "I've got a problem with a client, and I need to get back home. I'm sorry. I'm spoiling our date night."

"No, that's okay, I understand!" she assured him, reaching across the table to touch his hand.

Catching their waiter's attention, she asked, "Excuse me. We've had an emergency come up and will need our food to go. Would you mind taking care of that for us please?"

"Of course, ma'am, I'll go do that now. Your pizza is almost ready," the young man replied, quickly hurrying off in the direction of the kitchen.

Noticing the flush on the young waiter's cheeks when he spoke to Rebecca, Logan wondered if any man was able to say no to her.

"See? All taken care of, we'll be out of here lickety-split," she smiled at him.

Knowing that happy, beautiful smile wouldn't remain on her face for long, Logan smiled back at her and said. "Thank you for understanding."

"Always," she winked at him playfully.

"*We'll see,*" he thought sadly.

Chapter 42

Rhea stared at Logan, stunned into silence as he began to tell her the seemingly most outrageously unbelievable story. It was about him being an agent with the FBI who had been following her ex-husband for the past three years, and how he came to Blacksburg to see if she still had any connection to Zander. He further tried to explain how he never planned for things to happen the way they had and how much he cared for her. After a while, she no longer heard the words coming out of his mouth; she only heard the agonizing sound of her heart breaking into millions of tiny fragments.

Tears began to flow down her cheeks at the realization that Logan was a completely different man than the man she'd spent the last few weeks falling in love with, who she believed she could trust.

"Why? Why does this keep happening to me? What have I done to deserve having to go through this all over again?" her tormented thoughts plagued her. *"Is this Karma? Have I led such a disappointing life that God is punishing me?"*

"Rhea!" she heard Logan call out to her sternly.

Not used to hearing him use her real name, she slowly brought her eyes back to his, and whispered, "What?"

"I need you to talk to me, tell me what you're feeling?" he begged, hating the pain he saw in her eyes.

"Why?" she sighed in resignation. "So you can write it down in one of your reports?"

Cringing inside at the bitterness in her voice, he admitted, "because I love you and I hate myself for putting you in the position we're in, and because I want to believe we can still find a way to get through this together."

Searching his face, she asked, "I don't know what to believe anymore. Every word that's come out of your mouth the past hour has sounded like they belong to a man I don't even know. How do you expect me to feel? Do you expect me to believe you, to trust you? Is Logan Chase even your real name?" she exclaimed.

Logan walked over to his desk, unlocked the bottom drawer and retrieved his badge. Handing the badge to Rhea, he said, "Yes, that part is true."

Running her fingers over the embossed government seal, she read the inscription that read 'Federal Bureau of Investigation' along with the accompanying photo ID bearing Logan's name and picture. Rhea handed the badge back to him, and her eyes flicked over to his computer monitor, which still showed several lines of random code displayed on the screen. Hearing her unspoken question, Logan placed his badge on the desk and clicked a few keys on the keyboard, instantly changing the screen to the FBI logo.

Still unsure what to believe, Rhea sat on the couch, her mind trying to formulate a plan of what she should do. Suddenly she felt a cold, wet nose nudge her hand and she looked down at Scout sitting at her feet, wanting attention. *"It's still so uncanny how much he resembles Butler,"* she began to think when the realization hit her.

Looking back at Logan, she inclined her head in Scout's direction and asked, "Was he your lure? Did you intentionally select a dog that resembled my old dog to get my attention?"

"Do you mean Domino or Butler?" Logan gently reminded her she had lied to him too.

"I think it's time for me to go," Rhea advised with a note of indignation in her voice.

"I'm sorry, but I can't allow you to leave," Logan advised, cautiously.

Glaring at him angrily, Rhea stood up and approached him until she was just a few inches from him. "And just how do you plan to stop me?" she threatened coldly.

"I'm afraid I must insist," he replied as calmly as he could. "Please sit down, Rhea."

"I don't think so," she angrily replied, pushing past him, heading for the door.

"Rhea, please don't go," he said, reaching out to grab her by the wrist which was the worst thing he could have done.

Turning around to face him, Rhea's other hand, now clenched into a fist, swung out and firmly punched him in the nose.

"Ouch!" he cried out, letting go of her wrist as a stream of blood began flowing out of both nostrils. "I can't believe you just did that! You know I could charge you with assault for doing that!"

"You do, and I'll accuse you of misrepresentation and deception! Just stay away from me!" she fumed, walking quickly to the door and slamming it behind her as she left.

"What is with these men? I can't believe the pair on that guy! Why do I keep falling for these losers? Is there some black cloud over my head or something?" she mumbled to herself as she strode angrily across the lawn toward her apartment.

Having anticipated how Logan's talk with Rhea might go, unknown to Rhea, Tori and Goliath were within earshot of her ranting, waiting in the shadows of the stairwell near her apartment.

"Holy moly that is one pissed off woman right there," Tori thought. Allowing Rhea a few minutes to cool off, Tori dialed Logan's number. "Are you okay?" she asked when he answered.

"Other than possibly having a broken nose, sure I'm fine. Do you have eyes on Rhea?" Logan asked.

"Yes, she's back at her apartment. Wow is she pissed! Did she punch you in the nose?" Tori asked, trying not to laugh.

"Yep, I've got quite the gusher going on over here. It's too bad. I liked this shirt. Can I call you back?" Logan sniffed loudly.

"Yeah, you go take care of that nose. I've got things under control here at the moment," Tori assured him, ending the call. *"Girls got some spunk,"* she thought humorously.

Slipping her phone back in her pocket, she approached Rhea's door and softly knocked.

A few seconds later the door swung open, and a very angry Rhea answered, "I told you to stay aw…., oh, I'm sorry. I thought you were somebody else. May I help you?" she asked, briefly glancing down at Goliath.

"Hello Rhea, my name is Tori," Tori greeted her, waiting to see if Rhea knew who she was.

It took a moment for the connection to trigger, but when it did, Rhea's eyes darkened again, and she replied, "You're a friend of Logan's, right? Or wait, maybe that was a lie too, are you his girlfriend or something?"

"May we come in, please? I just want a few minutes of your time, and then I'll leave," Tori asked, not wanting to risk Zander seeing either woman out in the open.

"I don't want to hear anything you have to say," Rhea insisted, trying to close the door.

Quickly placing the toe of her boot in between the door and the door jamb, Tori pressed her hand against the door preventing it from closing and pleaded, "Please Rhea, just hear me out. If you still don't want to talk after you hear what I've said, I promise, we'll leave."

Debating for a moment, Rhea exhaled loudly and stepped aside, "Fine. Just for a few minutes, I have things I need to do," she agreed.

Tori glanced around the apartment and noticed two partially filled suitcases lying open on the couch. "Do you know where you're going yet?" she asked.

"As far away from him as possible," Rhea spat angrily, crossing her arms over her chest. "Why are you here?"

Inclining her head toward Rhea's dining table, Tori asked, "Would you please sit down at the table with me? I have a lot to tell you and hope it will help explain most of what Logan has done."

"Fine, you've got five minutes," Rhea agreed, taking a seat at the table.

Opting for the chair directly beside Rhea, Tori retrieved her badge from her pocket, placed it on the table in front of Rhea and sat down. "My full name is Agent Tori Cooper. I'm with the FBI Behavioral Analysis Unit Division Two, the same unit as Logan. He and I are partners along with a bigger team of seven other agents, including Goliath here."

Rhea looked over at Goliath, who was sitting patiently beside Tori. "Goliath is an agent with the FBI?"

"Yes. Goliath became one the day he took a bullet trying to save my life after your husband tried to kill me," Tori replied.

"What?" Rhea gasped, notably surprised.

Pulling the collar of her shirt aside, Tori showed Rhea the scar from the bullet wound below her shoulder. "It was a rifle shot from across a park where children were playing. I was eight months pregnant at the time."

"Oh!" Rhea exclaimed, bringing her hand to her mouth. "What happened to the baby?"

"They're both fine. The trauma from the gunshot forced me into early labor, and I delivered identical twins later that day," Tori assured her. "They just turned three a couple of months ago."

"Oh, thank God," Rhea breathed in relief. Turning to look at Goliath again, she reached out her hand to gently pet him on top of his head. "It's an amazing feeling to have a connection with an animal like you have with Goliath. To risk his life like that means, he really loves you."

"And to sacrifice Butler the way you did to keep him safe and put him in a good home means you really care about him. It was risky staying so close to him after you gave him up. Why did you do that?" Tori asked curiously.

"You know about Butler?" Rhea asked, wondering what else Tori knew about her.

"I do. I know Butler now belongs to a family here in town and that you've been working as a veterinary assistant at one of the clinics just so you can be near him," Tori replied.

"I just couldn't let him go," Rhea admitted sadly. "I made sure he had a good family I knew would love him, but once I did, I still couldn't leave him."

"That's because you have a caring and protective nature which from what several of your former clients told me, made you an excellent veterinarian. I'm sure you've missed it. Being an assistant can't be as rewarding for you," Tori noted.

"It's what I felt I needed to do," Rhea admitted. "What has Logan told you about me?"

"I know everything, Rhea," Tori admitted quietly.

"Including the things Zander has done?" Rhea asked.

"Yes," Tori replied. "Tell me what happened in your own words. How did you get to where you are now?" Tori asked curiously.

"It's funny that you mentioned my caring and protective nature," Rhea admitted. "That was one of the things that brought Zander and me together in the first place. He was just like me. He was hard working, honest, kind to strangers and always helped out where ever he was needed. That's the part I don't understand. Why would Zander do what he did? He faithfully served his country protecting people."

"I think you know, Rhea," Tori replied softly. "I think you knew the morning you saw your friends face on TV reporting his murder. You knew Zander had done it and you were terrified because the man you first fell in love with wasn't the same person anymore."

Rhea stared at Tori and shook her head slowly. "That seems to be the story of my life," she noted sarcastically.

"That's why you ran isn't it?" Tori prodded gently.

Rhea nodded her head guiltily and choked out a sob, "I couldn't even look at him anymore without thinking about what he did to my friend. Grant was such a nice man. He'd been through so much in his life and was finally happy. I just couldn't believe Zander would do something like that."

Gently placing her hand on Rhea's, Tori revealed, "Grant Albertson is not the only man Zander killed, Rhea. We know of three other murders over the past eight years."

"Three others....," Rhea whispered, her thoughts racing.

"Rhea," Tori called out to regain her attention. "It's very important that you listen to what I'm about to tell you okay? Some of it will be difficult to understand and may sound completely unbelievable, but I promise you everything I'm about to tell you is true, okay?"

Rhea nodded her head and whispered, "Okay."

"The men Zander murdered were all men like him, they each had a tragic life event in their past causing them to be slightly different afterward. Grant Albertson was the sole survivor of an accident that killed the rest of his family. Wade Hackett, the second victim, was the sole survivor of a small engine plane crash when he was in college. The third victim, Peyton Birch, was a former Marine who was the only survivor from the rest of his troop who died from an IED explosion."

"Just like Zander," Rhea noted, seeing the pattern. "They were all broken men like they cheated death somehow."

"Not all of the men were just like Zander," Tori replied. "Just because someone goes through a life changing event like those men did, means there was anything wrong with them. They just had a different perspective on life afterward than the rest of us."

"Then what made Zander kill them?" Rhea argued.

 "Rhea, are you a spiritual person?" Tori asked, testing the waters.

Rhea frowned, confused and asked, "Do you mean do I believe in God?"

"Both God and Satan," Tori added.

"Uh, yes, I guess so. I mean I've always believed in God, but I haven't thought much about the existence of the devil," Rhea admitted.

Taking a deep breath, Tori said, "I have a theory, and this is the strange part of the story I mentioned. I believe your estranged husband may be acting under the influence of the devil and may not be completely in control of his actions."

Rhea blinked in surprise, giving Tori a strange, doubtful look. "What? That's crazy! Is that even possible?"

"It is possible. I've seen it before with other serial killers my team has come into contact with," Tori admitted.

"I don't know how to process that information," Rhea admitted, sitting back wearily in her chair. "What makes you so sure?"

"For example, did Zander seem 'off' before you left?" Tori asked. "Did he ever look at you and you didn't think he saw you? Did he ever say things and then deny having said them when they came up in conversation later? Did he ever lose track of time? When he spoke to you, did it sound like someone else speaking?"

Rhea's eyes widened at Tori's last question, instantly recalling a night when Zander came home from being out and he seemed like a completely different person. "Yes he did," she admitted. "Is he sick? Is that why he did all of those horrible things? I turned my back on him and left when I should have stayed and helped him!"

"No, none of what has happened to Zander in the past or what he's doing today was your fault, do you understand?" Tori insisted, taking both of Rhea's hands in hers. "You aren't to blame for what's happened, nor could you have done anything to help him. There are powerful forces at work with Zander, and you're not equipped to fight them."

"And you are?" Rhea asked.

"Yes, I am, but that's a whole different story that we don't have time to go into right now. What matters right now is you believe you had no control over what Zander did," Tori insisted.

"Why?" Rhea asked. "Why is it so important I believe that?"

"Because Zander is in Blacksburg and he may be looking for you," Tori revealed.

Jumping up from her chair, Rhea looked toward the door and frantically cried out, "What? He's here? Why didn't Logan tell me?"

"Well, he was trying to tell you earlier but then you punched him in the nose," Tori pointed out.

"Well, he should have tried harder!" Rhea objected. "Does Zander know where I am? How did he find me?"

"I don't know for sure, I just arrived in Blacksburg this afternoon and saw him driving through town, but I lost him. Other than Butler, the only other connection to bring him here would be you," Tori admitted. "Look, I know you're really angry with Logan right now and you two have a lot to talk about, but you need to trust him and believe he cares about you and your safety. We both do. We need to leave town tonight. I'm here to take you with me."

"You know what's been going on between Logan and me?" Rhea asked, slightly embarrassed.

"Yes," Tori nodded. "I've known all along. Logan is a good man, but he can't keep a secret to save his life. He's one of mine and my husband's dearest friends, and I love him like a brother. Yes, he screws up sometimes, but he has a good heart."

"I don't know, Tori," Rhea sighed. "He lied to me."

"You both lied to each other," Tori pointed out bluntly. "His job was to find you, to stay close to you and to keep you safe. At some point during all of that, he also fell in love with you, and I think you fell in love with him too. That's why you're so angry with him right now. When things settle down, you both need to sit down and spend time getting to know each other. Meaning, the people you are, not who you've been pretending to be."

Dropping back down into the chair, Rhea shook her head in defeat, suddenly feeling very tired. "I've been Rebecca Stone for so long; I have no idea who Veronica Wells is anymore."

"I would be surprised if she isn't much different than the woman sitting in the chair across from me right now," Tori offered reassuringly.

"Thank you, Tori, I appreciate your kindness," Rhea said. Glancing back at her suitcases, she asked. "So what do I need to do?"

"You go ahead and pack your suitcases and only take what you need. Once we leave, I'll arrange to have the rest of your things packed up and taken somewhere safe. Then we need to go help Logan do the same thing," Tori advised.

"Oh, I don't know if I'm ready to talk to Logan just yet. Can I finish up here and then you both come get me when it's time to go?" Rhea pleaded, hoping Tori would understand.

Debating if she should risk leaving Rhea alone, Tori noticed all of the drapes on the windows were closed, and the front door didn't have any glass for someone to be able to see inside.

"Okay," she agreed, "but I'm only giving you thirty minutes, got it? And you have to promise me you won't look out of any of your windows, make any phone calls or open your door for any reason, understood? That includes not taking out the trash or checking your mail. You stay put until I get back. If someone knocks, don't answer it, it won't be me."

"How will I know it's you when you come back?" Rhea asked.

"Have your phone near you at all times. Logan will text you when we're outside your door, and you can come out then, got it?" Tori instructed.

"Got it," Rhea promised.

"Okay. I'm going to turn off your interior lights briefly, so nobody sees Goliath or me leaving your apartment. You can turn a few of them back on after we're gone so you can see what you're doing but try to avoid using any unnecessary lights," Tori instructed, clicking off the lights in the living room.

"Okay," Rhea agreed.

"We'll be back in thirty minutes. Be ready," Tori repeated as she and Goliath snuck out the door.

Chapter 43

"Are you sure it was okay leaving her alone?" Logan worried as he and Tori quickly packed up the computer equipment and enough things for Logan and Scout to survive for a few days. "I get that she doesn't want to see me right now, but I don't like leaving her unprotected."

"I had no other choice. Goliath has to stay with me at all times, and you needed help getting your stuff together," Tori replied, focusing on what she was doing.

"At least Goliath and Scout are getting along," Logan pointed out as he passed through the living room where both dogs were sitting patiently watching them.

"Agreed, she grunted, zipping the last suitcase shut. "Okay, are we ready to load all this into your car? We'll come back for the rest after this is over."

"What we've packed is all I need. The rest of it I don't care about," Logan admitted.

"Okay, then let's get going," Tori noted, looking at the clock on the stove. "Goliath, tell Scout no barking under any circumstances, okay? We need to do this quickly and quietly."

"Goliath will take care of Scout," she heard him promise.

"Good boy," she praised. Turning off the light switch, she slowly opened the door and looked around the surrounding area. "Okay, let's go," she whispered.

Quickly making their way down the stairs and into the parking lot, they were putting the last box into the trunk when suddenly they heard a woman screaming.

"That's Rhea! She's in trouble," Logan cried out, immediately running toward the sound.

"Logan, wait!" Tori exclaimed, running after him.

As they rounded the corner of the building, they saw Zander dragging Rhea by the arm toward the parking lot.

"Please let me go, Zander," Rhea begged, trying to pull away.

"Let go of her, Zander!" Logan yelled, drawing his weapon.

"Stop right there, or I'll kill her," Zander threatened, grabbing Rhea around the neck from behind and revealing a large kitchen knife in his other hand.

"Yes, that's good. Use her as a shield so the others can't shoot you," Lucifer applauded.

Recognizing the knife from the set in Rhea's kitchen, Logan immediately stopped a few feet from them.

"That wouldn't be a very good idea, Zander," Tori advised, coming up alongside Logan with her gun drawn. "I think you've hurt enough people."

Instantly recognizing Tori, Zander's eyes widened in surprise. "You! What are you doing here?" His eyes darted down to Tori's side, and he saw Goliath standing beside his master like a large grizzly bear, fur up, teeth bared and ready to spring into action.

"Are you not happy to see me again, Zander?" Tori asked, slowly advancing.

"I told you to stop!" Zander warned angrily. "And keep that dog back!" he growled, pulling Rhea's body closely against his. Then he saw Scout emerge from the shadows like a ghost beside Logan and he blinked hard, thinking his mind was playing tricks on him. "Butler?" he asked, wincing as a sharp pain passed through his head.

"Pay attention!" Lucifer chastised angrily.

Like a love struck fool, Logan rushed forward to grab the knife out of Zander's hand, taking advantage of the opportunity while Zander appeared off guard.

"Watch out!" Lucifer quickly warned Zander.

Seeming to anticipate the attack, in one quick motion, Zander pushed Rhea to the ground, turned and stabbed Logan in the stomach. The two men stood motionless, staring into each other's eyes for a brief moment before Logan's body slid to the ground.

"I told you to stay back!" Zander shouted angrily, holding the knife out, now stained with blood.

"Logan!" Rhea cried out when she saw the blood stain on Logan's shirt quickly start to spread.

No longer caring what Zander would do to her, all Rhea saw was the man she loved lying on the ground bleeding. She quickly crawled across the grass to where he lay and began applying pressure to the wound. "Logan, can you hear me?"

Shocked at how quickly Zander attacked, Tori was worried about Logan but knew she couldn't take her attention away from her target. Trying to keep her voice calm, she stepped forward and called out, "Drop the knife, Zander, now! I don't want to shoot you but I will if I have to."

"She's bluffing, she won't do it," Lucifer whispered.

Turning his attention to Tori, Zander smiled wickedly at her and began approaching her slowly. "I've got someone here with me telling me you're bluffing," Zander hissed at her. "You should be dead! I shot you myself." Taking another look at Goliath who was now poised directly in front of Tori protecting her. "I shot you too! You should both be dead."

"Alex!" a booming voice called out behind him. "Don't do it, son, put the knife down."

Turning his body so he could still see Tori yet also look behind him, Zander scowled when he saw Sheriff Ford approaching him with his weapon drawn. "Sheriff Ford? What are you doing here?"

"Considering I told you not to leave town, I decided to come pay you a visit and see what you were doing out here. So far, it doesn't look very good," Sheriff Ford replied calmly. Glancing over at Tori, he tipped his hat and added, "Good evening, Agent Cooper. It appears you could use some assistance."

"Good to see you, Sheriff Ford. I appreciate your help," Tori greeted him in return.

"Officer Poag, we're going to need an ambulance if you would please call that in," Sheriff Ford instructed, turning his head slightly to look behind him.

"Calling them now sir," another male voice replied a short distance away.

Completely baffled by what was going on, Zander looked back and forth between Tori and Sheriff Ford and exclaimed, "What's going on here? You two know each other?"

"Let's try to focus here, Zander," Tori replied, bringing his attention back to her. "This can go one of two ways. Either you drop your weapon and surrender so we can end this without anyone else getting hurt, or either Sheriff Ford or I disarm you by force. What's it going to be?"

"This is why I insisted you needed a gun, but no, you wouldn't listen to me!" Lucifer spat angrily.

"Quiet! I can't hear myself think with you in my head!" Zander demanded fiercely.

"No more running, Zander," Tori said calmly, knowing Lucifer currently held the reins. "It's time to bring you in."

"Don't do it! You can still get away! Let me take the knife and kill her for you," Lucifer insisted.

Realizing the chase was over and partly glad for it because he was so tired of running, Zander dropped the knife and his shoulders in defeat and placed his hands on the top of his head.

"What are you doing? Put your hands down and pick up that knife!" Lucifer demanded angrily.

Approaching him slowly, Tori kicked the knife out of Zander's reach and returned her gun to the holster on her hip. Then she removed her handcuffs from the clip on her belt and clasped Zander's hands behind his back.

"Is he secure?" Sheriff Ford asked, maintaining his stance with his gun pointed at Zander.

"All clear," Tori replied, turning Zander around to face her. "Alexander Wells," her voice slightly wavered when she saw his eyes were brimming with tears. "You're under arrest for the murders of Grant Albertson, Wade Hackett, Peyton Birch, the attempted murder of two Federal officers and three counts of aggravated assault with a deadly weapon. You have the right to remain silent. Anything you say can and will be used against you in a court of law. You have the right to an attorney. If you cannot afford an attorney, one will be appointed for you. Do you understand these rights as they've been given to you?"

Zander solemnly nodded his head in response.

"I said do you understand these rights as they've been given to you?" she demanded again sternly.

"Y-yes," he whispered, nodding his head again.

"Sheriff, may I borrow your car, sir, so I can take Mr. Wells to the police department and lock him up there for the night?" Tori asked.

Sheriff Ford approached Tori, handed her the keys and replied, "Absolutely. I'll call ahead for you and let them know you're coming. Officer Poag and I will make sure your partner makes it safely to the hospital."

"Thank you," Tori replied.

"You're welcome." Then he looked at Zander. "You made some bad choices here today, Alexander," the sheriff said quietly. "I wish things had turned out differently."

"Me too, sir," Zander admitted quietly.

"Come on," Tori commanded, leading Zander in the direction of the Sheriff's car. Walking around the vehicle, she opened both back doors and eased Zander carefully into the backseat while Goliath climbed in from the other side. Once she had Zander buckled in, she warned, "Don't try anything. Goliath knows who you are and that you're the one who shot him. He could rip your throat out in a second."

Zander gave Goliath one side-long glance and said, "I won't give you any trouble."

"Good," Tori replied. "I'm going to go check on Logan, Goliath, keep an eye on him."

"Goliath has him," she heard him growl as she walked away.

"How's he doing?" Tori asked Rhea, crouching down beside Logan to check his pulse. "Is his conscious?"

"No," Rhea whispered. "He hasn't said anything."

"There's the sound of the ambulance coming now," Tori assured her. "They'll take care of him."

"Can I go to the hospital with him?" Rhea asked hopefully.

"Of course you can. I think Logan would like you to be the first person he sees when he wakes up. Once I have Zander settled in a cell at the police station, I'll come to the hospital," Tori replied.

"Okay, thank you, Tori," Rhea said.

"You're welcome," Tori replied, standing back up. Turning to Sheriff Ford, she said, "I'm heading out. I'm thankful you were here to help. I'll want to know why later."

"Same goes for you. I'll be here," Sheriff Ford agreed.

"Scout, come," Tori commanded, opening the front passenger door of the squad car so he could get in. Sliding in behind the wheel, Tori turned the keys in the ignition, fastened her seat belt and adjusted the mirrors. Glancing behind her briefly to check on Zander and Goliath, she pulled out of the parking lot and began driving toward the police station.

"I'm sorry," Zander quietly murmured, stealing a glance at her.

"For which part, Zander?" she asked, keeping her eyes fixed on the road ahead of her. "Are you sorry about shooting me; for almost killing my dog; for just stabbing my partner or for those three men you murdered? Which part are you sorry for?"

"All of it," he sighed, turning to look out the window.

"Was that Lucifer talking to you back there?" she asked, glancing at him in the rearview mirror. "You seem different now, more in control. Do you still hear Lucifer talking to you?"

Zander gasped in surprise and asked, "How do you know about that?"

"Oh, you would be surprised how much I know about him and his little head games," she admitted. "You're not the only one I've met that he's done this to."

"There've been others?" he frowned.

"Since the day he set foot here on earth," Tori replied.

They drove in silence for several more minutes before Zander spoke again. "Does he talk to you too?"

"Sometimes," she revealed. "But Lucifer has never made me do things to other people."

"How have you been able to stop him?" Zander asked. "He's relentless. Once he grabs hold, I can't seem to stop him."

"He doesn't have that kind of a hold on me," she replied. "Is that why you started taking the Quetiapine? Has that helped keep him out?"

"You know about the Quetiapine too?" Zander asked.

"I know a lot more about you than you'd care to know, Zander. My life the past three years has been all about finding you," Tori declared.

"Well congratulations," he sighed. "What are you going to do now with all your free time?"

"It's never a victory when a life is lost in the process, Zander. You left a trail of bodies behind you, and you don't even seem remorseful," Tori challenged angrily.

"You have no idea how much remorse I have for the things I've done," he argued, looking back out the window.

"If that's true, why didn't you turn yourself in?" Tori demanded.

"I don't know," he admitted quietly.

"Well you'll have plenty of time to think about that when you're in prison," she noted bitterly. "You better hope Logan survives his injuries. The state of Virginia supports the death penalty and killing a federal officer would pretty much seal your fate."

"Yeah, well maybe that would be best all around," Zander sighed, thinking about Rhea and how quickly she had rushed to Logan's side. "I don't have anything keeping me here anymore."

Chapter 44

"It's been a while since we've all been on a private jet together," Piper chirped happily. "It feels good having the band back together again."

"I'll second that," Riley agreed, reaching over to take her hand in his.

"I agree!" Reagan nodded.

"This is a first for me. It's pretty cool! This plane is like a party bus in the sky!" Brice declared.

"That's funny; that's exactly what I was thinking," Rhea laughed.

Glancing over at the spotted puppy curled up on the floor by Logan's feet, Piper asked, "How's Scout handling his first flight?"

"Pretty good so far," Logan grinned. "It hasn't seemed to faze him at all. Well that and he has Goliath showing him the ropes," he added pointing to Goliath, sleeping on the floor by Tori's feet.

"Well, Goliath and I gave Scout a pretty good workout in the park earlier this morning. I would bet he'll sleep the rest of the way to Cheyenne," Ben affirmed.

"Speaking of sleeping the entire flight, I don't think I've seen Tori move since we took off. Is she okay?" Miranda asked quietly.

"Yeah, she's just really tired. That whole trip to Pikeville and Blacksburg wore her out. She'll be fine once she catches up on her rest," Ben assured her.

"Well she's earned her rest as far as I'm concerned," Agent Hunter proclaimed. "She managed to arrest one of the FBI's most wanted serial killers and assisted in another arrest of a serial arsonist in less than twenty-four hours."

"So between Sheriff Ford and Detective Daniels, they were able to find enough evidence to charge Pierce Andrews?" Piper asked.

"Enough to arrest and charge him," Agent Hunter nodded. "Now it will be up to a jury of his peers to decide if he's guilty."

"It's too bad they can't use the testimonies Tori obtained from Gretchen Mallory and Sam Cutler," Riley noted. "That's pretty damning evidence."

"I know, right?" Ben agreed. "Some days it feels like the bad guys have all the power, not us."

"Which is why we celebrate each victory we can," Agent Hunter admitted.

"Speaking of celebrations it was pretty cool of Tori's parents to invite everyone out to their place in Cheyenne for the weekend," Brice exclaimed.

"You're going to love Tori's parents; they're so much fun!" Piper sighed. "They're the coolest parents I've ever known."

"Yeah, they're pretty great," Ben agreed. "Tanner's been more like a father to me than my dad. That says a lot."

"And the twins have been behaving for them?" Reagan asked with a wry grin. "I haven't heard any horror stories so, either the twins are behaving for Grandma and Grandpa or Grandma and Grandpa aren't telling you!"

Chuckling lightly, Ben replied, "They've had their moments, but Grandma Sarah is pretty good at putting the hammer down when they get out of line."

"I've missed those little munchkins," Piper admitted.

"Same," Ben agreed.

"Ladies and gentlemen, this is the captain speaking. We have just been cleared to land at the Cheyenne Regional Airport. Please make sure one last time your seatbelt is securely fastened and that any remaining cups or glasses have been cleared away. We'll be on the ground shortly, thank you," the captain announced over the intercom.

"Here we go!" Piper exclaimed happily, always enjoying the descent back to the ground.

~~~~~~~~~~

"How's it going out here?" Tori asked, joining Ben on the driveway.

"This is the last suitcase, so I think we're in good shape!" Ben replied, closing the trunk on the rental car. "Did you get enough hugs from the twins to catch you up?" he grinned, wrapping his arm around her shoulder as they walked toward the front door.

"I don't think I could ever have enough hugs," Tori smiled, leaning her head on his shoulder.

"Are you sure you're feeling okay? You were in the bathroom a long time earlier," Ben worried, kissing her on the forehead. "You don't feel like you're running a fever, so that's good, but you still look a little tired around your eyes."

"Well, there is something we need to talk about...," Tori began to say when Brice and Reagan interrupted them.

"Okay, we've got everyone set up in rooms, couches, and tents in the backyard. What else can we do to help?" Brice offered.

"That's great, thanks! One second, Tori said she needed to talk to me about something," Ben replied.

"No, that's okay, we can talk later," Tori quickly answered. "You go ahead."

"Are you sure?" Ben asked.

"Yes, of course!" Tori assured him.

"Okay, ah Tanner has the grill under control, and Sarah and Piper are taking care of the food, how about you and Reagan stock the coolers and bring them out to the patio?" Ben suggested.

"Sounds good," Brice agreed.

"Are the coolers in the garage?" Reagan asked.

"Yep, everything you need should be in there. If you would also throw in a few juice boxes from the fridge for the kids, that would be great," Tori suggested.

"Will do," Reagan nodded. "Come on sweetie; I'll show you where we need to go."

"Okay," Brice agreed, following her.

As they entered the garage, they quickly found the coolers and began filling them with an assortment of beer, wine coolers, soda, water, and juice boxes.

"We should probably keep the beer and the wine coolers in one cooler and the non-alcoholic beverages in the other one. You know, for the kids," Brice suggested.

"That's one of the reasons I love you; you're always thinking!" Reagan smiled, leaning over to kiss him on the lips.

"Hmmm, I like the way you think too," he grinned, pulling her into his arms for a much longer, more passionate kiss.

Suddenly, one of the cans of soda in the refrigerator fell over and rolled out onto the garage floor.

Frowning slightly, Brice walked over to pick it up. "That was weird, neither one of us were anywhere near the fridge."

Immediately suspecting the culprit behind the incident, Reagan innocently replied, "I agree, that was pretty weird."

Then the lids on both coolers slammed shut at the same time.

His frown deepening, Brice walked over to the coolers and opened them back up. As soon as he let go of the lids, they slammed shut again. Turning to Reagan, he asked, "Is there something going on here I should know?"

Laughing out loud, Reagan nodded and revealed, "I believe Tori's sister, Aubrey, is here with us."

Brice raised his eyebrows in surprise and said, "Are you serious? I totally forgot about her sister, Aubrey! That is so cool!" Glancing around the garage, he added, "It's nice to meet you, Aubrey, I'm Brice!"

Hearing a squeaking sound of a marker writing on a whiteboard behind him, Brice turned and saw a note appear on the surface.

It's nice to meet you too, Brice!

"This is seriously, wicked cool," Brice grinned at Reagan. "What's with the whiteboard?"

"They're located in several places around the house. Sarah can see and talk to Aubrey but Tanner can't. Sarah installed the whiteboards so Aubrey and Tanner can communicate with one another," Reagan replied.

"What a great idea!" Brice exclaimed. "This family it so in tune with one another, I love it."

I agree!

"Even Aubrey agrees!" Brice laughed.

"I do too, they're awesome," Reagan smiled. "Okay, I think we're all set. Grab a handle and let's go," she directed, picking up one end of one of the coolers.

"Let's do it," Brice replied, picking up the other end.

"Where would you like us to put these?" Reagan asked Sarah as they made their way out to the patio.

"Umm, under those trees I think would be best. That way they're in the shade, and they're out of the way. Thank you both for doing that," Sarah praised.

"It's the least we could do for you putting up with all of us all weekend!" Brice grinned at Sarah.

"I second that," Reagan said as she and Brice set the cooler down on the grass. "Are you ready to get the other one?"

"I'm following you," Brice agreed, motioning for her to go first.

"I like him," Sarah said quietly to Tori as she walked up.

"Me too, he's good for her," Tori agreed, glancing across the lawn where Logan and Rhea were playing with the kids and the dogs. "I'll be back in a bit. I'm going to check on the kids."

"Okay sweetie," Sarah smiled.

"Hey everyone, how are you guys and gals doing?" Tori greeted the group as she joined them.

"We're good!" Rhea grinned. "Is it okay for me to say I love your family? I've never seen a group of people related to one another get along so well! And you look so much like your mom!"

"Thanks, we hear that a lot. And don't be fooled, we have our moments, but for the most part, we get along pretty well," Tori replied.

"Uncle Logan, pick me up and spin me!" Gemma begged and reached her arms up in the air.

"I can't pick you up today, sweetie, I'm sorry," Logan frowned down at her. "My stitches haven't healed yet."

"Let me see!" Gemma ordered, lifting up his shirt.

"Gemma, do not grab," Tori warned gently.

"She's okay," Logan chuckled, showing Gemma the row of stitches on his stomach.

Without saying a word, Gemma placed her hands over the wound, and after a few moments, her fingers began to glow. When she removed her hands, Logan's wound was completely healed.

"Now pick me up!" she ordered, raising her hands above her head.

"Did she just…," Rhea breathed in amazement.

"Yes, she did. Thank you, sweetie, I didn't even think about asking for your help," Logan acknowledged, picking Gemma up under her arms and slowly spinning her around in a circle.

"You're welcome," Gemma giggled. "Weeee!"

Giving Rhea a compassionate smile, Tori said, "You'll get used to it eventually. In the meantime, prepare to be amazed!"

"Consider me amazed," Rhea whispered, shaking her head in disbelief.

"Okay, I think we're ready!" Sarah called out, inviting everyone to the patio table.

While everyone jockeyed for position beside their spouse or significant other, Sarah and Tanner stood at the head of the large table, helping to direct people where possible.

"RJ, honey, try not to fidget," Tori whispered across the table.

"I'm trying not too, but my shoulders are really itching today," he complained, rubbing his back against his chair.

"Let me see," Gemma ordered, lifting up the back of RJ's shirt.

"Gemma, sweetie, don't grab," Tori reminded her gently.

When the chairs were filled, and everyone looked settled, Tanner raised his glass. "Thank you all for joining us this weekend. This celebration has been a long time coming, and Sarah and I are so blessed to have you all here with us, especially the new faces around our table," he added, glancing at Rhea and Brice. "Welcome."

"Ow, Gemma, that hurts," RJ whined, trying to pull away from his sister.

"Just let me finish!" Gemma exclaimed in concentration.

"Kids," Ben whispered in warning.

"Cheers!" Tanner exclaimed happily.

"Cheers!" everyone replied in unison, tapping their glasses against the people nearest to them.

"Well, I guess now is as good a time as any to share my news," Tori thought to herself, standing up in her chair.

Suddenly RJ cried out in pain, knocking his chair out from beneath him as he jumped to his feet. "Ouch! What did you do?" he screamed at his sister.

"It was time for them to come out!" Gemma replied, calmly.

"It was time for what to come out, sweetie?" Tori asked, rushing around the table toward RJ. "RJ, honey, what's wrong?"

Unable to take the pain any longer, RJ ripped off his shirt and twisted his body to try and look at his back. "What's happening?" he wailed, fearfully.

Suddenly before everyone's eyes, RJ's shoulder blades began to glow a bright white light, followed by the eruption of a pair of beautiful, white, feathered wings protruding from his shoulders.

"Oh my," Tori gasped in surprise. "Sweetie, are you okay?"

"What the…," Ben marveled in amazement, quickly getting up to help his son.

"I-I'm okay now. The pain is gone," RJ replied, his face beaming. "I want to see them!" he exclaimed, running toward the window so he could look at his reflection and see his wings. Testing the movement of his new appendages, he gently fluttered them back and forth like a bird. "Aren't they amazing?"

Staring in awe at the pristine white wings reaching down to RJ's waist, Tori admitted, "Yes, they are, honey."

"I told you they were ready to come out," Gemma announced, firmly.

"Tanner!" Sarah burst out.

"I see them!" Tanner blurted in shock.

"Holy cow," Piper breathed.

"I agree," Riley whispered in surprise.

"What on earth….," Brice asked, turning to Reagan.

"I'll explain later," she whispered, grinning happily.

"Is this kind of thing normal around here?" Rhea whispered to Logan.

"Totally," Logan grinned. "Way to go, RJ!"

"Agent Sullivan is going to be so disappointed he missed this," Agent Hunter shook his head incredulously.

"I think I'm going to want to hang out with your team more often if this is what it's like," Miranda whispered quietly to her husband.

"I told you they were special," he whispered back.

"I had no idea," she admitted, grinning happily.

Looking around at all the happy faces, especially RJ's, Tori decided today's big news belonged to her son. Resting her hand gently on her stomach, she looked down at the small rounding of her belly and whispered, "That's okay little one. We can wait a little longer to tell them about you."

Note from the author

Well, here we are, at the end of the Tori Cooper Novels. I hope you've enjoyed them. It's going to be hard for me to hear Tori and the others carry on conversations with one another in my head from now on without writing them down.

But fear not, another story has just emerged! I don't know about you, but I'm very much looking forward to finding out what God has in store for our Gemini twins, especially little RJ.

Thanks as always for joining me on this journey. It wouldn't have been the same without you!

God bless,

Vicki

Recipes from Changing of the Guard

Ben's Turkey Parmesan Sliders

Ingredients:

1 package wheat dinner rolls, sliced in half
1 pound ground turkey breast
1 medium onion, finely chopped
4 cloves garlic, finely chopped
4 tablespoons olive oil
2 tablespoons fresh basil, chopped
1 teaspoon salt
1 teaspoon fresh ground black pepper
1 teaspoon crushed red pepper
1 teaspoon dried oregano
1 cup marinara sauce
1 cup parmesan cheese, shredded
1 cup mozzarella cheese, shredded

Directions:

1) Pour 2 tablespoons of the olive oil to an oven-proof saucepan and warm it on the stove over medium heat.

2) Add the onion and garlic and cook for 6-8 minutes until soft.

3) Stir in the basil, oregano, crushed red pepper, salt, and pepper and cook for 2 more minutes.

4) Remove the pan from the heat and scrape the mixture into a large mixing bowl. Allow the mixture to cool for about 5 minutes.

5) Add the ground turkey, half of the marinara sauce and half of the parmesan cheese into the mixing bowl and combine the ingredients with your hands until fully incorporated.

6) Shape the mixture into 12 small patties, large enough to fit the size of the dinner rolls. Season the patties with salt and pepper.

7) Preheat your oven to broil.

8) Using the same saucepan, pour the remaining 2 tablespoons of olive oil into the pan and place the patties into the pan, seasoning side down. Season the patties with salt and pepper and cook them for 4 - 8 minutes or until browned on the bottom. Gently turn the patties over, cooking them for an additional 4 - 8 minutes until browned.

9) Arrange the bottom half of the rolls on a foiled lined baking sheet and place a patty on top of each half. Spoon a tablespoon of the marinara sauce on top of each patty, followed by a generous pinch of the parmesan and mozzarella. Place the tops of the rolls face up on the same tray.

10) Slide the pan under the broiler and broil the sliders for about 2 minutes or until the cheese is melted and the rolls are slightly toasted.

11) To serve, top each slider with fresh chopped basil and the top half of the roll.

Sarah's Seared Scallops with
Tori's Apple Wood Smoked Gouda Grits

Ingredients:

12 large sea scallops
2 cups chicken broth
1 cup fat-free half and half
1 cup dry white wine
1 cup uncooked quick-cooking grits
1 cup apple wood smoked Gouda cheese, shredded
2 tablespoons butter
1 tablespoon olive oil
1 tablespoon lemon juice
Salt and pepper

Directions:

1) Bring the broth and half and half to a boil in a saucepan over medium-high heat.

2) Whisk in the grits, cover, reducing the heat to low, and simmer for five minutes, stirring occasionally.

3) Stir in the cheese, 1 tablespoon of the butter and season with salt and pepper. Remove the pan from the heat.

4) Pat the scallops dry with a paper towel and season them with salt and pepper on both sides.

5) Heat the olive oil in a sauté pan over medium-high heat. When the pan is hot, place the scallops in the pan and sear them for two to three minutes on each side until golden brown. Transfer the scallops to a plate and cover them to keep them warm.

6) In the same sauté pan, add the wine and lemon juice and stir to loosen the browned bits into the sauce. Bring the mixture back to a boil for one minute. Stir in the remaining tablespoon of butter.

7) To serve, spoon a bed of the grits onto each plate, top with the scallops and then drizzle the sauce over the top.

Tori's Sugared Lemon and Rosemary Scones

Ingredients:

2 ½ cups flour
½ cup granulated sugar
1 ½ sticks, light butter
½ cup light cream
½ cup fat- free half-and-half
2 tablespoons fresh rosemary, finely chopped
2 tablespoons raw sugar
1 tablespoon baking powder
½ teaspoon kosher salt
Zest from one lemon

Directions:

1) Combine the flour, baking powder, salt, granulated sugar, rosemary and lemon zest in a large bowl.

2) Add the butter, sliced into tablespoon sized portions, to the bowl and using a pastry blender, cut the butter into the flour mixture until a course mixture remains with some small pieces of the butter still visible.

3) Stir in the cream and ¼ cup of the half-and-half until you have a loose dough.

4) Turn the dough out onto a lightly floured surface and work it into the shape of a log. Wrap the log in plastic wrap and refrigerate it for one hour, until firm.

5) Preheat your oven to 350 degrees and line a baking sheet with Parchment paper.

6) Remove the log from the refrigerator, discard the plastic wrap and cut the log into two-inch rounds.

7) Place the rounds on the Parchment paper, brush with the remaining ¼ cup of the half-and-half and then sprinkle the raw sugar on top of all of the scones.

8) Bake the scones in the oven for 25 minutes, until they are a light golden brown. Remove from oven and allow them to cool before serving.

Tori's Habañero, Bourbon and Pear Jam

Ingredients:

6 ripe Bartlett pears
3 golden habañero peppers, seeded and finely chopped
1 cup sugar
2 fresh vanilla beans, scraped
¼ cup bourbon
2 tbsp. pectin or unflavored, powdered gelatin

Directions:

1) Add the pears, peppers, and sugar to a medium sauce-pan and cook over moderate heat until the sugar is melted and the mixture begins to bubble.

2) Stir the scraped vanilla paste and whole vanilla beans into the mixture, reduce the heat to medium-low and allow the jam to cook for 30 minutes or until you see the color deepen to light amber.

3) Stir in the bourbon and cook an additional 15 minutes.

4) Remove the vanilla beans from the jam and using an immersion blender, blend the jam to the desired consistency (less to make chunkier, more to make smooth).

5) Stir in the pectin or gelatin and remove the pan from the stove.

6) Allow jam to cool thoroughly and then spoon it into glass jars. Don't forget to share a jar with your friends (they'll thank you). Store the jam in the refrigerator for up to two months.

Sarah's Red Quinoa and Bacon Salad with Balsamic Vinaigrette

Ingredients:

1 cup uncooked quinoa, rinsed
2 cups water
8 pieces of bacon, chopped
1/4 medium red onion, thinly sliced
1/4 cup chopped Italian parsley
1/2 cup extra-virgin olive oil
1/4 cup balsamic vinegar
2 tablespoons spicy brown mustard
2 tablespoons brown sugar
2 teaspoons kosher salt
1 teaspoon smoked paprika
1 teaspoon ground chipotle
1 teaspoon black pepper

Directions:

1) Combine the quinoa, water and 1 teaspoon of salt in a medium saucepan. Bring the water to a boil reduce the heat to low and cover the pan. Gently simmer, covered, for 15 minutes (there may still be some water not yet absorbed). Remove from the heat.

2) Keeping the pan covered, let it stand for 5 minutes, or until the remaining water is absorbed. After 5 minutes, gently fluff the quinoa with a fork and set it aside to cool.

3) Using another pan, cook the bacon on medium-high until it is browned and crispy. Remove the pan from the heat, drain the bacon and set aside.

4) Whisk the olive oil, balsamic vinegar, mustard, brown sugar, smoked paprika, chipotle, remaining teaspoon of salt and pepper in a small bowl.

5) In a large serving bowl, add the quinoa, bacon pieces, red onion and parsley, gently mixing them together. Stir in the dressing until all ingredients are fully incorporated.

6) Serve the salad at room temperature.

Rhea's Vietnamese Pork and Noodle Salad

Ingredients:

2 lbs. pork tenderloin, cut into 1/2 inch slices
1 package rice noodles
1 package fresh baby spinach, washed
1 red onion, thinly sliced
1 cup carrots, julienned
1 cup radishes, thinly sliced
1 jalapeno, seeded and thinly sliced
1/2 cup cilantro leaves
1/2 cup water
4 tablespoons olive oil
4 tablespoons, fresh garlic, minced
4 tablespoons fresh ginger, minced
4 tablespoons fish sauce
4 tablespoons soy sauce
4 tablespoons sugar
1 tablespoon crushed red pepper flakes
Kosher Salt
Freshly ground black pepper
Chopped peanuts
Juice from 2 limes

Directions:

1) Mix half of the lime juice, 2 tablespoons of the olive oil, fish sauce, soy sauce, garlic, ginger, and sugar in a large bowl.

2) Add the pork to the bowl and toss it with the marinade until coated. Cover the bowl and place it in the refrigerator, allowing the meat to marinate for a minimum of 30 minutes. (Two hours is ideal).

3) Cook the rice noodles according to package directions, rinse under cold water, drain and set aside.

4) Pre-heat your oven to broil.

5) Combine the water, the remaining olive oil, sugar, lime juice, fish sauce, soy sauce, garlic, ginger, and the jalapeno, crushed red pepper and black pepper in another large bowl and stir until the sugar has dissolved. Add the noodles, cilantro, onion, radishes, spinach, and carrots to the bowl and toss until the dressing is thoroughly incorporated.

6) Transfer the pork to a foil-lined baking sheet and season it with the salt and black pepper.

7) Place the baking sheet in the oven and broil the pork until browned, about 3-5 minutes. Turn the pork over and broil another 3-5 minute until browned.

8) To serve, distribute the noodle and salad mixture onto plates and top with a few slices of the pork. Garnish each plate with the chopped peanuts.

Grandma Chase's Classic Peanut Butter Cookies

Ingredients:

2 cups flour
1 cup vegetable shortening
1 cup creamy peanut butter
1 cup plus 2 tablespoons granulated sugar
1 cup powdered sugar
2 large eggs
2 teaspoons baking soda
2 teaspoons vanilla extract
1 teaspoon salt

Directions:

1) Add the shortening, peanut butter, cup of granulated sugar and powdered sugar in a large mixing bowl. Beat the ingredients at medium speed until well blended, about 3 minutes. Add the eggs and vanilla and continue mixing at medium speed for another minute until thoroughly combined.

2) Combine the flour, baking soda and salt in a separate bowl, and add the dry ingredients into the wet ingredients. Mix on low speed until combined. Cover the dough with plastic wrap and refrigerate for 1 hour.

3) Pre-heat your oven to 350 degrees, then line a baking sheet with Parchment paper.

4) Remove the dough from the refrigerator and pinch off sections of dough, rolling them into 1-inch dough balls.

5) Place each dough ball 1-inch apart on the baking sheet and sprinkle the remaining granulated sugar on top. Using a dinner fork, slightly flatten the tines into each dough ball in a crisscross pattern.

6) Place the baking sheet in the oven and bake the cookies for 12 to 15 minutes until golden but not browned.

7) Remove the pan from the oven and allow the cookies to cool for 3 minutes before transferring them to a wire rack to cool completely.

www.ingramcontent.com/pod-product-compliance
Lightning Source LLC
Chambersburg PA
CBHW050019030726
47506CB00001B/19